# MELLIFLUOUS

*Circle of Sixths, Part I*

## IMOGEN PYRE

*First published by Stories by Imogen Pyre*

*Copyright © 2025 by Imogen Pyre*

*Cover art by Laurent Reis*

*First edition*

*ISBN: 979-8-9996011-1-7*

# CONTENTS

This work contains many dark themes; sensitive readers should proceed with care.
Please visit imogenpyre.com to review a full list of potentially-triggering material.

\* \* \*

*In darkness, evil hides—*
*But only in our fear of darkness can it thrive.*

# 1

# DARK PRESENCE

Reuben kept his eyes closed as his fingers danced across the strings of his mother's old violin, trying to appear lost in the music.

In truth, he had never managed such a feat before. Even as his body swayed and the song flowed through and out of him with every kiss of his bow against the strings, Reuben was aware of the crowd watching. More than that, with the assistance of his crowdcraft, he could *feel* them.

The elvish woman near the front of the stage watched with admiration—but also a sprinkling of envy as Reuben's performing partner, Isolde, dipped backward and sang out a long, soulful note. Missing her own youth, the music whispered to him.

Further back in the crowd, disgruntlement emanated from a few customers of dwarvish descent. Upset at their obstructed view as Reuben and Isolde did a bit of synchronized footwork, he knew without even looking.

And then there was the infernal-blooded man exuding impatience on the sidelines—waiting for the next stellas to perform, Reuben's crowdcraft discerned for him.

It was overwhelming, tapping in to so many emotions and intentions over the course of a half-hour. But still well-worth the discomfort. With enough focus and his violin as a conduit, Reuben's crowdcraft could sift through the masses until he spied out those who watched his movements with particular interest—and lust.

Which would make his next job easy. By the time they played their last number, Reuben always knew which customers would welcome his attention, as sure as their apparel would soon tell him how much cantergold that attention might be worth.

No, Reuben never escaped his surroundings when he made music. Sometimes he became much, *much* too aware.

Tonight, one entity stood out of place, distracting him. His music echoed back an unusual, powerful presence in the crowd, focused solely on him—not admiring or lusting, though not carrying the rarer reactions of scorn or judgment either.

Instead, the sheer intensity of it felt malicious . . . and familiar, somehow.

And yet, to Reuben's growing unease, he could not spot its source with his own two eyes during any part of their act. Not even at its end, when he could scrutinize the sea of faces better whilst channeling the final riff of his violin into a small demonstration of crowdcraft, a sparkling burst of illusory petals falling over them in time with the applause.

Only his years of practice in this particular craft of magic kept him from doubting whether he'd imagined it entirely. So as Isolde collected their tip bowl from downstage, Reuben took the chance to scan the cheering masses more blatantly, searching for the dark presence in their midst. Watching Reuben fiercely in return.

His search proved useless. Isolde walked in front of Reuben's view as she waved one last time and hurried off the stage, breaking his focus before he could make any conclusions. And Reuben knew he should follow.

Still, he paused just in front of the curtains, his gaze lingering over the crowd right up until his friend pulled at the chiffon of his loose, slitted sleeve, raising a brow at him.

Reuben gave one last glance over the still-applauding audience—justifying it with a flirtatious wave and wink—before giving up on the search and ducking through.

"I wish you would sing and I accompany," Isolde groused the moment the curtain closed, muting the crowd. "My voice already needs a rest, and the night's just started."

Reuben swallowed down the remnants of his unease and let out a perfectly soft, light-hearted laugh. "Oh, I think our clientele would have my head if they never got to hear their *Songbird* again," he said while they walked the short distance to the backstage green room. Adding, as he placed the violin back in its case, "Although your lute doesn't require much upkeep—I'm about to run out of rosin yet again."

Isolde sat down in front of the mirror vanity, eyes narrowed at his bow through the reflection. "Hm. I'd wager the fraying hair on that is to blame."

Reuben hid the admittedly old horse-tail bow behind his back and gave her a look of scandal. "I think that's the first time anyone has *dared* to insult my hair," he scoffed, nodding down at his actual red-gold locks, still perfectly waved and swept over one shoulder.

"Good thing I'm here to keep you humble, then," she smirked, though didn't let the matter drop yet: "Surely it doesn't cost much to rehair a bow?"

Reuben shrugged, watching as she dumped the bowl and began splitting their earnings in half. Talk of personal expenses was one of his least favorite subjects, right next to hobbies and health and the future and—well, anything personal, really.

Luckily, just then two of their fellow stellas—the young dwarvish twins Bittie and Gringoll—burst through the door.

"Late as always," Reuben commented while the two hurried past them in their usual bright, coordinated outfits, Bittie still tying up her dark hair and Gringoll tucking his heel into a shoe.

"Can never tell when you're finally done soaking up the applause," Gringoll shot back, a playful smirk on his stubbled face.

"Wait, Bittie, don't forget—!" Isolde warned, just in time for the dwarvish girl to rush back and take the now-empty bowl from her, blowing Isolde a quick kiss in thanks.

"Not that you need it," Reuben teased, though that was an absolute lie. The twins were a crowd favorite ever since they'd been sent here to the Starlet Eye Bordello, almost five years ago now.

Bittie threw Reuben a rude finger gesture just before Gringoll parted the curtains, and with that, brother and sister both ran out together for the next act.

This time, just a brief glimpse of the crowd beyond made the hair at the back of Reuben's neck stand on end.

"Catch the eye of a promising potential?" he distantly heard Isolde asking.

The malice itself wasn't what made the presence familiar. Reuben had encountered plenty of terrible people with terrible intentions in the 46 years of his extended elvish life working at the bordello. Encounters he didn't wish to think about, names he never wanted to hear again, old games he had no desire to play. Only to be expected, after so many decades.

No, there was something else about it. Like a haunting melody he could only remember a few notes of.

"Reubie?"

Reuben blinked; the curtains had already fallen closed again.

Isolde frowned. "You're acting spooked. Is something the matter?"

4

"I'm certainly done performing for the night," Reuben side-stepped with a sheepish smile. Inwardly deciding that he wouldn't go fishing for the most agreeable, wealthiest customer he could find tonight, if it risked running into the person that malice belonged to. He might even leave a few hours of his schedule open despite the hit to his nightly income, and not look for trouble.

Unfortunately, Isolde noticed his tendency to dodge questions over the course of their friendship.

A flash of concern whitened her face. "Did you spot one of your old clients?"

"No! No, I didn't see anyone," Reuben denied, even as his stomach flipped at the thought.

But the bordello's security guards knew who to never let on the premises again, and truly Reuben *hadn't* spotted anyone at all. That was the unsettling part about it.

He reached out and squeezed one of her crossed forearms. "I'm probably just tired, Isi. Took on too many customers last night."

Isolde relaxed. "A lesson for tonight, I hope? I'm always telling you gold can't solve all our problems," she chided, waiting for his nod before she went back to counting coins.

His mother's stern wisdom often proved true: *In conflict, conceding a smaller, less-important thing often distracts the other party away from the original issue at hand,* she'd told him once, whilst smudging powder over her bruised cheekbone.

Reuben found the tactic worked wonders on stubborn customers and, over the last three years since Isolde started here, on his new, well-meaning friend.

After Isolde gave him his half of their earnings—a reasonable 20 cantergold—they exited into the back hallway, and Reuben resolved to put that dark presence out of his mind.

Just a trick of the music. Or another quirk of working at the Starlet

Eye Bordello, where people with all sorts of motives from nearly every walk of life could walk through its doors.

They entered the bordello's main hall from a side door just between the grand staircase and the main desk. While Isolde joined the masses, who were cheering as the twins performed another feat of acrobatics on stage, Reuben steeled himself and headed the opposite way. He didn't feel that unsettling presence anymore, but he wasn't about to linger in the crowd and find out exactly *how* familiar it actually was. No matter that he usually avoided this desk and the person behind it.

There stood a tall, slightly-stooped elvish man with receding brown hair and an easy, winning smile. Sidarchus—once a stella at the Starlet Eye, now the house manager—was busy scribbling into one of his ledgers, handing a key over to the person at the front of a surprisingly long line.

Of course, the bordello accommodated an array of overnight customers: some here just for a room with excellent balcony views of the city and mountainous skyline; some wanting a stella's company on top of that; and a spare few who paid for private showings of more sensual performances. With the crowd now spilling out under the vine-laced pergolas that wreathed the bordello outside, they would easily have every bed filled tonight.

Which gave Reuben hope he wouldn't need to posture and prance around to entice customers anyway. So he took no regard for the line, budging half in front of the horned, infernal-blooded woman about to approach Sidarchus next, and spoke loudly over the music and buzz of the crowd, "Sid! A moment?"

Sidarchus startled at the sight of him. "Is it Isolde again?" he said, half-shouting as well.

Reuben leaned in. "No, she's fine, just—open my appointment book tonight, when you can? I'm feeling a bit under the weather to mingle for myself."

Unsurprisingly, Sidarchus wasn't quick to agree. "That is highly irregular for you, Reubielocks," the older man replied with a grimace, opening a smaller book. He flipped through the pages holding the schedules of all 24 stellas who worked in the bordello, muttering, "And on a night like this, with every page and merchant and off-duty guard in a twenty-league radius here in Sazzera . . ."

The large woman behind Reuben blew out a breath and took an impatient step closer.

Reuben leaned further against the desk, both to avoid her and to argue back, "On a night like this, it should be easy to fill whatever openings I have, should it not?"

Sidarchus found Reuben's section, just then, and they both looked down to find an entirely blank column.

Reuben *did* often struggle to secure repeat customers these days.

Sidarchus made a short *tsk* sound. "I simply won't have the time. Now please," he gave Reuben a dismissive wave, "you're holding up my line."

The bordello house manager could be frustratingly hard to work with at times.

In his desperation, Reuben nearly resigned himself to what helped soften Sidarchus in the past. Whoever the dark presence belonged to, Reuben was in no mood to get threatened, he couldn't afford to be robbed, and he'd rather not get beaten by another old rejected customer with how his flimsy health liked to collapse of late. There were much safer, if more distasteful, options.

But before he could so much as grab Sidarchus's weathered hand in his, the infernal woman intervened.

She stepped forward with a gruff sound, nudging her shoulder into Reuben's—not with any considerable force, but plenty to throw *him* in particular off-balance. A twinge of pain followed down his always-aching spine, and by the time Reuben righted himself, she had placed a small envelope and sack of gold on the ledger in front of Sidarchus and turned his attention away.

Sidarchus began apologizing to her in that entreating, yet assured way of his, opened the letter at her decisive nod towards it, and entirely ignored Reuben's presence.

He would have to brave the crowds still. Either that, or waste an entire night of pay and use savings he desperately needed to hold onto for more dire times, like when his legs wouldn't work or Isolde had an episode.

Worry was not enough justification. It never had been. And if there was one thing anyone here could say about him—not the favorite or the most beautiful, but the most seasoned in the bright constellation of stellas working here—it was that there was little Reubielocks *wouldn't* do for a gold piece.

Reuben gave the woman's back a half-hearted glare before he looked towards the nearest willing body.

He made it just a few steps before Sidarchus called, "Reubielocks! Wait!"

Reuben paused and turned, brows raised. Approaching the desk again, he was just in time to see Sidarchus draw a line through every appointment slot on Reuben's schedule for the night.

"You've been requested for *especially*, stella." Sidarchus smiled proudly, gesturing at the woman Reuben had budged in front of. "For the whole night, too."

"Me?" Reuben repeated, glancing at her with incredulity. Taking in the gray horns that curled up from her forehead around a head of short, dark hair, the warm fuchsia tone to her skin, the forked tail behind her, the thick leather she wore as well as sheathed blades on either hip. Perhaps a lone traveler along the Red Road, or some kind of muscle for a merchant.

Most stark of her features—no pupils. Nothing but a flicker of icy white flame amidst black sclera, in the gaze that might or might not have been side-eying him now.

For a moment, he feared *this* was the source of the presence he'd felt earlier. Customers rarely booked for a full night with him, and it certainly seemed uncanny for two out-of-the-ordinary things to happen at once.

But even without humming a tune to channel his sharper intuition, Reuben could already feel a dutiful-if-disgruntled aura about her. Infernal heritage aside, there was nothing of uncanny intensity or malice, and certainly nothing . . . *familiar.*

"She will take you to her employer at a private location for the night," Sidarchus continued, halting Reuben's assumptions of this woman being the client. At hearing about a private location, however, a new wave of uncertainty washed over Reuben while Sidarchus gestured at the letter in his other hand. "500 canters up front, the other 500 upon appointment completion. Dear—this is only *half,*" he said, winking.

Reuben's eyes widened at the heavy sack on the desk.

The bordello naturally took half, not counting additional fees for rent, food, and other necessities. And most appointments earned Reuben 30 canters at best. When he ended the night with more than 50 pieces of cantergold in his actual pocket, he called himself grateful.

Still, even with the cut for his employer—*500 canters* of his own?

If Reuben could make half that amount every working night, he'd be free of this place in five years, not another forty. Or better yet, could pay off Isolde's debt before the job wore her down into the same shadow of a person he saw each day in the mirror.

Bright gold winked at him from the opened sack, and even from here he could see a couple of coins at the top stamped with the twelve-pronged, geometric symbol of the Zaldian Priesthood—designating it as the most precious, valuable substance across the entire continent of Monmark.

"Where to? With whom?" Reuben asked, reaching for the letter.

Sidarchus pulled it back out of reach. "They're paying so well for the sake of *privacy*," he answered, coldness leaking back into his tone. "Don't be difficult, dear."

Reuben glanced at the tall woman, but she still said nothing. Just watched their exchange with a vague sort of vexation on her face.

Maybe she didn't care to speak—or maybe, hidden behind her confident stance and strong figure, was a discomfort for this loud, boisterous crowd. Reuben could always get more out of someone when he talked to them one-on-one, in a place quiet enough for his voice to lull and soothe with the same lilting timbre as his violin strings.

And even if this job turned out a bit dangerous, that gold could mean *everything*.

Slowly, Reuben nodded. "Let me . . . fetch my things."

As he climbed up the stairs, Reuben tried to recall the last time he worked outside of the Starlet Eye. In all his four decades here, it couldn't be more than half a dozen times—and almost always for an event, not an entire night.

The one and only experience he'd met a new client in a private residence, Reuben tried never to think about.

But even in his coveted youth, Reuben never earned such a sum of gold at once either. That was for the concubines and courtesans of High Ring—a much smaller subsection of the vast city that the noble high houses and Zaldian Priesthood called home, where the Aureate Cathedral crowned the city's summit with its impressive bell tower.

The most Reuben could recall earning for a single appointment was 200 canters, and he lost the ability to walk for days after the experience.

His feet faltered at the thought. What worse things could this private client want for a *thousand* canters?

Reuben entered his chambers, taking a steadying breath. Even if their tastes turned out less savory than simple taboo, he couldn't pass the offer. Not if it meant escaping that malicious presence likely still in the crowd. Or if entertaining this rich new client might secure him a repeat customer, and actually make a dent in the debt that forever ruled Reuben's life—just as it ruled his mother's before him.

But Oriana had never given up: *Freedom is the only song a person must fight to sing*, she'd whispered just a few nights before her death, *and that is why we must. You must keep singing, Reuben, so long as your voice is still yours to lose.*

Most of the advice given to him by the distant, aloof woman he called mother was blunt and simple. These words, he never fully understood—but as he prepared for a night that could just as easily turn out a nightmare as a miracle, Reuben hoped he had some fight left in himself to lose.

# 2

# CHARMING WORDS

Reuben had done his three-fold preparations for the night already—rose oil on his neck and wrists to attract, base oil to loosen himself for penetration, and salve oil rubbed down the line of his spine to soothe the inevitable pains and aches.

But a little extra preparation never hurt. After entering his bedchamber, Reuben tied a small pouch to his beaded belt and stowed two additional items. First, an extra vial of base oil—in case the client offered none and asked for something that would physically injure him without it. Second, a tiny bottle of voleris—a potent, shimmering potion the Starlet Eye Bordello was famous for—in case the client demanded something Reuben couldn't *mentally* bear otherwise.

Only a few tasks remained. As he crossed to his personal vanity, Reuben smoothed a few stray curls in the mirror, then checked the gold dust at the corners of his eyes, which accented the gold ring in his otherwise-brown irises. But nothing looked smudged yet—the night was young, after all.

Next, Reuben pinned a sheer, beaded veil to fall over his face, a necessity in case he crossed paths with any Zaldian acolyte or priest in public. Then he slid his mother's ring onto his pinky finger, for good luck.

After picking up his violin case, Reuben couldn't stall further—and silently resolved to be brave for the sake of gold and his loved ones.

*An autumn crow knows, always where to go / A swan needn't wait, till dancing for its mate*, he sang silently to himself while heading back down, lyrics of his mother's favorite folk song from the southern heartlands. It still held some childish comfort after all these years: *The phoenix can feel—*

Reuben paused, noting the infernal woman waiting at the stairway's base. Her face was turned towards the crowd, though it was impossible to know what, if anything, her pupil-less eyes gazed at before she noticed his halted approach.

Reuben gave her a low bow. "A gilded blessing to meet you, saer," he started in a soft voice. "I had no idea I was jeopardizing my own prospects tonight, stepping in front of you like that. My sincerest apologies. Getting in my own way as usual, it seems." He offered a shy smile from under the sheer veil. "You can call me Reubielocks. Or Reubie for short, as you'd like."

She made another "Hm" sound, this time without annoyance at least.

After a short beat, Reuben added more flirtatiously, "Let me know if I can make it up to you, while you lead me to your master?"

The woman's neutral expression stiffened. She opened her mouth—then shut it, abruptly walking away towards the bordello's main doors.

Reuben quelled a frown before following.

It was a good thing his escort towered above most, or else he would have already lost her in the thick current of pedestrians as they walked out into the main ring's piazza—nearly as congested as the brothel tonight. Some sort of event or political happenings was likely to blame, Reuben thought dismissively.

As they moved west, she led him under stone archways and a labyrinth of lanes away from the main square. Ignoring the judgmental looks thrown his way by passing pedestrians, Reuben started, "So, may I ask what it's been like for you, working for this master? Are they a stricter sort, saer?"

The woman frowned tightly and looked down, walking faster.

Not that Reuben minded a fast pace on principle. The reason for the veil, according to the Gospel of Zald, was to shield clerics, children, and other innocents from impurity—though anyone could be influenced to sin just by looking into the eyes of someone like Reuben: whores, deviants, heretics.

Only once had someone thrown a rotting vegetable at him before, but he'd rather not experience it a second time—especially not prior to an important appointment. The smell was terribly hard to get out of one's clothing.

"Do you know any Dijheri hand gestures?" Reuben asked around slightly-labored breaths. "I'm not fluent, but I have a friend who's taught me enough of the basics, and if you'd be more comfortable—"

The woman came to a stop just then, however. Reuben barely avoided running into her on the unkempt stonework of the older street before he noticed the sight ahead: a pair of sentry guards speaking to a white-clad Zaldian cleric, standing between them and the main stair that led down to the Hollows—the poorest section of the city.

Her face danced through a complicated set of emotions before she took an abrupt left, long legs striding even faster. Reuben was forced to jog to keep the pace. And no matter the lean strength Reuben could claim, it did little for his endurance or the harsh impact of stone pounding an ache into his back.

"Wait!" he called between pants, when all but her tail had disappeared around one of the narrow switchbacks of stairs and

14

streets.

She came back into view with a disgruntled expression, though it faded the moment she took in his state.

Reuben tried to hide how fast his chest was moving, adjusting his veil and giving her a weak smile. "A moment, saer," he huffed. "I don't like sentry guards either, I just—need to catch my breath."

Then he glanced around them; built entirely on a mountainside, Sazzera's ancient, lowest tiers offered a breathtaking view of the mountains around Sazzera—currently a ragged line of snow-capped peaks reflecting the crescent moon with a ghostly sheen. Sentry guards were stationed to regulate who passed through each of the city's tiered levels, but the ones who guarded *this* part of the city were particularly unfriendly. The old hollowed dwellings saw little upkeep compared to the tiers of architectural splendor above them. The impoverished had been left to burrow deeper into the mountain, or otherwise collapse right where they worked in the Ravine mines below, with debtors and criminals beside them.

Which was where Reuben could have ended up, if not for Sidarchus's generosity—and a reminder of just how important his earnings tonight could be, Reuben reminded himself before pushing away from the old limestone wall.

"Ready," he lied.

The smell greeted him first, once they descended enough stairs into the Hollows. Thyme bush and mountain lilies gave way to the stink of poverty and worse, a sulfuric stench belching from the chasmic Ravine. The familiar sight greeted him next: steep staircases winding their way through jumbled rows of small, square dwellings layered on top of each other in honeycomb clusters. A life where the floor of one dwelling was very likely the roof of another, while its own roof helped to form the streets of the level above.

Decrepit and dirty; forgotten places filled with forgettable people.

Once, a neighborhood Reuben called home.

Though it had been a while since he snuck down to the Hollows himself, unveiled and in common attire. The few people out at this hour were soot-smudged, hollow-faced, and raggedly clothed. Likely just returning from their work in the Ravine. Most lowered their gazes—but the few who didn't passed Reuben with open, disbelieving stares.

In this case, Reuben didn't need any music to know these looks had more to do with the silk chiffon and beads adorning his body than any self-righteous piety.

Perhaps for that reason, he found them much harder to ignore.

To his relief, the woman stopped soon after, glancing around before she ducked into the next arched cave entrance. Reuben squinted into the dark as he took a few careful steps after her.

He smelled the animals stalled in the carved-out room before his eyes adjusted to see them: three swine, a mule, a chicken coop. But Reuben had no time to further assess the sight before his guide lit a waiting lantern and approached a wooden door at the back.

Behind it lay a narrow room with a bed, tiny window, and cooking area; on a table, Reuben noted strange playing cards left abandoned in a haphazard pattern. But they passed all of it by, this time through an open doorway into an even smaller space filled with storage shelves and crates.

Reuben's delicate sleeve caught on the scratchy side of one crate, nearly ripping it as he gingerly edged through the walkway. "Is this a, uh . . . short detour, of some kind?" he asked while carefully pulling himself free.

Her continued silence felt more ominous, this time.

At the back of the dark storage room, the woman stopped. Tall wooden shelves stood against the limestone wall in front of them, littered with sealed boxes and items draped in cloth which Reuben couldn't identify further in this dim. He did spot the concealed button on the furniture's side which his guide reached to press— but took a surprised step backward as the shelves made a groaning, clicking sound, and slowly parted straight down the middle.

Behind them, an innocuous wooden door awaited.

And Reuben's mind chose *now* to remind him of all the superstition surrounding what might still infest the deepest parts of the Hollows, where the city's half-collapsed catacombs remained: criminals, devilcrafters, and various monsters of the corrupted, undead, and bloodthirsty variety. Most of it was false—but not all.

Just how private did this customer need to be? And, most worrisome, *why?*

Reuben didn't like any of his guesses.

As the woman moved forward, he had to ask, "Is it much further?"

She at least acknowledged this question with a shake of her head, gesturing at the door as she opened it and stepped aside.

Reuben stiffened. "Not much further at all," he recovered with a forced laugh, peering hesitantly into the candlelit room beyond.

But hesitance wouldn't do—it wasn't what anyone paid a whore for.

So Reuben took off his veil, tied it to dangle from the side of his beaded belt, and smoothed down his hair. Nothing more, before he made his next few strides slow but confident walking into the unknown.

This room was better lit and far larger than the rooms before it. Cream and cobalt-dyed curtains draped over its tall limestone walls, the space outfitted not with more storage or the usual cluttered necessities of an impoverished family, but simple, sturdy oak furniture.

And there, writing at a candlelit desk positioned across from a large bed, sat a man.

The quill he held paused over the parchment, his posture stiffening as he half-turned to face Reuben. Who put on his prettiest, demurest of smiles in response. Reuben immediately set aside his surveillance of the room in favor of his new client's features and demeanor, profiling who exactly he would be entertaining tonight.

Dark, shoulder-length hair, round ears, and a standard but pale complexion gave the man the appearance of a full-blooded human, from Reuben's very limited experience—full humans were so uncommon in this city of mixed elvish, dwarvish, infernal, and even orkish descent, that Reuben only had Isolde to compare the man with. By that life span, the slight lines on this client's forehead and around his mouth would mark at least three decades of life, though the purplish circles under his dark green eyes betrayed another mark of age.

"Welcome, saer," he said in a low tone that carried a similar weariness, giving Reuben a formal nod as he set down his quill.

Unlike the pristine furnishings around him, he wore an old leather coat with a high collar, its bottom edges scuffed with mud. A large metal scabbard peeked from its length, as if he hadn't found either the time or interest in removing his sword belt before sitting to write. Thick shoulders and scarred hands promised he knew how to use the weapon. A stiff mouth and hard expression promised that he had used it, more times than he could count.

Handsome, but in an unkempt sort of way—much more importantly, still a potential danger.

Reuben heard the door shut behind him, cutting off his final chance to turn around and never find out.

For now Reuben didn't move any closer. Only bowed low, idly running fingers through the curls that fell down his chest. "The pleasure is *certainly* mine," he said, glancing up through his eyelashes. "But please—no need for any formalities with me. They call me Reubielocks, or Reubie if you'd like, my good saer."

"Reubie," the man repeated slowly, as if testing the word in his mouth. Then gave Reuben a stiff smile. "I am rusty in formalities myself."

His dark eyes traveled up and down Reuben's person with a sharp scrutiny. Whatever he saw—past an elvish whore draped in a lewd ensemble of sheer finery, Reuben thought—he seemed to have little opinion of, one way or the other.

"Call me Everic," he finished, before standing and shrugging off the long, dirty coat to be draped over his chair.

The gesture calmed Reuben. He always privately felt it a more comfortable experience, when his customers somewhat matched his own state of dress or undress.

Time would tell if that equality continued for the rest of the night, of course.

Now that he was standing Reuben assessed the likely-human further: just a little taller than him, but built like a soldier. If true, Reuben wondered which part of Sazzera's military this Everic had fought for, and if it was still his profession. Nothing but a few skirmishes had occurred in the past few decades, mostly with raiders along the coast. But given the last century of watching the far-off empire of Loethia expand again across the heartlands, Sazzeran soldiers were trained as if that could always change.

Besides that, Everic stood strangely . . . stiff. As if the man had mastered how to breathe without moving a muscle.

Luckily, Reuben was well-practiced in relaxing people. He set his violin case by the door and approached, stopping only a pace away from Everic to trace a finger along the top of his chair. "*Everic.* It's been a long time since I was called for out of my own chambers like this," he murmured, playing at vulnerability now. "I'm afraid I may need some . . . guidance, to best be of service to you, saer."

Reuben watched to see how his words affected the man, though

Everic's expression changed frustratingly little.

"And I thank you for coming." His words stayed short and formal—as if giving a report, not conversing with a prostitute—as he continued, "I appreciate this is not an area of the city most would care to venture down."

Not relaxed yet, by any means, but Reuben would never discourage a client's gratitude. He took a small step closer, grinning more freely as he gestured about them. "On the contrary, it's a cozy little oasis you have down here. I admit, when your servant brought me—"

"—friend," the man corrected.

Reuben kept smiling. "Of course, saer, forgive me—when your *friend* led me into the Hollows . . . well, I didn't know what to imagine. Maybe a quick tryst in a back alley, if I was lucky, or an assassination if I wasn't," he chuckled. When Everic didn't so much as smile in response, Reuben swallowed hard and hurried on, nodding at the room and furnishings, "But I daresay, save the lack of natural light, this place seems far more comfortable than my own bedchamber."

Instead of softening at the compliment, his client tensed—specifically right when Reuben's eyes swept over the desk as he spoke. Everic reacted without subtlety, gathering up the half-written parchment and tucking it under some books while asking, "Do prostitutes *often* fear assassination attempts in this city?"

A private customer indeed. But luckily for this man, Reuben had neither aspirations nor stupidity enough to pry into his clients' lives.

He waved a dismissive hand, leaning against the chair and angling his body—both to direct his gaze away from the desk and to show his form off better as he took a calculated step forward, baring a leg through the high slit of his silk dress.

Reuben had grown especially good at spotting the telltale signs of lust over the last few decades. The human paused at the display with small, yet undeniable signs of it: slightly wider eyes before his gaze flicked away; a small tick to his jaw.

"Oh, nothing so dramatic," Reuben said, meanwhile. Almost assured now that he had found himself a touch-starved recluse with an inheritance to waste, not another powerful, controlling sadist. "Just the occasional client with enemies. You don't live such an exciting life, do you, Everic?"

An uncommon amount of satisfaction filled Reuben, when his words finally cracked a true half-smile on Everic's stern face. "Me?" Everic said in a dry voice. "Oh, I try to be as boring as possible."

Reuben's smile widened. "Then again, what is life without a bit of danger?" he quipped in return. "Too often I'm the most titillating factor in someone's life. It's always a nice change of pace, to be the mundane thing."

Which was an outright lie. Truly, Reuben didn't mind pretending interest when all a client had to talk about was the most recent tax increase, or another low-born parlor party, or their petty familial drama, even if it grew dull.

Clients with dangerous lives tended to be . . . well, *dangerous*. Speaking of powerful, murderous sadists: an old customer of his named Waron had once been attacked right in the midst of their appointment, after Reuben had already taken voleris and laid tied to the bedposts. Luckily, Waron was quick to overpower the would-be-assassin. But instead of calling for bordello security, he'd taken out his large, dark-metaled blade, repeatedly stabbed her abdomen with it, then stalked out without another word. Leaving Reuben tied there with her gutted body on the floor until Isolde checked on him hours later—after the wound from the woman's belly bled out a necrotic black ichor that ate into the flooring.

It was the only time Reuben had seen a dead body since his mother's, though it didn't feature in his nightmares half as often as other, worse experiences with Waron.

Reuben blinked now, realizing they'd fallen into silence a few moments longer than he meant to allow. "Have I run my mouth long enough?" he said with a small laugh. Then lowered his voice into something velvet-soft, stepping closer and reaching to stroke a hand down Everic's remarkably-still chest. "Is there something else you'd rather it was busy with?"

Everic's face hardened, his ribcage finally moving around a sharp inhale. "Did you not read the letter?" he asked, taking a step back. Reuben's hand was left hovering in the air between them.

Reuben let his arm drop and swallowed down a bolt of frustration. He guessed this appointment wouldn't be easy, of course—but he still couldn't see the full shape of its difficulties.

"Oh, was that meant for *my* eyes, then?" he said, carefully lacing his tone with worry and hesitance. "My apologies, saer, if I come unprepared—"

"And Bev explained nothing further on the walk down?" Everic pressed.

Reuben tried not to grimace. "Bev, was it? I didn't have the pleasure. Was she the one meant to give instruction?"

He wasn't aware the infernal woman could or liked to speak *at all*, frankly, though he kept that part to himself.

"You're completely uninformed, then," Everic scoffed, pacing to his desk and back with clear frustration of his own—though at least no limbs had started swinging yet.

Reuben blew out a slow, silent breath and tried again to entreat, "Whatever error has been made, saer, I take full responsibility," regardless of his complete ignorance. Reuben wondered if he *was* partially to blame, if Bev's silence was her recompense for his initial disregard of her. "I would wish to rectify it now, if only you'd allow—"

"Stop, just—stop. Please sit, and I will explain," Everic interrupted yet again, though the rudeness was counterbalanced somewhat by the "*please*" and the fact he'd only slightly raised his voice to interrupt.

Then Reuben saw where Everic was pointing, and his entire body relaxed.

He made sure to flash Everic a sweet smile as he obeyed and walked towards the bed. The mattress was soft but firm under him when he sat, clearly of the same high quality as the rest of the furnishings. Reuben found himself wondering further at this man's current circumstances to have such riches on hand, and yet hide himself away in the most impoverished level of Sazzera.

Reuben abandoned his idle musing, however, upon realizing his customer still hadn't joined him. Instead, Everic had approached the door, and now pulled out a key from an inner coat pocket—turning it in the lock with a decisive *click*.

For the first time since entering the room, Reuben felt true unease. "Worried about an interruption all the way down here?" he said around a hesitant laugh.

The human didn't tense up before making an attack, at least. And why would anyone pay 500 cantergold upfront just to get Reuben here and kill him? No whore was so valuable as that, he tried to comfort himself.

Then again, Reuben hadn't been stupid enough to hope this Everic would pay such a price only for sex. He would likely need to drink the bottle of voleris during this appointment after all, if the mere explanation of Everic's desires was expected to send him running.

For now, he only gripped the bedsheets and pasted on a smile. "No need to worry, saer. I'm all bought and paid for, whatever you should desire," he pointed out—even whilst eyeing where he'd placed his violin case near the door, the best conduit for the few strong, defensive spells crowdcraft could offer.

Everic ran a hand through his dark hair, messing it further. He muttered to himself, just loud enough for Reuben's pointed ears to catch, "This had better *work*, Jophiel."

Then Reuben's stomach flooded with an ice-cold dread.

Reuben prided himself in reading people and their intentions well, particularly when his music could assist. But whenever he *didn't* pick a customer out from the crowd himself, their true intent was harder to parse. At hearing that name, one instance in particular took over—a painful, too-vivid memory drowning his senses, tightening like a chain around his lungs, holding his entire mind hostage:

*"My closest friends call me Jophiel," the voice whispered, smooth as silk in his ear—later sharp and menacing as it spoke in an arcane-laced tongue, while her body rocked above him—ignoring his protests, pinning his arms, binding his tongue as a strange, searing magic spasmed through his body—*

"You're with her," Reuben gasped, jumping to his feet.

There were worse things than Waron out there. Especially if *she* was back in the city.

And apparently one night of torment hadn't been enough. It wasn't a common name, but beyond that Reuben had no justification as to why he knew it was *the* Jophiel he'd once met.

But the insidious presence in the crowd tonight . . . it had to have been hers.

Reuben was breathing too fast, too disoriented by the awful flashbacks to manage a few lyrics of the complicated *Charming Words* spell and get himself out of here. Humming a quick *Friendship* tune would be easier, even in his panic. But that spell didn't last longer than a few minutes, and people tended to be *angrier* once a charm faded. Singing it to a strong, armed man—who could easily run him down before he made it back to the main ring, much less the bordello—was a laughable idea.

Reuben could channel longer-lasting magic through his violin, and with much more skill . . . but Everic stood in the way for now— looking uneasy, yet unsurprised at Reuben's abrupt reaction. "You

24

know Jophiel," he replied.

So Everic knew there was a connection. Had this just been some elaborate plot to allow her to use Reuben for her devilcraft again? If so, why *him*?

"I don't," said Reuben whilst he edged along the side of the bed, angling his steps slowly towards the locked door. "And I'm sorry, but I don't *want* to get to know her, saer. Our one evening together was quite enough—you seem like a fine person, but I'd rather have nothing to do with her or her friends, so—so I think it best I leave now, saer, and just get your money returned to you—"

"I'm not her friend," Everic cut in.

Reuben should have kept entreating. "Who are you, then?" he shot back instead. It was hard to remember the last time he'd spoken so harshly; Reuben's own ears rang with the grating, shrill sound. "It was her at the bordello tonight, I'm sure—why bring me all the way here?"

"This has nothing to do with her," Everic pressed instead of answering.

Reuben let out a shaky scoff of disbelief. "*Zaldus wept,*" he cursed, "if she thinks she can send someone else to finish the job—"

"Wait. Just listen a moment," Everic interrupted yet again, taking a step forward.

Reuben instinctively moved backward, and swallowed down a wince as his back hit the bedpost. As a proficient crowdcrafter, he knew better than most how much trust it cost to listen—how much power simple words could weave.

And yet Everic didn't launch into an explanation, or worse, an incantation. He just stood there in silence, until Reuben realized it had been an actual request.

"Fine . . . then *explain*."

The human didn't seem to be thrown off by Reuben's drastic shift in demeanor. Everic just sighed, "Thank you." His shoulders stayed stiff, his spine straight—but the lines on his face softened somewhat, as he took a breath and started, "My name is Everic Payne, and I arrived quite recently in the city. While I've known Jophiel for many years, she would not be involved in this agreement between you and I; she only recommended I hire you. I don't know what transpired between you two before, but I promise this is nothing personal. Nothing . . . intimate," and he gestured at Reuben's whole person.

Reuben was not assured. Sex, he could easily provide. Other intimacies, his persona had been painstakingly crafted for. But unwittingly playing part in a dark rite that sent his body into a minute-long seizure—would *that* count as intimate to this man?

"What plans have you, then?" he demanded. "Does my willingness factor at all into them?"

If Everic side-stepped the question, Reuben now readied himself to sing the *Charming Words* spell, reciting the first lines in his head: *Mellifluous, diaphanous / Illustrious, euphonious.*

For all that Reuben had been reduced to a simple whore for coin, he wasn't like his mother in every respect. He wouldn't go through the pain of that night ever again—no matter how much gold was thrown at him.

Everic looked upset by the question, however. "Your willingness is *required*," he answered with a deep frown.

Despite it all, Reuben still sensed none of the dark malice he had earlier this night. He even found himself begrudgingly starting to calm, hoping Everic might be agreeable enough to let him go.

Or at least, right up until Everic spoke the next words.

"I don't want your body . . . well, not in that sense, anyway." His eyes, suddenly so dark the irises seemed to match the pupils, flickered to Reuben's neck. "Just your blood."

# 3

# SIMPLE BUSINESS

Dwelling in a small, lavish retreat deep in the Hollows—likely not far from the infamous catacombs once infested with a myriad of devil-made monsters—should have already given Everic away. Not to mention his sickly complexion, or the unnatural stillness of his body. Reuben felt a bit slow for not considering this possibility sooner, blinded by his relief Everic had yet to act like a monster.

But why bother acting, if he simply was one?

Reuben knew little about vampires—they were a newer kind of monster, only appearing in the last few hundred years. But he'd heard the basic signs included a sickly pallor, a hunger for blood, a need to sleep underground, and a deadly aversion to the sun, all easily explaining the man in front of him. Unholy immortality was another feature to expect, if harder to spot. Only the tales of red eyes and fangs were entirely missing—for now, anyway.

And before Reuben could even consider other theories, the man removed all doubt: "I am a simple businessman . . . and a vampire, yes," he said, blunt and grim as ever. "I am new to this city, in need of a steady source of sustenance while I conduct my dealings here. I have no other intentions towards you, Reubie. I swear it."

"A steady source?" Reuben repeated, not enjoying how badly his voice shook or how tightly his hand clung to the bedpost. He tried to calm himself and stay rational, clarifying, "So, you—you're *not* wanting to kill me?"

The vampire's mouth turned down further. "No."

"Well . . . that's good," Reuben said with a faint chuckle, feeling lightheaded.

But the client being a vampire explained almost every quirk of this arrangement: the extra need for privacy, the reclusive, underground location, and even the amount of gold, considering a vampire's undead longevity to accumulate it.

The only thing it didn't explain was Jophiel. An elvish woman Reuben had serviced a little over a year ago now, a devilcrafting witch as far as he could surmise, who had used Reuben in some dark, experimental rite one night that left him bedridden for more than a week, and more prone to an aching spine ever since.

Reuben swallowed and made himself continue: "And what else? What is *her* involvement in this?"

Everic's frown hardened. "I need discretion, for obvious reasons," he replied, turning the key in his hands. "I don't prefer killing. But it is no easy thing, leaving someone alive and expecting news of a vampire in town not to spread. Especially here—this city once wiped out an entire coven in the catacombs."

Reuben numbly nodded in understanding. Vampires, devilcrafters, and shapeshifters—two hundred years ago, the followers of Zaldus saved the city from them all. It was not long after, that the people granted the Priesthood of Zald to take full rule of Sazzera and its surrounding lands. The previous gods of the mountains and sky, already losing followers, faded into obscurity in the *Brilliance of Zald, God of Gold and Light*, and He had been crowned Sazzera's patron god ever since.

It made sense for a devil-made creature of darkness to fear discovery here, of all places—a city governed by godcrafters of gold and light.

"I have no allegiance to the Priesthood," Reuben said—though he did have a healthy fear of them.

"Jophiel thought so. She recommended I seek those of your profession in the city, who deal in physical favors and discretion—Reubielocks of the Starlet Eye, she spoke highly of in particular," Everic said.

Reuben wanted to snarl. "How flattering," he replied in a deadpan voice instead.

It was true he had not reported her devilcraft to any Zaldian cleric. But that choice had more to do with how little a whore's word would count with them, than any respect for the woman's privacy. More likely, Reuben would have just been heavily fined or burned for admitting to his own unwilling participation.

How much more likely was the Priesthood to burn him for fraternization with a *vampire*, even if Reuben managed to get out of this appointment alive?

"But, whether you agree to give blood or not," Everic went on, his words slow and careful, ". . . I *will* need assurance of your silence, before I let you go."

"And if I can't give it to your satisfaction?" Reuben dared to ask.

He stiffened as Everic took a few slow steps closer, his expression somber. "It's best that you do," was the vampire's only reply.

Reuben swallowed. It was a very good thing he had some talent in eloquence, not just music, when he put his mind to it.

"Very well. Then I swear," he started, and bowed his head while holding out a hand, "on my life and perfect reputation for discretion, as the most senior stella of the Starlet Eye Bordello, that

I, Reubielocks, shall tell nary a *soul* regarding who or what you are, Saer Everic Payne."

For a moment, Everic only looked down at the extended hand. But then he did grasp it with his own—his skin unnaturally cold to the touch, Reuben noted with a small curl of fear tightening his throat. And when Everic twisted their clasped hands instead of letting go, Reuben feared he'd fallen right into some kind of trap.

But the vampire merely placed the room's key into his palm before carefully closing Reuben's fingers around it, then stepped back and let go.

A gentle monster, it seemed.

Reuben clenched his hand tight around the metal . . . and found himself wavering in his resolve to use it.

Everic had locked him in, but he didn't intend to kill him. Everic vaguely threatened Reuben if he did not swear silence about the man's nature, yet now he'd given Reuben the very key with which to turn his back on this proposal. Everic knew Jophiel—but all he wanted was a portion of Reuben's blood, in exchange for a ridiculous sum of cantergold, the purest, most valuable currency in all of Monmark.

It was all too disconcerting and contradictory. And still, despite the danger, Reuben didn't sense any insidious intent or malice from this man.

Was that enough to gamble on?

His mother had cautioned him about so many things—*never insult a sentry guard, never drink from the Hollow pools, never join the Zaldian Priesthood*—but she hadn't thought to mention this one. Probably because it was simply that obvious of a bad idea, letting a vampire get anywhere close to one's neck.

Reuben questioned further, "You . . . you don't mean to kill me, but you *do* want to drink my blood, what—every night?"

If Everic was surprised Reuben hadn't gone running out the door already, he didn't show it. "Every night would weaken you terribly," he denied, looking stern, "even still kill you after a while. It'd be twice a week at most, if you agree, though the frequency may fluctuate depending on . . ." His eyes wandered to Reuben's neck again. "Well, depending on when I need it."

Reuben blinked, unsure how to respond. Unsure how to react in general, after two startling, potentially life-threatening revelations had been shoved at him all at once, besides pull the neckline of his dress higher up on his throat.

Instead, he gripped the key tighter and continued: "And I—*in theory*, I would come here each time, but then be free to return to the bordello?"

Everic gave a business-like nod. "And I'd always pay for the full night, so that you have time to recover," he added, gesturing at the bed. "With high compensation, of course, for what I'm taking."

Reuben twisted the small gold ring on his pinky finger with his thumb, biting his lip. "How much blood?"

Everic motioned back at the desk and the small goblet resting on it. "Two cupfuls, no more."

Reuben felt some inkling of relief; it was much less than he would have guessed.

"From my neck?" he asked, glancing up at the vampire.

Everic's dark eyes lingered yet again on the part of Reuben's body in question, though he replied, "Your wrist," and shook his head as if to clear it. "That way we can measure properly."

Reuben raised a brow, glancing around the room. "Then, after . . . I would just lie here? For the night that remains?"

"And eat and drink, to restore your energy," Everic stipulated.

Reuben huffed out a shaky laugh, to his own surprise. "Ah yes, how remiss of me."

His aching spine was relaxing a bit, despite the lingering fear, as

Reuben imagined adding 1,000 cantergold a week to his savings. With that sort of income, he could get Isolde out of indenturement in half a year. His health might even *improve*, with more rest between usual working nights. And it would be easier to make his own private visits to the Hollows, if he was already here for an appointment.

All for the small price of a portion of his life blood. No sex, or torture, or degradation, or more likely all three, that even 100 cantergold would usually warrant.

Given his many bodily weaknesses, of course, Reuben wasn't sure if he'd recover from the former any better than he previously had with the latter. For that alone, he still wanted to say no.

But he was rather used to saying yes to things he had little desire for.

"And, Jophiel . . . ?" Reuben trailed off, waiting to see what Everic would answer the open-ended question with. But at her mention, the vampire's lips thinned. He said nothing.

Reuben supposed he could be more specific—make sure she wouldn't at any point show up and *pin him to the bed, smear her bright red blood in arcane glyphs over his lower abdomen and thighs again while riding his cock and spitting out words that had his bones aching, his nerves searing, his groin burning—*

"She will have nothing to do with this?" Reuben said simply instead, swallowing down the panic at each new flash of repressed memory.

Everic gave Reuben a sharp nod. "I swear it. She's nowhere near the Red Road anyway, at present."

Reuben almost hoped the man was lying. The Red Road was the only safe path out of the Sazzeran Pass, whether heading south to Dijher or north to the heartlands and Loethia beyond. If Everic spoke truthfully, there was no possible way she'd been in the city tonight.

Which meant that insidious, obscured person watching Reuben from the crowd tonight remained a mystery.

But even without the threat of Jophiel, Reuben would still be taking on one of her allies as his client. No matter how reasonable Everic seemed or his insistence that he was *not* a friend to her like he was to Bev, there was a high likelihood the vampire had a darker side under the surface as she did, matched by monstrous powers Reuben had only heard of in legend.

There was no way to know for certain . . . but Reuben did have one skill to help.

So he closed his eyes and hummed a short tune under his breath—*Did I catch you, little lie, in the apple of her eye? / Did she let me bury seed, and then make her lover pie?*—his spine straightening as he concentrated.

As always, Reuben's music opened his deeper senses to what else was in the room with him. In this case, a single presence, which echoed back an aura of grief, wariness, *hunger* . . . and little else, save perhaps growing confusion as Reuben's humming continued.

Nothing insidious. Nothing of particularly ill intent, unless Reuben counted the desire to drink his blood.

It was still uncanny. It was still a risk.

But freedom was always worth a fight, Reuben reminded himself as he opened his eyes.

Resolute, he held out the key back to Everic. After the vampire took it, Reuben started untying the cuff at one of his wrists.

"My blood probably isn't very strong," he warned, picking at the lacing with unsteady fingers as nervous energy fluttered up his spine. "My mother had some pains and illnesses she passed on to me, I'm not sure how it'll affect the, uh—taste, I suppose, or potency."

Then, before he lost his nerve, Reuben thrust his bare wrist out between them.

The previous age and weariness seemed to have melted off of the vampire. With his dark green eyes widened and lips slightly parted, Everic almost looked younger than Reuben, taking in the wrist presented up to him. And if not for the bodily injury about to ensue, Reuben would have enjoyed having such an effect on the otherwise stoic, controlled man.

But the look was fleeting before Everic took the offered appendage in one hand, considered it . . . and then gently pushed Reuben's arm back.

"I'll have Bev gather the food and drink," Everic said in a low tone. "Lie back and get comfortable, please."

Once Reuben gave a hesitant nod, the vampire crossed back to the door.

To better ignore the fears still inwardly screaming at him, Reuben focused his mind on the mundane task of propping up a few cushions along the nearest side of the bed's headboard. Then climbed on to sit himself against them, nervous but curious to see whether his client joined him on the mattress during the bloodletting.

Meanwhile, he heard Everic speak to Bev at the doorway, though quietly enough Reuben only caught innocent phrases like, "fruit as well," and "with the cinnamon."

What happened next—well, it all felt surprisingly procedural, despite Reuben's nerves. Perhaps Everic made a habit of commissioning whores' blood in every city he traveled through, Reuben mused as the vampire methodically gathered the needed supplies: a small side table and stool pushed up closer to the bed, a large piece of linen folded over the table, then clean strips of cloth and two small goblets placed upon it.

It reminded him somewhat of the routine charity visits Zaldian clerics made every few months to the Starlet Eye—save there was less undressing, prodding, or invitations to leave his sinful life, thus far.

After Everic sat on the small stool and held out a hand for Reuben's wrist, however, Reuben's entire stomach dropped: the vampire had pulled a knife from his belt.

Reuben gasped, tried to flinch away, but his wrist was already held fast. "I don't—" But he cut himself off, trying to quell the instinctive panic. "Not—not your teeth?" he recovered enough to ask, though his voice came out much too small for his liking.

Everic lowered Reuben's tensed arm, a cold thumb soothing over the thin, sensitive skin of his inner wrist. "It's cleaner this way," Everic explained. "Quicker, easier to gauge the blood flow. And . . . more controlled."

Reuben glanced at the man's face, wondering if he should worry about dying from a vampire's bloodlust tonight after all. But Everic's expression was hard to make conclusions about—he looked calm and assured, yet there was a sorrowful glint in his eyes, a downturn of his lips. Like the last admission reminded him of an unhappy past.

Reuben blew out a breath and considered his own comforts. Knives were one of his least favorite "toys" for customers to use, especially after Waron's over-enjoyment of them. Reuben had been lucky thus far that his body didn't retain any noticeable scars, and he hated the thought of enduring a blade cutting into his skin twice in a given week, for potentially months on end.

Then again, if something even more dangerous and *less* controlled was the only alternative, as Everic implied, he'd be a fool to turn this option down.

So Reuben bit his lip and forced himself to nod—looking away after Everic held his arm over one of the goblets and positioned the blade.

He bit down harder, sucking in a sharp breath around his teeth at the ripping, splitting pain that followed. Deeper than he'd expected for some reason.

Worry of how his wrists could ever heal whilst doing this twice a week flitted into his mind as hot blood cascaded down the side of his wrist, then began dribbling into the cup.

The first goblet filled without issue. It took less than a minute before Everic replaced the full cup swiftly with the next, only a single drop spilled.

The second goblet seemed to fill slower, though Reuben couldn't say for sure. A soft fog settled over his mind as more and more blood left him. His hand felt terribly cold too, though soft spikes of prickling sensation kept it from falling asleep entirely. Everic was holding onto his hand, Reuben noted when he dared to look, squeezing it gently every now and then where he held it above the goblet.

Maybe just to help the blood flow. All the same, Reuben's throat tightened at the accidental gesture.

He didn't notice much at all past that point, of course, unsure when his eyelids had slid shut before he opened them at a new, unexpected pain.

Everic's control *shouldn't* have been trusted, was Reuben's first hazy thought as he slowly understood it was a mouth he was feeling against his open wound. Then he wondered if this was it. He was going to die, and not unlike his mother had, so desperate for gold and freedom she sold off her frail body until it crumbled entirely from the strain.

At least *he* would have no offspring to pass his debt on to.

But all he felt next was the soft, lapping sensation of a tongue across the torn skin, nothing else before Everic pulled back. The vampire merely licked his lips as he straightened, then wrapped and tied Reuben's wound with the cloth strips.

"What did you just . . . ?" Reuben muttered, his head lolling forward.

Everic glanced at him with a concern that turned to sudden alarm. Quickly he knelt over Reuben's body, removing cushions before laying him back at a full recline.

As Everic continued to hover, cold fingers pressing at his neck, Reuben instinctively parted his lips and spread his legs. Through the murky fog in his head, he wished he'd taken some voleris so he wouldn't remember what came next, or at least could more easily pretend to enjoy Everic fucking him in this state.

But then the fingers left, and the vampire leaned back.

"My saliva helps the wound close," Everic murmured above him, the vampire's dark brows furrowed as he pressed the back of his hand against Reuben's cheek. "A good thing, too—it's been a long time since I've seen someone have an adverse reaction to losing that small amount."

Reuben blinked, struggling to process the words around the buzzing lightheadedness in his skull. "My body . . . I did warn you that's its favorite way to react."

Though his brows stayed furrowed, Everic's mouth curled up into a grim half-smile. "You warned me about the *taste*," he corrected, looking a bit—well, exasperated, if Reuben's bleary vision could still be trusted.

Then Everic let out a slow sigh and—unless Reuben was *truly* hallucinating now—brushed the back of his scarred knuckles briefly down Reuben's cheekbone before the vampire disappeared out of view.

Reuben's head only grew more woozy and lightheaded. He let his eyes slide shut to get through the worst of the dizziness, unaware for some time again until he processed Everic trying to prop his head up, and then the press of something sweet and citrus against his lips.

When Reuben groaned and turned his head away, a bolt of nausea striking his stomach, the fruit was replaced with the rim of a cup instead. This Reuben did manage to stomach: a thick, nutty drink with hints of cinnamon, smooth and soothing down his throat.

"I'd worry you put something in that," he said after taking intermittent sips with Everic's help, his head clearing some. "But that would taint the food, wouldn't it?"

"Only things to help you regain your strength," was Everic's mild reply.

When Reuben opened his eyes, his lips shaped around a retort—but he ended up just staring. If his body had any energy left, he might have jolted at the shock of seeing the vampire's irises—suddenly a bright, molten gold—looking down at him.

"What . . . ?" he whispered, too surprised to even formulate a question.

Everic lowered the drink, his now-golden eyes flickering away with what seemed to be uncertainty. The vampire's face wasn't so ghastly pale either, Reuben noted, the shadows under his eyes faded and his lips pinker while he clarified, "My eyes changed?"

Reuben nodded, drawn back to the vibrant color—and then remembered another strange oddity about vampires that would prevent Everic from being able to know for himself: there was no mirror next to the wardrobe for a reason.

But Everic didn't offer an explanation. "I'll leave you to rest," he said, his mouth narrowing back into its usual grim line before he stood and set down the cup. The two goblets of Reuben's blood were nowhere in sight.

It was strange, Reuben feeling the urge to protest. Not as a performance of feigned interest either. In his exhausted, clearly impaired state, the vampire's presence simply read more like a balm than a danger to Reuben's unmoored senses.

He bit his lip and swallowed the desire, however, especially since Everic didn't go very far. Just back to the desk he'd started at. And after a minute, Reuben's remaining anxieties quieted, the scratch of a quill and occasional rustle of paper the only sound in the quiet, candlelit hideaway.

He didn't notice as he fell into sleep, or when the remaining half of his payment was placed on the side table next to him. But when Reuben's eyes next opened, the pain in his wrist had completely disappeared—and so had the vampire.

# 4

# ANOTHER CHANCE

In many ways, Reuben's indentured life at the Starlet Eye Bordello offered him more freedoms than the impoverished in the Hollows would ever afford: access to the best tailors and suppliers that cantergold could provide, platters of the sweetest fruits, meats, and cakes the mountain city could import. Reuben could even pick and choose his clientele—so long as his expenses were covered, of course.

Once, he and Isolde joked that even the Zaldian clerics had more rules placed upon them than a stella of the Starlet Eye.

There were a few things forever forbidden, however: they could not marry, they could not miss a payment, and they could never, without express permission of the house manager, leave the bordello.

So Reuben had no way of knowing why the days passed with no word from Everic Payne.

He didn't have the energy to wonder at first, either. Ever since Bev escorted him back from the terrifying but lucrative appointment, the bordello's busy nights continued—quickly becoming more of a drain on Reuben than the literal one he'd taken from a vampire.

A pale line lingered on his inner arm only for a day before

miraculously disappearing, not even requiring a *Healing Song* spell to help it along. And the exhaustion afterward wasn't much more than Reuben's usual baseline, since Everic let him sleep there for the rest of his working night. No, Reuben blamed the unusual influx of customers for the increasing aches and pains that followed.

Luckily, Reuben's greatest talent was on his knees—his back didn't usually get involved more than once per work night, unless it was absolutely insisted on or heavily compensated for. And in those cases, he usually relied on a sip of voleris to relax his muscles, turn the pain into pleasure, and smooth out the discomfort from his mind.

When he added even more canters to the pile and did the numbers between Isolde and her freedom, mild discomfort felt well-worth the price. Reuben was more motivated than he'd been in years, strangely, after just one night of nearly doubling his small savings.

Of course, that came with repercussions. By the time they reached Repose, the single night the bordello closed each week and Sidarchus held accounting meetings, *everything* in Reuben ached—his hips, his legs, his throat, his back, his back entrance. Reuben had to hide a limp as he entered the house manager's office; idly, he wished he could justify a sip of voleris, if only to make it through this conversation.

Sidarchus gave a warm smile as Reuben gingerly sat down across from his desk. "I hardly think *we* need to have a meeting this week, Reubie," he said, dropping his quill over the financial logbook.

Its open page itemized not only the nightly amount of income the bordello received from Reuben's appointments, but tracked every payment he owed the Starlet Eye in return: the bedchamber, the performance space, the daily meals, the voleris, the contraceptive tea, the furniture, and anything else provided down to the candles; not to mention service fees for cooking, cleaning, laundry, security, management, tailoring, and more besides.

Reuben could remember fretting over and contesting the numbers, his first decade here.

Now, he tried hard not to even glance at them.

"You made almost as much progress in a day as you usually do in a given month!" Sidarchus continued, gesturing at the page. "Should I expect to transfer a payment to the Priesthood vaults on your behalf, soon?"

"Soon enough," Reuben agreed, though he internally corrected, on *Isolde's* behalf, to himself.

Sidarchus lifted a graying eyebrow. "And I trust you showed the client your other talents, on top of what *unusual needs* they had?"

Everic hadn't disclosed any specifics in his letter, then. But of course he wouldn't—he'd locked Reuben in a room with no other exits before daring to verbally disclose his vampirism.

Reuben returned his manager's smile. "Without trouble," he confirmed, and it was only half a lie.

Sidarchus's cheerful look faded, however. "Perhaps not entirely," he countered, then steepled his fingers, resting his chin on them in concerned contemplation. "In their letter, the client said it would be an arrangement of about twice a week—yet I have seen neither hide nor tail of that horned servant to pay and escort you to them. Was there a mistake made? One you haven't considered the gravity of?"

Reuben hesitated, considering. "I suppose I . . . I still have a problem with knives, at times."

Sidarchus gave a sympathetic nod. "That *devilspawn* Waron was quite the scourge on your poor senses—no relation to your new client's servant, I hope?"

*Friend,* Reuben corrected in his head, but did not comment on the older man's slur or frankly bigoted question. "I'm not sure it actually mattered, Sid; I only reacted for a moment. And they didn't seem to mind."

"Sometimes clients like a bit of struggle," Sidarchus chuckled in agreement, though he didn't look appeased quite yet. "Did voleris help?"

"Not needed," Reuben said, though he probably shouldn't have— Sidarchus gave him an unimpressed frown.

"Better safe than sorry next time," he said, waiting for Reuben's reluctant nod before pressing further: "Did the client say when to expect word next, at least?"

Reuben maintained an achingly-perfect posture, even if he felt the urge to shift in his seat. "They told me they have a changeable schedule," he paraphrased. And then assured, with all the confidence he didn't feel, "But I think it is a matter of when, not if, I am called for again, Sid. My services are truly a need for them, you understand."

"I think I do," Sidarchus smirked, though Reuben seriously doubted it. "Or at least, until they try another stella with less *fragility,* dear," he added before standing to show him out.

The fact that Reuben's knees almost buckled as he stood up from the chair certainly didn't contest that argument.

He knew how to keep himself useful, at least, Reuben thought as he passed by Isolde waiting for her own accounting meeting. Now 622 canters closer. If he could put away that much for her every week, he'd see his friend out of this place by next winter's final frost.

And he knew how to keep his body useful as well. For the rest of Repose, Reuben stretched and worked his sore muscles against his own body weight, and then rested under the sunlit window. He even played the violin later that night, wrote down a few lyrics, and—with help from just a sip of voleris—avoided ruminating over things he couldn't change.

*The soldiers and fighters / They always touch lighter,* he penned just before sleep the next morning, musing idly in his inebriated state about the stiff, painfully-private vampire. *For once in a battle / That grip squeezed much tighter . . .*

By the next evening, Reuben felt his health returned somewhat, though apparently not enough. One of his few regulars—an older dwarvish woman with an intricately braided, silver-streaked beard, named Caterina—took one look at him upon arriving at her appointment and *tsked.*

"Poor thing," she said while Reuben poured them wine at his small parlor table. "The influx of foreigners are wearing our stellas out already, I see."

Reuben gave her a playful look of affront as he sat himself across from her. "I will pinch my cheeks harder before next time, then, if you perceive me as *worn-looking,* saer. No worse thing for a stella to be called."

Caterina waved an unbothered hand. "You are still radiant, Reubielocks. It is not your fault the Dijheri have no sense of decorum surrounding these types of establishments. Just as they have none in the council," she huffed before taking a large pull from her cup.

Reuben raised a brow as he sipped from his. "Council?"

"Oh—some talk happening between the Zaldian Priesthood and a few Dijheri representatives over the next few months," she said with a grimace, though it relaxed as she gave him a fond look. "Nothing to worry *your* pretty head about, my dear."

But while he busied his mouth and fingers between her thighs minutes later, Reuben's mind couldn't help but wander, and then wonder. Could this have to do with the dubious business Everic was in the city for, and the vampire was from the vast lands of Dijher? And if Reuben was right about his military background—could that imply these council talks had to do with war?

As the new week continued, Reuben managed to get more out of his new, foreign clients—many of whom were happy to explain the reason for their visit.

"The council will meet twice a month, probably until winter at latest," said a cloth merchant native of Dijher, all whilst slowly stripping Reuben. "The goal, so I hear, is to create a more friendly trade relationship between our two nations. Easing the flow of commerce—though past that, I know our ambassadors will propose an official alliance to your high priests, given the ever-looming, mutual threat of our northern neighbor."

Reuben cocked his head, deciding to play dumb and stroke the man's ego at once: "Oh? Are you attending as well?"

The merchant's fingers paused where they'd been bunching up Reuben's silk chemise. He laughed lowly, "A cloth merchant? You *flatter* me, Reubielocks," and then the conversation was discarded with the last piece of clothing.

Reuben learned later that certain public figures, like magnatus— leaders of the high houses—and their household could attend to observe the conversations, though only by invitation. Meanwhile, the rest of the city relied solely on official public notices for news.

One businesswoman lost her relaxed smile during their pillow talk when Reuben asked about the most recently-published bulletin, her voice rising as she swore the council cared only for profit.

"Even simple trades like ore and wheat will be negotiated for so long! Is *security* not a more pressing matter?" she finished in a heated tone that emphasized her soft, short-voweled accent, common in the Sazzeran Steppes.

Considering the Steppes was the most northern area under the city-state's jurisdiction—and the one and only part of it that the Loethian Empire tried to invade a couple centuries prior—Reuben didn't blame her.

"Careful, saer, or you'll undo all my hard work," he teased anyway, giving her a salacious wink. And found himself redoing that work soon after.

In truth, Reuben did find the matter a bit dull the more he heard about it. But it was still a nice change of pace from the trite personal things he usually listened to—a harmless little mystery to distract himself with, whilst kneeling or laying back on a bed.

By the second week's end, things steadied into a new, exhausting normal. Reuben found no issue filling up his schedule and his purse for once, even if his heart sank to see only 106 extra canters to show for it.

It was odd, how easily he could forget the futility of his hard work after just one appointment with a stupidly-rich vampire.

Of course, Sidarchus took issue with the lack as well. "I didn't think you'd put our careful client off so badly they would not return, not even to sample our *other* stellas," he snapped in the midst of their next accounting meeting.

Reuben's throat tightened, though he played it up further— allowing tears to well up in his eyes at Sidarchus's words. "Sid, I'm *so* sorry," he whispered. "It seems I . . . I ruined this opportunity, somehow."

The tactic worked; Reuben watched with silent relief as Sidarchus sighed, shoulders lowering. "I might have prepared you better too, of the letter's contents—only I wished not to worry you without necessity, Reubie." He gave Reuben a small, nostalgic half-smile, adding, "You have always spooked easily, you know, much like a nervous colt."

Reuben didn't want to feel the sudden crawling sensation under his skin, or think about what it reminded him of. So instead he made himself feel nothing and concede, "It was my fault," while standing to go. "I swear, I'll do better next time."

Sidarchus nodded. "And even if not," he promised Reuben, tapping the open logbook with a fond twinkle in his eye, "there will always be a place for you here, my dear."

Reuben had heard the promise many times before, and maybe once, felt comforted by it. Now, he spent the entirety of Repose in his bed, curtains drawn, accomplishing nothing during his night off. Unable to stop Sidarchus's voice from echoing over and over again in his skull.

The busy, demanding nights weren't just affecting him, however. It was easier to ignore his own problems over the next few days, as his worry grew for Isolde.

Bittie and Gringoll shot him concerned glances, when Isolde didn't show up at their usual breaking-fast meal for yet another afternoon that week. Sidarchus pointedly said nothing, going over the performance order without a pause to question if Isolde would be on stage. Adina—a blue-haired, infernal beauty, arguably the *brightest* star of the bordello—even gave Reuben a pitying look, as he passed her with a loaded plate and cup of tea to bring to Isolde from their small dining hall.

Isolde was somewhat of a mystery in comparison to the other stellas. What Reuben knew was only thanks to Sidarchus's offhand comments to him, about her foreign origins and criminal status, or the 25,000 cantergold she owed in reparations—Reuben made a point never to pry further.

But whoever she was before her time in the Starlet Eye, when she *could* work, Isolde was a natural. Perhaps choosier with her clients, though he could only be proud of her for that; Reuben helped Isolde learn which types to avoid when she started here. Three years later, many regulars still gushed about the "Starlet's Songbird" more than they'd ever cared to engage with old "Reubielocks."

When she couldn't work, however, Reuben often ended up exactly where he was now—watching her push away the food he'd brought without touching it, mumbling nonsensically as she curled back into a fetal position.

Reuben sat near the side of her bed in vigil, his violin case open and ready at the bedside table, while she stared into space with a tired sort of defeat. At least not sobbing or screaming, or trying to scratch at her own skin this time. The instances Reuben found her like that, he always played a *Soothe* incantation until she calmed enough to fall into exhausted sleep. For now, he only hummed a soft, unenchanted melody, working on his new song lyrics.

"Sidarchus will sell me to the Ravine," she whispered that evening, when muffled sounds outside her door signaled the other stellas getting ready for the night.

"He's *never* done that, Isi. The ones who can't keep up the work have always been allowed to find another contract themselves, or join the Priesthood."

And thanks to the one-time anomaly that was the vampire Everic Payne, Reuben still had quite a bit of cantergold to make up for her missed work before that became a real threat, he didn't add. Plus knowledge of how *else* to bargain, when money wasn't enough to keep Sidarchus appeased.

Isolde's soft brown eyes flickered to him, red-rimmed but more coherent than they'd been the last few nights. "There's a first time for everything. *I* was the only one my captain ever took undercover to Sazzera, you know."

Reuben resisted the urge to hush her. Usually, Isolde was tight-lipped about her past, and rightly so—if word got out that she not only originated from somewhere in the Loethian Empire, but once worked for their government, she'd be quick to lose most if not all of her clientele.

In this mind-addled state, however, she often grew more brazen, loose-lipped; it was yet another reason among dozens as to why Reuben did everything in his power to keep her safe and hidden until she recovered.

"Sid might have turned my mother out when all she could do was lay in bed and waste away," he pointed out. "But he didn't. He let her stay until her final breath."

"And what's to thank for that, I wonder?"

Reuben frowned. "Has he said something that made you think . . . ?"

Isolde's eyes drifted from his. "A slayer in the dark whispered it to me," she murmured.

Reuben held in a sigh and glanced toward the door—but apparently Isolde wasn't so far gone into her own mind to not notice.

"You need to go," she stated, sounding at once scared and resigned.

Reuben tried to smile at her. "I'll come by and check on you between appointments," he promised, knowing half of her problem during these episodes was not having someone she trusted to ground her. "Just rest. Like you're always telling me to do, yes?"

She frowned at him. "Yes, I—"

A knock on the door interrupted her.

Reuben crossed the room and had to hold back a wince as he opened it—instead of another stella or bordello staff, of course it had to be Sidarchus standing on the other side.

Reuben's worry gave way to confused shock, however, when his eyes traveled next up to a tall, familiar horned woman looming behind Sidarchus.

"Reubielocks!" Sidarchus exclaimed, a hand over his heart. "We couldn't find you in your chambers or the common area! It's almost opening time—why aren't you presentable yet? Never know when an important client might come calling," he chided, his eyes darting meaningfully to the side of him.

Reuben flushed. With a half hour until the doors opened, his hair was still in a messy, slept-on braid, his face bare of any powder or rouge.

But a customer being allowed in here at such an hour was unheard of—long past when even overnight customers were directed out of the stella wing.

Reminding Sidarchus of that was out of the question, of course, so Reuben replied, "My most humblest apologies," looking directly at Bev's unreadable fiery eyes as he added, "Is there such a client tonight?"

Bev made no response like usual, only emitted a rather impatient aura while Sidarchus nodded enthusiastically. "Another payment from your private saer, Reubie," he said, winking as he patted his pocket. "They insist on *your* presence and no other, dear. Their servant will take you again—Isolde can manage tonight's performance just fine, I'm sure."

Reubie's interest in earning more gold died an abrupt death.

Carefully, he leaned in and murmured, "I'm afraid she's still unwell, Sid," edging the door closed so as little of Isolde's room was visible as possible. "She can't work, much less perform on her own—I'll pay her share again tonight, but you'll need to skip our act, or the appointment will have to wait—"

"She'll manage a few songs, at least," Sidarchus said, with a firmness that always left no room for argument. "And if she needs support with you gone, *I* can always speak with her." His eyes narrowed at Reuben. "Let's not waste another opportunity, yes?"

Before Reuben could even think of how to respond, Sidarchus answered for him: "Yes—here's your chance to *do better,* as you said." He smiled brightly at Bev, assuring, "Just give him a moment to dress, saer," before heading towards another stella down the corridor.

Reuben felt sick. Now Sidarchus wouldn't *let* him solo the performance tonight—but leaving Isolde to stumble through it or worse, try and refuse Sidarchus on her own, could have consequences he didn't want to even consider.

He turned back to face Bev and forced out a denial: "I . . . I really can't tonight, saer. At least, not yet. Please—if you can just wait for a couple hours, or tell your friend I'm happy to plan for another evening as soon as tomorrow . . ."

She didn't answer, of course. Briefly Reuben thought her mutism might even be to his advantage—until she shook her head in a frustrated motion, brows pulled together over wide, urgent eyes.

Reuben resisted the urge to slam the door in her face. No matter how terribly rude her insistence felt, it *was* her friend's money that had allowed him to cover Isolde for the last three nights.

"My dear friend is very ill, you see," Reuben entreated. "I can't in good conscience leave her here. Especially if our manager intends to put her on stage in her condition."

Bev's brows stayed wrinkled together as she opened her mouth, as if to finally speak. But then she shook her head again, even more insistently this time, and Reuben lost his patience.

"He can have any other whore's blood," he hissed, "I'm the only one *she* has," and then shut the door.

Or tried to, anyway. Bev threw an arm out to catch it right as he moved—and Reuben, for all the work he put into strengthening his body, stood little chance against such sheer mass. He'd only pulled it halfway closed before her wide grip grabbed a firm, unyielding hold around the edge.

"*I* can stay with her."

It took him a moment to realize the voice had come from Bev. Softer and higher than he expected, taking up none of the space or presence her physique did. Rough—likely thanks to how little she spoke—and insistent . . . but edged with fear, too.

"My—my friend, needs *you*," she continued in the same soft, halting tone, taking advantage of Reuben's surprise to reopen the door a fraction.

Reuben stared into her blank, fiery gaze, and finally realized the woman was acting this way out of *desperation*, not disregard.

"Why?" he asked. And this time, when her lips pursed and she only shook her head again, frustrated, he understood now that it was more likely frustration with *herself* than Reuben.

Sighing, he grabbed Bev's wide arm and pulled her into the room.

"I'm sorry, Isolde, this'll be just a moment," he turned to tell his friend, though was surprised to see Isolde already on her feet, wrapping a robe around herself. "There's been a slight . . . schedule misunderstanding."

Isolde stared at their sudden guest with wariness as he spoke, though at least no panicked fear yet. So Reuben turned back to Bev and whispered, "Shall I find you a quill and parchment, saer? Even if I *did* decide on a whim to trust you with guarding her door and fending off our manager, I'd need a proper reason to."

Bev shook her head harder. "Can't write," she said, though only in a whisper this time. Desperation returned to her voice as she forcefully pushed out each word, "I . . . please. Help him. He . . . *whatever* you'd want, just . . ." Then she trailed off and gave him a pleading look.

Reuben sighed. Not for the first time, he wanted to question why *him*. And he hated the idea of leaving Isolde alone, with only this woman . . . but perhaps they could still find some compromise.

Like going back to his own chambers and having Bev bleed him here and now. Without the strange healing Everic's mouth had provided, performing tonight might be difficult, but hopefully not impossible. And Bev would have to carry the blood discreetly down to the Hollows, somehow. But Reuben could ask the kitchens to spare an empty bottle—perhaps, if it truly *was* so urgent, he could find a way—

"Reubie," Isolde interrupted his thoughts, suddenly much closer. She stood just behind him, still looking at Bev, though with more curiosity than anxiety now. "I'll be fine, if you need to go."

Reuben scoffed. "Even if you're feeling better, you still need *rest* after today."

"No, I won't sing—but if she can ward off Sidarchus, that's all I need," Isolde said with a nod at Bev, looking more clear-headed than before. Still, not enough for Reuben's comfort. "You can help her friend, and she'll help yours. Right?" She turned to Bev at the last word.

Bev's brows rose, though she quickly nodded in agreement.

When Reuben still hesitated, Isolde pulled him a few steps away. "Unless you just don't want to?" she said softly, looking up at him with wide eyes. "Or it was a bad experience last time? Because in that case, *don't* go, Reubie. Not for any money they offer."

Her concern always grated, despite how sincerely she gave it. Maybe because Reuben wasn't used to such consideration. Even more likely, because he hated the thought of *anyone* being able to perceive when he was weak, or where he was vulnerable.

So he smirked at her, replied, "Oh, just dull, I'd say—no rope or whips or anything," quietly relieved as Isolde relaxed and rolled her eyes at him.

The brief levity between them died as Bev took a single step closer, however. There was a deep line between her brows as she pulled out a small leather bag and pressed it against his chest, giving a sharp nod towards the door.

Everic Payne needed blood, apparently without delay—and yet Bev had come all the way to the Starlet Eye Bordello, to *Reuben,* for it.

Once Reuben took the bag from her, she spoke one more time in a whisper: "Please . . . *hurry.*"

# 5

# GOLDEN INCENTIVES

Less than ten minutes later, Reuben had put on a ruffled silk shirt and trousers, coiffed his hair to one side, and draped a lavender wrap around his head and shoulders, which had a silver-fringed edge that could subtly fall over his eyes. He'd also managed a rush job of his three-fold oil preparations—just to be sure—slid his mother's ring back on his finger, readied his violin case, and pocketed a vial of both voleris and base oil.

Last, he inspected the contents of Bev's pouch: a key, which he recognized as the one to Everic's door, and a square, metal token embossed with an intricate, golden crest.

Reuben stared. It was surreal, after all this time, holding an official city pass.

He couldn't delay further—still, the small weight of the bag hung heavy at his hip as he hurried out of the bordello. A nagging reminder of just how different their lives might have been if his mother ever gained access to such a token, like she'd tried so hard to before getting ill. If she then *could* have made it past the High Ring gates to the family she said lived up there, who even might have helped, despite her debt and bastard child.

Unwittingly, Reuben glanced up at the higher tiers and imagined himself walking in the opposite direction . . . but more than 62 years later, there was surely no one left to aid. None save those with the purest of elvish or dwarvish bloodlines would still be alive to remember Oriana now.

Reuben didn't look much like her, either—the same lips and pointed ears, perhaps, but otherwise red hair where hers had been a lovely chestnut color, his brown irises ringed in gold where her eyes had been dark, and strong-jawed and sharp-nosed where she had been soft and rounded.

No remaining family of hers was likely to claim him, and his natural father was never spoken of, much less known by Reuben to turn to or rely on. From how Oriana's face would drop, her expression growing haunted whenever he asked about it, Reuben concluded from a young age that he was better off never knowing.

He ignored the weight at his hip after that and, whilst trekking down zigzagging alleys into the Hollows once more, kept his mind focused on earning the one thing he could rely on: gold.

It propelled him through fear, discomfort, and pain—and a good thing, too. With how much he'd pushed his body the last two and a half weeks, the long walk on its own reintroduced every ache to his senses. By the time Reuben reached the same doorless entrance a half hour later, he felt every step like a knife up his back.

A particularly loud bray of the mule and a sharp stable smell greeted him within. Reuben squinted to find a torch, but after a few seconds gave up and cast a simple *Light* spell on his wrapped shawl with the quick lyric: *"Quietly he waits / Torchlight at the gate."*

Soft light emanated from the fabric in a small circumference around him—enough to see where he was stepping, if not dispel the shadows. And with each step, he was closer to earning the equivalent of 10 long, fully-booked night shifts, all for the price of a small, draining cut. The thought helped Reuben brave crossing the quiet, strangely eerie underground room on his own.

When he entered the second room, an entire swine lay dead on the floor to greet him.

Reuben yelped, jumping back. But nothing jumped from the shadows; whatever killed it wasn't around. He swallowed hard, noting the twin puncture wounds weeping blood near its neck. A small smear of the blood traveled from where the dead carcass lay, deeper into the dwelling toward his destination.

Maybe Bev had been wrong and this wasn't urgent anymore, Reuben thought in desperation, terribly spooked now. Certainly he wasn't about to find Everic wasting away from a lack of blood, if the vampire already drank an entire animal of this size.

But then, what other emergency would require Everic to call on him?

Reuben pushed down the rising fear that this was some long, elaborate trap of Jophiel's after all, and told himself the urgency didn't matter. He'd only get his 500 cantergold if he kept going—and so he gingerly stepped around the trail, into the storage room, and finally to the shelf mechanism at the back where Everic's hidden door lay.

The shelves had already been shifted, the door exposed. Much more strange, another storage shelf on the adjacent wall had been moved too, revealing a blackened iron door with triple the amount of locks.

Reuben felt absolutely no desire to know what lay beyond it.

He forced his attention away before his aching feet sent him running and fumbled with shaky hands for the key in Bev's pouch. Once found, he tried to fit it into the lock—then winced, as the click of the key echoed throughout the otherwise deathly silent space.

Reuben didn't spare his shadowed, blood-streaked surroundings so much as a parting glance before hurrying in to meet the vampire Everic Payne once more.

Nothing jumped out to grab him as he walked inside. The same well-furnished room awaited him, though only a single candle burned at the desk this time. A faint chemical smell also greeted his nose, pungent and strangely familiar to Reuben.

Then Reuben heard a sharp, pained gasp to his left; he spun in alarm to face its source, grabbing for his violin case latch on instinct.

But it was nothing threatening. Unless Everic—slumped in one of the sitting area's chairs, one hand weakly clutching at his arm as it gushed out a dark shade of blood—should be considered as such.

Under the fall of hair obscuring half his face, he looked even paler than the first time they met. Sicklier too, despite the fact the smeared trail of swine blood ended quite close to where Everic sat. Half of his clothing was stained in the same color; worse, so were his eyes—bright red irises staring back at Reuben.

"Your eyes," Reuben blurted out, stumbling back a step.

Everic only blinked, regarding Reuben with sheer wonder in return. "You're . . . glowing?"

Reuben's confusion dampened the fear at least, until he realized what Everic meant: he was still emanating a magical light thanks to the spell on his shawl. It didn't seem to be burning Everic, but Reuben still hastily ended the spell with a quick tap to the fabric.

The vampire's irises shone a much brighter red in the dark, Reuben took in with a cold shiver, until Everic grimaced back down at his wound.

His *wound.*

"You're injured," Reuben gasped in sudden alarm, shrugging off the strap to his instrument's case with a very different intent now.

"Reubie?" he heard Everic question weakly while Reuben opened the case, quickly tightening up the screw of his bow and running the frayed hair over rosin.

"I can play something to heal you," Reuben assured, giving his violin strings a few testing plucks. Then he rested the old instrument on his collarbone and started the melody of a wordless *Healing Song* he knew better than the sound of his own name—a soft, melancholic tune he'd learned to play for Oriana once he lived with her at the bordello.

Music on its own could be a balm to the soul. But charged with crowdcraft, it could convince the body to heal minor injuries and sicknesses as well, so long as a person was conscious and willing to hear it.

But before Reuben could get more than a few notes in, Everic repeated in a firmer voice over the music, "Reubie." He wore a very grim smile when Reuben glanced his way. "Reubie—you can't heal me."

Then the vampire winced—and Reuben noted Everic's hand press a little harder over the bicep of his wounded arm, right as a shiny black ichor leaked from the wide gash.

Reuben's bow froze over the bridge of the violin. A cold shudder rattled through his ribcage, like he'd just swallowed an entire bowl of ice.

Unless vampiric blood always looked this way . . . Reuben had already seen this type of necrotic wound before, up close and personal.

He failed to keep his voice steady as he met Everic's ominously-red eyes, arguing, "If—if the wound was magically inflicted, you'll need more than bandages—I don't know greencraft, I'm afraid, but crowdcraft might still help—"

"Any type of healing magic is *useless* on something like me," Everic interrupted, his voice sharper than Reuben had ever heard it.

Although, that was based on extremely limited experience. They'd only spent an hour conversing up till now, Reuben dizzy and half-conscious for much of it. He didn't know Everic at all—maybe, just like a wounded animal, injured vampires were more prone to bite.

Reuben fully lowered his violin, keeping a safe distance. "When did you get the injury?" Grimacing, then, at how unsure his voice had sounded without his permission.

Everic shrugged, then winced as more black ichor dripped down, falling to splatter and hiss in a growing pool on the stone floor. "A few hours ago," he replied evenly despite that. "Bev already brought a pig from the stable to help me regain strength, but the wound *still* won't close up. Instead, it seems to be . . ."

"Widening," Reuben finished for him, swallowing hard. Remembering the woman's gut wound on his chamber floor after Waron stabbed her, as more ichor and blood ooze from between Everic's fingertips. He understood why he'd recognized that off-putting chemical smell in the air, now.

Admittedly, Reuben couldn't say who all had access to devilcrafted blades, outside of the Allunata—a powerful group of criminals and devilcrafters which Waron was currently the head of. But the reminder of his sadistic old client frightened Reuben far worse than anything else tonight.

He hid his fear with a shaky, self-deprecating laugh. "And you had Bev call for *me*, not a cleric?"

"*Godcraft* certainly won't work," Everic said, and if possible his voice held more vitriol than before.

Then his red eyes flickered to Reuben's neck.

For a moment, Reuben was about to scoff at him for thinking of food at a time like this—until he caught on. "So . . . you think the blood of a whore can do what celestial power can't?" he surmised.

"Are you willing to try and see?" Everic replied, wincing again while he attempted to sit more upright.

500 gold, Reuben silently chanted.

He stowed his instrument back in its case on the ground, blew out a breath, and willed himself a few steps closer. "Where's your blade?"

Quickly it was fetched from the draped belt on the desk Everic pointed to, along with cloth for bandaging and an empty goblet Reuben was pretty sure had contained his blood once before. Only after placing it all on the side table next to Everic's chair, rolling up his sleeve, and holding up the blade, however, did Reuben stop to think about the fact he'd never cut into flesh like this, much less his own.

Gold was a powerful incentive—enough to take him away from Isolde, on the painful journey down to the Hollows, through the shadowed, blood-streaked tunnels of a vampire's abode, and all the way up until this moment, positioning the edge of a knife at his wrist.

But Reuben wasn't quite sure, in the end, what it was inside of him that actually propelled him to dig the sharp point into his skin.

It hurt *worse* than the first time, strangely. Reuben bit hard on his lip, which only half-muffled the pained whimper that escaped. Meanwhile, Everic watched with a bleary, single-focused stare as the first beads of blood dripped, then poured down Reuben's wrist and into the cup. He seemed far less composed than their last encounter, his gaze hungrily following each droplet.

The flow was also much slower this time. Reuben must not have cut the right vein, he realized by the time the goblet just barely filled halfway. And he only felt a bit light-headed when the cup was full, having kept his mind busy with thoughts of what to add next to his lyrics for Everic. Something to do with the vampire's strange eyes—though more about the weary age in them than the indecisive coloring.

Finally, Reuben pulled his hand back, held the single bandage against his wrist, and nodded at Everic to drink.

Everic's ichor-stained hand left his wound to snatch the goblet a second later.

Reuben watched with equal parts fascination and disquiet as he caught a brief glimpse of the vampire's extended fangs. They clicked awkwardly against the cup rim before Reuben's blood was drunk in front of him, Everic's head leaning back near the end and exposing a long column of pale throat.

Then, just as Everic lowered the cup, the sickly pallor to his skin faded, the sharpness of his cheekbones softened. Even the black ichor leaking from his arm slowed.

When his dark lashes fluttered open, the eyes that regarded Reuben back were once again shining a bright gold.

The changing color *did* have something to do with what the vampire consumed, then. Reuben filed the observation away to ask about later, for now only remarking in a soft tone, "*Zald's balls . . . the common blood of a whore indeed.*"

Everic shook his head whilst licking the red tinge from his lips. "Your blood is anything but common," he replied in a very serious tone, though with the slightest smile curling his mouth.

Reuben didn't like how pleased he felt, on top of relieved, to hear it.

He waved his hand in a breezy, unbothered motion. "You're right. Who knows—maybe there's a rogue Dijheri prince somewhere back in my bloodline." And on that subject, Reuben stopped putting pressure on his own wound and reached out for the emptied goblet in Everic's grip, readying himself for the next round of bloodletting.

Everic didn't hand the goblet back, however. His bright gaze now flickered to the door Reuben had left open. "Where is Bev?"

"Oh! I had . . . unfinished *business* she offered to stay behind and take care of," Reuben said, hurrying over to the door to shut it with his uninjured arm. "Nothing unsavory, don't worry, just assisting a friend—I don't usually start work before dusk, you know."

He turned and flashed a reassuring smile at the vampire, putting pressure back on his wound, only to then note *Everic's* injury. Everic followed his gaze downward, and both of them watched as the gash shrunk and lost its ink-like discoloring. Then, right before their eyes, Everic's skin knit itself back together entirely, leaving nothing but a pale patch of finely-muscled arm.

Everic set down the goblet. "Neither do I. Nor do I intend to make a repeat of this particular venture," he said as he stood and shrugged off his long, ichor-and-blood-stained shirt.

Reuben took in the words, though he simultaneously took in the vampire's form whilst Everic strode over to the wardrobe. He'd seen far too many bare bodies over the last four decades—but on *occasion*, Reuben could still appreciate the shape of some.

The shift of Everic's neck and shoulders as he walked, for instance, or the curve of his chest in contrast to the flat board of his stomach. A bit of dark hair covering his pectorals and trailing down from his navel; a thin slash of a scar wrapped around his abdomen to his waist and a larger puncture scar just under his shoulder blade. How his wide back rounded and moved with sharp, muscled lines as he knelt to open one of the wardrobe's bottom drawers.

Reuben felt rueful at the sight. Everic's blunt attitude and occasional sharp tone aside, there would have been no need to pretend attraction if he was a typical customer. Physical beauty wasn't everything—but it certainly *helped*.

Normally, anyway. It didn't make the knife sting any less, Reuben thought as he knelt down and busied himself putting away his violin one-handed.

He held his injured arm close to his chest, saying, "May I ask where you've been, the last three weeks?" as Everic changed clothes in Reuben's peripheral. And because Sidarchus's worries had slowly taken over his own, Reuben clarified, "Or at least—if I did something wrong, that you went elsewhere for a 'steady source' since then?"

Everic stiffened and threw Reuben a sharp look, though it was dulled by the fact he had one arm halfway through a sleeve. "Unless you broke your vow and told someone of my nature," he replied in a testing, suspicious tone, "what wrong could have been done?"

Reuben's eyes widened. "I haven't breathed a word to *anyone*, I swear it."

His mounting panic halted as he saw Everic relax at the words.

"Thank you," the vampire said with a small incline of his head, finishing his change into the fresh linen shirt.

Reuben had never struggled so hard to keep his mouth shut and not pry further.

He didn't care about his clients' lives, generally. But right now, his mind burned with a thousand questions: what Everic had been up to these last two weeks, who the other attacker was, if they survived. *Why* they stabbed Everic in the first place.

As he latched his violin case closed, he heard Everic say, "And also . . . thank you, for coming this evening as well."

Reuben looked up to respond—and startled at their sudden proximity. Everic was holding out a hand to him, palm up, his expression perfectly neutral.

Hesitantly, Reuben took it, and shivered at the cold touch.

Everic kept hold of Reuben's hand after he helped him to his feet, walking them over to the bed. "I haven't sent for you because I've been trying a less *official* way of establishing contacts. No invitations and frilly collars required, at least."

He gestured at the bed, and Reuben obediently sat down at its edge as he listened, even if he didn't feel half so tired or light-headed as the first bloodletting. Though that also meant he was much more distracted by the sharp, pulsing pain in his wrist, despite his interest in Everic's cryptic explanation.

"I thought it would be more efficient, more . . . conducive to my personal talents," Everic finished, gesturing at himself.

Reuben eyed where Everic's arm had just been leaking necrotic ichor, then raised a brow. "As a 'simple businessman,' you said?"

And there came that feeling of satisfaction again, as his question cracked another half-smile on the vampire's face. This one made Everic's eyes crinkle into half-moon shapes, the grim lines around his mouth softening as he responded wryly, "Well—I never said what *kind* of business."

Reuben chuckled, louder and less graceful than his usual practiced giggles. Just for a second until he quelled it, of course, watching Everic walk over to his desk.

The vampire sighed down at the half-written papers littered on it. "But it's slow, frustrating work, going the proper routes for the right connections to society. Slower than I have time for."

Reuben raised both brows this time. "High Ring society?"

Everic turned back to him with sharp alarm—though it relaxed into a considering look, as if rethinking something as he beheld Reuben.

Reuben hurried to amend, "Not that it matters of course, saer. I only wish to know if I can be of further service."

Everic's eyes narrowed. "Do you have connections there?"

"Oh, not at all," Reuben denied, even if it was a *bit* more complicated than that. "Only a handful of magnatus and high priests have ever entered the bordello in all my time there, and usually just to view a private performance." He gestured at himself with a self-deprecating laugh. "I don't exactly run in the same circles as them."

Everic didn't laugh with him. "And they're nothing a person *should* aspire to know," he answered sternly. "My aims only make it an ugly necessity."

"Less ugly than getting stabbed, I'd say," Reuben teased. "Though I can't imagine how such contrary methods of establishing contacts could achieve the same goal."

Everic's lips thinned into a single, tensed line, not offering to elaborate.

Reuben *could* imagine the disaster of Everic Payne in a High Ring socialite atmosphere, however. Given the vampire's stiff demeanor, direct words, and intensely serious attitude, Reuben didn't blame him for trying the bloodier path for his mysterious business. The vampire's disposition encapsulated everything high society *wasn't*.

Even in this city of riches and opportunity, all the gold in the world couldn't make up for a *tarnished* personality.

Gold which Reuben never received the second portion of tonight— reminding him, then, that there was still another goblet of blood to mete out.

"I don't think I could cut quite so deeply as needed, by the way," he admitted, nodding at his own arm. "You may have to use the knife again when you'd like the rest of it."

Everic frowned and glanced over at the goblet across the room. Instead of retrieving it, however, he approached the bed again, holding a hand out.

Maybe he would drink straight from the wound, since the cut was already open. Reuben didn't argue—just bit his lip and placed his arm into Everic's waiting palm.

The vampire's dark brows furrowed once he started inspecting the wound. "You've butchered yourself," Everic said in a very disapproving tone.

"Not as much as I needed to, apparently," Reuben tried to laugh— only to choke on the first chuckle, when Everic did lean down and put his mouth against Reuben's wrist.

But only to seal the cut with his mouth, as he did the first night. More coherent this time, Reuben found it strange how painful and yet soothing Everic's cool lips felt, quickly replaced with a tingling numbness as his tongue swiped along the jagged seam of the open cut. Besides letting out a pained gust of breath, Reuben kept very still through the conflicting sensations.

His wound didn't heal miraculously, of course—but the pain had already eased by the time Everic finished.

"Enough for tonight," Everic said, even as his eyes lingered on Reuben's wrist.

Reuben wanted to simply be grateful. Instead, an anxious static started buzzing in his head. "Come now—no need to deny yourself with *me*, saer."

"I was already filled, as you probably saw walking in," Everic dismissed. "Just in need of something . . . stronger."

Reuben forced out a laugh as Everic walked away, speaking after him, "A kind compliment—but if it was merely a matter of cutting myself wrong, I can always try again now."

Everic glanced back, a sharp frown on his face. "Really? And if you rendered your arm useless on a second try?"

He was angry now, for whatever reason, and Reuben could feel his anxiety climbing in response. "My magic may be weaker than some, but it can heal a simple wound," he replied, wincing a bit as it came out too defensive. As Everic crossed over to the desk, Reuben switched back to entreating, "I assure you, saer, I came prepared to give you all of what was agreed to before."

What had he done wrong, Reuben inwardly panicked all the while, for a vampire to already be losing desire for his blood?

When Everic returned, it was with a few more bandages in hand. "Well, I am not so keen on having you faint *every* time you come here," he responded in an abruptly mild tone, and began binding Reuben's wound in tight layers of cloth. "You don't look like you're in a state to be weakened further."

Reuben's heart sank. *There* it was, then—the mistake he made the first night, just as Sidarchus suspected.

But for all the lies Reuben could compose, his health was much harder to hide. And this was even sooner than usual for a new client to clock Reuben as weak, unreliable, and ultimately undesirable. Usually, the disinterest came after he had to cancel one too many appointments, or denied a request that he wasn't fit for.

Reuben never blamed them; pity, by nature, wasn't an arousing emotion. Only the ones who *liked* using a weak thing ever put up with him for long—and too often, were the type to like weakening him further.

Which was the reason Reuben had yet to keep a single wealthy returning customer. And why, despite the extended life his elvish lineage would supposedly grant him, in his heart of hearts Reuben suspected the only way he'd leave the bordello for good was in oil-soaked wrappings, another body to dispose of in the public pyre.

Just like his mother before him.

Reuben painted an easy smile across his lips and resolved to mask any adverse reactions better in the future. "A single goblet for 1,000 gold? I don't think even the Voice of Zald herself could claim to drink such an expensive vintage."

After a belated pause, Everic corrected, "Just 500 for you, isn't it?" When Reuben glanced up, the vampire met his gaze with a single raised brow. "If Bev was correct in observing you only receive half," he amended whilst tying off another bandage.

Reuben had rarely been questioned about such a thing, though he still kept a practiced response ready. "I would never see a quarter of it without the generosity of the bordello," he murmured, his arm quick to drop once Everic was finished. "Thank you, saer."

"I believe the gratitude is mine to express," Everic responded, before heading over to the desk and retrieving a small bag resting there.

Reuben deflated in relief at the sight. "I'll just hope I can earn it better next time then, saer," he sighed.

And yet, after Everic returned and the sizable weight of 500 cantergold lay on his lap, Reuben's contentment at the fruit of his meager labor all at once soured. Ruined, the moment Everic spoke the words: "And I'll hope you find many ways to enjoy the gold. Less work, and more rest and revelry, perhaps? Besides all the silk and finery you seem to like," and he gestured offhandedly at Reuben's person.

It wasn't said with derision. Everic didn't even seem bothered at the thought of so much cantergold being *wasted* like that.

But Reuben was. Shame, defeat, indignation at Everic's false perception of him—despite the fact Reuben had painstakingly crafted the flippant, carefree persona of "Reubielocks" himself—it all swirled into one large toxic brew of discontent, burning sharp and angry in his gut.

Never for long before the anger was doused by fear and fatigue, of course. So Reuben just swallowed down the feeling for now and mustered up his prettiest, most bashful smile for his promising new client.

"Something like that," he agreed.

# 6

# MORE MISTAKES

With less blood taken, less recovery was needed. Reuben left earlier this time, carrying a bag of gold at his hip and a lingering disquiet in his heart.

Outside in the open air, however, with hours before his needed return to the bordello, Reuben refused to waste this rare break on angry rumination. He glanced to his left at the stairway winding up towards the main ring of the city . . . then, taking a deep breath, turned right.

The expansive city hugged Mount Sazzo's slope at a gradual decline, right up until the last row of hollowed dwellings where Reuben was headed. From there, it dropped straight down into the darkness that was the Ravine, a wide crack in the earth where everything from granite to iron to cantergold was mined and refined. The workers with a home to return to would soon wake and take a metal lift down for another day of grueling labor—though not for another hour, with dawn still no more than a distant, deep-gray thought.

Reuben was tempted to lower his shawl at such a miniscule chance of crossing a Zaldian cleric or sentry guard. His face, while a public spectacle thanks to their nightly performances, was hardly recognizable in this dark. But the deathly beating a previous stella once had taken for "publicly exposing" herself, decades ago now, still lived on in Reuben's mind as if it was yesterday.

So he kept the fringed shawl over his eyes until he approached a small, well-worn door along the lowest row of dwellings. Here, the most ancient burrows remained, abandoned to all but the horribly impoverished.

And yet a small smile lifted his lips at the sight. After all, it was here, in the city's utmost squalor, that the last of his known family lived.

Nahlia and Daxus lay asleep when Reuben entered the one-room abode carved into the mountainside. Rats scattered at his arrival; a couple of chickens let out sleepy, disgruntled clucks. Daxus's thunderous snores paused, the ancient dwarf shifting, and then picked up again a moment later.

All of it just as it was since Reuben's childhood, as if the passing decades were nothing more than a bad dream.

Reuben shut the door as carefully as he'd opened it, tied his hair back with some loose twine, grabbed Nahlia's apron from its wall hook—and slowly let out the breath he'd been holding for the last three months.

He started with gathering up the dirty linen and dishes into differing piles. Wishing, not for the first time, that he knew how to create a song that would purify water, as he used murky liquid from their tiny cistern and an old lump of soap for the job. For all that crowdcraft was useful on people, chord progressions couldn't bend the elements like they did a person's mind.

Reuben saved cleaning the chicken coop for last, after the laundry had been scrubbed and hung to dry. It was past time to head back by then, from what pale light the tiny carved window above the door provided. So he cleaned quickly around the squawking protests of the hens, ignoring the knife-like sensations in his spine, the lingering pain in his wrist, the lightheadedness threatening his equilibrium.

Who knew when any of this would get done otherwise?

Reuben scrubbed his hands thoroughly afterward, then reached up to the carved niche above the washbasin, taking an inconspicuous piece of crockery from the makeshift shelf and shaking it. A bit surprised, when the pot felt light and empty—not even the smallest jangle of coin sounding from within.

He'd left the equivalent of 100 canters last time, Reuben was almost positive, even if in the lesser form of silvers and foreign coinage. He glanced over at the old couple worriedly whilst filling the little pot again, this time to the brim, wondering what on earth had cost them so much with only water and food to pay for.

But daylight was approaching, and Reuben had no time to get these two coherent enough for questions.

He stayed only a moment longer—for his own sake.

Daxus's snores paused again, his eyelids flickering as Reuben leaned down and pressed a quick kiss on the dwarf's bald head. Then he moved around to Nahlia, though her long, drooped ear twitched at his approach, the elf's eyes cracking open.

Wrinkled lips stretched into a sleepy smile. "Reuben?" she whispered. "Is that you, sunshine?"

All at once, Reuben wanted to collapse. He wanted to burrow in between these two, on this same prickly straw mattress where he'd once slept beside them as a child. He wanted to shut out the world, never hear the name *Reubielocks* or worry about clients or managers or *gold* again. He wanted nothing at all, save to have everything taken care of for him.

But these two were the ones who needed taking care of, now.

"I'm sorry I couldn't visit sooner," he replied, grasping her hand when it reached for his.

She sighed, looking up at him with such open adoration it made Reuben's chest ache. "You always come back, my sweet boy."

"I'll bring water again next time," he promised. "There's plenty of gold in the coin pot now, so you can keep paying for an errand runner to get it too, alright? And try to remember to search the coop a little more carefully. I found a few rotten eggs, and that'll attract much worse than rats."

Reuben paused to make sure she understood, though all Nahlia responded with was, "Daxus keeps wanting to walk the rim with you again," in a disapproving tone.

Reuben leaned down and, after pressing a kiss to her forehead, murmured, "Make sure he doesn't get into too much trouble?"

"That old fool never listens to me," she grouched with a jerk of her chin towards Daxus's snoring form—acting much closer to the sharp-witted, no-nonsense old woman who watched over him as a child. Though Nahlia's weathered face softened back into something guileless as she asked, "Come back to us soon?"

It was always uncertain when Reuben could. Days of Repose gave him the best chance to slip away, sneaking out in the plainest attire he owned right after his accounting meeting. The true risk was in getting *back*. Reuben had to manage it without crossing a sentry guard or bordello security, and in time before Sidarchus noticed. With how closely their manager kept an eye on things these days, a monthly excursion to the Hollows had seemed too risky to justify of late.

But if Reuben kept seeing Everic, and could on occasion take advantage of being sent to the Hollows anyway . . . it was a reason *better* than gold, for Reuben to make their agreement last.

"Soon," Reuben agreed—and hoped that he wasn't lying, for once.

By the time he returned to the Starlet Eye, his spine sent painful twitches down his legs with every step. Still, Reuben checked on his friend before heading to bed—sighing in relief when he opened her door and found Isolde peacefully asleep.

Bev was slumped in the chair at her bedside, blinking tired eyes open at the sound of the door. And then they widened, the woman quick to stand and cross the short distance to him before he'd even entered the room.

Bev stepped outside of it, glancing around worriedly before whispering, "Is . . . i-is he . . . ?"

"He's alright," Reuben finished for her.

Her shoulders sagged with relief. Then, to his surprise, the infernal woman raised a hand and made a slow, simple motion—communicating one of the few Dijheri gestures he knew outside of what was useful for his work; words like "yes," "no," "stop," and "hurts."

This one meant, "Thank you."

Briefly he wondered if she had known the language all this time and simply hadn't deigned to use it with him. Then Bev directed a fond glance at the half-open doorway, toward the one person Reuben knew who *did* have a full knowledge of the language, and he put two-and-two together.

"Thank *you* for helping her," he said with a small, genuine smile. Which widened when Bev quickly shook her head, then nodded in Isolde's direction.

She raised both hands this time, though after making a halting motion Bev just sighed and gave up the attempt, offering him another short nod instead. Nothing more was communicated, before Reuben gave back the key and city token, and Bev went on her way.

Reuben returned to his own chamber just down the corridor with heavy, pained steps. He didn't risk even sitting down to count the remaining precious gold. Small spasms running down his legs warned that time was short before he'd lose function of them entirely;

all Reuben managed was a quick wash of his face and change into a silk chemise before the pain grew unbearable and he collapsed into bed.

The fat sack of gold, dropped on the bedside table next to him, didn't appease his mind from the pain. For all that he'd risked his health and Isolde's safety for it, Reuben only felt weary now as he thought of the meager ten days he'd just bought her. On top of that, Daxus and Nahlia's little coin pot ran empty far too quickly these days, cutting into Reuben's savings further to keep them somewhat healthy and off the streets. Beyond *that*, there was the exhausting futility of it all, working and paying and working even more, only to lie here in pain for his efforts.

Maybe he *should* spend the rest on revelry, feasting, and luxury like Everic had assumed, and give up on any notion of his or Isolde's freedom.

The thought only made him want to give up on himself.

Reuben had an effective way of halting such dark musings *and* muting the pain, luckily. He reached over and fumbled to open the gold bag where he'd transferred the unused vials, spilling coins onto the floor before he finally grasped the voleris bottle in their midst.

He told himself he'd stop at a few sips, at first. But the pain kept coming; it wasn't until Reuben drank down every last drop that the ache of his limbs and the shooting nerve-pain in his spine finally dulled into far-off nebulous things his mind could float away from.

Though he didn't expect what memories it floated towards: Everic greedily drinking Reuben's blood from the goblet; the scar under Everic's shoulder blade rippling under the motions of his arms; Everic bringing Reuben's wounded wrist up to his parted lips.

The memories held no conscious thread between them save for the vampire himself. Still, Reuben's addled mind found it all a rather pleasant wave to drift on until a fitful sleep finally found him.

Grunting and heavy breathing behind him, the oiled slide of a cock filling him. A hand pressing down on his shoulder, silk sheets beneath him.

A position Reuben knew, easy as breathing.

And Zurnick had turned out to be the affectionate sort. After the orkish man let out a harsher grunt, pinning Reuben's hips to the mattress with his own as he ground out a deep, shuddering orgasm, he brushed away a few curls that had fallen into Reuben's eyes. Letting out a pleased hum, before giving Reuben's arse a pat and carefully pulling out.

It was always nice to finish the work night with a gentler client like this. Reuben didn't feel more than the usual pains as he grabbed a rag and twisted around. The soft smile came easily to his face, while he cleaned himself and his new repeat customer dressed.

"Might be able to see you sooner than next week, Reubielocks," Zurnick said as he finished tying his boots.

Reuben raised a brow. "Are your wool sales increasing, then?"

"About to be," the man answered around a gummy, tusk-mouthed grin. "Didn't you hear? Tariffs with Dijher have been cut in half."

Reuben sat up more, feeling an idle interest at this news. "The trade meetings are going well, then," he murmured.

"Splendidly! I may even get to try out that fancy potion your locals always talk about when I mention this place," Zurnick said.

Reuben smiled, even as he tried to dissuade, "Oh, it's nothing too special; just a concoction to relax the body, help things along. *You* certainly have no trouble with virility, saer," he added with a wiggle of his brows.

"For you, then," Zurnick smiled, flipping a Dijheri silver piece onto the bed. "The Loethians may have been on to something all this time—war is *great* for business."

While no declaration of military alliance had been made, much less a war against the Loethian Empire, the lifted spirits throughout the city after the recent trade agreement translated into even better business for the stellas. When Sidarchus took personal orders for the month during breaking-fast one afternoon, many of them indulged in a bit of finery: Adina bought a silver-laced canopy; an older stella called Jemeye added a large Dijheri rug to her order; Bittie requested a new set of silk ropes and a priest to come inspect Gringoll's aching tooth.

Once Sidarchus reached where Reuben and Isolde sat, Reuben said, "An extra stock of my usual," thinking of how much more oil and voleris his influx of customers necessitated, "and . . . my bow, it needs to be rehaired again."

"Again?" Sidarchus asked, as he always did. But the house manager didn't gripe about sending for the luthier, for once—his mouth split into a wide smile. "Why not a polish too? On the house!" Sidarchus declared as he added it to the list.

At that, all eyes in their small dining hall turned in Reuben's direction. Some, like Adina and Jemeye, just looked curious and surprised. Reuben could feel envy emanating from others like Gringoll and Bittie, however, who were indentured as well.

Reuben doubted they'd feel so envious if they also received a personal visit from Sidarchus later that evening, however.

Too often, Sidarchus didn't knock—like in this case, startling Reuben in the midst of dusting rouge onto his cheekbones.

"Reubielocks," Sidarchus said warmly as he walked in without a care—an unspoken reminder of who owned the place and carried each room key. "I'm so pleased your private client came back to us. And even requested *you* alone! You must have left an impression." He stopped behind Reuben's chair, leaning against it.

"I expect to hear from them regularly," Reuben agreed, finishing off his blush.

Sidarchus nodded, though his gaze tightened. "And . . . their servant staying behind—did she explain to you what all *that* was about?"

Reuben tried to feign confusion. "She stayed behind, yes—though I have no idea why," he shrugged, then pointed out, "she doesn't seem to talk much."

*A lie is best served between two easy, digestible truths,* his mother once advised him. In her case, after claiming a contagious sickness to get rid of a disliked client.

"A good quality in a servant, most of the time," Sidarchus agreed. Then he leaned in further, eyes narrowing. "I trust *your* silence to keep too, as your client instructed. Do not speak of them, or the money you receive, or any concerns that may arise, with Isolde or anyone—but me. Is that understood, Reubie?"

Once, Reuben might have *wanted* to confide in Sidarchus over this precarious situation. The older elvish man had enjoyed a long, successful career at the bordello, before he used his saved-up earnings to buy the pleasure house. Now the wine tasted richer, the stellas looked prettier, and the old days of the Starlet Eye—when their security guards dealt out brute punishment for the manager, whenever a stella did not behave as told—were a fading stain of the past.

As dead as Oriana, who suffered such treatment every day of Reuben's life until her last few years, when it was too late to save her.

As a young man, Reuben had admired and trusted Sidarchus for his considerate behavior. But here and now, his smile was entirely contrived as he met the older man's eyes in the mirror and replied, "Of course, Sid. No one but you."

Sidarchus put a hand on Reuben's shoulder, squeezing it before he turned to go. "Good boy. Keep up the great work—that debt won't undo itself!"

And, just three nights later, it seemed Reuben would have another chance.

Barely two songs into his and Isolde's act, he noticed Bev joining the crowd. With none of the urgency of the last occurrence emanating from her, the music told him—just an anxious discomfort about her surroundings, and a quiet fascination as she watched Isolde's performance in particular.

Reuben approached her immediately after. "Only five days, and your friend sends you back for more?" he asked, mostly to make sure of her purpose here. Given how Bev's head had not lowered in his direction still—turning to follow Isolde's path as she joined the crowd—it was obvious the Starlet's Songbird had ensnared yet another admirer.

Belatedly she blinked and did face Reuben, however, giving a short nod.

Reuben put on a smile. "Excellent timing, then, as I have no engagements arranged yet tonight. Did you already inform my manager?"

To his relief, Bev nodded her head again—so Reuben didn't approach Sidarchus's desk, only went up to fetch his things from upstairs. And threw a reassuring smile towards Isolde a minute later, when she watched him and Bev leave the bordello with a questioning gaze.

Reuben had no intentions to share details with her, however, whether Sidarchus forbade it or not. Telling her any specifics about this job would only add unnecessary worries on her shoulders, and *Zaldus knew* Isolde didn't need any more.

Besides, he had yet to gather many details himself. Reuben spent almost the entirety of his third appointment with Everic in silence as the man cut his wrist with a slow, careful precision, filled the two goblets and not a drop more, and ensured Reuben was given sustenance before leaving him there on the bed. Any of Reuben's attempts at small talk were met with a short, curt response or nonverbal acknowledgement. The only moment of interest was after the vampire drained a goblet of Reuben's blood—and his eyes, starting out a deep emerald color that night, quickly changed back to molten gold.

A week later the cycle repeated, with Bev fetching him, Everic draining him, and Reuben spending the remainder of the visit alone to recover. With the exception of him inquiring about Everic's eyes, earning the vague reply that "the diet of the prey usually affects the coloring," Everic interacted with him only to get his meal.

That was all there was to it. Nothing complicated, nothing intimate, just as Everic had promised—save for the fleeting moments his mouth traced the line of Reuben's bleeding wrist.

Reuben tried to be grateful. He enjoyed the chance to leave the bordello, certainly, and even the secluded tranquility of the vampire's candlelit hideaway, so different from the ruckus and revelry of the bordello. The bloodletting only made him dizzy and nauseous, not so weakening that Reuben couldn't feel back to normal after a day or two.

But the cutting itself seemed to take much longer now, in comparison to the first time Everic used the knife. If Everic was fucking him while he did it, Reuben idly thought, he'd at least be half-distracted from the sting. With sex and flattery there was a performance to focus on, something to divert his attention during. Especially in moments of pain.

In contrast, offering a donation of blood involved an uncomfortable *absence* of effort. Reuben had but to sit there, present his wrist, and hold still. Which he could only manage by biting his lip hard and clawing a hand into the bedcover until the slow, deep cutting finished.

Even then, during the fourth visit it was painful enough to ask, "Saer . . . if you could . . ."

Everic raised a brow whilst handing him the cinnamon drink. "Yes?"

"Perhaps next time, no need to cut so slow? Or—unless you desire it, of course."

Everic's eyes narrowed. He looked angry, then tired, then contemplative, saying nothing as Reuben dutifully drank.

When he did finally speak, it was just to ask, "You're a musician, correct?" He nodded back at the violin case Reuben left near the entrance like always. Just in case he ran into danger on the streets, or Everic requested a performance—or, of course, Everic *did* change tune and try to kill him.

"I . . . yes, among other things," Reuben shrugged.

Everic's mouth tightened into a thin line. "Then all the more reason to be careful. I'd prefer to leave you without a mark, at the end of all this."

The next morning, Reuben walked back to the bordello rather . . . melancholic. Grateful for Everic's seeming carefulness—though at a loss, now that the fear of dying had waned, at the fact that Everic had not originally requested Reuben for his persona, or his talents, or the attractiveness of his body. Only because *she* had told Everic that Reubielocks wouldn't make trouble for him.

*At the end of all this,* Everic had just said.

There was an entire city of necks to choose from. How long *could* Reuben hope to keep this agreement going, if all Everic wanted from him was blood?

"Does much of your business involve writing?" Reuben asked during the fifth visit, distracting himself from his newly-opened wrist. "You're usually in the midst of a letter, when I arrive—I assume they aren't love notes?"

"Refined society seems to entail just as much written correspondence, as it does balls and parlor parties," Everic replied distractedly, brows furrowed in concentration as he watched for the moment to switch the goblets. "I find I am at least *adequate* at participating in the former, if not the latter."

Well, at least the man was self-aware.

"Still seeking entry into High Ring social circles, then?" Reuben guessed, and at Everic's grimace, correctly. Reuben gave a nod towards Everic's dark, frankly drab clothing and offered, "I've heard the right lapels can get you places, just as well as the right name."

Everic huffed—then raised Reuben's forearm before swapping out the full goblet with the empty one. "I have access to all the utterly ridiculous fashion they sport," he said in a low, contemptuous voice. "Unfortunately, through pen or in person, it comes down to the right *words.* The correct intonation, charms, flattery. Things I was never trained for, or ever found an instance to care about."

With how fuzzy his thoughts were growing, it was easier to not take offense at Everic's clear derision whilst describing the few talents *Reuben* had to his name.

And yet harder, not to think before he spoke and pushed too far: "Oh? What *were* you trained for, then?"

Everic's mouth opened—then snapped shut. "That's enough, I think," he nodded at the second goblet, only half full.

He left Reuben in the chamber soon after hastily setting down a platter of food and drink, not returning before Reuben had to head back to the bordello.

In the days that followed, Reuben felt terribly foolish for letting curiosity get the better of him. He'd only intended to offer *help*, not pry. And of all people, he should understand Everic's distaste for getting personal with others—even if he wasn't used to his clients sharing the sentiment.

Reuben resolved to never again test Everic's need for privacy. *If* he was ever sent for again, of course.

When Bev did indeed return to collect him, this time less than a week later, Reuben was partly relieved—but also hesitant, given the bad state his friend was in once again.

"Isolde?" Bev signed once he finished a solo performance, waiting right outside the backstage door for him. Her hands were only a little uncertain as they moved into Isolde's name sign.

"Resting," Reuben admitted. "If your friend wants me tonight, well . . . I may need someone to guard her door again."

Bev stood up just a bit taller.

With Isolde's blessing and Bev's key handed over a few minutes later, Reuben left the bordello alone, glad that his prying question to Everic hadn't been an irreparable mistake. Regardless, he planned to ask for Everic's forgiveness. Perhaps the apology would make Everic soften, even relax just a little, and the two could engage in some interesting conversation to better distract him from the pain.

As Reuben walked out under the pergolas of the bordello, however, he instantly regretted his desire for an interesting night.

The hooded figure amidst the piazza's evening crowds wouldn't have stood out to Reuben, if not for the way their head stood above the masses or the definitive curl of horns under the low hood. But it wasn't until Reuben noticed a familiar weapon at their hip that he realized who the figure was—the intricate silver hilt of their sword catching the last rays of dusk with every step they took towards the bordello.

Reuben ducked behind the nearest pillar of the wooden pergola, breaths coming in sharp and fast. He could only hope he'd spotted Waron first. A hot flash of fear ran through him as he fumbled to open his violin case with sweaty hands, clutching the neck of the instrument still secured within as he waited for his old client to either pass the bordello by, enter it, or approach him.

At this busy time of evening Reuben couldn't rely on the sound of feet to guess which. So he carefully angled his head just enough around the pillar to watch the bordello entrance, trying to calm his breathing as he waited.

A small, sudden flash lit up against the wall to his left. Reuben flinched, instinctively ducking his head—a reflection from Waron's sword hilt, no doubt.

But Waron didn't round the pillar and confront him. After a few seconds, Reuben snuck another glance, and sent a quick prayer of thanks to Zald when he caught a glimpse of Waron walking into the bordello through the wide double doors, the infernal man miraculously oblivious to Reuben just a few paces away.

Reuben waited only a moment longer before making his escape.

A panicked, fizzling energy quickened his feet as he switched between a dash and a brisk walk weaving through the streets, urging him out of the main ring of Sazzera and down the winding steps that took him to Everic's hideaway.

On a normal night, he'd have little to fear. Sidarchus would simply tell bordello security to remove Waron from the premises, as he promised they would ever since Reuben convinced the house manager his life had been threatened by Waron.

Out on the street, in these rundown, forgotten places where the Allunata were said to patrol the night, rob passersby, and kill for gold, however . . . Reuben ran a little bit faster at the thought.

Everic looked curious at his state of disarray when Reuben stepped inside, though he only greeted, "Good evening," setting down a quill as Reuben hurriedly locked the door. "I hope you've been able to recover since our last session?"

Reuben headed straight to the bed, fixing his hair as he answered breathlessly, "Quite recovered, thank you."

Everic frowned—but stood up to gather the necessary things.

Meanwhile, Reuben tried to catch his breath. He couldn't let his fear sour the evening, or ruin the apologies he'd carefully prepared in advance. So he stayed quiet as Everic readied everything, and then leaned forward to present the arm before it could be asked for—only to gasp out a cry, doubling over as a sudden knifing pain stabbed through his spine and down his left leg.

Everic dropped the dagger, eyes wide. "What's happened?" he said, his usual low, careful voice taking on a commanding tone.

Reuben shifted as he clutched his thigh, opened his mouth to answer—then whimpered when an even harsher pain seized his nerves. "It'll—pass," he hissed, even if he had no idea of when.

When Reuben attempted to lie back, he froze at the vampire quickly leaning over him. But only to grab a few more pillows and soften the fall behind him, he realized. Reuben winced hard before he finally reclined and could relax his back muscles, breathing harshly through the grating spasms still shooting down his leg.

"This happens often?" Everic surmised as he watched with a grim frown, his eyes—dark green again, tonight—flicking over Reuben's person in assessment.

Reuben, as usual, lied. "Not often," he said through gritted teeth. And then, after a pained chuckle, admitted, "It's my own fault, truly, for running here on a whim."

Everic frowned harder. "You ran?"

Reuben shouldn't have said that. He wasn't about to explain Waron; Reuben wasn't sure he even knew *how* to without lowering Everic's opinion of him, or worse, outing himself as a liability. "It seems my delicate bones—*ah*—couldn't handle my enthusiasm to see you, saer," he said, then sighed as the jolting pain at last started to lessen.

A small thrill of satisfaction ran through him despite the pain, when Reuben saw Everic's face change. In particular, how the frown faded almost into something as personable as *fond* exasperation.

That brief moment ended, however, before the vampire replied, "Or at least to see my gold—I hope your payments are being used to visit a healer about this problem?"

Reuben should have kept insisting it *wasn't* a problem. But he had no control over his own tone right now—it was difficult to spin so many lies, with half his head already spinning in pain. "We have charity visits from the Zaldian Priesthood, every few months," he said, deeming this to be a harmless truth.

He was wrong. Everic's face twisted, then hardened into something sharp and bitter. "Their practice has *never* been about healing."

In a better state, Reuben would have apologized, even if he didn't know for what. The pain was flaring again, however, and his aggravation with it—enough he snapped back, "Do you care *so much* where the money goes?" He moved a hand under his thigh to try and massage at the back of it, grimacing in pain before continuing, "Is that it? Would you like me to bring an itemized list of everything I did with my 500 next time, Everic?"

Everic's eyes narrowed, and for a second Reuben regretted every word—until he pulled Reuben's hand away and replaced it with his own wide palm.

It was cold, even through the fabric of Reuben's loose trousers. But the temperature felt soothing as Everic half-knelt on the bed and pressed at the rigidly tensed muscles of Reuben's thigh instead. With much more strength, of course, but also a slower, methodical effort, digging the heel of his thumb over and over into the deepest aches. Reuben had to hold in a moan of relief.

"I would like to see your circumstances improved, whatever that may look like," Everic finally answered in a neutral tone. His eyes were trained down at Reuben's leg, impossible to read.

Reuben blinked while taking this in. Then forced himself not to sit up, rip Everic's hand away, and laugh in his face. For the sake of the gold he would miss out on, if nothing else.

He'd wanted better conversations with this strange, interesting man to distract from the pain—not a savior.

Reuben had seen a few of that type in his time, and learned to trust them the least of all his clients. It was hard to get hurt by someone who never tried to care in the first place. But with those few who first managed to convince Reuben he was worthy of aid, or worse, *important* to them?

For all his aches and bodily woes, loss still counted as Reuben's least favorite type of pain.

Where he once might have softened at the kindness, now he only muttered, "I'm afraid I would run even *your* ample coffers dry before I saw any improvement, saer."

Everic's hand stopped. "What could cost you so much?"

Reuben really shouldn't have said that. Mentions of his indenturement were never received well—it tended to sour the fantasy of Reuben's eagerness for customers. Or worse, they behaved as Waron had: like it didn't matter, only to later use the knowledge as leverage against him.

Fear made Reuben short-tempered, however. Worse, fear *and* pain made him sloppy. "Nothing at all, saer," was all Reuben could think to reply with, whilst trying and failing to muster a teasing smile. His face could only manage something less pained.

It was too late anyway. Just a moment later, Everic's hand dropped away. He stood abruptly from the bed and stared down at Reuben, his eyes widening in horror. His lips curling back with growing *disgust.*

"You . . . you're not a prostitute at all, are you," he accused. "You're a *slave."*

# 7

# PRIVATE PERFORMANCE

The stout dwarvish children of the earth god, Sazzo, climbed out of their holes to trade with the much taller elvish progeny of the sun and sky goddess, Klera, out of necessity at first. Slowly, the little trading post at the highest mountain's base became a small settlement of both dwarves and elves, established on the principles of fair trade and cultural tolerance—a sentiment which allowed the migration of other mortal-kind over time, and also soured the residents towards discriminatory practices such as slavery.

Unity of mortal-kind brought mutual prosperity, from what early Sazzeran history exhibited. Just as the union of the old gods of light and earth begat true gold, the ultimate mark of prosperity and godly favor: the *Brilliance of Zald*.

Since the Zaldian Priesthood came into power, indenturement had grown more and more common over the last two centuries—most of the time, however, the indentured person was a criminal unable to pay their fine, or deeply in debt, or both.

In a city whose patron was the god of gold, certainly no one *admired* those in such a lowly position. But these days it was impossible to even walk down a street of Sazzera's main ring without passing one or two indebted workers. And they were far better off than slaves—if Everic was here to do "business" as he first claimed, he should already be well aware of how these things worked in Sazzera.

"No!" Reuben denied. "*No, of course I'm not, saer.*"

Everic's gaze narrowed—and then darkened. "And now you'd lie to me?"

Reuben's mouth snapped shut around the next placation, though he couldn't very well say, *This is more honest than I've been since the first night you drank my blood.*

"Slavery is illegal here," he assured instead. "I am indentured, yes—though I've never opened a loan myself—and I'm *not* a criminal—it's only, in my case, there were . . . well, extenuating circumstances . . ." Reuben trailed off, realizing just how unconvincing the details would be.

"Then not even this rotten city's usual *farce* of consent can deny the term," Everic concluded in a low, biting tone. From where he stood above Reuben, there wasn't a hint of green left in the dark eyes half-shaded under his brow.

They weren't red, at least, though part of Reuben wanted to shrink from the gaze anyway. Contrarily, the other half of him was still raw with irritation from the lingering pain in his nerves, ready to snap at Everic in answer.

But he hadn't even fulfilled the part of their agreement that would earn him gold and end this horrid conversation. "Perhaps we can argue the details later," Reuben tried to gently persuade, and offered his arm again with the underside exposed. "You have not had your supper yet, saer. I assure you, I am *quite* willing to supply it."

Everic took his wrist—and pulled Reuben to his feet. All at once there was frighteningly little distance between them, the vampire's expression thunderous as he coldly replied, "Your assurances mean nothing now."

Reuben's already-weak knees nearly gave out when the vampire let go. He managed to steady himself despite the recent fit of pain, but it was embarrassing how low his stomach sank at Everic's words, how fast his eyes began to burn with the threat of tears.

He tried again, "I swear to you, saer, there's no—"

"I will not be a participant in *any* shape or form of this disgusting practice," Everic spat out, glaring at Reuben. "Nor will I feed gold back into the *Priesthood vaults*."

Reuben took the answer like a blow to the stomach.

He'd never expected this to last. He'd resigned himself to thinking he ruined his chances after the very first appointment. He'd upset Everic with the wrong question plenty of times since, made mistakes over and over again despite his best efforts.

Yet even whilst fearing its futility, he'd appreciated the quiet, safe seclusion this job provided from the rest of his life. He'd come to tolerate the blood loss and pain in exchange for securing his dear friend's standing at the bordello and his remaining family's livelihood in the Hollows. He'd come to somewhat enjoy the presence of this man before him, even—or at least feel enough at ease to ask questions and prompt conversation, as if he was the vampire's equal.

Everic's stark, visible disgust looking at him now was a necessary reminder of just how deluded Reuben had allowed himself to become.

Part of him wished to simply go. He didn't want to find out just how loud Everic could shout or how hard his hands could hit, if Reuben crossed a line by pressing the matter further.

And yet, for all his blunt words and harsh tones, Everic had yet to react with violence through all the ups and downs of their short exchanges thus far.

A gentle monster, Reuben reminded himself before taking a gamble—and falling to his knees.

He didn't hide his wince at the impact with the hard stone before grasping at the thickly-woven material of Everic's trousers with shaky hands. He looked up through wet lashes, letting the tears slip down his cheeks as he started, *"Please."*

*Your beauty is always improved when customers can look down upon it, Reubielocks,* he heard echoing in his head meanwhile—not his mother's words, for once.

"Please, don't send me away," Reuben begged, the emotion behind it entirely too genuine for his own comfort.

Perhaps Everic could sense that sincerity. At last, the disgusted curl of his mouth lessened, brow relaxing as he looked down at Reuben. Not with interest, yet—but Reuben still counted pity as a step up from pure revulsion.

He thought of just how disappointed Sidarchus would be when this amount of money stopped coming in. He thought of Isolde getting sent to work in the Ravine. He thought of Daxus and Nahlia being turned out of their little hollow and forced to survive on the streets—and Reuben's grip on Everic tightened.

"Tell me how to change your mind, saer, I beg you," he whispered. "I . . . I would do *anything.*"

Reuben would already have started nuzzling the inner seam of Everic's trousers, if his client had given him a single indication towards favoring it. But Reuben doubted such a bold move would receive a warm reception from the closed-off man. Instead he just let his lips part an increment and looked up at Everic with wide, teary eyes.

Everic moved—though not to unbutton his own trousers. Instead, his hands carefully extracted Reuben's fingers from gripping the fabric. Then he bent down, one hand grasping Reuben's arm just under the elbow and encouraging him to rise.

Meanwhile, Everic said quietly, "That was harsh of me. My

apologies."

Reuben wasn't about to fight the assistance, even if the small apology worried him. He wanted Everic to feel attraction towards him, not *regret*.

Then again, when had Everic once cared about his beauty? The only consistent desire Reuben had seen flare in the man's eyes was for his blood. Once he was upright, Reuben considered laying his exposed arm up against Everic's chest, or maybe resting one cheek on the man's shoulder so the line of his neck was more visible.

Everic kept hold of the undersides of Reuben's forearms, however, quite literally holding him at arm's length. "Though . . . not *quite* so harsh as you just dropping to your knees like that, so soon after a spasm," Everic added with a nod down at Reuben's legs. And for just a moment, a ghost of that same fond exasperation softened his gaze.

"It hurt less than it would having to walk back up to the bordello, saer," Reuben pointed out, wiping at the tears on his face.

"You're right." Everic's frown returned. "Would you like assistance to run? A new, safe place to go?"

"What . . . ?" Reuben stared at Everic. When the vampire provided no further explanation, he had to ask: "Why?"

Everic gave him the strangest, saddest look. "To be free."

Reuben blinked, caught off guard. But that feeling was quickly replaced by disbelief. "Just *run* from my debt?" he repeated, incredulous. "You think it so simple as that?"

"Of course. These so-called *sentry* are the least competent guard the city has ever seen. You could leave, start a new life—with Bev's assistance, if you'd like it."

Reuben stared at him a bit longer. If Everic was just saying all this to entrap Reuben somehow later, he was better at hiding dark intentions than anyone Reuben had ever met. But worse, if he actually *meant* what he was saying . . .

Reuben knew his answer regardless.

"You're too kind, saer—but I am not looking for alternatives," he said softly. Then lowered his gaze, idly noticing where Everic was still touching him. "My life is in this city. And the bordello is a coveted spot out of all places an indentured servant could work. I can assure you, I'd much rather be there—be *here* with you—than trying to pay off my debt manning the city canals or doing any of the work in the Ravine mines." He chuckled weakly, adding, "You can imagine how long I'd last at that."

Suddenly Reuben's breath caught in his throat, as Everic lifted his chin with the soft, barely-there pressure of two fingers.

Reuben expected a kiss as Everic leaned in, his gaze flitting between Reuben's eyes as if in search of something. But as the seconds dragged on, Reuben felt more exposed under the vampire's sharp scrutiny than he ever did naked on his back. It took everything not to shrink away from that gaze—or to lean in and prematurely end it with a kiss himself, his instincts begging him to fall back into a simpler intimacy he understood.

Finally, Everic dropped both his hands and leaned back. "You *need* to stay, then?"

Reuben nodded, blinking hard as the strange moment passed. "I . . . yes—yes, I do. And I understand your distaste for where some of the money goes," he lied, "but I promise, it has helped me and those I love more than you could ever know, saer."

"I believe you," Everic answered, even as his lips twitched into a grimace.

To reassure him further, Reuben placed a hand lightly against the vampire's chest—and bit down a smile at the jump of breath he felt, as if Everic's lungs had jolted alive in response.

Despite the sharp reaction, Everic wasn't leaning away from the touch.

Reuben could only hope the spidery state of his still-wet eyelashes didn't detract from his way of coyly looking up through them as he spoke, his voice feather-soft: "You see, your gold is even *more* appreciated by someone like me than a usual whore, saer. But if I can show further appreciation, just tell me how. I would offer you *five* goblets of my blood for what you pay . . ."

Everic's eyes flashed to his neck in response, emboldening Reuben to continue, "I'd play you love songs all night; I'd help you word your letters with the utmost charm and flattery . . ." and then he stepped into Everic's space entirely, leaning in to spill words like pearls into the man's ear, "I've been *aching* to give you the simple pleasures as well, Everic, if ever you desired—"

"How much?" Everic interrupted, his voice nearly unrecognizable in how hoarse it sounded.

"How *much* have I ached for you?" Reuben guessed, smoothing both hands down Everic's chest and nestling his nose into the sharp line of the man's jaw—stalling to quickly fabricate an answer.

Something like, *With more passion than poets can convey*—or even bolder, *I'd much rather show you, saer.*

Before Reuben could decide, however, Everic replied, "No, no," his voice evening out some.

Then Everic took Reuben by the arms and steered him to sit back on the bed. Which Reuben didn't resist, both for the sake of his leg and, if desired, to consummate the continuation of their expanded deal.

But then Everic let go with a grim frown. "No—I mean, *how much* is the Priesthood holding you hostage for?"

Reuben's lips pressed together. He leaned back against his hands, silently wishing Everic would just act normally—Reuben would *much* rather appease with the simple, transactional act of sex right now than continue this fraught topic of conversation.

Especially considering he didn't know the original amount, or who exactly his mother had first contracted such an astronomical debt with, or why. She'd grown angry with him when he asked, or worse, detailed every part of his birth and rearing that had added to that amount until he begged her to stop.

When she died, the debt that then fell under his name was a little under 100,000 cantergold. The kind of money only a high house would ever see at once, and even in High Ring, it probably equaled close to a year's worth of asset increases. Now his debt was somewhere just below 80,000 cantergold the last time he checked with Sidarchus, only slowly decreasing over time—worse, *stagnating,* thanks to interest and other fees always piling on top.

"I don't know," Reuben murmured when Everic kept waiting for an answer. He reached forward to stroke his fingertips along the man's hip.

Everic just gave him a look and caught the hand. "Then for how long? And on what grounds?"

Reuben wanted to wrench from the vampire's grip in frustration— instead, he let out a soft sigh. "I don't see any point in discussing this further." Then he carefully drew Everic in by their joined hands, brushing the vampire's scarred knuckles up the side of his throat. "I'd rather you let me stay and show my appreciation, saer . . . *however* you would like."

Everic quietly allowed his hand to be brushed along Reuben's skin. But when Reuben glanced up, he didn't see lust or interest or even consideration—only something unexpectedly sad and *disappointed* in the vampire's weary eyes.

Reuben dropped Everic's hand himself, all at once uncomfortable. Even a bit ashamed.

After a beat of silence, Everic sighed too. "I'd like to see your circumstances improved," he repeated himself—and then reached forward of his own accord, brushing the back of his knuckles ever-so-briefly down the edge of Reuben's cheekbone.

It was rather pathetic, how just the small gesture made Reuben's throat ache with an unexplainable despair.

Reuben should have said something about feeling an improvement anytime Everic was near, or that more appointments should do the trick. Anything, but the same, useless word that slipped from his mouth yet again: *"Why?"*

Everic's eyes flitted to the side. For once, the curve of his frown was slight, gentle, even *unsure,* as he admitted, "I've wished at times to give up on my business in this corrupted city; instead, I keep finding more reasons to stay. To try a little longer." Then he met Reuben's gaze with a rueful smile. "Perhaps that is the curse of Sazzera for us both."

Reuben went very still. "Then . . . you will continue to call for me?"

"So long as you are *choosing* to be beholden to your indenturement, and find the money beneficial, yes," Everic stipulated. "And I . . . I wouldn't decline assistance, if you have any advice on improving my letters, helping me gain access to High Ring. So long as you don't expect many answers to your questions."

A jolt of excitement traveled through Reuben—quickly accompanied by nerves.

He hid it with a tease, lounging more provocatively on the bed: "Just the *simple pleasures* of correcting grammar, then . . . nothing else?"

Only because he was watching carefully, did Reuben catch the moment the vampire's gaze flitted over his body, lingering a second too long in certain places.

It was strange, given how brazenly Reuben had offered his body tonight without success—but still clear enough. No matter his special appetites, Everic wasn't *so* far from a living man as to not carnally desire Reuben this way as well.

There was security in that truth. Safety, in the expectation that it would only be a matter of time before Everic gave up whatever misgivings held him back, and he took pleasure in Reubielocks. Allowing Reuben's chance, in return, to further secure the vampire's attention and ensure gold filled his pockets for many more months to come.

And so Reuben swallowed down the strangely bitter taste in his mouth at the knowledge, when even without music he could detect the evasion in Everic's voice as the vampire replied, "I couldn't wish for more."

Voleris always left a sour, earthy flavor on the tongue, which lingered for as long as one had the presence of mind to notice it. Reuben had to drink close to a full vial these days to reach a place where he didn't. But he couldn't risk much more without the possibility of overdoing it—even if he was about to endure one of his least favorite parts of working at the Starlet Eye.

"Consider it a reward for all your hard work," Sidarchus had told Reuben the night after his sixth appointment with Everic, whilst carrying in Reuben's extra order of oil and voleris. "You should make twice our usual rate—apparently some sentry official is celebrating a promotion! I even gave you Adina to be your scene partner."

Two nights later, Adina shot Reuben a disapproving look from where she powdered her dark blue skin at the other mirror, her horns and shoulders adorned in bright, tinkling silver. "Strange that Sidarchus would pair us for such important clients," she pointed out.

Reuben swished the last sip an extra moment within his mouth and then swallowed. "I certainly wouldn't," he agreed shortly, shaking out the last, gritty dregs from the vial onto his finger and rubbing it into his lower gums. Then he leaned back and waited for the draught to lift the dread from his gut.

There was no excuse for the feeling. He would make close to 100 canters tonight; he hadn't lost Everic as a client yet—even if he'd had to act *pitiful* to manage it, Reuben thought sourly, as it didn't seem possible to be desirable enough—and, much more a comfort, Sidarchus had confirmed that Waron had been turned away yet again, with no sign of the man since.

Perhaps Waron would finally give up and pick another whore from the hundreds in this city to cut his knives into, Reuben told himself.

Adina was brushing a shimmering dust along her cheekbones as she added, "Sid *did* insinuate you found yourself a wealthy client of late. Perhaps your talents are finally getting recognized."

"I'll have to work on returning to mediocrity, then."

Adina *tsked* and stood, taking one of their selected props for the night from where it hung on the wall. Reuben obligingly lifted his chin as she threaded the thick leather collar around his neck, buckling it snugly against his skin before handing him the end of the chain attached to it.

By the time she finished, Reuben's body felt looser, his mind just a bit quieter. "Shouldn't this be in your hand, *saer?*" he nodded at the dangling chain she'd handed to him, letting out a soft chuckle.

"We have a few more minutes." Adina moved back to the vanity, touching up the kohl around her fiery eyes as she added, "Just let me lead? Whatever the group requests, I'll guide you through it."

"I'm no stranger to private performances, Adina," Reuben replied, sinking further back into his chair.

Adina gave him a very unimpressed look before dabbing herself with more powder. "Maybe not—but you've taken enough voleris to be an absolutely useless scene partner."

Reuben wanted to protest. But despite the distracting fascination growing in him at how the small chain links dangled and slipped along his palm, he was cognizant enough to realize he would lose that argument.

And also still present enough to hear Adina mutter, "I *told* Sid I didn't want to be partnered with stellas like you."

"Like *me?*"

Adina shot him a flat look. "And the twins, and Eniss, and Isolde, and the other half-dozen of you. I wanted to be here. I *chose* this."

"Well—then no one's stopping *you* from leaving, are they?" Reuben said with a loose wave toward the door, idly noting how his words came out slurred.

Adina dropped the powder brush and put her head in her hands, long enough a hazy sort of guilt filled Reuben for whatever he'd said. Then the woman murmured, "I plan to, as soon as I can. This place . . ." She didn't finish, only lifted her head to give Reuben a thin smile. "For now, I'll just hope you don't black out before we reach the bed."

Bright, magically-lit spotlights illuminated the low platform at one end of the viewing room Adina and Reuben entered, some unmeasured amount of time later. A bed, a bench, a rack, and a chest of toys had already been staged there like usual. But Reuben focused on the lights as she introduced them both as "*Reubielocks* and *the Devonaire!*" and didn't bother to squint for a glimpse of the dark, purposefully-obscured audience on the room's other side.

He *hated* this part of their job—even if it usually made him more cantergold than a musical performance and a full schedule of appointments combined. Whether with Adina or Gringoll or any of the other stellas, even Isolde with her helpful hand signs, it didn't matter. Reuben would always prefer a one-on-one, pseudo-intimate performance where the customer became a bit vulnerable too, over being ordered around by a shadowed, voyeuristic crowd like he was no more than a marionette to be puppetted.

At least with voleris the misery was muted. Reuben let his mind wander in pleasant, aimless circles about the lights reflecting off Adina's jewelry before she moved his body to lay doubled over the bench and fingered him open. He pondered how strange and fascinating the polished grooves of the wood floor looked instead of thinking about the paddle hitting his arse. He let his body react however it liked to the stings of pain and pleasure as he clenched around something, all the while his mind floated away.

The next thing he registered was the tight constriction of his collar being tugged by its chain, a soft hand bringing his cock to attention at the same time. And, also thanks to the voleris, he felt himself harden after just a few seconds, even as he focused on mentally playing out a few possible chord progressions to go with the lyrics he'd been writing.

Reuben truly *had* taken too much of the potion for this type of work, however. He knew it after realizing he had no memory of when he'd ended up in the bed, on his back, dried candle wax streaked over his chest, Adina sinking down to envelop him in her warm tightness while still pulling at the chain. The lights were too bright now, glaring behind her profile and making his head ache. And the small crowd draped in shadow felt too *loud*—as if he could hear the desire many of them held to take Adina's place, to watch him writhe in pain or pleasure or both for hours longer.

To their eyes, he had no personhood. And they were right: Reubielocks *was* nothing and no one, whether others around him had realized it yet or not.

Life was so much easier, when Reuben managed to believe it as well.

But he couldn't always keep himself separated from his persona—

especially at times like this, when his hazy, drug-addled mind caught an eerily familiar presence amidst their onlookers. With that same faint, but terribly *malicious* intent, directed straight at him.

Reuben froze underneath Adina.

"No," he whispered, even as his heart began to pound and his thoughts moved in sudden, rapid circles—the dark presence was back, *Jophiel* was back, or maybe Waron was back, it was a terrible person whoever it was, and it had returned, trained on him, it was *back*—"Stop!"

Reuben tried to roll away, but the woman above him was too heavy, her hold on the chain too firm. And even as he heard Adina murmur, "Reubie? Reubie, calm down," the angle of her jaw narrowed in his mind's eye, her face lost its bluish hue, her eyes burned a bright, devilish red—*it was Jophiel, the crowd was cheering her on as she cried out some strange incantation—and Reuben was going to die from the seizure she left him in this time, his heart was already pounding hard enough it echoed through his bones—*

—and then time slowed down again.

Distantly, Reuben was aware of Adina climbing off of him and taking a bow, the shuffle of feet and clothing as some of their audience left before she took him out of the viewing room. Speaking words he couldn't process in a low, upset voice, nearly dragging him on his stumbling feet before at last she took him into a place Reuben belatedly recognized as his own room, and left him to collapse on his bed.

Reuben went in and out of consciousness after that, unsure if minutes passed or days. Unsure if *anything* was real at all: the scene that had just played out, or the presence he'd recognized, or the occasional hitching in his chest that was just as likely to be laughter as sobs.

That was, until the voleris worked its way out of his system. Then, finally, Reuben found himself lying alone in the darkness of his own chambers.

A few tears rolled down from his eyes, over the bridge of his nose and onto the pillow.

It would be a surprise if Sidarchus gave him any portion of the performance's earnings, once he caught wind of what just happened. Though Reuben couldn't say *he* knew, given how much reality and delusion had blended together, just how much of a spectacle he'd made tonight.

His head still felt too heavy, too unfocused, like it was stuffed with cotton. Even the recollection that he'd sensed the same malicious presence again did little to stir his senses. Of course, it was probably just another hallucination, like the moments Jophiel had taken Adina's place in his mind.

Really, all Reuben wanted to do was drink another dose of voleris and slide back into oblivion.

His self-flagellating melancholy stuttered to a halt, however, at hearing a voice hiss from the corner of his room: *"Reubie."*

Reuben didn't need his violin for every spell. Even in his intoxicated state, he managed to roll onto his side to face where the voice came from, trying to recall the crippling incantation of a quick *Insult to Injury* spell as he squinted at the shadows.

But then he recognized who it was.

By first appearances, Isolde looked perfectly presentable for the night—her face painted, her hair curled and plaited, her slip of a dress artfully falling over one shoulder. It was only the pale state of her face under the rouge and the wide, glossy look in her eyes as she staggered toward him, that told Reuben his friend was likely in an even worse state than him.

"How—how did you get in here?" he asked, glancing at the still-closed door.

Isolde grabbed at his arm, fingernails digging harshly into his skin. "Someone is watching you," she hissed. "You are *not* safe."

Usually Reuben would focus on calming and orienting her, not paying attention to ramblings she wouldn't remember herself in a couple of hours—but her words hit too close to his own fears, tonight.

"Wh-what . . . what did you hear, Isi?" he asked, wincing as he did it.

"Oriana waited too long to warn you." Isolde pointed at the shadowed corner she'd come from, her eyes wide with insistence. Reuben recoiled just at hearing her say his mother's name—but Isolde wasn't done yet: "Now you can't hear it, but it's waiting there in your heart, in your blood. The woeteller says you keep playing, when you should be *singing*."

From that point, however, the little clarity left in her brown eyes clouded over, and she repeated between them in a jumbled rush, "Can't hear, go sing, can't hear go sing, can't-hear . . ."

By the lack of light from his window, Reuben assumed their working shift hadn't ended yet—but neither of them would please a customer tonight. He took both of Isolde's hands and helped her lie down with him, trying to hush her and when that didn't work, repeating, "Can't hear, go sing," with her until Isolde seemed to believe he understood.

Then her whole body sagged into the mattress. "Virtues and vices, gods and devils," she muttered before burrowing into his arms, a phrase he'd heard her say to herself many a time in these states. Though this time, Isolde added in a whisper once Reuben had pulled her in, "She couldn't hide you forever."

An old ache panged in Reuben's chest.

Hesitantly, he asked, "Oriana couldn't?"

A small, indelicate snore answered him.

With a sigh Reuben drew the blankets over them. His own nerves finally began to settle after Isolde half-consciously pulled him back into an embrace, her short but sturdy body keeping him grounded through the fitful sleep voleris always gave him, her steady breath in his ear a reminder he was not so alone as he often felt.

The first time they'd slept like this together, just a year into knowing one another, Reuben had cried after she'd snuggled in and fallen asleep—and then decided he would help her. Even try to save her, the way he wasn't able to save his mother.

But he'd never told her about Oriana.

The next day Reuben woke to the shift of his friend sitting up in the bed, Isolde glancing around with a disoriented frown. When their eyes met, she whispered, "Did I scare anyone?"

Reuben propped an elbow under his head and tried to smile. "If so, not badly enough—Sidarchus hasn't come barging down the door yet with complaints. You likely came in here soon after it started," he assured, and then, wondering if he'd imagined it, asked: "Do you . . . do you remember any of what you said this time?"

Isolde wrapped arms around her shoulders and looked down. "Of course not."

Reuben quickly nodded—there was no reason for this time to be different than any other before, and every chance that the voleris had been affecting *his* head still. How else could Reuben have heard Isolde not only voice his own fears about a dark presence watching him, but speak the name of his mother?

Isolde reached a hand out then, interlacing it with Reuben's before giving an affectionate squeeze. "Did the private session with Adina go alright?"

"Of course not," Reuben quipped back, trying to smile when Isolde gave him a look. "But here we are—both made it through a rough night, and awake to enjoy the day," he tried to reassure whilst getting out of bed and pulling her up with him. When his friend still looked tense, he smiled wider and started, *"One less day to tarry . . ."*

Isolde rolled her eyes, pulling free of his hand. But after a moment she let out a long sigh and finished the line from the first song they'd ever written together: *"One day less to bury."*

As they headed to their breaking-fast meal, however, Reuben had to ask: "Do you know where you might have heard of the name Oriana?" And when Isolde frowned over at him, he clarified, "Like from Sid? Or one of the older stellas?"

Isolde's brows furrowed. "Did I say that name last night?"

"Just the once."

"I've never heard it," she shook her head, looking genuinely lost. "Do *you* know someone by the name?"

Reuben opened his mouth—then, thinking twice, shut it.

He tried to keep his face neutral, even as foreboding pooled in his gut. He couldn't in good conscience start encouraging her to *listen* to the voices that at times made her want to claw her skin off. Nor did Reuben have any desire to entertain the idea of his mother still watching him from the Embrace of Zald, likely disapproving of every choice he made. Even if he had no other explanation for Isolde's words.

"No . . . not very well, anyway," he said after a belated moment— and it was hardly a lie at all.

# 8

# PERSONAL QUESTIONS

**I**f ever you cannot present a work of art, show them a mirror instead, Oriana had told Reuben once.

And when Bev came for him that very night, Reuben was in no state to attempt his usual eager exterior—especially considering Sidarchus had handed him only half the amount expected after the poor performance, and ignored him entirely since. So, once he arrived, Reuben simply mirrored Everic's behavior, quiet and cordial as the vampire gathered the needed supplies.

But after the bloodletting Everic interrupted the silence. "Bev told me you often perform the violin on stage, at the bordello," he said.

His words startled Reuben out of a blank, unfocused haze. The vampire had just returned with the food platter—this time featuring dried dates, fresh blueberries, and pine nuts. A fine array, if Reuben had any stomach for it.

Everic sat back at the stool and held out the cup of that cinnamon drink Reuben always started with, continuing, "When did you learn?"

Reuben took the cup and forced down a few sips, blinking as he waited for his head to clear. He felt light-headed, nauseous, and oversensitized, besides befuddled at the sudden interest. This bloodletting left him with a particular case of nausea—likely because he'd eaten little whilst recovering from the voleris.

But at least the personal question wasn't about his indenturement. "Every time my mother visited," he shrugged. "Her friends raised me when I was very young, but she came during her Repose to teach me letters, maths, music. I learned how to pluck out chords and tunes years before I was big enough to hold a bow."

Everic looked surprised. "She was well-learned, then."

"Well enough," Reuben agreed. Then, after a moment of hesitation: "Most of the knowledge I can give you about High Ring society came from her, actually—she grew up and spent the majority of her life there, until I was conceived."

Everic's brows rose. "So you're *nobility* of some kind? From a notable house of High Ring?"

An incredulous scoff burst from Reuben in the midst of taking another drink, nearly choking him. "I'm a bastard, I'm afraid," he corrected, chuckling once he'd cleared his throat. "And hold no claim to their hierarchy of inheritance for that alone."

"Ah yes—I'd forgotten about that part of this city's contrived nonsense," Everic said, face going dark as it ever did talking about Sazzera.

Reuben plucked a dried date from the platter and busied himself with biting it and removing the pit within. When Everic still didn't turn to go, watching Reuben eat the fruit, it was no hardship to mirror the man's interest and ask in return: "Is this your first time in the golden city of opportunity, then? Did you grow up very far from our backward ways?"

He had to force down an aggravated sigh of frustration, watching as Everic's face tightened, eyes shifting away. Ever hesitant and closed off when the personal questions turned his direction.

"Oh come now, Everic," Reuben tried to tease instead. "Surely you can trust me with a *little* insight about my generous benefactor? You've already let me leave with knowledge of your condition multiple times now, and I've yet to send sentry guards knocking on your door."

To his surprise, the tease somewhat worked; Everic's tension faded, his lips twisting into a reluctant smirk as he answered, "That could have just as much to do with their tendency to piss over the rim and shirk their duties, as it does you."

Reuben put a fluttering hand over his heart. "My good saer, are you questioning my discretion *still?*"

Everic's smile faded. "No. I simply don't want to damn you with knowledge," he said, low and serious once again.

"In the case your 'business' here goes badly," Reuben guessed.

"In case it goes much too well," Everic responded, as cryptic as ever. Then his head turned towards the desk currently littered with parchment. "But once you've recovered, if you are willing . . . I *do* have an important reply to send by the morning that I could use a second pair of eyes on."

Reuben sat up straighter, the haze fully cleared from his mind now. "So long as I can review it while lounging here," he stipulated, if only to not seem overeager.

Which was how he ended up looking over a very short, very lackluster letter a minute later, which seemed to be accepting an invitation to a small gathering for drinks.

"The closing salutations should be 'Zald bless,' or 'Zaldus guide us,'" Reuben started with the easiest change—or so he thought.

"No," Everic responded, short and sharp.

Reuben glanced up from the parchment as he opened his mouth to protest, to explain the cultural convention behind it . . . and on seeing the stubborn set of Everic's jaw, decided to pick his battles. Whatever the man held against this city, its government, and patron god, it was clearly not to be underestimated.

Perhaps he should start considering *Loethia* as a possible origin for the vampire, Reuben silently worried.

"Alright," he allowed, then tapped the parchment. "If you received a token from a high house or guild, you'd also press their seals at the bottom here—they're like social coinage, just as esteemed as cantergold. Otherwise, well . . ."

Everic raised a brow. "Well?"

"It's just a bit abrupt, isn't it?" Reuben glanced over the words a second time, then suggested, "Perhaps sharing your appreciation more would help, if you are hoping to make them like you. Mention something you look forward to about the gathering, a topic you hope to chat with them regarding. Say how *sorry* you are, after this explanation about needing to be an hour late. That sort of thing."

Everic nodded slowly, though he didn't necessarily look pleased at the suggestions. "Did your mother have any experience going to parlor parties?" he asked, eyeing Reuben.

"That's where she once used to perform for her peers, yes," Reuben nodded, setting down the letter to pick up another fruit. "Music of all types—though usually the harpsichord, the viol, or the harp—is an important part of the gathering for both upper rings of the city. Sometimes musicians are hired, like at balls, but usually half the point of a *parlor* besides party games is for nobles to lug in their various instruments and showcase everyone's elitist talents around drinks and refreshments."

"It's only more unfortunate that I am attending these peacocking affairs, then, rather than someone like you," Everic answered. Then he watched Reuben eat the date for a moment, eyes flickering down to Reuben's neck when he swallowed.

Usually Reuben had an easy guess as to what a man was thinking about whilst watching him eat, but in this case, it was a toss up.

"You've yet to join me," Reuben pointed out, nodding at the two goblets uncharacteristically still full of blood next to the platter.

Everic snapped out of his focus, blinking. "Yes," he agreed, though he didn't reach for one of them. He only gave Reuben a scrutinizing look, continuing, "Which brings me to another question—what did you consume in the past day?"

"Besides everything right here?" Reuben raised a brow, then ticked off his fingers while listing, "Porridge with fruit to start, then I snuck in bread and olive spread before the night began."

Everic didn't look satisfied. "And to drink?"

"Table wine, I suppose?" Reuben said, growing a bit defensive. "Some water—perhaps less than I *should* have, but . . ." and then he trailed off, realizing all at once what else might be lingering in his blood after the previous night's performance.

Everic watched whatever was happening on Reuben's face with a grim, knowing look. "I didn't notice until after it hit the open air, but your blood smells faintly of *poison,* whether willingly or unknowingly consumed," he said. "I'm not sure which I hope to be the case, but—"

"I'm sorry," Reuben blurted in horror, his nausea back with a vengeance as it sunk in just how bad of an idea that amount of voleris had been. He threw a hand out and grasped Everic's forearm, pleading, "I didn't *think,* when I took it, how it would affect things for you, saer—but I could try playing a healing spell and see if that might purge it from my system, have you try again—"

"It's likely fine, Reubie," Everic cut in, though his voice was strangely soft. Even more strange, he placed a hand over Reuben's—and Reuben couldn't be sure if it was the soothing tone of the vampire's voice or the cooling temperature of his skin that calmed him as Everic continued, "It smells faint, as I said. I just need to know what it is before I decide whether to risk drinking."

Reuben managed a shaky smile, nodding. "It *shouldn't* be dangerous," he started, though he couldn't be sure how things translated for vampires. "It's just a potion that Sidarchus sources for us, called voleris. A mixture of compounds that can mute pain and anxiety, increase pleasure." Reuben grimaced, thinking of the adverse reaction he'd experienced with it the previous night, but still promised, "Nothing harmful, unless in very high dosages. I try not to take it often these days, but if you can warn me in advance somehow, I'll make sure to *never* use it before our appointments."

Everic didn't look appeased—rather, to Reuben's dismay, the explanation seemed to have made the vampire *angry.*

Yet without another word Everic took the first goblet and drained it down. The second quickly followed, while Reuben watched in anxious silence.

Everic didn't remark on the taste or the effect, if there was any of either. He simply stood and cleared the cups from the table, leaving the chamber presumably to take them into the kitchen area. Minutes passed in silence, Reuben's anxiety ticking up with each one. But by the time the vampire returned, Everic looked no worse for wear, his irises shining gold once more—just upset still, if his tight frown was any indication.

"How do you feel?" Reuben had to ask.

Everic shook his head while crossing over to his desk. "No change."

"I'm glad to hear it," said Reuben, forcing a smile, "though *terribly* sorry to have inconvenienced you like this, saer."

The apology didn't soothe the disquiet on the man's face, though neither did he argue. "I will do my best to give you more advance notice for future appointments . . . though they may increase, with you now assisting my letters as well." Everic nodded at the parchment still in Reuben's lap and asked, "Can you orate to me how you would answer this one—without the Zaldus reference, please—and then I'll leave you to rest for the night?"

111

Reuben relaxed at the request. "But of course. Your pleasure is my command—and your command, my pleasure, saer," he promised, his smile genuine now as he leaned back against the pillows.

And that smile only widened, when Reuben caught another flicker of fond exasperation pass over Everic's face before the vampire sat down and picked up his quill.

Reuben couldn't recall the last time he'd so looked forward to an appointment.

Bev had returned with a missive from her employer, Sidarchus informed Reuben just a day after their last session, his private client requesting to book Reuben again in only two nights' time. Giving advance notice, as promised.

Despite the lack of voleris, Reuben had been in a good mood ever since. He found spare energy to do his strength exercises *twice* outside of Repose; he spent an hour before work collaborating with Isolde on a new performance number. He even wrote more: *Oh, have you met the souls / Whose eyes live far away / Deep in the bloodstained trails / Of darker yesterdays?*

The prospect of getting to do more for Everic now, not just offer his wrist up, filled Reuben with an eager excitement. Partly because it ensured Reuben's usefulness and longevity in this arrangement— the more Everic needed Reubielocks, and him only, the better. Otherwise, well . . . Reuben had grown fond of plenty of customers over the years, he reasoned with himself. What danger was there in allowing the feeling now?

In his good mood, he reacted much better than he might have otherwise, when Bev showed up to take him only for Isolde to intervene.

"You know how to get there on your own, Reubie," Isolde pointed out whilst stepping between them in the main hall, grabbing one of Bev's hands in both of hers. "Would you mind if I steal your escort another night?"

Reuben narrowed his eyes, glancing between the two—seeing for the first time just how pink Bev's skin could glow as she looked down at Isolde with clear surprise. But her hand didn't pull from Isolde's grip; the proposition was a *welcome* surprise, it seemed.

"The whole night? I hope your coffers run half as deep as your friend's, saer," he warned Bev, only half-joking. "Once our Songbird takes someone into her nest, they are loathe to leave it long."

Isolde waved a hand dismissively. "He exaggerates."

"I'd believe it," Bev answered out loud then, in that high, soft voice. Though it oddly suited the quiet woman more each time he heard it.

Reuben didn't put up any further argument, even if he silently worried. Not about how Bev would treat her, really—but how Isolde taking on a client tied to Everic's business might put *her* in danger as well.

How much danger, though, he couldn't guess. It would be easier to assess if Reuben knew just a little more about Everic's plans, besides needing access to High Ring. But that was yet another reason to look forward to the appointment ahead and get another chance to help with Everic's correspondences.

Indeed, it was one of the first things Everic asked upon Reuben's arrival: "I need to write an invitation tonight, if you'd be willing to help?"

"*You're* the one making the invitation?" Reuben said, not hiding his surprise. Then teased, "I hope it's not to visit the Hollows—I know that worked out with me, saer, but not everyone is so open-minded."

The side of Everic's mouth pulled up, slightly. "Perhaps you can help me iron out the details too."

113

Soon enough, Everic had the stool moved over for Reuben to sit next to him at the desk. And the moment Reuben sat down he noted the same flowing cursive as the last letter, signed by Everic already. "Started without me, I see."

Everic nodded. "Just a draft," he said, flipping the parchment to show a few crossed out sections and smudges. "I often write two or three, before I'm satisfied enough to have Bev send them."

Reuben gave the letter a cursory look-over, skimming Everic's proposal to a "Saer Aldo Delvanzus" to meet for an evening drink. It was a rather blunt invitation to discuss what worthy investments one might make in Sazzera, with plenty of awkward, tactless phrases littered throughout the inquiry.

"Clearly you've trained in penmanship," Reuben started with a compliment as he leaned back.

"Nothing formal," Everic grimaced. Then, to Reuben's surprise, opened up further: "I didn't know how to read or write at all, well into my adulthood."

Reuben raised a brow. Given the man's wealth, it was rather odd he'd been uneducated for so long—stranger even than Reuben getting education despite his sore *deficit* of gold. "Took advantage of a vampire's extended life, then?"

Everic hesitated; a few fingers stroked along the edge of the page as he looked down. "No . . . no, my husband taught me, actually," he said, his voice soft and quiet.

Reuben always quietly despised the unfaithful customers—which was why he didn't understand, when disappointment curdled in his stomach at the news.

After all, Everic had made *sure* not to touch Reuben beyond offering polite assistance on occasion. The brief looks of interest at Reuben's body aside—which Reuben could take all the blame for, with his clothing and strategically provocative posing—Everic had not verbally given any hints yet that he would take Reuben up on his offer for simple pleasure. He had stayed faithful to this husband admirably.

"He must be a very patient man," Reuben replied, keeping his voice light and unbothered. Continuing, when Everic didn't reply, "I know I run my friend Isolde to her wit's end, any time she's tried to teach me the more complicated Dijheri signs. We'll have to hope Bev is a better pupil. Now," he pointedly turned to the draft in front of him, "I'd word these first few sentences here different . . ."

With Reuben's help, an hour later Everic's next draft was much more robust, taking up the entirety of the page. No longer simply asking, for instance, *I can meet after the sun sets to discuss future investments. What location would you prefer?* but instead offering, *My recent ventures in this city lead me to believe you and I could have a mutually profitable conversation. I'm available anytime after sunset in the coming week, if you'd care to join me over a glass of wine—you need only say where.*

As they took a break—Everic fetching a platter of food for Reuben as always, despite the fact he hadn't been drained tonight—and the vampire watched him eat, Reuben found himself more self-conscious than he usually felt whilst woozy and faint-headed. "Does . . . does food taste like anything to you, still?" he found himself asking after Everic's eyes tracked his hand lifting a small grape to his lips.

"In a way," Everic said, still watching Reuben chew on the ripe morsel with an intensity that made him swallow hard. "It affects the blood's taste—I can tell who is surviving on crumbs, who is eating like a king. Sometimes there's an echo of a certain flavor, if they are sick, or they simply glutton themselves on one particular thing too often. But food on its own?" He nodded at the platter in front of Reuben, finishing, "I'm better served simply watching your enjoyment of this."

Not quite an answer, but a much more thorough reply than Reuben was used to hoping for from this man.

"Did you used to have a favorite, then?" he followed up with, tucking his chin down to give Everic a sultry look. "I could always *glutton* myself on it, as you say, before our next meeting."

He was quite pleased, as that startled a laugh out of Everic—and only a little unsettled when he saw an edge of fang. It helped that the vampire's laugh was a quiet, low sound, somehow carrying warmth in it as well.

Everic's eyes stayed crinkled in crescent shapes after, making his long, dark lashes more noticeable when he replied, "I liked raspberries, if I remember right."

Reuben tried not to act shocked at getting two personal answers in a row, and mentally filed away the new clue regarding Everic's origins. Such berries weren't inclined to grow in hot, Dijheri temperatures, after all. Which left the heartlands . . . and Loethia.

"Raspberries, hm . . ." Reuben pretended to think, tapping his mouth. "Easier than most fruits, to source in the mountains. I can procure a whole basketful to eat before one of our appointments, if you'd like."

Everic raised a brow. "For what purpose?"

Reuben gave him a mock-affronted look. "I told you—I'm here at your *pleasure,* Everic," he said. "Whatever that may look like."

Dark green eyes slid to Reuben's neck, for just a moment, before darting away. "Perhaps," Everic allowed. "But you need not offer more than I'm already asking. Your blood, your discretion—and now your occasional assistance, with these correspondences—is plenty for what I'm paying."

"As an expression of gratitude, then," Reuben argued, exasperated. "A 'thank you for still hiring me despite viewing me as a slave,' sort of gesture."

He regretted it a little, watching how fast Everic's face hardened.

"Your standing is no better than one," the vampire said, stiffening in his chair. It was only then that Reuben realized Everic had leaned towards him throughout the conversation, and Reuben instinctively had in return.

He didn't have the excuse of pain this time to be an ass and snipe back at the man, no matter how much he wanted to. Instead he tried to soften—sighing and plucking a cherry next from the assortment as he leaned back, shoulders loose and rounded. After he bit off half of it from the stem, exposing its center, Reuben murmured, "My apologies . . . I'm usually much better with my words. I *am* grateful you haven't turned me aside." He plucked the pit out and tossed it on the platter, sighing, "It's kept me, and those closest to me, more secure than we've been in a long time."

Everic relaxed ever-so-slightly. "Including this friend, 'Isolde,' correct?"

Reuben raised a brow, nodding as he finished off the cherry.

He was unable to read the vampire's stonelike expression, though it slightly cracked around the next question: "Are you and she . . . very *closely* bonded?"

"Bonded? Hm. Despite the few years we've known each other, I'd say we're quite close," Reuben shrugged. "We are performing partners; we share tips and advice with each other, write songs together. She goes to me first, when something is wrong." Everic said nothing, as if waiting for further information. Reuben hesitated to give it—but what harm was there, truly? "She's the closest thing I've ever had to a sister," he admitted, voice softened.

"Blood has little to do with the bonds of love, from what I've seen," Everic agreed somberly, whilst an old grief flashed behind his eyes.

Reuben's curiosity grew just a bit more. He tried to lift the mood, however, teasing, "Well, it rather *shouldn't* with romantic love. From what I hear, mind you—I can't say I've experienced it myself. This business leaves little space for the heart." He gestured at Everic's person vaguely, before finishing, "I've found it best to leave such things to people like yourself, and that *patient* husband of yours."

Everic was quiet for a long while. When Reuben glanced over, he immediately felt guilty for what he'd said, though he had no idea why—only that his words had cracked the ever-stalwart countenance of the vampire open, exposing a raw, pained interior.

Reuben didn't think further before reaching out a hand. He placed it over Everic's where it was clenched into a fist on the desk between them, apologizing softly, "I'm sorry. Did I say something—?"

"Not at all," Everic denied, though his hand stayed stiff under Reuben's touch.

The vampire cleared his throat, blinking his eyes a few times until the anguish behind them had faded. And then it was as if the moment had never occurred, only the same grim, closed-off expression Reuben had grown familiar with looking back at him now.

"Vampirism leaves little space for the heart as well," Everic explained simply, before moving out from under Reuben's hand to pull the new draft's parchment back to the center of the desk. "Shall we?"

Reuben wondered if he'd ruined the short progress they'd made throughout the conversation—and without his curiosity to blame, for once. But upon reflection, Everic's response did muddy Reuben's assumptions about him yet again. How *could* a vampire have any sort of long-term partner with hurdles like conflicting waking hours, diet, and ultimately differing lifespans in the way?

More than likely this patient husband of Everic's was long dead, Reuben realized with a conflicted mix of sympathy and relief.

They didn't finish the missive until late that night, though it still left hours before morning. Once Everic readied it for delivery— using a handheld seal with an engraved, looping "P" to keep the envelope shut—he cleared away the desk and picked-over food platter, returning with a strange look on his face.

"What takes up the rest of your time, usually, when you spend the night with a customer?" Everic asked as he neared Reuben again.

Reuben raised a brow. "Besides the time devoted to sex?" he clarified needlessly, cocking his head and unfolding his legs to prop up a leg on Everic's chair.

The trousers he'd worn tonight were loose, billowy things, just pieces of half-opaque fabric laced together at the sides that left little to the imagination. And perhaps it was a bit cruel of Reuben, to position himself so Everic would *have* to notice his form, the subtle outline of his groin. But given the vampire's earlier gloom about the heart, Reuben felt little worry he was seducing a married man anymore.

Everic *did* take in the sight for a moment, to Reuben's satisfaction. Eyes tracing up his leg, lingering between his thighs before pulling away. "Yes . . . besides that," he muttered, giving Reuben's foot an expectant look until Reuben chuckled and lowered it off the chair.

"It depends," Reuben admitted. He busied himself with examining his nails as he continued, "I don't usually have one customer all night like this, you know. But when it's a longer appointment, sometimes they want to sit and talk about their lives. Sometimes we share a meal or drink together. *Sometimes,* I play for them, if they're willing to pay extra."

"I'm sorry to have cut the free sample short during your second visit, then," Everic said, and only after Reuben glanced up to see the vampire's expression did he realize Everic was trying to joke.

Reuben smiled. "A lesson learned," he teased back. *"Never* interrupt a musician, if you know what's good for you."

At his words, Everic nearly looked wistful. "I haven't had the pleasure to listen to one," he replied, eyes far away. "At least, not in a very, very long time."

Reuben would usually have tried a few persuasive words to change that. But at this admission, he was also faced with the fact he had no idea how old this once-human actually was. "Is it the *damning* sort of knowledge for me to know if you mean years, or centuries?" he said, watching as the vampire blinked back into the present at his words. "How long you've been 'stalking the night,' so to speak?"

Everic's mouth thinned into a grim line. "I died at the age of 37. Since then . . . I believe it's been another 220 years?"

"Give or take a few decades?" Reuben said with a weak laugh, mostly to hide what he actually felt about the news. A healthy amount of shock and awe, to be sure, at the realization that Everic's youthful visage housed a soul even older than Daxus or Nahlia. But maybe a bit of envy too, given how short and unfruitful *Reuben's* life was likely to end up being. "Strange, being the young one around a full human," he recovered, thinking of Isolde, "usually it's your folk gawking at *me* for being a youthful, spry 62 years."

Everic gave a small shake of his head before turning to put away his quill and inkwell. "It's been a long time since I felt human," he muttered.

Reuben bit his lip around more questions. That was the problem, it seemed, with getting to know this man. One question answered only opened the door to a dozen more—he itched to ask *how* Everic had become like this, if he asked for it or had no choice, if he'd followed a vampire master like the coven that once terrorized the city was said to be led by. If his husband had left him for it, or simply died while Everic lived on. Not to mention all the other questions about the man that Reuben already knew wouldn't be well-received, like how Everic met Jophiel, how he had so much cantergold to waste, and what he was *really* doing here in the city.

"How much extra?" Everic said, long after Reuben had tangled himself in too many potential questions to remember their current conversation thread. Everic was finished cleaning off the desk, standing now. When Reuben gave him a look of confusion, the vampire clarified, "To play your violin next time, I mean."

Reuben let out a genuine, delighted laugh. "For *you?* Nothing, saer."

Everic frowned down at him. "You don't want compensation? I may not always have extra cantergold on hand, but I could gather up some other coinage—"

"Everic, I helped you write a *letter* for 1,000 cantergold tonight," Reuben felt bold enough to point out, then corrected before Everic could, "Or 500, however you'd like to frame it. Regardless—it would bring *me* great pleasure, to finally sing properly for my supper."

He meant it, too. Reuben felt an unreasonable amount of excitement for the next appointment they scheduled in just another two nights' time—where he would offer a goblet of blood, review any needed letters, *and* finally use his instrument.

It was more effort, technically, than most of his appointments where Reuben mindlessly moved his mouth as expected, or laid back and moaned in the correct cadences. But he liked this sort of effort. He enjoyed engaging his mind, his charms, on someone not so easily swayed by them. The blood was a mundane necessity, but the other parts of visiting Everic of late . . . they were beginning to make Reuben count the hours until the next appointment arrived.

Of course, the other stellas noticed. Besides the general abnormality of a stella leaving the bordello for the whole night, Reuben hadn't ever had a wealthy, faithful client like this before. Gringoll gave him an encouraging smile upon his return that morning, even as he teased, "A good thing your gold-blooded client doesn't come here, Reubie, or I'd have snatched them away by now."

The next evening, Adina's eyes narrowed as they ran into one another grabbing food in the dining hall. Though she only said, "You look better—I trust they're keeping your delicate frame in mind," in the same tone she always had, which Reuben could never quite read between genuine or snide.

It seemed they just wouldn't acknowledge what happened at the private performance—which was how Reuben preferred to handle such things anyway.

Sidarchus finally acted happy with him again as well, remarking to Reuben, "Your absence has been noted by our regulars in a wonderfully positive way, stella. I have lots of hour slots already filled for you in the coming week—we can't disregard a bit of scarcity marketing."

"An excellent point, Sid," Reuben smiled back.

With roughly 4,300 cantergold saved from the last two months of extra foreign customers, a semi-successful private performance, and eight sessions with a vampire, Reuben even started keeping his own health in mind. Or at least, he stopped trying to fill up *every* hour of his nightly schedule. And he felt better than he had in at least a year. Still weak every time Everic took his blood, still aching with every other step some nights. But when he gathered the amount into three small sacks tucked in his vanity drawer—equal to the amount of years he would soon remove from Isolde's sentence—Reuben thought it might have more to do with the bright sense of *hope*, burning slow but persistently brighter in him of late.

Especially when Bev came, but only to give him a copy of Everic's chamber key and a city pass for Reuben to use from then on.

As the evening of their next appointment arrived, Reuben on a whim decided to put on one of his more intricate outfits—a delicate web of gold chains first clasped around his neck from a leather band, then dangling in threading loops down his chest and around his shoulders before connecting with white, blouse-like sleeves, which started midway down his upper arms. The tight, high-waisted trousers with amber embroidery were rather boring in comparison, but Reuben couldn't be *entirely* indecent along the path down to the Hollows, or he might get stopped whether he wore a veil or not.

With a bit of gold powder to the corners of his eyes and extra application of his oils—only two of them now when he went to see Everic, though Reuben still pocketed the base oil just in case—he slipped on his mother's ring, pinned on his veil, and took his violin case, only giving the extra bottles of voleris lined up on his vanity one look of longing before he told himself he could always take a sip when he got back.

But Sidarchus stopped Reuben before he'd made it out of the pleasure house. "Your private client again, yes?" the older man said at the bottom of the main stairway, giving Reuben a concerned smile.

"I'll return with the bordello's half," Reuben assured with a nod.

Sidarchus didn't nod back. "I should have told you—there was another saer wishing to book you for tonight, Reubie. Their servant was *very* insistent."

Reuben frowned. "What was the name?"

"Oh, who's to say—I wrote it down," Sidarchus sighed with a click of his tongue, gesturing towards the front desk area. "But the last two times I've scheduled something for them, you end up being gone for the night. You *will* be here tomorrow, I hope?"

"Who's to say," Reuben echoed with a shrug, unable to help a bit of smugness at this reversal of roles with Sidarchus as he finished descending the stairs. "I simply can't know when I'll have time at the moment, with my client's changeable schedule."

"This one is willing to pay 200 for three hours and a vial of voleris," Sidarchus said whilst Reuben walked down the last few steps. "Nearly as much as you'd get for a private performance, Reubie."

Reuben bit his lip, both to hide his grimace at the potion's mention and to stop himself from explaining he *couldn't* take voleris most of the time now, unless he wanted to risk tainting Everic's food.

Still, 200 cantergold was nothing to scoff at. "I'll do my best to be there," he allowed.

Sidarchus stepped in his path. "You *will* be there," he corrected, his wisened-but-handsome features sharpening into something stern. "For all their gold, this private client of yours is just one of many. And the second they are gone, you will still need to make payments, stella."

Reuben stiffened. He was proud of himself for not taking a step back, at least, even as he complied, "Of course, Sid."

Sidarchus deflated, sighing as he stepped aside. "Just . . . remember what you are, Reubielocks," he nodded at Reuben's outfit. "No matter how special this client is treating you, for now. Don't expect an exception to turn out exceptional. Alright?"

It was funny—besides the amount of gold, it didn't feel like Everic *was* treating him special. Only like a person. Just as an equal. And that was why, perhaps, the vampire's presence ironically felt like a breath of fresh air.

But Sidarchus was usually right about these things, Reuben reminded himself, his stomach sinking slightly.

He gave his old teacher a thin smile. "I know exactly what I am, Sid."

Sidarchus returned it. "You always were a smart boy," he said, squeezing Reuben's arm once before he walked away.

# 9

# UNPLEASANT ANSWERS

Reuben couldn't help but rub at the skin Sidarchus had touched after he left the pleasure house, as if some imaginary film was left behind. He rolled the thick key in his hands many times over while he walked through the streets with his eyes trained on the ground ahead, silently fuming.

*Remember what you are, Reubielocks.*

As if he could go an entire second of his life without a reminder, Reuben thought as he squinted to see through the veil.

Sidarchus always meant well, of course. He had been good to Reuben and his mother when no one else would have. Extended her loan payment deadlines, allowed Reuben to stay at her sick bed. Protected Reuben from needing to take on harsh manual labor and ruin his already fragile health at the young age of 14, ensuring he was allowed to stay in the one place he could still call home. Taught him how to succeed as a stella the same way Sidarchus had, showing him how best to bring others pleasure until he was grown enough to take on his own clients.

Reuben used to be more grateful to him. Up to a certain age, he'd even thought himself in *love* with the older man. But over time, he tended to avoid Sidarchus at every opportunity, kept their interactions friendly but short, and just ignored the sick feeling he had anytime he stayed in his old mentor's presence too long.

The unpleasant interaction faded from his mind, at least, after he entered the hollowed hideaway, hit the mechanism to part the shelves, and turned his key into Everic's door.

The vampire wasn't at his usual spot at the desk—though neither was he slumped in a chair bleeding black ichor, to Reuben's relief. Instead, he found Everic sitting at the foot of the bed wearing remarkably fine, clean clothes, his hair less messy than usual, though still falling forward to obscure his face as he looked down at something small and metal in his hands.

Only for a split second, of course, before his head lifted at Reuben's arrival, the eyes that met his an uncanny, almost *cheery* green today. Even the lines around them were much less noticeable than usual.

Recently fed, Reuben surmised as he shut and relocked the door, giving the vampire an intrigued grin in response. He held up his violin case with a suggestive waggle of a brow and said, "Good evening—I would ask 'business or pleasure first,' saer, but it looks as though you've already drunk well without me."

Everic blinked, his gaze sliding away. Ultimately he nodded, however, shoulders relaxing before he answered, "I met with Saer Delvanzus last night. It was . . . interesting, to say the least."

Reuben was too invested not to ask for more details. "Interesting how? Did *they* seem interested? Did you offer to arrange another meeting like I suggested, or should we send another inquiry—?" He paused when Everic raised a staying hand.

Then Everic lifted up his other hand, laying his palm out to show the metal thing he'd been holding. An octagonal, coin-like token made from a swirling, white-gray marble, Reuben surveyed as he crossed the room for a closer look—with an intricate symbol of a hammer and stone block wreathed by oak leaves engraved into its center.

A guild token, Reuben realized, right as Everic stated, "They invited me to a parlor party the morning of next Repose, hosted by the masonry guild here. This will give me admittance if I show it at the door."

It would do more than that. Though Reuben would never hope to earn one himself, he knew they were a coveted social currency only guilds and high houses bestowed. Besides giving access to an event, a person could expend the token to visit that guild or house at their leisure, or even ask for a favor.

Reuben glanced up with an excited grin—only to find trepidation and uncertainty written across Everic's usual stoic expression.

"But then—this is *great* news, is it not?" Reuben said, trying to encourage him. "Just one meeting, and you're on your way to the wealthiest parts of the main city. Before you know it, you'll be invited to a High Ring ball!"

Everic grew paler, if that was possible.

"Perhaps I gave up on the forceful method too soon," he muttered. "I'm much better suited for it."

"Oh, you're *suited* for ending up in a pool of your own blood and necrotic waste?" Reuben huffed, waving a hand at the vampire's arm. "You'd need to invest in a personal harem—or at least have a willing neck at your *constant* beck and call—to have a hope of surviving the underbelly of this city."

Everic glanced up through the dark strands falling in his face. "I have you, don't I?"

Reuben opened his mouth . . . then, his cheeks warming, shut it after a few seconds of looking utterly foolish.

But how could he argue, when he didn't actually *want* Everic to rely on anyone else for non-animal blood?

Everic raised a brow and stood, when Reuben stayed quiet. And then they were suddenly much closer—the air just a bit charged, as he looked Reuben in the eyes and continued in a low, sincere tone, "Thank you again, for coming so quickly to my aid before."

For a moment, the vampire's body shifted in a way that seemed like he was about to reach out and touch Reuben.

Perhaps if Reuben had stayed quiet long enough, he would have.

But Reuben refused to let Everic's proximity distract him from the argument at hand. "I'm glad my blood could somehow do what that *entire swine* couldn't," he said around a hollow chuckle. "But I'm serious. You're much better off dealing with the elite social ladder, using all that money you keep pulling out of thin air, to get at whatever your goals are in High Ring. You'd need more than just Bev and the occasional hired neck to risk crossing assassins with devilcrafted blades. "

"You know of the Allunata, then?" Everic said, watching him with a hint of curiosity in his usual stern gaze.

Reuben stiffened; he probably should have left the *"devilcrafted"* part out if he didn't want follow-up questions or the possibility of having to explain Waron.

He ignored the icy flood of fear in his gut and tried to shrug. "Who doesn't? I've lived here all my life, been privy to gossip for most of it—and their group has grown more brazen in the last decade. Destroying water channels; leaving a dead acolyte displayed in the piazza."

Reuben should have turned Waron away the moment he realized what the man was a part of, given everything. He would have saved himself a lot of grief.

He couldn't quite tell if Everic noticed the side step to his question, but either way, the vampire didn't press further. "Perhaps you could give me some pointers, then, on how to enchant an audience besides declaring the amount of gold I can offer," Everic carried on. "I assumed that would help me bypass such useless games, but instead it seems to be . . . off-putting."

"Those who are rich never just *say* so," Reuben replied, another direct quote from his mother. He ran idle fingers through the ends of his hair while explaining, "They will tell you not just in how they dress, but what words they use, when and where they do things, what tastes they have. While some unconventionality is appreciated, it's always balanced by enough of the conventional to signal their status to other elites."

"Wearing their foppish clothes is not enough," Everic surmised, sounding almost . . . grumpy, if a vampire could be called something so undignified.

Reuben hid a smile. "It's a start," he encouraged. "But if you wish to climb your way into high society—especially with only money to your name—you'll need something more. My mother said the merchants and craftsmen allowed amongst the high houses' circles always had some sort of *interest* to them beyond their success."

"Such as?"

Reuben shrugged, moving over to set his violin case on the bed. "She only mentioned this in the context of a wealthy young merchant she'd liked; apparently he had the largest collection of books in the city outside the Aureate Cathedral, and shared them much more freely than the Priesthood."

One side of Everic's mouth pulled into a sardonic smile, showing the edge of his teeth. "If only society was not so opposed to vampirism. What could be more interesting than that?"

Reuben wasn't sure if he felt more unsettled or flustered at the flash of fang this time, for whatever reason, but he tried to take the answer seriously as he sat down on the bed: "It wouldn't be good to admit to it, no . . . but encouraging some air of mystery or rakishness about you as a person couldn't hurt. It can even grant you privilege to forego some of polite society's customs. *Some,* being the keyword there—it's a delicate balance."

Everic sat down as well, to Reuben's surprise, his expression thoughtful. "Something to balance me out . . ." Slowly, his gaze narrowed and moved over to Reuben. He patted the case between them, requesting, "Play for me, would you?"

Reuben perked up at the prospect, purring, "*Of course,*" as he reached down and undid the latches.

Of course, there was every chance he ended up regretting this offer—for all that Reuben had mastered the overwhelm of playing to crowds with his violin, a solo performance could still feel like a terribly intimate thing, at times.

He would always do it, though, and happily over other special requests clients could make. And this time he felt *especially* curious what the music would reveal about the quiet, reserved, long-lived man next to him.

Curious, and perhaps a bit nervous.

Reuben focused on tightening the bow, rosining the sleek, new hair, and tuning the strings to soothe his nerves. "Do you mind if I stand, saer?" he asked last, laying his mother's old violin over his lap as he waited for Everic's verdict.

Everic's face twisted into one of his characteristic frowns, however.

"I *can* play sitting," Reuben hurried to explain, "it's no bother either way."

"No, no, I . . . what I mind is hearing you call me 'saer' still, I think," Everic admitted, looking down between them with an unhappy grimace.

Reuben's eyes widened. "My apologies, Everic; most people *like* when I use the honorific on occasion, but if you don't—"

"Keep using it," Everic said over him, his expression going hard all

130

at once. He met Reuben's gaze with a new resolve. "It is a necessary reminder, I think."

"Are you sure?"

"Yes," Everic replied sternly. Then, much softer: "Please—play however you'd like, Reubielocks."

Reuben nodded slowly, even if he felt rather thrown off by Everic's strange reaction and at a loss about what *"reminder"* the man could need. Without further ado he stood, rested his violin on the right side of his collarbone, and tried to focus his mind instead on what he should play.

The answer came quickly to mind: *The First Sunset*, a ballad about the tragic, distant love fabled between the two old gods of the city, Sazzo and Klera. While Reuben's performative, flirty numbers were always a hit, his more sensitive clients tended to enjoy the slower, more wistful melodies like this one—and Reuben knew Everic well enough by now to guess which would have a greater effect on the vampire.

Indeed, by just the second note he started to *feel* Everic through it.

The brief glimpse Reuben's short tune had given him, the night they met, was nothing compared to the encompassing waves of emotion washing over his senses this time. Everic was attracted to him, yes, not that Reuben needed further confirmation. But past that, there were strong currents of both anger and melancholy, shadows of ever-creeping hunger, and even deeper than that, a bottomless ocean of incomprehensible grief.

Reuben thought of the most-likely dead husband, but the grief was far too deep and permanent to be explained by simply outliving a loved one. And more an ingrained *part* of the man, rather than a feeling Reuben could discern the specifics of.

He tried anyway—pouring everything he had into the final move-ment of the ballad, feeling more than seeing when Everic's melancholy ballooned into an overwhelm of emotion. A single tear ran down the vampire's pale cheek as Reuben stroked out one final high, lingering tone slowly with his bow.

But then the last note faded into silence.

Reuben blinked, coming back to himself. Belatedly he lowered the violin, realizing that though he hadn't managed to feel lost in the music, he *had* gotten a bit lost . . . in Everic.

"'Beautiful' is far too insufficient a word," Everic said slowly. "But I'm afraid it's the only one I have."

The moment their eyes met, it was too much for Reuben. He'd delved too far, too quickly, and couldn't shake the lingering echo of Everic's grief in his own heart. It was hard to even face Everic without tears beginning to prick in his own eyes.

So Reuben looked away. His voice came out soft and shaky as he replied, "Thank you, saer—*Everic,*" and hurried back to the bedside to put away the instrument. And in the resultant silence, felt compelled to fill it, adding, "The best music does not require words. It is a greater compliment, I think, if words cannot define it."

"What does it require?" Everic asked.

*Emotion,* Oriana would have answered.

*Conviction,* Sidarchus would probably argue.

As for Reuben: "I couldn't say."

Everic didn't respond. But when Reuben glanced over, the vampire was watching him with an intensity he'd never seen before—almost as if he knew what Reuben's music had just allowed him to see, and was trying to peer inside Reuben in return.

With his mother's old instrument put away and the case gently deposited at the foot of the bed, Reuben tried to shake off the last traces of Everic's melancholy and offer the man a simple, pretty smile. Though his voice still came out too subdued for his liking as he held out a wrist and said, "I haven't touched any voleris since you sent your request."

Everic's gaze almost felt like a tangible caress as it traveled down Reuben's arm. Narrowing in on his inner wrist for a drawn-out moment, before reaching out a hand.

Reuben stayed pliant, even took a step closer when the vampire cupped one side of his wrist and pulled it toward him. Though he did have to stifle a small gasp when Everic leaned forward and took a deep, lingering breath in right against the skin.

"You didn't," Everic murmured, sounding pleased—then, with the faintest, gossamer touch, traced his lips down the thin, veined skin. Almost, if not quite, a kiss.

Reuben held his breath, resolving to not put up a struggle.

But then Everic leaned his head back. "We'll save your strength for when I truly need your blood," he said, practical as always. Though, unless Reuben's eyes deceived him, with a bit of regret too before he squeezed Reuben's wrist and let go.

Reuben felt terribly light-headed, and he hadn't lost a single drop of blood.

Then his mind belatedly registered what Everic had said. "Should I hope to be called again by you soon?" he asked.

Everic stood and crossed over to the wardrobe, agreeing, "Very soon," whilst opening its doors.

He stood there in unhurried contemplation before picking out a simple, elegant doublet from the various clothing items. Made of a thick, silver-woven fabric with an off-gold sheen to it, Reuben saw as Everic held it out for him, with pearl buttons, embroidered sleeves, and the left side of the collar fashionably flaring just so, the way Reuben had seen on rare glimpses of rich merchants and High Ring elite in the piazza.

"Tonight, however, I'd like you to try a few things on," Everic said as he draped it on the bed. "This one was tight in the arms for me, but perhaps you're more suited for it."

Reuben stared at it. For all his silk and lace, the sheer *quality* of the pattern, cut, and fabric before him told Reuben this single item alone was worth more than the amount Everic gave him each night. He was nearly afraid his touch would taint it, like the Zaldian Priesthood warned of deviants and heretics.

"Saer, I . . . couldn't."

"Why not, if you are here at my pleasure?" Everic pointed out, raising a brow. "At my whim, I could take you now for a stroll in the piazza markets, or sit in a high terrace garden and be served the finest wine, or have you play for me the rest of the night, and more. Could I not?"

"Of course," said Reuben.

"Then why not this?"

Reuben opened his mouth, then shut it. Everic wasn't playing fair— but ultimately, what could he do but give in to his customer's desire? Even if putting on such lovely, respectable items meant for *dignified* society would pain him?

Everic's eyes stayed admirably to himself when Reuben undressed without further protest. And he spent the next hour having Reuben try on nearly half the things in his wardrobe, remarking about each item either that he didn't like the color on himself, or some part of it was too snug, or he simply couldn't stomach the style. He didn't try to outright give any of the pieces to Reuben, at least—though why he was so insistent otherwise didn't make sense to Reuben until he noted Everic pinching at any ill-fit, loose fabric, taking care to see where exactly a too-long sleeve or trouser leg should be cut back to better fit Reuben.

Then all at once, Reuben realized the man's intentions went far beyond just gifting him a few items of much-too-fine clothing.

"You wouldn't want me present at any party or ball," he warned, just as Everic was checking the sleeve length of a navy overdress called a pellanda, which Reuben had tried on next.

Everic looked surprised—then his eyes narrowed as he challenged in a low tone, "You know all my wants, then?"

Reuben ignored the very inconvenient, very unusual shiver that traveled down his spine and pulled off the pellanda, holding it out for Everic to take. "I am not my mother, I'm afraid," he said. "I've only been brought to these sorts of events to look pretty and . . . well, provide my client pleasure at the end—certainly not to perform music or actually converse with people."

"Then your talents have been sorely underutilized."

Reuben swallowed down his growing anxiety and argued, "Because they are not *wanted.* Especially at a high society occasion? Even wearing this sort of clothing, a low-born whore like me should not set foot in such places."

Everic did not look persuaded. "High Ring cannot be so pure as that," he frowned, still not taking the garment from Reuben.

"They do have courtesans and concubines," Reuben allowed, "but I work in the main city, for common people—far below them in every respect."

"As do I," Everic argued, gesturing around them. "And yet *I've* been led to believe enough canters can get a person anywhere in the great, golden city of Zald. Unless you say differently, now?"

Reuben grimaced. He didn't want to encourage Everic to fall back to whatever his *forceful* methods had been—underground, illegal, highly dangerous ones, he could guess—and most likely meet the end of an Allunata's devilcrafted blade once more. Truly, Everic *did* have a chance to rise up in society with the seemingly never-ending amount of cantergold he had on hand, if only he played his pieces well.

But there was no way to know without a doubt that adding

*Reubielocks of the Starlet Eye* as another piece on the board would help Everic win the game, or lose it entirely.

To stall for an answer, Reuben moved past Everic to hang the overdress back up himself—only for the vampire to place a hand on his arm.

"Reubie?" Everic murmured. So softly, Reuben almost thought he'd heard his true name.

Hesitantly, he met Everic's questioning gaze. "I . . . I only fear that eventually, my presence would become a terrible hindrance to the social ladders you are trying to climb, saer."

Everic's eyes flickered over his face, contemplative. "*Or*, it could create just the sort of interest you've said I need."

Reuben's shoulders slowly lowered. He sighed, then conceded, "It could be." Everic's small but genuine smile in return almost made it feel worth the risk, whilst he finally took the clothing item back and hung it back in the wardrobe. But Reuben still had to stipulate, "*If* I came with you, though, it would only be a trial run. And even assuming it goes well, if at any point in future I feel my presence *is* becoming a hindrance, you must let me discontinue this part of our agreement."

Everic turned back and crossed his arms over his chest. "Any other stipulations?"

Briefly, Reuben worried the vampire was angry—but when Everic only cocked a brow at him, still waiting, a slow smile tugged at the corners of Reuben's mouth.

". . . *if* I'm allowed to pick out the ensemble I wear," he bargained.

Everic smirked back, then gestured freely at the wardrobe.

Reuben could feel a small trace of a smile linger on his face all the way back to the bordello.

All things considered, it had been a wonderfully successful night. Reuben spent the remainder of it giving Everic a few extra pointers on what card games to know, what sort of people to expect, what greetings to give, and it was quite gratifying to see his client listen with such apt attention, even taking a few notes. After Reuben had chosen from the clothing, Everic promised to have the outfit altered for him by Repose. Bev would arrive at dawn to bring Reuben to a small property in the main ring where he could dress and give Everic a small drink, before Bev drove them to the location by carriage.

Now, all Reuben had to do was look forward to Repose, just two short days away.

Some part of him was nervous he was right—that Reuben would ruin Everic's chances, and even lose this entire arrangement for good. But most of him could too easily imagine himself at Everic's arm, finely dressed, using the charming facade he'd crafted over the last four decades for something *grand*.

With the help of Reubielocks, Everic would win over the right people with ease, receive even more exclusive invitations with elite social circles, until finally he got access to High Ring for whatever he needed to do, and then . . .

Well, Reuben didn't care to think about the end of something potentially good when it had only just begun. He walked with a spring in his step up the stairs and opened the door to his dark chambers with an audible sigh, ready to fall asleep thinking of the future, and maybe reimagine the sparks of sensation he'd felt when Everic's lips ghosted over his inner wrist.

Reuben only made it to the vanity, however, when he sat and noticed a tall, dark shape in the mirror—the shadowed figure of a man leaning against the opposite wall.

All at once Reuben's body froze to ice.

"Reubie, my elusive little dove," Waron said as Reuben met his gaze through the reflection, pushing away from the wall.

The infernal man's height was an uncanny thing. It required that he stoop through most doorways, his curling horns just exacerbating the problem, and meant even from a great distance he was able to look down at someone. But much more unsettling than that, had always been the contrast between the pupil-less, entirely black sclera of his eyes and the pale, spider-veined gray of his skin, which had only grown more sickly-looking over the years.

Reuben stood and forced his stiff lips to move, his breath to rush through his vocal chords and shakily spit out the words: *"M-mellifluous, diaphanous—illustrious, eu-euphon—"*

He wasn't even close to being fast enough. And his *Charming Words* spell likely wouldn't have worked anyway, given how badly his shaky voice served as a focus. Reuben had yet to finish the first line before Waron was upon him, a wide hand over his mouth and the other threading a tight grip into his hair.

That was the problem—the true reason Reuben had asked Sidarchus to send Waron away. Not the increasing demands, or the depraved humiliation, or most damaging of all, his pushing Reuben to use more and more voleris each time. So long as he could charm Waron into easing up or conceding when it had gone too far, Reuben told himself it was worth the higher pay. Maybe for a time, he even believed it.

But the moment Waron realized what Reuben was doing, he started covering his mouth, and *any* defense Reuben had disappeared.

Reubielocks would do most anything for gold—but Reuben wasn't ready to die for it.

He tried to rip Waron's hand away now with no success. Dark, fathomless sclera stared into his eyes as his old client watched him struggle, unmoved as Reuben beat hard fists against his chest. When Reuben grabbed at his throat, however, Waron finally reacted further.

The tight grip in Reuben's hair yanked his head back, his scalp burning and neck aching from the force of it. Waron's other hand briefly disappeared, but Reuben's freed mouth had only started shaping a word before Waron shoved a large handkerchief into it, abruptly making him gag and forcing his jaw to painfully lock on itself.

Reuben's eyes widened in panic, his hands scrabbling against Waron's to reach up and dislodge it—but Waron used the grip on Reuben's hair to wrench him entirely backwards, slamming his head hard against the vanity dresser's edge as he fell.

Reuben blinked, then found himself staring at the ceiling. Only belatedly did he notice his limp hands were pulled together, and that his own silk rope from the dresser was being used to tie his wrists.

But of course, how could Waron forget the location of his second favorite toy?

"I've missed this," he heard Waron sigh, right as Reuben registered a sharp, throbbing pain in the side of his skull. "Even whilst watching from afar . . . I missed *you*, Reubielocks. It's unfortunate I couldn't return sooner."

Reuben started crying, then. Not because of the pain, or even at the knowledge of who exactly had been watching for the last two months—but because Waron began to half-drag, half-carry him to the bed, and Reuben's attempts to fight were laughable compared to the other man's strength.

And that was just it, wasn't it? He was powerless. Too slow to use magic, too frail to give a proper fight, too feeble-minded to do anything but go lax and try to minimize the damage from here on out as he was thrown onto the mattress. Because even if he *could* charm Waron and force him to leave, what hope did Reuben have to stop Waron from trying this again and again?

For all Sidarchus's reassurances, Waron had gotten past the bordello's security guards without an issue. Reuben's pleas hadn't been taken seriously—probably because he should have *lied*, invented a story that Sidarchus would actually care about, like Waron stealing gold or threatening Reuben's future ability to earn Sidarchus money.

When had the truth ever been enough to protect him?

"There are so many whores and courtesans in Sazzera," Waron remarked as he flipped Reuben onto his back and straddled his hips—and Reuben inwardly bemoaned having to face the man through this as Waron pulled his wrists up to the bedpost, retying them there amidst Reuben's struggles. "So many in this holy city, and yet someone out there wants to keep an eye on *you*. Willing to pay a crooked canter for it, too. Isn't that strange?"

Reuben stopped short. It *was* strange—disturbing, that Waron's sick obsession wasn't simply to blame for his reappearance.

"Keep track of little Reubielocks' habits, they say, report back on the foreign scum he services, take note of *every* place he goes," Waron mocked. "Not a problem, of course—until recently."

At that, he paused, reaching down to trace Reuben's lips, which were currently bloated by the cloth forcing his jaw half-open and his throat to constantly constrict and try to swallow. Meanwhile, Reuben's heart paced out a wild, galloping beat against his ribcage as he thought of Waron or one of his underlings following him through the Hollows. Taking note of the place he entered to see Everic, or worse—Daxus and Nahlia's little hollow.

Waron's lips twisted up into a soft, gentle smile. "I'm a busy man, you know," he continued, "especially with so much happening in the city. I've wondered if I might just find you a new cage to chirp from; much simpler for the Allunata to keep track of you that way, keep our client happy. And things were so much *better* when you had me, weren't they? Admit it—I can see how sickly you've grown." He traced the skin under Reuben's eyes, chuckling when Reuben tightly shut them and flinched away. "I see how scared you are, too. Isn't it better to *face* what you're afraid of, not constantly live in fear of it?"

More tears leaked from the corners of Reuben's eyes, now falling down his temples.

Waron briefly stroked a hand down Reuben's wet cheekbone—then reached for his knife belt. "I don't think you fear me, either. Deep down, what you're *truly* afraid of is how I make you feel," he mused while pulling out the first blade.

Reuben started to sob then, despite himself, shaking his head and gagging harder as he tried even more desperately to dislodge the thick cloth with his tongue. A dozen terrible memories flashed through his mind, each worse than the last. He used to only be anxious when Waron started adding knives to their appointments—now, even after weeks of Everic's careful cuts, his heart picked up in animalistic fear just at watching Waron handle the blade.

But crying and twisting away were short-lived privileges. When Waron held it up against his neck, Reuben grew very, very still.

"Unfortunately I didn't just slip past your brothel's security for my own amusement, Reubielocks," Waron leaned down and whispered playfully, as if letting him in on a secret. "We all need to earn our bread—and booking you under a different name without success has grown tiresome."

Waron dug the point of the knife in, though only to cut the leather band free from Reuben's neck. He did similarly to the bands on Reuben's arms, tiny gold chains spilling loose into Reuben's hair as the frivolous outfit he'd worn for the night was cut to pieces.

Once Waron set the sharp edge against the underside of Reuben's upper arm, however, he cocked his head. "I assumed you'd wish to be the innocent little victim tonight—but would you prefer voleris like before?" he asked, looking down at Reuben curiously. "Give in to the pleasure of it all, after so long without? You're always more yourself, you know."

He'd never given Reuben the option before, only paid the potion's extra cost in advance and made sure Reuben took it. Sometimes he had even paid for two vials, as if to consume one himself, and then made Reuben drink *both*. The bad reaction Reuben had experienced at his last private performance was child's play in comparison to what those amounts had done to his mind and body.

But voleris was probably his best option to make it through the next few hours—the only way to give himself some escape. Plus, if Waron freed his mouth, Reuben could ready himself to spit out a much quicker incantation than before.

Reuben couldn't resist the chance. He nodded his head desperately, making a weak, whimpering sound in case that helped convince the man.

Waron gave him a much wider smile before pulling out a familiar vial he must have taken from Reuben's vanity, uncorking it and sticking two fingers into Reuben's mouth with the other hand—only pushing the gag to the side, Reuben noted with a sinking in his gut. He was still thankful for the familiar sharp, earthy tang of the potion pouring into his mouth, choking only a little before he managed to swallow.

But then Reuben felt as if the surface under him had dropped out, his stomach making harsh somersaults when he saw Waron pull out two *more* vials from his belt pouch.

"No whore likes to admit what they are," Waron sighed over Reuben's wordless, muffled shouting, forcing his jaw open whilst Reuben fruitlessly tried to bite down, to wrench his head away. "I know it's not easy, to realize you enjoy something like this." He shoved the second vial so far back into Reuben's mouth he wretched—then choked, nearly drowning on the potion as it gushed directly down his throat. "But it only takes you a little extra encouragement before you relax and start admitting the truth, Reubielocks. You always do. And now, tonight, I need you to be extra truthful—and tell me *everything* you know about that man you meet in the Hollows, including why my blade didn't end his wretched existence."

Reuben choked again, coughing so hard that stomach acid burned up his throat. He doubted his voice would be intelligible by the time Waron let him speak.

But that wouldn't lessen the amount of pain inflicted until the man was satisfied.

As Waron dislodged the second vial from Reuben's mouth, it moved the handkerchief enough Reuben did manage to unlock his jaw and get in a bite, finally. His jaw snapped down hard, feeling a satisfying *crunch* in the fingers his teeth found purchase on.

Still, it probably wasn't the smartest choice. Waron let out a pained, angry roar before his free hand slammed into Reuben's jugular. The handkerchief was dislodged when Waron pulled his wounded hand free—but all Reuben could manage in the aftermath of his throat getting punched was an indelicate wheeze. Then the third vial was shoved into his open mouth, and he had to focus on not drowning again.

"I was doing you a kindness," Waron said, his voice suddenly ice-cold. He looked down at Reuben like a child might inspect a pinned insect now, as if to consider which wing to rip off first. "But it seems you'll have to *earn* the use of that whore-mouth, tonight."

The vial was too long and far back for Reuben's tongue to dislodge. He could only lay there, swallowing over and over again at the jabbing pressure of it so he wouldn't gag and drown in his own vomit, while Waron watched impassively. Then—as if a cloud had just blown past and uncovered the sun—the same presence Reuben noticed months ago in the crowd, and again a week ago during the private performance, suddenly radiated from where Waron knelt over him, this time searing down with an even harsher, scrutinizing intensity.

Malicious. *Familiar.*

When Waron pulled out a tiny knife from the many on his belt and replaced the vial with it against Reuben's tongue, Reuben prayed to Zaldus that the voleris would kick in soon.

# 10

# PRETTY LIE

Waking up after expecting to be dead wasn't quite so relieving as one might think, Reuben had learned more than once. Mostly, because it *hurt*. But also, because it meant you still had to face whatever came next.

The first time he woke in pain and confusion, Reuben's mind utterly rejected it—plunging him back into darkness before he could sense anything else. The second time, it started like the beginning of another convoluted dream, thoughts and images swimming in lazy, distorted swirls through his mind. Lulling him more gently back to the waking world this time, so that Reuben only gradually became aware of the insistent, angry ache of his back, shoulders, and legs. Even pain in his arms—still draped above his head, though no longer tied to the bedpost, he realized an hour or a second later.

But he couldn't get himself to move. Reuben's mind stayed floating and distant for a long time like that, right up until the moment he managed to shift his mouth. Then a white-hot, daggering pain flared deep into his tongue and the back of his throat, and Reuben remembered what Waron had put there. Later, *tied* around Reuben's head by the handle to stay inside, after Reuben ripped up his mouth further to spit the short knife out.

Unsurprisingly, his mouth still tasted like blood, even more so now that he'd jostled the dozens of cuts inside.

Perhaps Everic would finally want to kiss it, Reuben thought in a half-daze.

After that, his thoughts stopped their buzzing and bumbling about like bees drunk on smoke. But Reuben wasn't grateful. In their relative stillness, hazier memories resurfaced: Waron using a blade on Reuben's chest whilst commenting on how well he seemed to heal; the painful, bloody extraction of the knife from his mouth at last; the questions Waron asked as he cut further down Reuben's body, threatening to put the knife back between Reuben's teeth if he tried an incantation or his slurred, convoluted answers weren't satisfactory.

Worst of all, the ugly truth of what he'd heard spill from his own lips, once the pain grew intolerable: *"He . . . h-he's a—vampire.* That's *why, Waron. No, please—that's why, I swear it!"*

Reuben could no longer recall if he was trying to explain the reason behind Everic's miraculous survival of a devilcrafted blade, or why Everic hired Reuben in the first place. Nor could he recall the details around why Waron responded in answer, *"I wonder what would happen if* Soul Bleeder *touched* your *skin, little dove,"* whilst fingering the silver handle of his longsword.

Everic could kill Reuben for this betrayal.

A few weeks ago, Reuben would simply have expected it of the vampire. Now, his mind flashed briefly to Everic's hand on his arm, Everic's voice asking, "Reubie?" so soft and gentle . . . but he pushed the memory aside. Reuben couldn't expect exceptions from the vampire forever. Really, he should send Bev away the next time she fetched him and end this before it ended him.

But how on earth would he explain it to Sidarchus? Even more, what tale would he have to spin to make the house manager *believe* the danger and not hold the decision against him, without breaking his vow to Everic a second time?

Slowly, Reuben sat up and shook off the tattered remains of the clothing Waron had ripped apart, feeling sick from the motion. He stared ahead at nothing until the nausea settled, then tried to view the rest of himself objectively.

Given the state of his body, Reuben was grateful he didn't remember much else, even if he also felt terrified, confused, and disoriented as he surveyed the damage. Tacky dried blood scabbed and smeared over multiple new cuts that ran between Reuben's ribs, a dozen more littering his inner arms and legs. More blood smeared into the silk sheets under him, Reuben leaned further to see, as well as some off-white, telling stains.

A tacky feeling between his legs and an inert twinge inside him confirmed further that Waron's strangely fixated obsession for him still very much involved lust. Which was probably gratified near the end, once Waron got all the information he wanted and the high dosage of voleris left Reuben little more than a mindless, starry-eyed doll.

Reuben stared at the evidence, feeling nothing. Then all at once his mouth grew terribly dry—and he had just enough time to twist and lean over the side of the bed before his stomach clenched, expelling the little fluid left in it onto the floor. He spent the next minute dry-heaving until his body was finally convinced it had purged all it could.

Reuben collapsed and curled into himself afterward. He had no desire to face reality. Truly, his only desire was for *more* voleris. But his mind drifted back into sleep before the urge could grow strong enough to get him on his feet.

The third time he woke, it was to the warmth of a blanket being laid over his bare form, and Sidarchus's voice saying, ". . . an unfortunate outcome, and we've all had the need for an extended Repose before, dear. I'm proud of Reubielocks for so stalwartly earning his."

"You'll let him rest, then?" the low, concerned voice of his dear friend asked, a hand gently laid on his arm.

"I'm sure he has enough cantergold to rest for quite some time, Songbird . . . so long as he doesn't lose his most *important* customer."

Meaning the one customer he was bound to lose, Reuben thought bitterly. And worried yet again about what he'd say, how he could spin a lie convincing enough to avoid Sidarchus's disfavor.

At the same time, he kept his breathing silent and even, his eyelids relaxed and limbs heavy. Even when he heard Sidarchus leave the room, Isolde draping another blanket over top of the first and moving about the chamber for a few minutes, Reuben didn't feel ready to be present with her. Not without pain and fear and despair bursting out of him like rain torrenting down from a storm-swollen sky.

He acted asleep so long he convinced his own body it was—and woke up with his body washed, the floor cleaned of his vomit and blood, the sheets underneath him changed, and the empty potion bottles, ripped clothing remains, and rope gone from sight. The only physical indication of Waron's assault that remained, Reuben found as he slowly got up and looked around, was a small dent in the wooden vanity's side from its impact with his skull.

Which barely twinged when he pressed at the spot, though his throat ached every time he moved his head, his spine was terribly stiff, and his entire mouth felt swollen. The cuts on his chest and limbs had already scabbed over, at least, looking to be healing quite well as usual. Regardless, Reuben went to his mother's violin and played the *Healing Song* to speed the process, managing the familiar tune despite his sheer exhaustion. Hoping against hope that his luck would come through at least for this, and he could still avoid gaining any noticeable scars.

The wounds closed up and disappeared in seconds, the discomfort in his mouth fading. But without the immediate physical pain to distract him, Reuben's remaining aches asked for a different kind of relief.

With shaky hands he inspected the vanity drawer, heart picking up when he couldn't find any more voleris despite his recent stock-up.

Waron had *stolen* from him on top of everything else, Reuben realized, and at last some of his fear flared into anger.

The rage faded just as quickly as it came, however. What could feed something so hungry as anger, when a person was entirely starved of power to fuel it? Reuben couldn't think much past the burgeoning need to dull his pain as it was, especially after noting his room was even out of table wine—just a pitcher of water near the bedside.

He barely remembered to shrug on a day robe before moving with heavy feet down the corridor to the stellas' little dining hall. There, Reuben grabbed two bottles of the weak alcohol—then, despite the constant low-grade nausea in his gut, swept up a pile of whatever food he saw first on the little trays always left there in the dim of pre-dawn. Which Reuben could assume meant an entire day had already passed since he'd walked back from Everic's appointment and found Waron in his bedchamber.

Reuben almost dropped the meal on his way out, as he walked straight into Bittie.

"Woah! Careful there," she laughed, helping him snatch the rogue corner of napkin before things could tumble out. Then the dwarf looked up at him with tired but curious eyes, still wearing one of her usual brightly-colored ensembles—always one of the last ones to turn in for the morning. "Enjoying your little vacation?" she teased with a nod at Reuben's bundle. "I hope you saved me a few rowan berries."

Reuben blinked slowly, half-understanding and struggling to formulate a response. After an awkward beat of silence, however, he felt himself take three mental steps backward, the hollow shell that remained attempting a tease back: "I'm afraid you'll have to take it up with the kitchens."

Bittie looked a bit confused, though only for a moment before she shrugged and patted her pockets. "I can always make a personal order. With how excited the new proposals have made the city, I have more Dijheri silver than I know what to do with—did you hear? The Voice of Zald might even let piazza businesses stay open this evening!"

Reuben didn't care to question what Bittie meant. His head and spine pounded with every step he took back to his room, his mind swinging between an anxious panic and a murky daze. He didn't realize until an hour later, picking at his food and watching the window from where he'd collapsed back into bed, that the sunrise actually marked the morning of Repose itself.

Not until a knock came from the door.

As Reuben opened it, he had already started, "Sid, I'm sorry, but—"

But it was Bev standing there, wearing a considerably smaller amount of leather and weapons than usual. Only a thick, corset-like leather belt fashioned around her waist, with a single blade holstered in it. The rest of her ensemble was made up of a green overcoat, a high-collared shirt, and darker green trousers that complimented her skin tone well. She gave him a quick nod, though her eyes narrowed while taking in his state in comparison: hair tied in a ragged, out-of-the-way knot, a loose robe on, still barefoot.

Somehow *two* days had passed, Reuben realized with an abrupt, nauseous twist of his stomach. He hadn't even had the time to warn Sidarchus about the unusual working hours, much less think about how to style his hair or face or practice his lines for what might be the most pivotal moment of Everic's mysterious goals thus far.

Much worse, he hadn't even decided what to say or do, to stop Everic from killing him.

"Bev! A-are you looking for our Songbird?" he asked in an attempt to stall, desperately surveying her for any signs that she, and by extension Everic, might already know what Reuben had done and planned to silence him forever. He was sorely tempted to hum a quick tune and more accurately take in her emotions to make sure.

She shook her head, brow furrowing—but for all that her eyes were still a bit hard to read, Reuben had seen the infernal woman look confused enough to clock that same emotion now on her face. Nothing less, nothing more, he was relieved to see.

And with the fear for his own life quieted, Reuben's next worry was for *Everic.*

"Oh—*oh*, it seems I've entirely lost track of the days," he tried to laugh, opening the door wide and gesturing at her to come in. "How is your friend? Ready for our morning social?"

Bev raised a brow as she entered, her shoulders relaxing once he shut the door. "I . . . he seems nervous," she answered quietly. Then added with her hands, "But fine."

Reuben blew out a breath of relief. "I'll have to relax those nerves of his, then—just give me a few minutes, I'll be ready," he promised, swallowing down his fear. Moving to the water basin and gesturing at his hair as he added, "These locks don't need much more than water to bounce back."

His curls *did* need a bit more help after two days of fitful sleeping and no care, it turned out. Reuben hurriedly combed a combination of water and oil through his limp, knotted mane with a comb and then his fingers, while Bev watched in silence. Once it was finally detangled, tousled, and resembling something uniform, he looked in the mirror and felt his stomach deflate.

Reuben met weary, bloodshot eyes with purplish circles under them, darker than he'd even seen on *Everic*, much less himself. Reuben smudged a neutral powder over both areas and dabbed furiously until the discolored skin looked concealed enough. Finally, he added gold powder to his eyelids and threw on the loose wrap of a dress from his first meeting with Everic, ignoring Bev's curious gaze on him the whole time as he tied its belt.

All the while, he wondered if he had it in him to survive the next few hours without collapsing or breaking down. Even if Waron had taken no action in the last few days, and Everic was none the wiser about Reuben's betrayal, could he look the man in the eye and pretend nothing had happened since their last terribly enjoyable appointment?

Should he *warn* Everic, and depend upon his mercy? Or keep his instrument close to charm the vampire, should Everic bring it up?

Did Reuben still have enough fight left in himself to lose over this precarious arrangement?

Finally, with one of his longer veils securely tied behind his ears, Reuben was as ready as he'd ever be. Which was to say, nervously biting his lip and twisting fingers into his drying hair all the way down the staircase as he followed Bev out.

"Reubie?" Sidarchus called after them, having just emerged from the main hall's backstage as they reached the exit. He looked Reuben up and down with concern—till his eyes lit up with recognition at Bev. "This is an unexpected delight, and on Repose no less!" he chuckled, hurriedly walking over. "I'm glad Reubielocks so impressed at his last appointment—though, please *do* tell your master to take more care this time? Reubie is more resilient than any other stella I know, but everyone has limits."

Reuben could feel Bev tensing up with every step Sidarchus took nearer, like a coiling spring about to snap. So he stepped between them and pasted on a smile. "You're so very kind, Sid, but I *thoroughly* enjoyed my last session." And, to help ensure Bev didn't worry enough to inform Everic about this later, clarified, "It was another client that tired me out—though I'm gilded as gold now, as you can see."

Sidarchus's eyebrows rose at the words *"another client,"* but he slowly nodded, stopping just a step away. "Very well. I won't keep you longer, then. We'll discuss your . . . *limits* later, stella."

But as Bev briskly opened the doors, Sidarchus caught Reuben by the wrist—pushing a small vial into Reuben's palm as he murmured, "In case you're in need of it," before letting go.

Just the shape of the bottle in his grip made Reuben's heart pick up a beat.

Perhaps he'd take only a tiny sip, in case his headache or back pain grew too hard to ignore during the parlor party. Reuben held it in one clenched fist as they walked further around the terraced edges of the main ring, wondering how he could transfer the vial into a pocket of his new outfit without Everic noticing.

Or maybe he shouldn't wait. It might be better to just drink the whole thing and discard the bottle before they arrived. Reuben looked around the busy morning street from under his veil, waiting till they neared enough clustered market shops so he could discreetly dispose of it after.

But Bev led him straight out of the piazza and its wider streets, heading toward the western edge of the main ring where residential buildings were more common and the street noise was less likely to disguise the sound of shattering glass. Rays of the late summer morning prickled on his neck, the heat already exhausting him as he struggled to keep up with Bev. When she turned another corner, he had nearly decided to risk drinking and tossing it to the side regardless.

Then Reuben recognized the street ahead, and halted in his tracks.

He knew this small property Everic had mentioned all too well, it turned out.

*"She specifically requested you be freshly washed, recently fed, and well-rested before you arrive tomorrow, stella," Sidarchus said, more than a year before. "And warned that she expects the night to be rigorous."*

*Reuben ignored both the nerves fizzing up in his stomach at such a warning and the dubious look Sidarchus was giving him. He brightly replied, "For 200 gold? I'd expect no less."*

*"Then are you up for the challenge?" Sidarchus pressed, and at Reuben's confident nod, continued, "Good boy. I'll assign someone from security to escort you, dear. It's not a far walk . . ."*

Only ten minutes, it turned out, both then and now.

Reuben paused, leaned a hand against the cold stone of the wall nearest him, and focused on staying upright as his stomach heaved out the little wine and food he'd consumed in the past hour.

Everic didn't consider Jophiel a *friend*, he had insisted during their first meeting, at least not by his own definition. But clearly there was still a great deal of trust between them, for him to borrow this same little property she'd once brought a whore from the Starlet Eye within. Everic was borrowing that whore as well, after all.

Reuben wanted to scream. He wanted to collapse.

He was so, so tired of fighting.

Bev was rushing back when Reuben tried to stand up on his own again, frowning worriedly at him. "What's wrong?" she signed—hand gestures he recognized well thanks to his performances with Isolde.

Reuben wished he had learned more of them. Maybe then he'd be able to explain without breaking down into tears, exactly why he never wanted to enter this residence again.

"I think my last meal disagreed with me," he managed faintly, inching around the mess he'd made to lean his back against the wall.

Bev's hands kept moving, both impressing and confusing Reuben in their speed. Seeing his bleary lack of comprehension, she sighed and pointed—first at the direction they were going, then back where they'd come from—finishing with a few basic signs that Reuben was pretty sure meant, "Where do you want to go?"

Reuben thought of the lumpy bit of straw mattress where he used to fit between Nahlia and Daxus as a child, and breathed out a faint laugh.

He slumped further against the stone and asked in a whisper, "Please, just tell me—is Jophiel there?"

Bev was quick to shake her head. The worried line between her brows remained, though the rest of her expression twisted at hearing the name. With that and the way her body stiffened, Reuben wondered now if he wasn't the *only* one who had a bad opinion of the woman.

It was enough for him to believe her.

Even if he didn't, of course—what hope could he have in escaping yet another dangerous old client. potentially even more powerful than Waron?

Reuben tried to shut down his mind and all but the most basic functions of watching the ground ahead of his feet. He took it in as if from a great distance when they entered the small first-floor terrace house and its simple, refined living area, approaching a door he'd already entered once before and mechanically removing his veil just as he had a year ago.

Then the door opened to a candlelit room, and dark red, softly-glowing eyes met Reuben's as Everic stood from the bed.

It was startling how put-together he looked compared to usual—wearing a perfectly-tailored, sleek overcoat in black that hugged his broad shoulders and flared out at the bottom, with small gold accents at the cuffs and collar. Even his hair for once looked only tousled, not tangled, like it had been neatly brushed before he ran a hand through it one-too-many times.

"Reubie," Everic greeted, a slight smile lifting the corners of his lips before he gave a thankful nod at Bev and she headed back towards the front door. The pleased look faded as the seconds passed, however, and Reuben realized he should have already returned the greeting by the time Everic continued in a more formal tone, "Please, come in."

Reuben obeyed, belatedly attempting to mirror back the smile. But the moment he entered the dark, curtained room, reality warped and smeared across his vision—Everic replaced with a shorter but equally-beautiful Jophiel, who once *led him to the bed with a friendly, conversational tone at the start, saying, "I've heard many great things about you."*

*"About me? You flatter me, saer," Reuben chuckled, sitting on the mattress edge.*

*"Your mother, the 'Summer Lily,' she was formerly of High Ring, was she not?" Jophiel inquired whilst she untied the few gathers keeping his ensemble together. "Quite the legacy to continue here."*

*Reuben didn't stiffen, though he was immediately on guard at this stranger having such knowledge about him. A past client of his mother's, perhaps?*

*"If you know anything of her, you'd know I couldn't hope to," he laughed breezily to hide his sudden discomfort. "I'm only trying to earn my daily bread, saer."*

*"And your father offered no support," she tutted, pushing his bare chest down with a surprising amount of strength. "A pity," she continued once he'd fallen back onto the mattress. "Did he live much lower on the mountain?"*

*"Yes. Very low, I'm afraid," Reuben decided to fabricate, shifting to lay more comfortably on his back while watching his new client undress above*

him. "*He worked in the Ravine and was trapped under a collapse just before my birth, from what my mother told me . . . it's no matter, saer. I've found a good life here, as you can see.*"

"Still—what tragic timing," she murmured whilst crawling over him. Then reached out a hand to stroke his chest, her dark gaze flitting between his eyes. "But you carry him with you in many ways, I'm sure."

"Who's to know," he smiled. "I'll have to prove my own talents with you tonight, saer."

Jophiel smiled back. "Oh, I look forward to you doing just that."

"Reubie?"

Reuben blinked, finding himself standing in front of the same bed he dragged himself out of over a year prior. His fists were clenched, the top of the voleris vial biting harshly into his palm.

The outfit he'd chosen for himself innocently laid out over top the bed: the silver doublet with its off-gold sheen, a pair of tall, violet boots, and slate gray trousers, which now looked more taken in at the waist and sported near-identical pearl buttons as those that detailed the doublet's fabric.

"Apologies," Reuben said, keeping that smile fixed to his expression whilst slipping the vial in his belt and reaching to undo the ties at the back of his neck. "It looks lovely, saer."

He'd only shrugged out of the sleeves and exposed the upper half of his chest, however, before Everic put a staying hand on his bare arm. "I'll need to do the bloodletting now—the doublet you chose is not as versatile as your usual wardrobe." Everic nodded down at the top and its thick, layered sleeves.

"Oh—of course," Reuben said with a weak chuckle, hands freezing at his beaded belt.

Somehow he had forgotten about this part. Or perhaps, his mind shielded him from its reality until the last possible moment, when Everic unsheathed a small knife from the inner side of his coat.

At the sight, Reuben stumbled back until the underside of his knees hit the bedside frame, landing him in a seated position. Instinctively his fingers twisted into the bedcovers, his eyes flickering to his violin case. His mind flashed through a dozen ways to get out of this service, to never get near a steel blade again.

But he couldn't anger Everic now, and in so doing endanger himself even further after betraying the man.

Everic hadn't noticed the small reaction, busy retrieving bandages and a shallow bowl from a nearby cabinet. "Does . . . does it need to be a knife?" Reuben asked, just as Everic returned with the items.

Everic frowned, dark red eyes shadowed under his brow as he glanced Reuben's way. "Is there a reason it should not be?"

He didn't sound very pleased—uncomfortable, even a tad defensive—and in this fragile state just that reaction alone was enough to scare Reuben out of further protests with a sharp shake of his head.

So he retreated even further from reality. Only distantly aware as his hands rotely removed his belt and the voleris tucked in it, keeping his lips tilted upwards, humming in agreement at whatever Everic was saying about cutting the other wrist this time. Allowing his right arm to be handled, hurt, and bled into a shallow bowl as if the appendage belonged to someone else.

Not even the touch of Everic's cool lips managed to rouse his senses.

It was the sudden sharpness to Everic's voice that forced Reuben back into himself. And only then did he notice the tears slipping down his own cheeks.

"What's happened?" the vampire demanded with bloodied lips, and a bright gold, piercing gaze now narrowed at Reuben.

Reuben's heart fluttered weakly in fear. He wiped at the tears with his free hand. "I—what? It, it just hurt a b-bit more than usual, saer,

I'm sorry—"

"There is voleris in your blood."

*Voleris.* How badly Reuben wanted to unroll the belt next to him, just at the reminder, and drink down the entire vial hidden within.

"Oh . . . I took it two days ago, just after our appointment," Reuben started with a half-truth, not having to fake the regret in his voice. Then he laced in the lie: "More than usual, I admit, as my legs were acting up after the walk from our appointment. I *truly* didn't think voleris would still be present in my blood by now. The mixture is never exact, it isn't always easy to tell how potent it will be—but in this case a terrible mistake, saer. I deeply apologize. "

Everic sighed, still looking cross as he nodded.

Reuben felt a rare twinge of guilt for his dishonesty, and added, "Please, let me see if I can purge it with magic somehow," reaching for his violin case.

Everic put a staying hand over Reuben's. "It shouldn't have an effect on me at this point," he said with a frown. "But is the walk down into the Hollows too much for you? We can meet in this residence on occasion, if that's easier; I will just have to plan the previous night to come sleep here for the day—"

"*No!*" Reuben blurted out. He grabbed at Everic's hand, entreating, "No, no, *please* don't. Not here. I can't . . . I would *very* much prefer it, saer, if we could please meet in the Hollows, as often as possible," he tried to finish in a steadier, less desperate tone.

Everic stared back at him with an unreadable expression, for long enough Reuben questioned all over again whether the vampire somehow knew of his betrayal.

Then Everic sat down on the bed next to him, and pulled the hand clutching his sleeve free—only to interlace it with his own.

A deep line formed between his brows, his gaze searching as he asked, "Is everything alright, Reubie?"

Reuben's breath caught in his throat. Just five years ago, he might have been stupid enough still to risk admitting the truth.

But even if Everic proved a vampire could be kinder than any cleric, and Reuben *didn't* end up as dead as that swine on the floor had, Everic would still stop their arrangement. Reuben already should have. And then he would be back to only having a prayer of getting Isolde out of the Starlet Eye, and pinching silver to bring to his family in the Hollows. His blood wouldn't be there to aid either, when Everic was inevitably attacked by the Allunata once more.

Obvious, but most visceral at the moment: he would never see Everic again.

Reuben blamed Everic for barging in on his life and being such a kind, intriguing exception thus far, for how miserable *everything* about that old reality sounded now.

There was little Reubielocks wouldn't do for a gold piece, Reuben reminded himself before swallowing down the last lump of guilt. Then he blatantly leveraged Everic's desire to feel like a savior, looking up slightly through his eyelashes as he murmured, "Everic . . . everything is *much* better of late, thanks to you."

Everic's features softened, to Reuben's relief, before he nodded and let go of Reuben's hand. And, after quickly drinking down the rest of the bowl and bandaging his healing wound, the vampire started helping him dress. Simply holding out the stockings and trousers for Reuben to change into, at first, and then stepping in when Reuben's hair snagged on a button.

But as the small, innocent touches continued, they soothed Reuben into the first semblance of calm he'd experienced in days—the brush of hands exchanging items, the small tugs on his doublet to situate it better over the white shirt underneath. Next, the bare trace of fingers on his neck, as Everic carefully moved Reuben's hair back to tighten the laced front.

Reuben held onto his next exhale, however, when Everic finished tying the laces at the bottom of the doublet and his pale, scarred fingers lingered there, idly tracing outward along the seam. The vampire paused at feeling the jut of Reuben's hipbones against his fingertips, before he realized what he was doing and his hands abruptly dropped.

Reuben released the breath—disappointment and relief swirling together in his already-nauseous stomach.

With just a bit of voleris to relax him, it would be easier to just spread his legs and let Everic take him by the hips right now. Certainly more feasible for Reuben than trying to impress a party full of strangers in his current state. Healthier even, than returning to the bordello and being left alone, given where his thoughts would likely descend.

Despite his stiff exterior, Everic even seemed like the type who might hold Reuben after.

"Do you *never* indulge in your own pleasure, saer?" Reuben asked, feeling wistful as Everic knelt down to help him into his boots.

Everic's golden eyes narrowed, just before the vampire ducked his face out of sight. "I indulge far too much," he replied, low and stern.

Reuben wondered, if he could get Everic to act on his desires, whether the vampire was also the type to grow sentimental about whoever he had sex with, even if that person was a whore. If so, Reuben might actually earn himself a better chance of not getting killed, hurt, or tossed aside, when the ugly truth was found out . . .

Then again, it might just make Everic feel *more* betrayed.

Once the vampire rose back up, Reuben's uncertainty was the only reason he didn't push into Everic's space and kiss him right then.

Instead, whilst Everic was distracted putting on gloves, Reuben quietly turned and fished the voleris bottle from his discarded belt, tucking it into his boot. And when Everic turned to the door, Reuben retrieved his veil and rushed to grab Everic's hand before the man reached it.

Reuben said, "Well, I'm too practical to self-indulge often—so *thank you*, Everic, for letting me borrow this fine ensemble. I almost don't feel like a prostitute," and chuckled whilst gesturing at himself.

Briefly he wondered if he'd lost his touch, when the vampire glanced back at him with that stubbornly persistent frown on his face. But then Everic raised a brow, scoffing, *"Borrow?"* in such a mock-affronted tone that Reuben's mouth split unbidden into a surprised smile, an unpracticed giggle bubbling up from his throat before he had time to tame it.

Everic's stern face relaxed into something fond as he watched Reuben laugh. And, for just a moment, the pains in Reuben's head and spine were forgotten, the despair and misery of the last two days grew muted, and the future didn't look *quite* so bleak.

All Reuben felt right then was the overwhelming desire to give up all his pretty lies and collapse into Everic's chest.

Yet if there was one thing he knew—not from his mother's teachings or Sidarchus's guidance, but his own hard-won experience over the last four decades becoming Reubielocks—it was that a pretty lie was *always* worth more than an ugly truth.

So Reuben just amended, "My mistake. For *gifting* it to me then, saer."

A half-smile on his lips, Everic shifted his hand to interlace their fingers and gave a brief nod to the door, responding, "Come. I think I will be in great need of your practical nature this morning, if we are to combat my tendency to make enemies more than friends."

# 11

# NEW COMPANY

E veric walked out of the residence with such nonchalance, Reuben didn't question it for the first few steps. He blamed it on his still-foggy mind for forgetting—right up until he noticed Everic squint, anyway—that the vampire should be *melting* under the late morning sun.

Everic only held Reuben's hand tighter as they approached a horse-drawn covered carriage just down the street. No melting, smoking, disintegrating, or however else vampires were supposed to be killed under the most concentrated source of the *Brilliance of Zald*.

Then again, maybe that vampiric feature had just been a myth—modern conjecture of how the Zaldian Priesthood defeated the vampire coven in the catacombs, given how many centuries ago the actual event occurred. Reuben filed away the observation to ask about later, busy squinting himself as the light made his aching head throb.

Bev had been leaning casually up against the side of the carriage, at odds with how her head turned, continuously checking up and down the small street even after noting their approach. When they stopped and Everic reached for the carriage door, the infernal woman pushed his arm away with a small noise of protest before doing it herself.

"That's not necessary *yet,* Bev," Everic scolded her, though he looked amused when she just offered a deep, flourishing bow and waved at them to enter.

With a helping hand from Everic, Reuben stepped onto the single stair of the high carriage and into the cabin. Which was small with cushioned benches, padded walls, and a curtain half-draped over a tiny window opposite the door.

Reuben could only guess what this sort of luxury would cost. At least a few days of what Everic paid him—more likely, a full week's worth. Reuben had only ever seen these large-wheeled, passenger-only carriages from his window or the street, on the rare occasions they traveled down from the higher tiers of the main ring to visit the piazza. If not for the respectable clothing adorning him now—rather than his usual thin, sheer, provocative wardrobe—Reuben would feel very out of place in such an expensive vehicle.

Meanwhile, Everic was muttering something quietly in Bev's ear. She nodded and gave him a smile as he ducked inside after Reuben, then shut and locked the carriage's small door behind them.

"Bev is quite the friend to be helping you like this," Reuben remarked once Everic sat on the opposite-facing bench, trying to distract himself from his nerves.

"Our goals are conveniently aligned, such that I aid with her efforts in the Hollows, and she aids me here," Everic agreed. "Though, I *much* prefer her business over mine."

Reuben swallowed down a spike of nausea as the carriage jumped into motion. He clutched the violin case in his lap and put on a smile, responding, "More blood and swords than foppish clothing, I would gather?"

Everic shook his head. "More . . . helping people."

*You could leave, start a new life, easily with the help of Bev,* Reuben then remembered Everic offering a couple weeks ago.

If he was in a better state of body or mind, Reuben might have tried asking further questions—this was to do with *Bev's* business, after all, not Everic's, and might be deemed less dangerous for Reuben to know about. But given the amount of social interaction he was about to take on, plus the state of his roiling stomach, Reuben decided not to prompt any further conversation. For once, he was grateful when Everic didn't speak for the first half of the ride either.

Reuben focused on slow, even breaths and stared out the tiny carriage window as Bev drove them out of the residential area and through the piazza, which looked quite busy for a day of Repose, when even businesses like the Starlet Eye closed. Up the gradual incline of the main roadway, eventually they reached the second tier of the main ring which Reuben had only visited for occasions such as this. Far fewer pedestrians traveled these streets than carriages, though Reuben still caught glimpse of a few entering a Zaldian chapel—one of many smaller, ornate buildings similar in construction to the Aureate Cathedral, but where various rites were performed and offerings made—and even a Zaldian cleric, the bare simplicity of the man's gold-and-white garb suggesting he was an acolyte, still in training to reach the title of priest.

Whilst wearing such fine, respectable clothing himself, Reuben hadn't thought he should already have his veil on—but as the acolyte glanced up at their windowed carriage rolling past, he felt a bolt of unease.

Everic watched Reuben hurriedly pull out the long, sheer fabric and tie it into place with a growing frown. "Is that *truly* enforced around here?"

It was surprising how strangely Everic was looking at him, up until Reuben remembered he'd always removed his veil prior to entering the man's chamber. "Not in every case—but I would rather not find out," Reuben admitted. "The Priesthood do like their rules."

"They like their gold," Everic corrected, eyes tightening.

Reuben shrugged, relaxing now that the veil was in place. "Gold *is* a sign of Zald's favor."

"And therefore, poverty and debt are signs of immorality."

"As are heresy, blasphemy, adultery, and harlotry," Reuben added, gesturing towards himself at the last word.

Everic scoffed. "The first two they *may* burn someone for, especially if they are infernal-kind—but the rest? Adultery is as common as horn fever and never punished; you've said even High Ring employs courtesans and concubines. And why would the Priesthood allow indentured servants in bordellos to begin with, if they so dearly hate the practice?"

"In that sense, we *are* given a choice on how we pay off debt," Reuben argued. "I had other options, but they would be too hard on me."

Everic's frown grew thoughtful before he asked, "Did you consider any others?"

Reuben tried not to get defensive. "Not really," he admitted. "It's only thanks to the house manager, Sidarchus, that I secured a spot in a place that isn't so physically demanding."

"*Isn't* physically demanding," Everic repeated, looking Reuben up and down. "Just two days, and you return to me poisoned and near-feverish."

Reuben felt warmth spread over his cheeks, shame curdling in his already-nauseous stomach. "It won't be an issue at the party, saer, I swear it."

"I didn't say it would be," Everic pointed out, giving Reuben a look that made him feel uncomfortably perceived.

Reuben quickly moved his eyes back to the window, shrinking back into his seat. "Well—it isn't physically demanding for *most* people, anyway. And if it grows too hard for me . . . well, I can always fall back on retiring into the Zaldian Priesthood," he muttered.

Though his mother's words rang in his head in answer, admonishing him in a soft, trembling voice after rejecting a priest's invitation yet again herself: *Never join the Priesthood, Reuben, understand? Even when it seems like the only option.*

A gloved hand reached out, firmly gripping Reuben's knee and dispersing the vision of Oriana's wide, desperate eyes.

The face that replaced it in Reuben's sights was no less somber. Everic had ducked his chin, looking at Reuben from under low, furrowed brows as he said, "You will come to *me*. I'll help you leave, as I said."

Reuben never trusted the savior types anymore—but as he beheld neither infatuation nor lust nor even self-importance, but a fierce *conviction* in Everic's eyes, Reuben knew he'd only have himself to blame when the vampire inevitably went back on his word.

"I do so enjoy coming to you," he murmured with a smile, then quickly changed the subject: "Now, let's make sure this group enjoys making your acquaintance as well—we should practice your greetings and expressions for the rest of the ride."

They'd gone over everything from the hierarchy of introductions and greetings, to what was an appropriate amount of times to blink per minute, to what signals might indicate a person's interest in business dealings, by the time the carriage jostled to a halt ten minutes later.

Reuben glanced out the window as he shouldered his case's strap, and was briefly startled by how much larger and taller the gilded white tower of the Aureate Cathedral loomed in the city skyline here—almost like a mountain peak of its own. Then, after Bev opened their door and Everic climbed out, Reuben's eyes caught on how deathly pale the vampire looked under the late morning sunshine, his frown even deeper than usual as he helped Reuben down from the carriage.

"Last chance to forget this nonsense," Everic muttered, glancing back at the carriage with longing.

The guild hall just ahead, while it didn't match the Cathedral's majesty, was still considerable in height and size—a marble structure rising above the various buildings around it with a platform base and six thick columns holding up an intricately-carved entablature. Feeling at ease in a fancy carriage had been hard enough; Reuben felt entirely out of place just standing in front of the remarkable structure.

But, for whatever reason, he found he could swallow down his own reluctance much easier at seeing it mirrored in Everic's expression. "The masonry guild is one of the wealthiest in Sazzera," Reuben reminded, then looped his arm around Everic's before prompting them to step forward. "High houses should be among their best customers—they certainly aren't building anything grand in the Hollows."

Everic gave a nod to Bev and then moved forward at a stiff, halting pace up the stone steps. "Saer Delvanzus might be persuaded to," he answered, his eyes staying trained ahead when Reuben shot him an intrigued look. But before Reuben could inquire further, they were stopped at the landing in front of the stationed door greeter, who Everic gave the guild token to between two gloved fingers.

After a quick inspection, the servant pocketed the token and gave him a short bow before opening the doors, ignoring Reuben as she directed Everic to take the first stairs on the right.

Guilds in Sazzera were quite common; the largest ones boasted of existing long before the crowning of Zald as the city's patron god. Even the Zaldian Priesthood had once been a simple guild, from what Reuben heard—made up of miners and goldsmiths that had originally found and refined the first precious, god-given piece of metal they termed "cantergold" in the Ravine.

The masonry guild of Sazzera had not elevated itself *quite* so high, but its halls certainly put the Starlet Eye to shame. Reuben subtly glanced around as they entered, taking in the four alabaster pillars on either side of them. Each one was engraved and inlaid with threaded cantergold, depicting scenes of builders gradually carving a city out of Mount Sazzo with hammer, stone block, and oak leaf motifs present throughout, the same as what featured on the guild's token. Different stairways led upward between each of the pillars, while just ahead wider steps descended toward an unlit grand hall.

Everic had been invited to a parlor party, of course, not a ball. When the vampire stood there in rigid stillness for long enough, staring out at the darkened ballroom, Reuben gently tugged him to their right towards the stairs, murmuring with a tilt of his head, "Up we go, then."

As they ascended, Reuben felt crossed between worried and grateful for Everic's clear unease. It would make things difficult during the inevitable social interactions to come—but provided Reuben with an enforced sense of purpose that helped to override his own doubts. Even more, a distraction from both the pain in his body and the building dread in his mind about anything but the immediate present.

When they reached the stairs' landing, oak doors lay open in welcome to the guild's lavish parlor room and a party within that already looked well-attended. Reuben pulled Everic through the doors and took in the landscape with a scrutinous eye: two people playing cards in one corner; four round tables filled with the remaining guests, a nearby music area left alone for now.

At the largest table, a half-dozen guests engaged in a game with a ball and brightly-colored wooden pieces without notice of the newcomers, drinking wine and laughing together. At the other occupied table nearest to the door, however, a straw-haired dwarf with a pronounced jaw and even more pronounced dimples quickly stood up from their chair and hurried over to Everic and Reuben.

A wide grin split their face as they said with exuberant enthusiasm, "Saer Payne, welcome! What a delight to see you!"

"Thank you for your refined invitation," Everic said, and made a stiff bow—the correct greeting Reuben had taught him, though with a terribly flat delivery.

Luckily, Everic seemed to have found the most cheerful, unbothered person of significance in all of Sazzera, Reuben thought as he bowed as well, then took in the person who must be Saer Aldo Delvanzus, an extra symbol pinned on their right-flared lapel that clearly marked them as guild master.

"And you've brought a companion," Saer Delvanzus continued with a smaller, inquisitive smile at Reuben—though before either Everic or Reuben could respond, the dwarf twisted to call back to the rest at the table, most eyes in the room on them now: "See! I *told* you all I wasn't telling a story."

"Hm. A mysterious man shows up and immediately offers to invest in one of your most tarnished ideas?" an elvish man with long blond hair put in, seated next to the spot Delvanzus had abandoned. His dark eyes narrowed at Everic and Reuben while Delvanzus led them over—though they gentled as he smiled. "I suppose these people put you in charge for *some* reason, guild master," he said, tipping his glass of wine at Delvanzus before taking a drink.

With how warmly Saer Delvanzus received them, it wasn't hard to keep the etiquette Reuben had been most worried about impeding Everic: only introduce oneself to guests who the host visibly welcomes.

Now, many gathered to see the stranger Delvanzus had so enthusiastically greeted, quick to bow and introduce their names and rank within the guild. Of particular note was the outspoken elvish man, who called himself, "Saer Micah Artris," was not of the guild, and came to discuss possible projects with them just like Everic.

Everic remembered the formal responses each time, at least, always replying, "A gilded blessing." But he only ever inhaled to speak the words. More worrisome, he said nothing else, his arm so tightly looped around Reuben's as the introductions continued that Reuben couldn't have separated from him if he tried.

Unlike Delvanzus, the other party goers were quick to note Everic's stiff stance, shifting eyes, and unenthusiastic, cordial replies. When one orkish woman asked if he was also from the heartlands, for instance, Everic's face twisted into a deep grimace.

"No," he said, short and frank, "I've only seen their outskirts," before decidedly looking away from her.

Reuben wanted to step in right then. But Everic had yet to introduce him, and as only a guest's companion at this social event *and* a veil-covered harlot, speaking up now would only make things worse.

By the time the guild master had the two of them take seats, the other guests seemed entirely unimpressed by the short spectacle of Delvanzus's strange, unfriendly guest. And if they looked at Reuben at all, it was in the same lingering, impersonal way potential customers at the bordello did. Despite his formal outfit today, the veil still allowed everyone around him to see Reuben for exactly what he was.

*Remember what you are, Reubielocks*—but clearly, he had forgotten. Why else would Reuben ever imagine his presence here might be a good idea?

"There's plenty of food and wine to go around, so make yourselves comfortable!" Delvanzus said as they sat on the other side of Everic.

Then, the guild master turned and unconventionally addressed Reuben: "No priests invited here today, by the way—you're in private company now, love," with a small dip of their head towards him.

Reuben felt his face flush, though he gratefully removed the veil without argument. Ignoring the nerves fluttering in his already-queasy stomach, he responded with a soft smile at Delvanzus, "And what *lovely* company Saer Payne seems to make."

Everic's eyes widened in realization. "My apologies, Saer Delvanzus—*this* is Reubielocks of the Starlet Eye," he finally introduced Reuben in a hurry, looking sheepish. "My chosen companion since arriving in the city."

Delvanzus cocked their head. "My, I've heard much of the Starlet Eye," they said with a glance at Everic, and by their tone, had not necessarily been impressed by the rumors. "Though, not quite *how* lovely their stellas are," they finished with a smiling nod at Reuben.

Reuben didn't spy any blatant disdain or ill intent in the guild master's attention. Of course, that didn't mean it wasn't hiding under the surface. His music would have to tell him later—a few eyes at the table had turned their way again now, and Reuben needed to take full advantage.

"You are far too kind, saer. Please, but I'm so curious," he started, glancing between Everic and Delvanzus, "how exactly *did* the two of you come to be acquainted? My good saer knows many an important person and spreads his assets far and wide, of course," and at that, he rubbed a hand down Everic's forearm on the table, playfully unfurling his tensed fist, "but I had no idea *masonry* might take up his interest."

Everic sucked in a breath and took Reuben's opening, repeating a phrase they'd practiced in the carriage: "My interests are vast," he said, and finally gave everyone at the table a glance from under his shadowed brow. "I'm interested in people, more than I am in any specific venture."

The unsure expressions of the guests at the table smoothed out, a few even loosening and leaning forward in interest. Among them, Saer Artris asked, "Oh? Anyone we would know?"

Reuben didn't need to glance at Everic to know how unwelcome the question was. "No," Everic replied much too bluntly, eyes shifting away again.

In a split-second decision, Reuben reached up and stroked the back of his hand along the line of Everic's jaw. He spoke in a soft voice just loud enough for their audience, using his random knowledge from so many clients over the years to fabricate, "Oh, these ones *might* be well-traveled for once, saer. Who knows? Perhaps one of them has met that Prince Oliphos you told me about, or the greencraft guild in the Steppes, or at least one of your favorite Dijheri art curators, hm?"

Everic turned his head, the motion inclining his face against Reuben's hand as he gave Reuben a questioning look.

In return, Reuben hoped he managed to communicate both vapid adoration for the sake of their onlookers, and enough conviction to convince Everic to play along.

Everic's golden eyes peered deeply into Reuben's—and then narrowed. He caught Reuben's hand and rested it on the table instead. Replying, "Doubtful," in a dismissive, slightly over-the-top tone.

But it still worked. Reuben fought down a smile when a woman to their left piped in a second later, "Well, I've *heard* of the prince," and another across the table started, "Dijheri art is unparalleled; I'll have to gather you all for a parlor party sometime so you can view *my* collection." And just like that, the social dynamics in the room began to shift.

Even Delvanzus protested after a minute, "I can't leave the poor man in suspense! You see, Reubielocks, Saer Payne and I met just over a week ago at a mutual friend's little gathering . . ." and began singing Everic's praises to the group as they explained the unlikely, but highly fortunate first encounter.

From that point on, Everic's short, brusque attitude was increasingly received with something close to acceptance, even approaching respect. So long as Reuben reframed each of Everic's curt, closed-off replies as something that implied higher standing or more refined taste, the rest of the parlor party ate it up as quickly as the food platters around them.

Reuben took a few things onto his plate, though he was starting to feel too light-headed on top of nauseous to stomach anything. Likely thanks to the blood loss, plus his body still recovering from voleris. But instead of the potion in his boot, Reuben found himself now wishing for the thick, nut-and-cinnamon drink Everic always fetched for him to soothe the discomfort.

As the conversation at their table moved on to discuss the recent trade council proposal and Everic was asked less questions, the vampire glanced over at Reuben and subtly nudged the plate closer to him.

Reuben *would* need his strength, were he to perform as planned today. He gave Everic a small smile and pointedly picked up one of the fresh late-summer raspberries, biting half into it so the juice would linger on his lips. Reuben smirked wider as Everic watched him intently, the vampire's body leaning just a bit more in his direction.

Meanwhile, the talk around them had grown more animated, guests discussing the potential advantages and disadvantages of Dijher including minted Sazzeran cantergold pieces as part of their own currency. Saer Artris pulled away Everic's focus as he spoke above the conversation, "No doubt on the benefits for those with deep pockets, ay?" with a smile of camaraderie towards the vampire.

Reuben was quite proud of him when Everic's shoulders stayed relaxed and he simply lifted his wine goblet in answer.

Just after Saer Delvanzus announced it was time for a little musical revue, Reuben and Everic stood to follow the group only for Saer Artris to step in their path.

"Unfortunate to be sitting too far away for conversation," the elvish man said with a small incline of his head. "I am the gold keeper of House Luthur—and I must say, you seem *strangely* familiar, saer."

"I've just arrived in the city for the trade council," Everic replied, "but it is a gilded blessing to meet." Then he stiffened, seeming to take in the implications of Artris's words just as Reuben did. "*House* Luthur?" he repeated.

"Just a small, unimportant house in the grand circle of High Ring," Artris brushed off, though his lips curved upward at Everic's reaction. "Forgive my forwardness, but are *you* connected with any from High Ring? That vivid gold in your eyes is a feature I've only seen in the most blessed of Zald," he chuckled.

Reuben almost wished he was still wearing his veil—it was terribly hard to keep his expression neutral despite his surprise.

Everic visibly stiffened at Saer Artris's words. "I am curious who you think I'd be connected to," was all he said.

"I'm sure," Artris replied, just as cryptic in answer. "Well . . . I'd love to share a bottle of wine sometime before the next trade council, Saer Payne, and hear how exactly you've built up your assets. Especially now that Dijher may be adopting our city's cantergold for currency— if yesterday's exciting trade proposal goes through. I'm sure my employer could make it *well* worth your time."

Everic slowly nodded. "I'll give your footmen my address and await your word."

Artris offered a sharp smile. "I look forward to it," he replied in a purring voice, before his eyes slid over to Reuben and, with a casual movement, stroked a hand through the locks of hair falling down his chest. Adding, "*And* to hearing this sweet morsel of yours play for us, now," before turning back to join where the group had gathered.

Everic didn't move after the man. Reuben glanced at him when enough seconds had passed—and was shocked to see *rage* twisting the lines on Everic's face.

Things had been going so well, he'd nearly forgotten how quick the vampire was to anger. Reuben swallowed down a flash of panic and murmured, "Everic?" Then, when Everic gave no reply, Reuben gently stroked a hand up and down the man's arm.

To his relief, Everic gusted out a sharp, shuddering breath and no longer seemed about to storm out of the parlor room, leaning into the touch.

Still, he had only just relaxed before Reuben felt him tense all over again as Saer Delvanzus called across the room, "Saer Payne! I've saved you and your companion a seat—can't miss the *best* part of this little get-together."

# 12

# SOOTHING MELODIES

veric didn't resist when Reuben led them over to sit next to the guild master, taking two of the cushioned chairs that were situated in rows facing one end of the room. A moment later, a dwarvish man from the small audience stood up to laughter and cheers, bowing dramatically before he moved to the floor's center, a finely-polished lute in hand.

Reuben was proud of himself for not visibly wincing through the next few minutes whilst the player tortured sounds out of the poor, innocent instrument. He could only imagine what Isolde would have to say after hearing such a travesty.

An infernal woman with a viol took the floor next and at least played in tune, if not with any great skill or finesse. But this was only a parlor party in the main ring—these people had the misfortune of *working* for their livelihood, instead of spending their days mastering all the refined arts while their gold earned them gold, as most of High Ring society could boast.

All the while, Everic stayed unnaturally still, an alabaster-skinned statue that fit uncannily well with the guild hall's decor. The only sign of life was from his eyes, blinking dutifully every ten seconds or so as Reuben had gently recommended—though Reuben now chided himself for not thinking to have Everic work on his lack of breathing habits as well. If anyone watched him long enough, it was *quite* apparent the man hadn't used his lungs in minutes.

Luckily, Reuben had the excuse of his occupation to lean brazenly into Everic's space and smooth a hand up and down the man's tensed thigh. *"Relax,"* he whispered into Everic's ear. "I don't think you've taken more than a dozen breaths since we arrived."

Everic pulled in a sudden, sharp breath—which drew a few curious gazes.

Reuben nuzzled his nose against the man's ear lobe to insinuate a much different reason for the sound, then whispered, "Just a little longer—you've done *so* well."

Everic was breathing at an even, overly-controlled pace by the time Reuben pulled back, though he muttered, "No, I haven't."

His brows wrinkled at an upward tilt as he stared back at Reuben— clear, open gratitude in his golden gaze.

Reuben didn't like how much his chest welled up with warmth in response.

So he broke eye contact and busied himself with opening up his case, pulling out his bow and running rosin over its new hair.

And handling Oriana's old violin, imagining her young and healthy, beautifully but respectably dressed amidst High Ring elite and playing her heart out, getting *lost in the music* as she always termed it, before a debt and a child ruined her life . . . well, it provided Reuben a melancholic sort of distraction, at least.

Then the person currently plucking at harp strings finished their little tune. Delvanzus cheered loudly, along with a few giggles and sporadic claps from others in the crowd. Reuben stood up next with a small, "May I?" to the guild master—whose dimples indented all the deeper as they gestured towards the empty floor.

After giving his violin a quick tuning, Reuben stood before them all, made a small bow, and declared, "This song is dedicated to my most generous, discerning, stalwart client: Saer Everic Payne. May you *all* be so lucky as to receive a small portion of his considerate patronage."

He watched with smug satisfaction at how eyes flickered Everic's way again, though only for a moment before he lifted up the violin to rest on his collarbone. Ignoring the twinge in his still-healing right hand, he raised the bow and then drew out the first, long note.

Reuben had the chord progression established in his mind now, if not all the words. But the melody was even less standardized as of yet—he allowed himself to wander through the chords at a slow, cautious tempo at first, lingering an extra beat on the major seventh before dipping his bow to create a sharp double stop into the minor fourth.

Already, by the time he finished the first progression, he could tell he'd ensnared his audience.

Which gave Reuben freedom to reach out with his music as the tempo increased. Delvanzus, to his relief, came across just as amiable on the inside as they looked on the outside, though more assessing of their partygoers than their dimpled smile let on. The woman who'd played her viol sat there with a polite smile—but she felt both in awe and embarrassed at Reuben's talent. And Everic . . .

Everic was *so* difficult not to spend the rest of the song tuning into, with how greedily Reuben drank in the vampire's attraction towards him, misplaced admiration for him, and blatant disregard of everyone else in the room.

But Reuben couldn't disregard the crowd. He'd done this to prove himself *useful*. So that maybe, just maybe, he could help Everic enough not to lose everything.

Likely a fool's hope—but Reuben was glad he made the effort

179

regardless, once his focus moved on to the aura of Saer Artris.

The gold keeper from High Ring was perfectly at ease on the surface, attracted to Reuben's body as well. But behind that emanated distrust and suspicion—directed at *Everic*, Reuben discerned after he focused harder.

For all Artris's seeming friendliness, he had no actual interest in doing business with Everic. Rather, he wanted to know *everything* of Everic's history, background, and purpose here.

Reuben finished the song with a dramatic, improvised resolution, smiling as the whole group loudly clapped for him. Delvanzus even protested, "Another! Oh please, that went by *far* too quickly," as Reuben returned to his seat next to them and Everic.

"I'm afraid I can only provide a sample—have to save the best for my good saer," he responded in a light, flirtatious tone, even as his eyes flitted to Artris in his peripheral.

"You should be our final performance next time, then," Delvanzus chuckled, looking around them as well before leaning in to whisper, "for it seems you've intimidated my poor circle of friends out of any more musical numbers."

Reuben chuckled with them at first, though in the next moment his eyes widened, both at realizing Saer Delvanzus had mentioned a *"next time"* and at the token the guildmaster now pressed into Reuben's hand with a knowing smile.

"But—saer, I'm a—" he protested, not quick enough. Delvanzus was already standing up and thanking everyone for coming, saying they'd have to do this again after the next trade council meeting.

The parlor party was soon after adjourned, though many of the guild members stayed past the official activities to talk more over wine. Reuben was relieved when Everic told Delvanzus he would need to be on his way. He and the guild master quickly agreed to schedule another private chat soon, before Reuben looped his arm in Everic's once more and the two left the gathering behind.

Noting many interested eyes on them as they departed, Reuben felt a momentary pride at all he'd helped Everic to accomplish despite the rough start.

Still, they'd only made the beginnings of progress. Being in a guild master's favor would help Everic receive invitations, but he'd need to use that to build even more prestigious connections. Connections like a gold keeper of a high house, certainly—though perhaps not the *particular* one they'd met this morning.

The moment they reached the stairs, Reuben said softly, "Don't see that man."

"Saer Artris?" Everic asked, then looked angry again. "I hadn't planned to."

"Good. He was too interested," Reuben said, anxious at the thought of *another* target on Everic's back. "And if he's seen others with the same color of eyes, who knows? He might even guess at what you are."

Everic stayed quiet for a time, seeming contemplative as they reached the entrance. Then, just outside the door, he gave a sideways glance at Reuben and admitted in a quiet tone, "Vampiric eyes . . . they don't normally turn this sort of color."

Reuben searched Everic's face, though the vampire looked as stern and closed-off as ever. "Then . . . why do yours?"

Just then they reached the exit, and passed the servants stationed outside in silence while heading towards the carriage. After that Everic opened his mouth, as if to speak and maybe even address Reuben's question—but then he paused, frowning as his eyes searched about. Bev wasn't visible near the horses or vehicle, Reuben realized.

Everic walked faster to the carriage, saying, "You wait inside—I'll take a look to see where she's gone."

Reuben didn't argue. He was concerned himself, glancing around the street for Bev even as Everic helped him into the carriage.

For that reason, Reuben only turned his head to see within it for a split second before a hand grabbed him from the shadows.

An elvish woman, he had just enough time to see before she pulled him in. And, by the sickly pallor and dark veins crawling up her neck, another Allunata who'd played with devilcraft to forge their necrotic weaponry—likely the cold metal now kissing the exposed skin of his throat.

He was faster to act this time, at least, spitting out a quick, crude incantation of *Insult to Injury* with the lyrics, *"Swamp-haired, mud-for-brains / Wankshaft, mirror's bane!"*

Reuben could feel her visibly wince and recoil, and took advantage to try and blindly wrench the blade away from his throat. But the Allunata threw him unceremoniously on the carriage floor anyway—not the intended target.

"Everic!" Reuben rolled over and shouted, in case the man had turned his back and not noticed the brief scuffle. Just then, however, the light streaming in from the carriage door was eclipsed into shadow by a wide, imposing figure.

The Allunata lunged forward with a dark blade, and Everic met her with only his gloved hands.

Reuben stumbled back right as the two collided in a brief, inter-locked spiral, Everic ending up on top as they crashed against one of the carriage benches. The Allunata let out a snarl of primal rage, however, and with a flash of steel tried to slash at one of his arms.

Only a second had passed by the time Everic ripped the short sword from her hand, and the woman in reply pulled a strange, glowing bottle from her belt with her other hand and smashed it against his face.

The glass broke easily as it connected with Everic's cheek, a few pieces embedding in his face. But then—unless Reuben's eyes somehow deceived him—it looked like *fire* started rapidly spreading from the impact. Too pale, bright, and fast to be natural, with a chemical smell that soured the air as it hissed and made contact with Everic's skin. The vampire gasped and staggered backward against the opposite bench as he clutched at his face, smoke billowing up from it.

The woman's mouth widened into a sharp smile. She picked her blade back up while Everic was distracted, the glass shards in his face now clattering onto the bench—though he dropped in time to dodge when she stabbed the sword forward again, this time landing to hover just above Reuben in this tiny compartment.

Reuben stared in horror. Now that Everic's face was exposed again, he could see the damage this strange fire had reaped after mere seconds: his skin crumbling to ash as quickly as a flame to paper, the white of his cheekbone and teeth exposed, his nose half-disintegrated and his eye perpetually wide in its socket.

He'd heard of this, Reuben realized—forged fire, it was called, fire enchanted with godcraft to burn twice as hot and target anything unnatural. Including vampires, clearly.

Just then the flames flared and dripped down from where it ate at Everic's jaw, landing on Reuben's clothes. Everic's working eye widened, his mouth hissing in a garbled voice, "Put that out!" before whipping around—kicking the woman's feet out from under her just as she tried to stab him from behind.

Reuben batted at the unnatural flames charring his clothing, surprised when he felt no heat on his skin before he extinguished them. Still, he was too slow, too *fearful* for fast-paced violence like this—his mother had taught him how to use crowdcraft for influence and protection, not quick defense. He could only clutch his violin case to ground himself as he desperately tried to hum the major melody of the *Soothe* incantation he'd made up for Isolde, and quickly enough to aid Everic before the forged fire consumed the vampire entirely.

To his relief, Reuben tuned right away into the tension, hostility, and bloodlust in the two fighting in front of him—targeting the woman as he hummed louder.

She had just been sitting up to strike at Everic again, stabbing forward with a snarling face . . . then, slowed.

Her shoulders relaxed. Her head cocked, body beginning to sway ever-so-slightly along with Reuben's tune.

It gave Everic a moment to slump, smoke billowing from one half of his person—and, with a single mumbled word, suddenly apparate into a dark cloud that filled up the inner cabin.

Reuben stopped the song in shock.

Unfortunately, that allowed the woman's faculties to return. "Coward!" he heard her hiss into the absolute darkness—then ducked his head at the sound of her sword whacking blindly against the interior walls.

Everic's voice seemed to come from nowhere and everywhere all at once, hanging from above and yet speaking straight into Reuben's ear as the vampire answered: "Why have you come?"

Her swinging stopped. "*Soul Bleeder* knows what you are now," she shot back in a hoarse, grating voice. "But the ending dark comes for all."

"We might have been allies," Everic said in answer, as if not surprised, but disappointed.

"There's only room for *one* devil in the Hollows," she hissed.

The dark mist curled in on itself and pooled back into human form, Everic's golden eyes molten from the shadows.

Then they flashed a fiery red, and fear ran down Reuben's spine like ice as the vampire spoke with sharp, ringing authority, "*Drop your blade."*

Just like that, the knife slipped from the woman's hand.

The anger quickly faded from her eyes, replaced by something dull and lifeless as her shoulders slumped. She stayed listless in her stooped, mindless stance while Everic produced a knife somewhere hidden in his fine coat, which was now irreparably burnt.

When Everic extended his arm back, the next motion was clear.

Reuben squeezed his eyes shut, nausea returning with a vengeance at the slicing squelch, splattering of liquid, and guttural, breathless groan that followed—just before an even harsher noise indicated the blade being wrenched back out.

Reuben's breathing came out shaky in the silence that followed. He hadn't yet dared to look again, when the feeling of hands on his shoulders startled him.

Everic quickly retracted the touch as Reuben jumped, eyes shooting open. Only to see the vampire crouched down on one knee, examining him with a searching, urgent expression—even whilst his own skin was reforming and tendons snapping back together before Reuben's very eyes.

"Did you get burned at all?" Everic demanded, hands hovering over Reuben's middle.

Reuben blinked and looked for himself—an emotion besides fear and horror finally surfacing, as he took in the warped, burnt state of his doublet and swallowed down a pang of loss. He'd never felt any pain, however, and so shook his head mutely.

"Alright . . . alright." Everic looked torn, glancing between Reuben and the carriage door. But then his rapidly-healing face hardened with resolve. "Listen to me, Reubie: stay here, keep away from the window, and don't make a sound," he ordered in quick succession. "I'll be locking the door from the outside to go look for Bev—don't let anyone else in or try to leave, even if it sounds important, understood?"

Reuben gave a jerking nod. "Yes, saer."

He felt frozen until Everic left; the only sounds were his own heavy breathing and the blood dripping from the Allunata assassin on the bench next to him. Reuben wasn't sure when he'd be able to relax in the vampire's presence again, after seeing Everic's eyes glow the same fiery, *devilish* color that Jophiel's had while she practiced devilcraft on him.

But a vampire—however more modern, palatable, and frankly beautiful a monster—was still devilcrafted like the rest, Reuben reminded himself. The fact that Everic could and did practice devilcraft should be a given. The insinuation that he'd attempted to *ally* with the Allunata, the most dangerous group to plague Sazzera with devilcraft since the old, destroyed coven, should not be surprising.

At least Everic knew his secret was out and could prepare himself, now.

Given Reuben had never disclosed his connection to Waron, there was a good chance he didn't get coined as the culprit either.

The woman's body kept leaking blood, pulling him from his worried thoughts as it pooled closer. Reuben reached to carefully leverage his hands on the benches and lift himself up—then hissed at the contact, pain flaring in his left palm.

Upon inspection, Reuben didn't find any serious injury. Only a tiny, discolored cut on his palm. Confused, he squinted to look at it closer and see if he'd gotten a splinter. But that confusion quickly shifted into a new kind of fear when he prodded at it and a single bead of blackened blood welled from one edge.

A devilcrafted blade. His skin must have just caught the edge of the woman's sword when he first wrenched free from her grasp. Reuben propped his palm up with his other hand, desperately watching for any sign of the wound widening or deepening.

For a tense minute, there seemed to be no change. Then Reuben saw a tiny flash of light beam from the wound and felt a quick warming sensation, before the cut lost its small discoloration. Almost as if he'd imagined the signs of ichor and necrotic rot in the first place.

Reuben didn't have time to wonder. All at once, the entirety of his spine lit up with *blinding* pain, shooting nerve twinges through both of his legs and even the upper half of his arms. Reuben cried out in agony, doubling over—then arched his back instead when that only intensified the pain.

No position helped. And over the next few agonizing seconds his entire body began to writhe, so badly Reuben couldn't even take control of his limbs enough to clumsily dig into his high boot and pull out the voleris. He could only lay there, cry out, and try not to twist so harshly he worsened the pain—or jostled the dead body precariously slumped on the bench above him.

The body-encompassing agony reminded him of the aftermath of Jophiel's devilcraft, though this lessened after a minute instead of an hour, and at least didn't include a seizure. Eventually, Reuben was able to curl into a ball and swallow his cries until they came out as whimpers, only twitching every now and then. He was too scared of uncurling his limbs to reach for his voleris, in case that triggered things all over again, until many minutes later.

But that was also around when Everic's muffled voice came from outside: "Reubie? I'm coming in."

Luckily, it didn't require a response. Unluckily, Reuben had only just gotten a shaky grip on the voleris vial in his boot as he heard the door unlock.

The devilish glow of the vampire's gaze jumped to mind—though in this state, with lingering pain still present in every one of his limbs,

Reuben's mind could only register a mute sort of dread about Everic's return.

Everic's eyes were only a soft gold, Reuben was relieved to see once the vampire ducked into the cabin much less menacingly this time. Though they did narrow at seeing Reuben curled down between the benches.

"Let's get you off the floor," he said in a firm, decisive tone, if less commanding than before.

Reuben bit hard on his lip to hold in any sounds of pain as Everic reached down to help him up. A hissing exhale still escaped as he got to his feet, staggering as a spike of pain stabbed down both legs.

Reuben ended up leaning against Everic to keep himself upright, breathing out heavy and slow through it. And—despite the unsurprisingly tense state of the vampire—was happy to find the surface of Everic's chest quite comfortable. Light-headed and dizzy with pain, Reuben thought no further before bowing his head to rest on Everic's shoulder, pleased at the audible breath Everic let out in response.

Slowly, a gentle arm wrapped around his aching back in return.

"It's safe now," he heard Everic murmur softly—his stern, commanding persona faded. "Bev had only been drawn away by a harmless distraction. No one outside has noticed, and won't, so long as we leave quickly."

Reuben only hummed, enjoying the vibrations of Everic's chest as he spoke. The pain finally receded so long as he didn't move a muscle, and Reuben had no qualms about staying still, exactly where he was.

It was hard to tell for how long, or if Reuben was even conscious in the meantime, before he heard Everic ask in his ear, "Reubie?"

Reuben blinked, then moved his sluggish arms to loosely wrap around the vampire's waist. "I call you saer, you call me Reubie," he pointed out in a slightly-slurred voice, all at once finding the parallel quite fitting. And then let out a sharp sigh when Everic stiffened in response, the strong arm around him dropping. "Issit *so* hard . . . to just *touch* me?" he complained, right before his knees buckled.

Everic was back to touching him again, Reuben noticed happily some indeterminate amount of time later—even whilst wincing at the bump of the carriage wheels that had brought him back to coherence.

They were on the opposite bench from the dead Allunata woman now, Reuben's legs draped over Everic's lap and his head tucked under the man's chin. And the carriage must have reached the lower tier of the main ring, the harsher bumps under its wheels triggering painful twinges and flares in his spine despite Everic's arm around his back, trying to hold him steady.

Then he registered the small, thin bottle Everic held in his other hand.

Reuben's eyes widened. "Please . . . please, saer," he heard himself whisper. "I just wanted a sip, for the pain."

Everic's hand closed tighter around the vial Reuben must have dropped. "You brought it with you," he said with a flat, contained sort of anger in his voice.

Reuben attempted to sit up straighter, to try to explain—maybe even to reach for the voleris before it could be taken away—and then let out a pathetic cry as the carriage hit a very large bump, tears springing to his eyes as it jostled his spine.

Then he sagged back against the vampire, his breath hissing out through gritted teeth as he begged, "Just a *sip*."

But he held no hope of Everic relenting, especially when the commanding tone returned to Everic's voice with the order, "Reubie, look at me."

Reuben obediently twisted his aching neck, just enough for his tear-filled gaze to meet Everic's unreadable, golden one.

Then it flared darker with devilish flame.

"Reubie: *Sleep,*" the vampire said, the last word echoing louder and louder in Reuben's skull—vibrating into his very bones until the nerve-deep pain and sluggish thoughts both came to a stuttering, staggering *halt.*

# 13

# GENTLE MONSTER

The next things Reuben registered were soft linen sheets under him, a dull, lingering ache in his back, and sweat sticking to his skin.

He was nestled deep under three layers of blankets, with a large pillow cushioning his head and a loose nightshirt clothing him. Reuben didn't think further before kicking the blankets off and pushing his sweaty hair out of his face to see where he'd ended up— breathing out a slow sigh as he recognized Everic's little hideaway, dimly illuminated by a single candle flickering on the desk.

The sigh caught at the end, however, as Reuben remembered *why* he was here. What all Everic had done in the carriage: turning into smoke, disarming the Allunata assassin with a simple command, and finally compelling Reuben's aching body the same exact way.

Not that he minded a quick way to fall asleep, on principle. Reuben had composed a spell he simply called *Lullaby* decades ago to help with that, though it only lasted for a minute if his aches were too sharp. Even a full bottle of voleris couldn't give him more than a fitful sleep when he was in enough pain. This dark, complete sort of unconsciousness he'd just surfaced from had been bliss in comparison.

But then the vivid image intruded of Everic charming him with no more than a word and a devilish flash of his eyes. At that, Reuben felt the drafty underground air chill his damp skin and force a shiver down his neck.

While Reuben did use crowdcraft whenever necessary with clients, and occasionally employed the magic-laced toys the bordello offered for sex, he had little experience with a client using magic on *him*. Only his one appointment with Jophiel came to mind. Even then, she had to cut her hand and draw arcane runes across his body in blood before whatever she did to him commenced. Powerful magic had to be summoned with some form of conduit, not just evoked by a single word.

Everic wasn't simply a *user* of magic, however. From what Reuben knew, the very essence of the vampire's undead, unholy existence had been created by devilcraft, like any monster. His powers were likely innate, just like his immortality or hunger—perhaps he himself was the conduit for them.

The things he could force Reuben to do, with nothing save a word . . .

Reuben shivered again. He pulled one layer of the blankets back over his bare legs to fight off the sudden chill, his body both too cold and overheated at once.

Maybe—most *likely*, given how the vampire treated others thus far—Everic was not the type to casually abuse the powers he'd been bestowed.

More than likely, he hadn't asked for becoming what he was.

In any case, all he'd done after compelling Reuben to sleep was bring him here somehow, dress him into something comfortable, and leave him to rest.

Reuben checked the sheets to make sure, but wasn't surprised when he didn't find any evidence to the contrary. And he felt no aches to signify sex either. Just that now-familiar tightening in his throat, as he noted a goblet of water and his violin case considerately laid on the bedside table next to him.

Just then, the door opened, revealing the considerate man in question.

Everic had changed as well, back in plain trousers and a linen shirt with the sleeves rolled up. His brow was furrowed in focus as he entered with a long-handled, heavy pan held out carefully in front of him, and shut the door with his elbow. Dark gold eyes glanced up when he turned with the metal object in Reuben's direction—and then did a double take, widening.

"You're awake," Everic stated.

Reuben smiled, and despite every new reason to be afraid, felt himself relax at the vampire's presence. "Good morning—or evening, perhaps."

Everic didn't change tune then and compel Reuben to do something vile, of course, just like he hadn't in more than two months of appointments. He recovered from his surprise with a slight frown, walking to the foot of the bed and remarking, "I didn't consider how drafty it can be down here. This should help better than the blankets," and he lifted the object slightly in show before leaning down.

Reuben belatedly recognized it as a rather antique-looking, ornate warming pan, right as Everic lifted the mattress's end and pushed it underneath. "Thank you," he said softly, pulling the blanket closer over his lap. "How long *has* it been, exactly?"

"Since the party? It is now past sunset of the same day," Everic reported as he smoothed the covers back into place. "I only meant to help you sleep through the carriage ride, but given how long you've stayed unconscious in and out of a mild fever, it's clear you needed more rest."

Not quite long enough for Sidarchus to send bordello security out looking for Reuben, or worse, sentry guards. Though it wouldn't do to push his luck further.

"Oh, I'd best head back then—I'd hate to take up your whole bed during the day *and* night," he chuckled, slowly swinging his legs over the bedside and making to stand.

For one moment, Everic watched him from the foot of the bed. But by the next, he already stood blocking Reuben's way, a pair of strong hands firmly pushing Reuben's shoulders until he fell back to sit on the mattress's edge again.

"I have no need of the bed tonight," Everic stated, firm and short.

Reuben was torn for a second between fears. Even with a vivid showcase of Everic's power at the front of his mind, however, he found himself more afraid still of Sidarchus's disapproval. "Surely even vampires need sleep?" he protested.

Everic looked down at him with a peculiar expression on his face. He reached forward and gently tucked a loose curl of Reuben's bed-frazzled hair behind his pointed ear, answering, "It will be hard to rest until I know with surety that you are recovered."

Reuben's heart made a strange, sharp clench inside his ribcage.

He ignored the sensation and widened his eyes, propping up on the back of his elbows as he assured, "I feel *much* better now, saer. A bit achy still, but that's only to be expected. Really, you could have just dropped me off at the bordello to rest there—I'm sure Sidarchus is worried."

Everic's expression darkened. "I've already sent word and more gold to your slaver," he said curtly, and Reuben bit his lip instead of making a useless protest of the crude terminology. "I'd rather you rest uninterrupted here for the next day or two, than be pushed back into work there. You'll return when you're *ready*, and I will cover the absence."

Reuben swallowed hard, half of him wanting to keep up his protests—half of him wishing to collapse back onto the mattress, and *never* let Everic make him leave.

"I . . . thank you, saer," he whispered, "but there's no need, truly."

Everic didn't answer right away. He sat down next to Reuben and reached into his trouser pocket, retrieving a thin, long vial Reuben immediately recognized. *Empty* now, he was forlorn to see, as Everic lightly tossed it onto the covers between them. "If you returned now, would you be drinking more of this?"

Reuben winced at the obvious disapproval in his voice. "I didn't mean to bring that along, I swear," he hurried to lie. "I'd entirely forgotten it was in my pocket, saer. It's just . . . well, at *times*, a customer may request it. Or I'll have a spasm, like you've seen, and can't get through the appointment otherwise."

Everic's eyes flashed in anger. "Then there is every need to give you time away from this *poison*. Bev tells me they put something similar in the food of Ravine workers, did you know?"

Reuben blinked in surprise, shaking his head. And truly he hadn't heard, though it made some sense—from what Sidarchus said in the past, one of the main ingredients of voleris was sourced from a fungi common in the Ravine itself.

Regardless, this was not an argument he could win. He had worked hard over the years to make sure his use of the potion remained sparing, but all it had taken was a single bad night with Waron for the occasional craving to descend back into this incessant desire.

Because of that desire, he had to bite his tongue to not protest more on the subject. "You are too generous, saer," he conceded instead.

Reuben was glad he did, when Everic sighed and put a hand on Reuben's arm. "I am too careless—I must apologize for what happened this afternoon. When I attempted to speak with the Allunata after our first appointment, I received that knife wound for my trouble. But I did not anticipate further danger from them—I truly don't know how they learned about my condition, or why they would take my vampirism so . . . personally." His eyes narrowed, voice darkening as he finished, "I will simply have to find out."

Reuben wasn't *quite* past the nausea symptoms, it seemed. He doubled over and groaned as a sudden spike of it made his empty stomach clench, his body achy and cold and hot all at once. His mind, all the while, screamed at him in fear over the terrifying chance Everic *did* find out.

He felt Everic's hand move to his back, smoothing up and down his shaky spine as he breathed through the last waves of it. "I hope I don't hear any more protests about resting," he heard Everic say in a wry tone.

At any other time, Reuben might have laughed. Now he blew out a breath and tried to diffuse his panic, at least until he had the time and privacy to process it.

"No, saer," he agreed after another minute, slowly uncurling to sit upright again. "Though, I can rest *and* talk—and I'd urge you not to provoke them further. The Allunata are a formidable organization, from the little I know of them."

"Yes, and seem to be left entirely *un*provoked by the Hollow's sentry guard as well," Everic said in a disapproving tone, though Reuben was pleased to feel the man's cool hand remain on his back, for now. "Not badly trained, I'd say . . . though they're very used to their blades giving them the advantage."

He looked troubled—not afraid, or suspicious, or even fully concerned, Reuben was both relieved and exasperated to see.

"Maybe their blades are less deadly to you than most, but clearly it's not all they have up their sleeves," Reuben tried to warn. "You should invest in more security. Especially if more than one Allunata member attacks, next time."

*"If* there is a next time," Everic said, a grim smile curling his lips. "With how we left the assassin they sent . . . well, perhaps they're as smart as they are formidable, and will know when to cut their losses."

Reuben stared at him. Then he sat up more, stressing, "Everic, whatever she dumped on you, your *face* was burning off. You looked . . ."

"Dead?"

Reuben flushed, but continued crossly, "I was *worried*."

"Not enough for yourself—you were much more vulnerable than I, in that fight," Everic replied as his hand dropped from Reuben's back, tucking the vial back into his pocket. "The Allunata were quite misinformed, if they thought so little forged fire would kill me." His face sobered, a faraway grief returning to his eyes as he added, "Though on a normal person, or even a lesser vampire, it might have been enough."

"Good thing it only ruined your lovely outfit for me, then," Reuben reasoned, putting on a bright tone.

Everic glanced at Reuben's middle where the fire landed with a worried expression, though he just agreed, "A very good thing." Then his lips thinned, his eyes flickering away. "I am confident they will not be any *real* danger to me—but you're right. I'll plan to hire more protection when I'm publicly moving through the city if Bev can vet them, especially as her own goals take her attention elsewhere. I will keep a closer eye as well, so that you are protected. But . . . " He met Reuben's gaze again, finishing, "I entirely understand if that is not enough, and you consider this a failed experiment, given the dangers."

Reuben frowned, confused until he remembered: Everic had agreed that Reuben could take back his consent if his public presence proved disastrous. That, if he wished to, Reuben could stick with bloodletting and letter-writing, and Everic would not hold it against him.

It seemed that assurance had not been an empty one—even if it was clearly not *Everic's* wish.

Reuben said nothing for a long moment as he considered, and found himself grateful at how comfortable Everic always was with silence. It gave Reuben time to process his feelings—past the fear from being attacked and then compelled and then reminded of his betrayal, at present—without worry of his client growing impatient in the meantime.

Given it was his fault the Allunata were after Everic now, and the high chance *he* was how the woman had tracked down their carriage, Reuben couldn't even blame Everic's dangerous business for this attack. Certainly, he didn't enjoy Everic exercising such power over him, but how could he complain if it was for his own good?

Despite his nausea and nerves, Reuben couldn't deny that he'd *enjoyed* the party as well, for the rare chance it gave him to wield his wits and charms without sex being the ultimate aim—and even help someone he admittedly liked.

"You'd understand . . ." Reuben repeated whilst reaching forward to stroke fingers down Everic's pale forearm, tracing the prominent veins that stood out from the muscle, ". . . but was my presence not helpful?"

Everic didn't chase after Reuben's retreating hand like he'd hoped, though the vampire replied, "I didn't say that," with a tone of reproach.

Reuben smiled and shrugged. "Well. Then I'd say it was a rather *successful* experiment."

Everic returned the smile ever-so-slightly. "Very well." His jaw clenched a moment later, however, smile fading as something seemed to cross his mind. "Though, if you are coming along from here on out, you'll need more understanding of what I'm trying to accomplish," he said in a very slow, serious tone.

Just a few days prior, Reuben would have struggled to temper his excitement. Now, Waron's words hissed harshly into his mind: *Tell me everything you know about that man you meet in the Hollows.*

"Damning me with knowledge now?" he tried to laugh, though it came out more like a weak chuckle. Reuben's gaze wandered down to his hands combing nervously through his hair, even whilst he assured, "I know I've asked far too many questions in the past, saer. But I swear, I *am* happy to remain in the dark on anything past the basics of your goal to access High Ring, and simply do as you say otherwise."

Finally, Everic did reach out for Reuben's hand—just in time to make Reuben's gut pang with guilt, when Everic ducked his head to catch Reuben's eyes with a warm, affectionate look in his burnished gaze.

The guilt started gnawing at Reuben's insides when the vampire squeezed his hand and stated so confidently, "I trust you."

Reuben could only manage a tiny smile in response.

"It will come up soon enough anyway, if you continue helping me," Everic explained, "that my aim is not merely an invitation into High Ring society. That goal in itself is only a gateway, a key to a locked door behind which an entire labyrinth must be braved." At that, his gaze hardened. "What I need, is access to the Voice of Zald."

Reuben blinked hard. "The Voice?" he repeated, even though he knew he'd heard correctly. "The *direct mouthpiece* of Zald?"

When Everic just nodded, Reuben felt dread slowly begin to pool inside his gut. At such a bold assertion, he simply had to remove any hope of Everic's origin being the ungoverned, rolling hills of the heartlands—if so, he would have grown up right around when The Voice that Spoke from the Golden Mount came to be.

More commonly called The Voice of Zald, she was the hero that saved the Sazzeran Steppes during a major Loethian attack—now simply called the *Battle of the Steppes*—halting their invasion that threatened to seize the whole body of land known as Monmark. And following Sazzera's victory, the Voice had been exalted by Zald and revered by the city ever since.

Everic should already know the Voice of Zald was not a mere mortal to "*access*" anymore, if she ever was to begin with.

"Everic . . . you might as well desire to speak with Zaldus Himself," Reuben replied with a slow shake of his head. "She never leaves the Aureate Cathedral. She isn't *supposed* to—and even in the Cathedral, there hasn't been a public appearance since before I was born."

Everic raised a brow, his head tilting. "That may have been true . . . until recently."

Reuben opened his mouth to argue—but as he thought of recent events, at once his mind put two and two together. "She is participating in the trade council?" he asked in disbelief, wondering how *none* of his clients had deigned to mention this.

"Not officially." Everic stood and moved over to the desk, returning with a parchment Reuben recognized as one of the few precious public flyers tossed into the piazza after every council meeting—of late, quickly snatched and fought over by the literate to rewrite for profit, the original copies sold to the highest buyer.

This one was clearly an original, headlined with the words: *GOLD FOR ALL.*

"From what Jophiel told me before I started my business here, there was a very good chance the Voice would attend concealed amidst the other high priests on the council," Everic said as he laid the paper on the bed between them—and Reuben was proud of himself for not stiffening at mention of the woman's name. Everic pointed to the signatures at the bottom, continuing, "This was confirmed to me by the very first bulletin and each one since; there is a discrepancy between the number of council members the report says are attending, and the number that actually sign each proposal. Four signatures—*five* priests masked in gold."

Reuben frowned down at the bottom of the sheet crowded with looping names, quietly impressed at the crowdcraft that had duplicated the differing penmanship so well as he skimmed over titles like *vault keeper*, *general of security*, and *head emissary*.

"There's a chance the extra priest is simply lower in station, and there only as an aid," Reuben suggested.

Everic shook his head emphatically, arguing, "From talks I've heard in the main ring, *every* single one of the priests over this city's main areas of governance is in attendance save her, and she outranks them all—and yet there is no delay in approval, no missives being sent to their leader before the papers are signed." Everic tapped a paragraph at the top of the parchment and explained, "Talks are happening in a place the whole public agrees is unusual as well: not the embassy hall, but a place called the Cantara Circle. It's an amphitheater across from the Cathedral's smallest side pavilion, where private religious performances are usually held."

As he spoke, the vampire's eyes were bright and alive with keen interest, despite only the faintest hint of gold remaining around his dark pupils. He spoke firmly as usual, but with an assured confidence entirely disparate from the stiff awkwardness at the party. Clearly in his element here, carrying out a mission and disseminating its plan.

"And . . . you want to be among those invited to attend and observe, in case she is," Reuben filled in, even as more dread pooled inside him.

For what reason would a foreigner like Everic want an audience with the Voice?  He didn't worship Zald, and spoke ill of the Priesthood in general.  He didn't approve of their laws or societal structure, and made no mention of planting roots here. He didn't even seem to care about the trade agreements being proposed and signed each month.

"From what I heard, only the most elite magnatus and public officials receive invitations," Reuben pointed out. "That's *quite* the social ladder to climb before winter's end."

Everic seemed undeterred. "Which is why I am grateful to have you. I made more connections at that parlor party than I have in two months, this morning—entirely thanks to your charms."

Reuben usually considered himself numb to compliments. Here and now, however, he felt his face warm. "Well, well," he deflected with a teasing smirk, "look who *can* be a flatterer after all."

"I only speak the truth," Everic said with an almost-smile, though it was brief before he grimly nodded down at the signatures. "But, if this method fails . . . I will still have to find a way to scale the wall, ladder or not."

Reuben bit his lip. "To . . . speak with her?"

In answer, the light in the vampire's eyes changed from a glimmer to an ember-like glow. As he merely regarded Reuben in return, Reuben was reminded of the imposing form that eclipsed the light streaming from the carriage doorway, and later swallowed the entire cabin in a thick, blinding darkness.

It was only thanks to the warming pan now noticeably heating the mattress from below, that Reuben could suppress his shiver.

Gentle at times—but monstrous still.

"You told me once, you had no allegiance to the Priesthood," Everic spoke at last.

Reuben swallowed hard. "I don't, of course not, saer," he assured, even as his inner dread threatened to upsurge like bile.

Because he *knew*, even if he had made an effort not to think about it. How could Reuben *not* have assumed already, that whatever business awaited the vampire in High Ring would involve bloodshed?

"I . . . I don't need to know. I probably shouldn't," Reuben admitted, more truthfully than Everic could know.

Everic's lips thinned in a sharp, down-turned frown, every other line on his face deepening around it. Then he rolled the parchment up in a quick motion, his voice clipped and short as he replied, "I will leave it up to your imagination, then."

In the silence that followed, the vampire stood up and returned the rolled paper back to his desk. But Everic stayed there leaning over the wood and its ever-cluttered surface for a long moment, the tension slowly draining from his shoulders. His head stooped, hair falling forward to obscure his face.

Eventually, Everic spoke in a much softer, regretful tone, "I wish to be honest with you—but not endanger you needlessly, Reubie. I never intended for anyone to face such perils but myself. And yet, Bev easily could have been attacked today as well, and you had a *knife* put to your throat, got thrown on your back, were nearly burned and stabbed . . ."

At those words, Reuben remembered the woman's devilcrafted blade *had* broken skin—but too slightly for proper necrosis, he could only guess.

"My back feels fine," he said. "Only . . ."

When Everic's head turned, allowing a glimmer of eye to be visible between the tangled strands of hair, Reuben tried to keep his voice steady and forced himself to continue, "Only . . . next time? Just— just, give me a bit of warning, should you wish to use a charm on me?" When Everic stiffened all over again, Reuben hurried to assure, "It's not that I didn't appreciate the rest, saer, *of course*, and I'm sure I was in no state to be asked, but . . ."

Reuben's next words died in his throat when Everic stood upright with fierce eyes and an angry line between his brows. Reuben felt his body shrink in on itself as the vampire briskly crossed the room, his mind going into a blank panic at a tall figure approaching—*soon to reach him and put a wide hand over his mouth, a tight grip in his hair—*

But Everic stopped just in front of the bed, then lowered himself to kneel.

Positioned to look up at Reuben now, Everic replied, "I won't warn you," around a deep frown. "Should such an action ever be considered again, I will *ask*—though only after I first ask forgiveness, yet again, for another needlessly harsh reaction on my part." His eyes went distant once more, the man's voice softening as he admitted, "I am often too quick to act, not pausing to consider other solutions."

Reuben recalled then how Everic had softened after almost dismissing Reuben for being indentured—the vampire admitting, *That was harsh of me,* as he helped Reuben back up from his knees.

But if *this* was the behavior the vampire considered harsh or inconsiderate, Reuben wanted to laugh at him. He thought of the careful way Everic had just held him in the carriage, the three blankets laid overtop of him while he slept . . . and felt a terrifyingly soft place inside him crack open, vulnerable and raw.

It was something a bit of levity would have to rebury for now, Reuben thought before tamping down the feeling.

So he put on a smirk. "Perhaps not entirely needless," Reuben said in a slow, warning tone. "I think I was close to pinning you down and *wrestling* for that vial, delirious with pain or not . . . then you truly would have had a fight on your hands, saer."

Everic blinked. Then his eyes crinkled, narrowed into crescent-like shapes as the vampire let out a low chuckle. And Reuben didn't quite understand it, how just the sound managed to turn his own smile into something genuine.

"Best it didn't come to that, then—for my own sake," Everic agreed wryly, looking up at him.

# 14

# UNDERGROUND TALKS

For the remainder of the evening Everic left Reuben alone, citing business in the main ring as he shrugged on his old coat and headed for the door. Despite the long hours he'd already slept, Reuben felt a wave of exhaustion come over him soon after. He laid down with the intention of gathering his thoughts, but ended up dozing through the next few hours.

Still not recovered from three vials of voleris, it seemed. Losing blood, putting on airs at a social event, and then going delirious with pain after getting physically attacked *probably* hadn't helped matters either, of course.

When Reuben fully came to, the candle at Everic's desk must have sputtered out, for he opened his eyes only to be met by complete darkness. Not unlike what Everic had devilcrafted, really, where Reuben couldn't see so much as his hand waving in front of his face. But to his surprise, he wasn't afraid—only glad to be waking in the hideaway again, rather than a place Waron clearly had little trouble sneaking into.

Reuben's back still ached more than usual, but otherwise, the constant nausea, lightheadedness, and headaches had finally relented.

His body temperature didn't feel so in flux either. Reuben laid there in the dark and decided to just enjoy the perfect silence for a while, so different from the muffled sounds of the bordello and faint noises of the piazza he was used to waking up to each evening.

Here, the quiet was only broken up by his breathing as Reuben twisted the gold ring on his pinky finger and found his mind playing out his most recent memories of Everic again: the press of Everic's hand on his spine; Everic kneeling at the bedside to look up at him with soft, apologetic eyes; the sound of his voice elevated and formidable in the crafted darkness, yet also reverberating right in Reuben's ear.

Lacking his usual exhaustion, however, recollection only had Reuben itching for his instrument. With a small touch and hum of the spell for *Light,* he illuminated his mother's ring and then knelt on the bed, pulling out the violin from its case and plucking out a few tunes by the warm, homey light the ring emanated.

First, he tried out an altered, more contemplative melody than the one he'd improvised at the parlor party that morning. Then he thought out a few more lyrics—after the line about darker yesterdays, settling on the words, *"Oh, have you seen the calm / They cling to, lest they storm / Or climbed the icy walls / They build to guard their warmth?"*

*"But lucky are those . . ."* Reuben continued to sing, in the midst of working out a line for the chorus when the door was unlocked with a click.

Everic squinted at the warm, sunny light at first entering, a hand quick to shield his eyes, although it slowly lowered a second later. Reminding Reuben of *another* curiosity he was itching to ask the vampire about himself.

As Everic revealed his face again, however, Reuben noted the vampire's eyes had switched to a deep green in their short hours apart and chose a simpler, teasing question for now: "Had a drink without me, saer?"

Everic huffed as he crossed over to his desk and shrugged off his coat. "I'm surprised you didn't hear—though perhaps your singing muted the sound for you. The mule always protests the loudest."

Reuben raised a brow. "The *same* mule, repeatedly?"

Everic nodded. "It would be rather blatant, to have a dozen animals every month disappearing into one little hollow," he said as he laid the coat over his chair like usual. Lighting a few candles, while adding, "Wasteful, too—I need not drain anything entirely, so long as it is large enough and I have multiple alternatives. And . . . Bev found the mule *does* stand still, if you distract her with enough fruit and carrots."

An unpracticed laugh escaped from Reuben at the image. "It appears I have some competition, then," he said, smiling wider when Everic scoffed. "Perhaps you'll have to put me on the same diet so long as I'm tucked away here, so your eyes stay that lovely green."

Everic shook his head and crossed over to the wardrobe. "I doubt that would make a difference," he said as he undressed.

"A shame," Reuben answered as he put his instrument away, trying to sound nonchalant. "Though that reminds me . . . you mentioned gold was an uncommon color for a vampire's eyes to be?"

Everic paused halfway through untying his boots. "From what I know, yes," he replied after a belated moment, though not half so guarded as he used to be. Just hesitant while continuing, "Generally, drinking from a creature whose diet includes meat guarantees some kind of red coloration, or green if they exclusively eat plants. In this case . . . I don't pretend to be an expert on these matters."

Reuben finished latching the case and abandoned any pretense of casual interest, turning fully toward the vampire from where he knelt on the bed. He stiffened a little at the sight of Everic half-clothed— which he'd already seen, Reuben chided himself, even as he couldn't help enjoying the sight more this time—but quickly recovered, "Then, you *don't* know what makes them change to gold?"

"Not for sure," said Everic with a grimace. "Not unless you do."

Reuben stared at him in confusion. "What?"

The vampire blew out a breath. "I told you, Jophiel spoke highly of you," he started, gesturing at Reuben, "but . . . specifically, of your *blood*. She said it was particularly potent, strong. Capable of protecting me."

Reuben laughed without a trace of humor. "*My* blood, strong?"

Just at the mention of her, his hands curled into fists, his breathing hastened. Reuben realized now, he'd filled in the blanks too confidently before—just assuming that Jophiel had recommended Reuben only for his discretion, when no sentry guards came breaking down her door.

Although, given it'd been *her* blood smeared in strange runes across his lower body—not a drop of his own spilled, much less tasted or tested—how could Reuben have assumed any differently?

Reuben didn't care to filter his voice at the moment, which came out sharp and angry as he remarked, "I didn't know she had such a sense of humor."

Everic's grimace twisted. "She's rather an expert on the subject of blood," he said. "Though I didn't believe her until after your first visit. And . . . I didn't *want* to become dependent on it, even then." When Reuben just gave him a look of guarded confusion, Everic said, "Like the devilcrafted knife—I don't think I would have healed from its necrosis without you. And you've seen me out in daylight now, not a hair singed."

"*That*—you mean *I*—?"

Reuben probably looked ridiculous, opening and closing his mouth multiple times as he struggled to understand, much less respond.

His musical talent, his skills with people, his mental resilience, they were all things Reuben counted as strengths; metaphorical armor he had to thank for getting him this far. Even the physical appearance of his body was an asset, if not one Reuben held many good feelings towards since his youth.

But the *strength* of his body?

"I'm . . . that's simply not possible, saer," he ended lamely, though even as he said it, Reuben wondered about the devilcraft rite. He'd been too optimistic when the only change he noticed after whatever Jophiel used him for was a weakening of his health. Too presumptuous that he had just been an unfortunate tool for her devilcraft, not the subject itself.

Everic took a few steps closer. Still barefoot and bare-chested—and Reuben felt a little twinge of nerves singe through him, despite the sheer unlikelihood of the vampire joining him on the bed this moment—as he gave Reuben a long, considering look. "You don't have any idea why, then?"

Reuben huffed. "Everic, I—I'm an *indentured prostitute*, like my mother before me."

"But you've said she grew up in High Ring," Everic pointed out. "And apparently there are others who share a similar golden gaze. 'The most blessed of Zald' according to that pig, Micah Artris."

Reuben thought of Jophiel's passing interest in his lineage, but shut down the useless musing. Where would it get them, when his natural father was absent and Oriana was dead?

"*My* eyes aren't that color, last I checked," he argued, crossing his arms a bit petulantly.

Everic examined Reuben for one drawn-out, increasingly uncomfortable moment. But finally he nodded and turned back to the wardrobe, selecting another white shirt of nicer quality to pull over his head.

"Very well," he said as he finished dressing. "I'm grateful regardless.

And I could ask for more details, if you'd like, the next time Jophiel visits the city."

Reuben's breath froze in his lungs. His immediate thought was *no*, along with a few expletives. But his mind caught onto the foreboding promise of *"next time,"* and he demanded instead, "When is she coming? *Why?*"

Everic turned, a concerned wrinkle in his brow. "She's sent no word," he assured. "I swore to you, she's not involved in what I'm doing here. She only visits this city on occasion—her . . . *business* often keeps her in Loethia."

Loethia. Reuben should have been grateful for how relatively upfront Everic was being, and proud of himself that his client would trust him with even more, however ill-advised.

At the least, he should have just smiled, then thanked Everic for the reassurance.

*Zaldus wept*, but all he could do was try to ignore the cold dread nearly drowning him now, as the truth stared Reuben in the face: the vampire in front of him not only meant to *kill* Sazzera's leader as he'd insinuated in their last conversation, but—based on his connections— was very likely doing it on the Loethian Empire's behalf. Probably to stop an alliance forming between Sazzera and Dijher, leaving them more vulnerable to attack.

And Reuben was right here, helping him.

Not hiding how badly he was handling the realization either, it seemed. The concerned line between Everic's brows deepened as he watched whatever was happening on Reuben's face. "Reubie—"

"What are you dressing up for?" Reuben quickly changed the subject, rising from the bed. "Another fancy parlor party on the horizon?"

He couldn't process this information right now. *Especially* right in front of Everic.

"A short meeting with Saer Delvanzus, just after sunset," said Everic as Reuben approached. He hesitated, then continued in a softer tone, "They said you'd be welcome to join—though I didn't expect you to feel well enough."

If it had been anyone else, maybe Reuben would have considered further. But at hearing Delvanzus's name, he was quick to agree, "I'm sure it'd do me some good; the fresh air, stretching my limbs a bit."

Then Reuben turned to do just that: making sure Everic could view it in profile as he raised his arms and let his head fall back, curving his spine in a subtly sensual manner. Enjoying too much, the way Everic's throat visibly bobbed, his eyes flickering down at the movement.

"Especially when I have a strong arm to lean on now, should I grow faint," Reuben finished, smirking at his distraction's success.

And once Reuben selected a plainer, dark outfit from the wardrobe that almost fit, and then stripped off the borrowed sleep shirt, something in Everic's posture—or else, in the overly careful yet *lingering* way he helped Reuben dress again—confirmed that Reuben's physical beauty was affecting the vampire much more of late.

Everic was close to initiating sex, Reuben surmised, or at least *some* kind of intimacy at last.

It was terribly strange to wait this long, but not unheard of in Reuben's line of work. Or at least, a gradual build with gift-giving and romancing was typical for courtesans and concubines, even if Reuben was far lower in station than them. He knew better than to be anything but flattered, of course—acting like it was a courtship at first was the only way some clients felt *comfortable* initiating something.

Up until now, Reuben found it hard to swallow most games his clients requested, particularly if they involved playing pretend; his whole life already felt like one big stage act as it was. He made sure to give them a terrible performance if they wanted more than

Reubielocks, so he was never asked a second time to play as someone's partner, or rejected infatuation, or angry abuser, or victim.

But this game felt dangerously *easy* to stomach . . . perhaps because, too often, he found himself not acting at all.

Less than an hour later they left the hideaway together. Reuben stayed quiet while they walked, grateful when Everic said nothing either, the vampire only offering his hand as the settling shadows of dusk grew deeper around them. Reuben returned the grip tightly. With how Waron, and then his assassin, had appeared out of the dark to surprise Reuben of late, he didn't feel at ease even as they returned to the more lit areas of the main ring.

By the time they reached the main entertainment district of the city, the Starlet Eye not far, night had fully descended. Everic led them down a narrow street off of the piazza to a small tavern. *The Lonely Lantern*, Reuben squinted to read as they neared the old sign above its door.

Indeed, a single lantern lit the small room they entered. Two patrons sat at an unmanned bar. Both glanced up at the new arrivals and, after meeting Everic's eyes, quickly went back to staring down their tankards.

Everic gave Reuben's hand a reassuring squeeze before crossing over to the lantern resting on a stone platform near the bar, twisting a small mechanism at its top—once, twice, thrice.

Then Reuben flinched, the only one to react at the rough, scraping sound of grinding stone that interrupted the quiet.

A slab of the floor had sunk and begun shifting underneath itself near the bar, even whilst the two tavern patrons drank on, unbothered. And without further ado, Everic led Reuben over to the opening the stone left, revealing a set of stone stairs that retreated into darkness.

As Reuben squinted down at the revealed hideaway through his veil, he felt a sudden urge to laugh. He'd been foolish to think even something so innocent as *a short meeting* would turn out normal, or safe, or above-board, if Everic Payne was involved.

At least Saer Delvanzus was as bright and cheery as ever once the stairs ended and Reuben followed Everic into a *much* more populated lounge and bar. The guild master sat up from where they'd been leaning back on a cushioned chaise near the back of the lounge, setting down a book and waving the two over with a large, dimpled smile.

Reuben took in the strange conglomeration of individuals around as he followed Everic over: more infernal-kind than he'd ever seen together in one place; some patrons wearing thin, weathered clothes, while others sported finer attire, either out in the open or visible under plain cloaks. And many of them sat brazenly side by side, despite their clear differences in prosperity.

"Ah, my many-eyed friend!" Aldo Delvanzus said first to Everic, clasping his arm in a hearty grip. The dwarf turned next to Reuben, smiling. "And his talented companion returns—you've found yourself a businessman you'll get *trusted* advice from, saer," they winked at Reuben while informing Everic, "if you can earn his honest opinions, of course."

Reuben flushed at the dwarf's astute assessment. "I'm sure no better than your own, saer."

After they sat, he found himself mostly silent, taking everything in with wary but undeniable interest as Everic and Delvanzus launched into business. The talk started with the amount Delvanzus could expect Everic to invest for a project in the Hollows, numbers in the thousands being tossed around and deliberated. The details of it were never laid out, though Reuben did find Delvanzus's lament that they were "used to building up these days, not tunneling down," rather curious.

Next, the conversation moved to the guild members Delvanzus trusted, or at least had begun to suspect "might have a like mind," during which Reuben took mental note of each name. Last, Delvanzus started asking vaguely but eagerly about measurement estimations, though Everic only replied, "Soon—my friend is still scoping out the right areas."

The guild master deflated. "I should have *realized* something was wrong a long time ago," they sighed, looking the least cheerful Reuben had seen them up to this point. Even defeated, as they continued, "Ever since I took over for my father, I've guaranteed our workers a paid, extended Repose if they sustain an injury in the quarry—but more and more over the last few years, my managers report that if they're Hollows folk and seriously injured, they rarely return; most don't even send someone to pick up the canters. Just disappear."

"The truth would not be natural for *anyone* to assume," Everic said, his voice low and filled with vitriol.

Delvanzus gave him a sad smile. "Well, now I know. And have the privilege to help where I can." They brightened a moment later, adding, "And I'd *love* to see you both at the grand ball the guild is hosting, the week after next. You can expect an invitation shortly—so get your capes, caps, and pelanda fit for a grand event!"

Reuben perked up at the ball's description, even whilst Everic grimaced.

Everic let out a slow sigh, responding, "I appreciate your help, Aldo."

"As do I, friend," Delvanzus chuckled, leaning in before they added, "It's not every day that one meets a fellow heretic."

The conversation had likely not taken more than an hour. Still, Reuben was relieved when Everic and Delvanzus said their farewells soon after. It'd been years since he wore a veil for this long—though Reuben's discomfort had much more to do with the high likelihood

Zaldian clerics would burn every person found visiting this secret, clearly-sacrilegious lounge.

He'd never been a zealous worshipper of Zaldus. From a very young age, he never had *time* to do much besides listen to Nahlia's retellings of the Gospel of Zald, learn the laws, customs, and beliefs surrounding the god, and shape his worldview around that understanding. But Reuben had never found a point in questioning any of it either. Even now, he felt an anxious disquiet over the implications of Delvanzus and Everic's heresy.

Even if Reuben was right about Loethia's involvement, Everic didn't seem motivated by someone else's orders or a gold ransom. For whatever reason, this was *deeply* personal.

As they walked back, Everic observed, "I've never seen you so quiet."

Reuben knew better than to paste on a cheery facade. "I . . . didn't feel you needed my help in that situation, saer," he replied, attempting a deflection instead. "What Saer Delvanzus said was kind, but I'm not actually practiced much in *this* sort of business. Though I'm always happy to join you as simple company, of course."

Everic mulled this over for a while. "I'm not in need of simple company," he said once they reached the winding path down to the Hollows' southern side. "I told you—I planned to do this entirely alone at first. But, knowing what you know, if you *are* still willing to help me . . . then I would value your input in the future."

Reuben's eyes widened as he realized his mistake. "No, *of course*, saer—and seeing how trusting Saer Delvanzus was with you tonight, hearing somewhat of your plans, all of it has given me important context for the upcoming ball, where I'm sure I can be of much better use."

At that, Everic made a small hum of acknowledgement, though Reuben wondered if he still hadn't said the right thing.

Once they arrived back and returned to Everic's hidden room,

Reuben tried again: "I feel quite recovered now, saer, thanks to your kindness. Whatever you need me for in the days to come—blood, letters, social events, or otherwise—I am more than happy to help." He ducked his chin as he turned towards Everic, glancing up through his eyelashes and adding softly, "I'd *prefer* it, over my usual work."

It wasn't a lie. Which may have explained why Reuben's stomach made a small, nervous flip as he spoke, even if the words were meant to manipulate.

Contrary to what Reuben expected, however, it was a quiet sadness that softened Everic's eyes, not gratification at the intended compliment. "Then you can finish out the night here, before you go," he responded, reaching up and briefly brushing two knuckles down Reuben's cheekbone. "I will have need of you often. Just—in the meantime, please . . . do try to take care of yourself, Reubie."

Reuben thought yet again of that lumpy bit of mattress between Nahlia and Daxus, before he nodded with a rueful smile.

Early the next morning, Reuben exited the hollow and turned right for entirely selfish reasons, down the stairway toward his old neighborhood.

Nahlia and Daxus shouldn't have run out of 100 canters so soon. Even at their advanced age, they would keep things livable a while longer. Really, Reuben's only excuse was to keep his promise to Nahlia that he'd visit again soon. He had no plans to worry them about Everic, or the Allunata—only to be held and comforted.

Unlike his last venture to the rim, the sun had almost peeked over Mount Sazzo's southern slope. Small shops were opening; many folk dressed in miner's caps and aprons were trudging down ahead of Reuben. Others hauling buckets or in servant garb headed up the stairways, and Reuben recalled doing the same each morning as a child, his first chore to fetch cleaner water from the main city pools.

On the surface, so little had changed.

With the conversation between Everic and Aldo Delvanzus fresh in his mind, however, Reuben walked among his old neighbors and noticed quiet differences: sentry guards posted on nearly every street, more vagrants huddled in corners, a few shops and hollows boarded up or simply abandoned. There was a tension in the air despite the morning crowd—as if to linger out in the open, even for a second, was to invite unwanted scrutiny.

When he rounded a switchback of stairs, Reuben got just an inkling as to why. Three sentry guards stood outside a hollowed dwelling, one of them nailing a piece of parchment into the door. Reuben couldn't read what it said from here. The other two glanced his way—noted a veiled harlot watching their official business with narrowed eyes—and he was quick to duck his head and hasten his pace, heartbeat thundering in his ears even after he made it around the next corner.

Still, he had every intention of visiting his family. Reuben just took a slightly-longer route to the northern edge to avoid the congestion at the rim, where workers waited their turn down the metal lift—and more guards would likely be present. The only deliberation left was what little he should share about recent events, and maybe which new song to play them, right up until a sound startled him.

A pained groan, it sounded like, under the shadowed arch up ahead. And the brief tension from his run-in with sentry guards was nothing compared to how Reuben's entire body froze up now, still as stone while he watched a dark-cloaked figure crouch over a collapsed body, then slink away—nearly as if they'd melted into the shadows.

*The shadowed figure of a man in his mirror, leaning against the wall . .*
.

Reuben was a fool. He already should have started running in the opposite direction. He never should have come here in the first place, when he *knew* the Allunata were being paid to track his every step.

From what Waron said, they found Reuben's movements harder to track when he was away with Everic—but all it would take was one time, before he led them straight to Nahlia and Daxus.

Reuben swallowed around the lump in his throat and gave up on any brief notion of rest, or comfort, or safety from his old parental figures. *They* were the ones that needed taking care of now, he reminded himself sternly.

"Are you alright?" he called toward the infernal-kind now rising on shaky limbs. But the thin man flinched at Reuben's voice, shaking his head and staggering into a nearby hollowed dwelling. The door shut harshly behind him.

Left alone on the narrow street, Reuben felt a phantom prickling along the back of his neck—and perhaps the Allunata had just spotted him. Perhaps, they'd been following him this whole time.

*So many in this holy city, and yet someone out there wants to keep an eye on you* . . .

More than likely, of course, this had nothing to do with him. The Allunata for many decades had held sway over businesses, conducted illegal trade, practiced devilcraft, and—especially in recent years–inspired fear in these parts. Even a few days ago, Reuben would have thought little of it after witnessing this altercation.

But it wasn't worth the risk.

Reuben swallowed down guilt for the second time in less than a day, knowing it might be a *very* long time before he could visit Nahlia and Daxus again, and turned his back on the street's sloping descent.

A half hour and many steps up the main stair later, he reached the bustling piazza—only two full nights since he left for the parlor party. So there was no reason for him to feel so strange, even out of place, after a security guard let him in and Reuben slowly entered the Starlet Eye Bordello.

Perhaps it was just the dusty light intruding from the windows, exposing the washed-out, faded state of the wooden panels and beams that the glow of candles and magical spotlights usually hid. Reuben wasn't often down here at this time, either—it was approaching midday, just after overnight customers had been ushered out, but hours before the stellas were expected for their breaking-fast meal. Even Sidarchus wasn't around to fill the silence. Which, on the bright side, meant Reuben could put off their inevitable conversation about his extended absence until later.

Or so he thought. As he finished climbing the stairway, Reuben was distracted thinking about whether to check on Isolde now or later—until a door unlatched to his right.

He turned, then stiffened at the sight: Sidarchus exiting from the viewing room for private performances, looking tired but pleased, followed by a disheveled Bittie with dirty tear tracks stained down her cheeks.

Reuben should have turned away and kept walking to the stella wing. There was little he hated more than staring into the face of something he detested, that he had no power to change.

But they were about to notice him anyway. Reuben planted his feet and called down the corridor, "Sidarchus?"

Sidarchus jumped as if caught, though his stooped shoulders relaxed at seeing Reuben. "Oh! Reubie, what a relief," he sighed, putting a hand against his heart. The other rested on Bittie's shoulder. "I was just telling your fellow stella here how worried I was."

"Are you alright, Bittie?" Reuben asked as he approached, though he wasn't surprised when Bittie immediately nodded.

"Yes—though, if you don't mind, Sid, Reubie, I should get back to my brother," she offered them both a wavering smile before shrugging off Sidarchus's hand. Her bleary, kohl-smudged eyes stayed down, avoiding contact with Reuben's gaze as she passed him.

Reuben didn't like to think about how young the twins were—just 15 when they first arrived, now only 20—but it was hard not to, right then, with how much smaller her hunched shoulders made her already-short frame. It was hard not to be upset at Sidarchus either for whatever had made Bittie cry, even if *he* wasn't the reason the twins were sent here after their parents died in so much debt.

Sidarchus had helped them too, the same way he did Reuben and any other young stellas that ended up in the Starlet Eye over the last four decades. Reuben always felt ill thinking about it, ever since the first youth that came after him. But by the time the twins arrived he could no longer bear it in silence. After all, if they were unable to legally work as a prostitute until they turned 16, wouldn't it be best to wait to train them until that age as well? Only have them work in the household, run errands and fill baths, and simply acclimate to the environment until they'd matured?

He finally found enough bravery to bring up his concerns with the house manager—but Sidarchus had just smiled, and said he'd be happy to oversee *Reuben* train them instead.

Sidarchus was smiling at Reuben now as he neared. "I'm relieved to see your private client didn't wear you out so terribly this time, stella."

"I told you, it wasn't them," Reuben replied, sharper than he usually dared with Sidarchus. "*Waron* attacked me. He'd snuck into my room before I returned from the last appointment, then stole my voleris, took pleasure without payment, and ruined two nights of work for me," he listed off in terms Sidarchus might actually be sympathetic towards. "I'm fortunate I recovered enough to attend my private client's event on Repose—I could have lost *them* as well."

It was somewhat satisfying to watch the house manager's face whiten, eyes widening in shock, even if Sidarchus was quick to defend, "I gave our security guards explicit orders to always escort him from the premises, Reubie. I'll question them and see if any door was left unattended that night, but—"

"That's not enough," Reuben argued. "Get sentry involved. Tell them we were robbed, attacked. You *saw*, w-what—what he—" He cut himself off as his voice cracked, his throat tightening up too much to speak.

Then Sidarchus wrapped arms around him, and so quickly Reuben's defenses crumbled, a small sob catching in his chest as he dropped his head onto his old mentor's shoulder. It was too easy to break down when he and Sidarchus were alone—the old man had already seen him pathetic and crying like this many times before. What was once more?

"I'm glad you healed yourself so well," Sidarchus hushed, patting Reuben's back. "You are so strong, dear, handling all of this with *such* grace. I'll see if the piazza sentry unit can be persuaded to keep an extra eye out—you know how they are about this place, but it won't hurt to try."

"Thank you," Reuben breathed out.

"Of *course*. Though . . . I admit, I was sure your private client had been to blame, and planned worse for you, with such an extended absence. Is all well in that regard? No true dangers to worry about?" When Reuben hesitated, Sidarchus pulled back, his eyes dark and scrutinizing. "He's some kind of criminal too, then?"

Reuben thought of Everic's dubious, bloody intent for the Voice of Zald, and shivered. "I don't know for sure," he whispered. "But . . . I am scared, Sid."

Sidarchus made a short *tsk* sound and led Reuben back into the viewing room. "Tell me what you *do* know," he said, sitting down on one of the cushioned sofas usually reserved for their audience, and patted his thigh for Reuben to join. "Then we can parse out if it's quite *so* bad as you fear."

It'd been a long time since Reuben felt comfortable, sitting intimately like this on his old mentor's lap—but less than a year since the last time. Needing help with a client, asking for leniency on Isolde's behalf, explaining that his body wouldn't let him work . . . it all came down to appeasing Sidarchus, often by complying with some belittling request like this. A subtle reminder of the much more intimate dynamic they used to share.

But Reuben never really had anyone else to turn to, did he?

Isolde was a great friend, but she wasn't practical. She would tell him to stop seeing Everic right this moment, and probably be angry at him for letting it go on this long–and for watching *her* take on Bev as a client without saying anything.

Reuben thought of Nahlia and Daxus next. But even were it safe to visit them still, the two already winced in pain at any mention of his sinful occupation or his neverending debt. They'd apologize to him over and over for the circumstances his mother left him in, and probably tell him to never leave them gold again.

Besides them . . . Reuben's mind flashed, however pointlessly, to Everic.

At that, he let out a broken laugh and shook his head at himself, before sitting on Sidarchus's knee with tears obscuring his vision.

Sidarchus pulled Reuben to rest more fully against him. "That's it, sweet Reubielocks," he murmured, one hand gently squeezing Reuben's thigh. "I'm here, now . . . tell good old Sid what's happened."

# 15

# TOO CARELESS

E veric hadn't lied about sending for Reuben often. Just two nights later, Reuben finished a performance only to feel Bev's quiet, waiting presence join the crowd.

He only made it a single step up the stairwell to fetch his things, however, before Isolde grabbed at his wrist. "I know you said it was Waron, not this one," she whispered, her face pinched with worry, "but do you really think it's *safe* to go out there so often? Can't Bev's friend leave his home for once?"

Reuben thought of the attack from within the carriage's dim, the shadowed figure assaulting a man in the Hollows, the series of subterranean rooms that Everic hid sequestered away in . . . and then the dark figure in his own mirror's reflection.

"Safer than here," he replied, raising a brow. *"Particularly* when you don't steal my escort."

Isolde flushed and let go of him, though she didn't look quite appeased.

Reuben felt much less anxiety over his circumstances, however. For all that Sidarchus's presence made Reuben uncomfortable at times, the older man could always offer a more practical mindset,

223

a piece of wisdom hardwon from his own decades of experience. Reuben hadn't told him *everything*—not about the vampirism, or the specifics of *who* Everic sought in High Ring—but Sidarchus had heard everything else. And had congratulated Reuben on making himself so invaluable to Everic.

Keeping their agreement was more of a risk than he'd even imagined at the start, just for fraternizing with a vampire. But still a worthy one, for now. Once Everic's intentions were about to be uncovered or Everic came close to reaching his goal—only *then* should Reuben cut off all contact, Sidarchus had emphasized.

Everic would understand. He might even be glad, given his genuine worry over endangering anyone else.

In the meantime, Reuben enjoyed the small outing Everic took him on that evening, involving a handful of guild members from Delvanzus's parlor party and a few new faces, who were all meeting for drinks after dusk. From the moment they sat down in a secluded, reserved area of a fancy inn, Reuben used every charm he could as the conversation moved from the best silk imports of the West Isles, to what food *should* be prepared at a ball, to the best parties they'd all attended. He giggled at or reframed most of Everic's responses to such questions—though it was already much easier now, with help from the five who'd been won over at the parlor party.

Like when Everic said, "I find *most* parties aren't to my tastes," Reuben didn't even need to verbally step in—the new attendants looked a bit miffed, but the masons just nodded their heads sagely as if he'd spoken wisdom. Already bought into the persona of the mysterious, refined Saer Payne.

"Is that why you bring your own entertainment?" asked an unknown man with dark brown skin and pointed, gold-capped horns, nodding slyly at Reuben.

"Oh, but you haven't heard him play, Randal!" said an elvish woman named Saer Blanca Orlyn. She turned to Reuben with very large, beseeching brown eyes, adding, "*Please* tell me you didn't bring your instrument just as an accessory tonight, Reubielocks."

*Orlyn* was a name Delvanzus had mentioned trusting, Reuben recalled. And quickly everyone who had seen his last performance at Delvanzus's party were echoing her desire to hear him play again.

Reuben looked to Everic, smoothing a hand down his arm. "Well, my good saer, what say you?" he said, making sure to keep Everic at center focus. "Will you have me play for everyone, or keep me to yourself tonight?"

The side of Everic's mouth twitched, before he allowed, "*One* song."

And so Reuben played them one of his jaunty crowd-pleasers, adding a simpler version of the quick footwork he and Isolde usually included as accents to the sharp stops in the bridge and chorus. Which allowed him to more easily tune into the small group around him—and calm further, when there was only the usual garden variety of intents behind the dozen faces. Some enthralled, some attracted, some impatient for conversation to pick up again; all eventually clapping or heel-tapping along.

He saved Everic for last, this time. And immediately Reuben startled, taken aback at the overwhelming desire that emanated from the vampire. Born of *lust*, not hunger—and without a trace of grief in the background.

His violin bow froze briefly over the bridge, before Reuben snapped out of the secondhand haze. Then he accented the pause with a brief whip of his hair and dove into the final iteration of the chorus.

"My my! Count me as thoroughly impressed," the infernal man conceded with a laugh once the number was over, turning to Everic. "He's a man of *many* talents, then?"

Everic only gave a stiff nod in answer, studiously avoiding eye contact as Reuben returned to his seat.

Part of Reuben wanted to investigate further, puzzle out if it was the small dancing he added, or the song, or the outfit he wore tonight that seemed to have affected Everic so profoundly. But the conversation turned to leaders of the high houses, and Reuben forced himself to pay closer attention to their purpose here instead.

"Oh, but you haven't met Magnatus Vyllorence," one dwarvish woman scoffed. "I offered him a sample of every silk this remote city could *hope* to access, and still he said none were soft enough for his sensitive arse!"

"We oversaw the construction of House Fiorett's garden pavilion," an elvish individual countered. "It was supposed to take six months. Magnatus Anello changed her mind so often, it wasn't finished for *three years*."

Reuben tried to remember the names for the sake of later interactions. Of course, throughout the conversation he also couldn't help wondering which, if any, of these high houses he technically shared blood with. Or if his mother would agree with any of these scathing remarks, and might have offered her own.

She talked so little about her life before her debt—before his conception left her life in ruins. It all had seemed irreparably wrapped up in so much despair and grief and anger, and trying to unravel the truth from their tight grip only made those same emotions lash out at *him* until he managed to sufficiently appease her.

Reuben had always told himself it didn't matter. But with his current charge to help Everic get into High Ring, and the possibility Jophiel singled out his bastard blood for both her rite and later, Everic's protection, Reuben wished more than ever his mother had told him more.

The next morning, he woke up remembering Isolde's delirious

warnings in part as well: *Oriana waited too long to warn you . . . you can't hear it, but it's waiting in your heart, in your blood . . .*

Admittedly, Reuben couldn't remember much else from the jumbled words Isolde said that night. He'd barely been coherent himself at the time. Something about a song? Or to *sing* more often?

He was too busy to spend much time contemplating it. Everic sent for him that night as well, needing help with his reply to another parlor party invitation, this one hosted by the infernal man they'd met at the previous get-together. Who had *an interest in finding and supporting the city's most creative innovators, and may know a few who'd be interested in your canters in return,* according to the personalized invite signed by a Saer Randal Kapriyah.

"I'll need your blood again, just before the party," Everic said after he finished penning the final draft, speaking slowly and carefully—as if to *warn* Reuben.

Reuben tried not to look confused. "But of course," he smiled, then tried to lean in and tease, "It's been almost a week since your last *taste* of me. And I've had no voleris, saer, I promise."

Everic didn't seem to notice the flirtation at all. He finished sealing the envelope and faced Reuben sternly. "Last I did, it deeply upset you."

A flash of panic ran through him as Reuben recalled cringing and crying over the small pain. "I'm sorry about that. I was sick and out of my head, I think. Usually I don't mind the pain—so long as it isn't too drawn out."

"You asked me if it had to be a knife," Everic pressed further, his brows furrowing low over his eyes.

A knife. Reuben winced at the thought—and then mentally cursed himself when Everic's eyes narrowed at the reaction.

"I . . . don't love the use of blades, generally," Reuben admitted, knowing further lies would just lose him precious trust at this point.

"But I've handled it alright thus far. I'll be fine."

Everic wore one of his characteristic frowns. "I'm not sure you'd find fangs any better of an experience," he said, slow and guarded.

But *almost*, like he was asking Reuben to convince him otherwise.

"I'm not sure either," Reuben agreed, trying not to grow hopeful. "Although . . . it couldn't hurt to try once—not more than *usual*, anyway," he amended around a soft, hesitant laugh.

"It shouldn't hurt as much," Everic said, though he didn't disclose the information as if it was good news. "At least, from what others have told me."

It sounded like good news to Reuben. He perked up, pressing, *"Really?"*

Everic's dark eyes flickered to Reuben's neck for a long moment instead of answering, before he physically wrenched them away. "But it is a higher risk," he continued in a sharp tone. "I will have to pay very close attention to what I'm taking—and avoid *any* distraction."

Reuben gestured at the quiet, closed-off room around them, smiling as he remarked, "In that regard . . . it seems we have the perfect setup already."

Two evenings later, Reuben left with the warning to Sidarchus he would be gone a full day, and headed to the Hollows just as dusk fell with nervous excitement squirming in his gut.

They agreed for him to come and be bled the night before the parlor party this time, to ensure Reuben's recovery—especially "should anything go amiss," as Everic put it. He didn't look like he'd changed his mind now, only behaved stiffer than usual when Reuben arrived. Soon enough he pulled the stool over to the bedside table and brought over half of the usual supplies: linen to lay over the surface and a few clean bandages, no knife or goblet needed.

Everic met Reuben's eyes with a firm, grim nod when Reuben held out his bare arm. Then he gently cupped his hands under Reuben's wrist and elbow, pulling the exposed limb closer over the table.

Next, Everic leaned down—and hesitated, glancing back up at Reuben with apprehension again.

"I won't talk unless necessary," Reuben assured, "and keep very still. *No* distractions."

Everic just grimaced. "I apologize, if . . . for *any* of the effects it might have," he said in very cryptic terms. Then, once Reuben gave a confused nod in return, finally put his open mouth against the fragile wrist skin and bit down.

Reuben sucked in a harsh breath, his whole body tensing at the two sudden, foreign intrusions.

Everic's fangs were sharp enough it had only stung for a brief instant. But Reuben's instincts seemed to realize he had been caught in the maw of a dangerous predator—his death inevitable unless he somehow wrenched this creature's jaw free.

He was a dead man, was all Reuben thought in his panic, his whole body beginning to tremble as if caught between instincts to either fight or flee. It had always been inevitable—*but he still wasn't ready to face the cold, dark, damned eternity that awaited him*—

Then both instincts, all at once, went to sleep.

Everic's fangs had retracted, the punctured skin left tingling and sensitive as his mouth remained to gently suck at it instead. And yet, despite the miniscule pressure, Reuben could feel his blood flow fast and thin from the wound.

Reuben's next breath hitched as the vampire continued with a bit more strength, the sucking sensation sharp and somewhat painful. Though also strangely . . . *enjoyable* in a way, soothing him even as it continued for much longer than Reuben was ever bled by the knife.

But this was not a savage, crude opening of his veins that a blade necessitated—just a decisive prick that left their structure otherwise undisturbed as Everic drank. Eventually, Reuben let his head fall back against the pillows and just enjoyed the slow, incessant pressure, the tingling sensitivity of his skin against Everic's lips, even the firm hold the vampire had his arm locked in.

Reuben had worn a decorative, sleeveless top, in case fangs made things messier. But when the suck of Everic's mouth receded, Reuben didn't see a drop wasted.

Of course, his senses couldn't altogether be trusted. He felt as lightheaded as ever from the blood loss. Perhaps even worse than usual, considering how sharply an uninhibited gasp escaped him as he felt Everic's tongue next. Which wasn't *anything* like the painful, tingling numbness Reuben always felt when Everic did the same to his knife wounds. He licked at the puncture marks much more slowly, with his mouth still sealed over them. Spending his time laving at the same spot over and over, where the sensitivity from the bite itself had yet to fade.

Reuben was aroused, he realized then with a sleepy curiosity. He could feel the warm current of it low in his belly, even if an erection hadn't developed quite yet—perhaps because of the blood loss. But if Everic's tongue continued like *that* for much longer . . .

It felt like a loss, when Everic's mouth finally did leave his skin.

"That was too much," he heard the vampire hiss out soon after, though from a murky distance that only seemed to lengthen, making whatever Everic said next indecipherable.

Reuben tried to see why the vampire sounded like he was underwater, but found his eyelids too heavy to open.

There was a cold pressure at his neck. Reuben tried to warn that he was too weak for another bite—but only managed a soft, hurt noise. Then, still as if through water, he heard the sound of Everic sighing and felt the cold touch at his neck leaving.

Reuben wasn't aware of much after that, until he registered a hand propping up his head and a familiar cinnamon taste at his tongue.

It was habit now, at the taste alone, to dutifully begin drinking and trying to clear his head. Over the next few minutes he did his best, though it was harder than usual to eat whatever Everic's fingers pressed against his lips even as Reuben's mind painfully came back to awareness.

It made perfect sense now, why Everic found cutting more controlled, though not in the way Reuben had imagined. The vampire hadn't turned into some bloodthirsty, violent devil, ignoring his prey's resistance. He simply couldn't gauge as well how much he was taking—and Reuben provided *no* resistance.

After the initial prick of pain and fear, there was only slow, stimulating pleasure, and then a peaceful descent towards dreamless sleep.

Which was all Reuben really wanted now, still. The moment he felt cognizant enough to speak, he said, "I'm alright . . . just need rest."

"You *need* more fluids."

So Reuben took dutiful sips from the water pressed to his lips, and then more of the cinnamon drink. After Everic relented, however, Reuben felt himself begin to slip towards unconsciousness—only to be interrupted by the insistent press of fingers at his neck once again, cold and jarring.

"Just tired," Reuben assured, though it came out a bit slurred.

"I don't want to leave you here and not notice if you grow worse," he heard Everic say, his voice tight with anger now.

Reuben was too exhausted, for once, to worry he'd done something wrong.

"Then don't leave," he said, forcing his heavy eyelids open. Smiling, as he met the bright gold, worried gaze of the vampire hovered over him. Reuben shifted to his left side and moved a heavy arm to pat the mattress behind him. Murmuring, just as his eyes slipped shut,

"Just . . . stay a while."

He grew somewhat aware again later, at the feeling of a body joining him on the bed. Fingers pressed at his neck again, followed by a mournful sigh from the chest he gladly leaned his back against. "Your heart is returned to normal, at least," Everic said, quiet but tense.

Reuben hummed in reply, happy when he reached up in time to catch the hand moving away from his neck and pull it over his chest. Even happier, when Everic's arm relaxed and stayed curled there, essentially tricked into hugging him from behind.

No louder than a whisper, Everic breathed out, "I am forever too careless," into his hair. It was the last thing Reuben heard before he drifted off.

The disappointment was hard to swallow, when Reuben woke later to find the arm around him missing.

Reuben recovered well enough to attend Saer Kapriyah's parlor party the next morning, though he played a shorter song for his audience and focused his minimal energy otherwise on smoothing out the inevitable bumps in Everic's social interactions. And Everic was especially quiet and curt the whole morning—though by the end of the event was still gifted with more guild tokens, this time from the masonry guild *and* a high-ranked member of the silk merchant guild.

On the carriage ride back, Reuben offered, "I would call this a resounding success, by the way. Even the bite—I may need another nap soon, but it was a *very* pleasant experience, saer."

Everic kept his eyes on the window. "We won't be doing that again," he replied firmly. Reuben felt his mouth drop open, a protest on his lips, but Everic continued, "*Not* until I absolutely require it. And with how many invitations I'm receiving now, I have my pick of the ones that take place after dusk."

Reuben bit his lip, then tried, "Everic—I'm sorry if I did something, or distracted you, but I swear—"

"I'm not sacking you," Everic interrupted, finally meeting Reuben's gaze. "Clearly I still need your help, if today was anything to go by, and the amount I give will not change. That's all that matters, isn't it?"

It should have been. Even so, Reuben knew he'd made a terrible mistake somewhere in all of this—perhaps his weak body's over-reactive response, or admitting he'd enjoyed it. Or maybe, Everic simply preferred the distance a knife afforded. The fact that Reuben couldn't pinpoint the reason made him all the more anxious.

Not that he would show it. "As you wish, saer—I'll just have to make it up with a private recital, every now and then," Reuben answered in a light, unbothered tone.

What followed was a series of social parties, gatherings, and preparations all leading up to the grand ball at the Mason Guild Hall. Which would mark the eve of the seventh trade council, the penultimate meeting before the Dijheri representatives and high priests of Zald finalized all trade proposals—then turned their talks to political alliance, and war.

Delvanzus had sent an additional invitation to the ball, addressed to "Reubielocks of the Starlet Eye." A guild token was included within as well, meaning Reuben now had *two* of the coveted social coins in his possession. Gifted by anyone else, Reuben would have assumed it to be a proposition—in getting to know Delvanzus, however, he had a strange feeling the gesture was simply the guild master being *kind*.

Everic stayed short and stiff during the next outing, and left the shop as Reuben was fitted for a small wardrobe of his own. Of course, he also seemed distracted by his new protection detail—both infernal-kind, from the Hollows, and approved of by Bev, from what Reuben gathered. Everic gave them firm orders to stand watch, but still had his eye on them for the entirety of the short trip.

By the next occasion he was somewhat relaxed again, at least, and even leaned into Reuben's casual touches when they attended another gathering for drinks and left with two more guild tokens bestowed. So Reuben kept a firm, constricting grip on his worry over what had upset the vampire, and simply made sure to remain as amiable and unassuming as ever in return.

And if the new reality of only attending events together made Reuben *miss* the vampire, given what limited time was given for private conversation, that was for him alone to know.

At the next evening party, dedicated to "cue sports," they ran into Saer Micah Artris again—or, more accurately, Artris approached Everic as soon as he spotted the vampire.

"Aldo's mysterious new friend, so we meet again!" he said, glancing only briefly at Reuben before continuing, "I am glad to see you have not *entirely* quit society, saer, even if I was forlorn to receive no missive in return about our proposed meeting. Perhaps it was sent to the wrong address?"

Reuben glanced at Everic in the corner of his eye, surprised to see Everic cool and at ease despite the veiled accusation. "Perhaps," he replied evenly. "Though Saer Delvanzus and their circle keep my days rather busy, anyway—if you'd excuse us," he nodded toward the other guests gathering around the game tables, taking Reuben's hand and brushing past the gold keeper.

Apparently the games had grown popular over the past decade in High Ring and only more recently been adopted by the lower tiers of society, which explained why Reuben had no familiarity with it. But what Everic lacked in social grace, he made up for in this area—it quickly became a spectacle of the whole party, how accurately he could aim his cue ball, knocking down every wooden piece save his own no matter where his opponents placed theirs. Some of the players gave up on any bets against his move, while others placed more and more cantergold on the table, arguing that at *some* point he would miss or knock down his own.

After he proved them wrong enough times, Everic gathered up his winnings and reached into Reuben's low blouse, taking a moment to tuck the coin into his breast pocket. Then offered him a faint smile, as Reuben's face warmed and a few other attendants giggled at the two of them.

Artris never participated in the game—but he did approach Everic again with two wine glasses in hand, once the tables had been covered with their tops and everyone finished the night playing card games. "Very impressive," Artris said, nodding at the table as he offered one of the filled glasses to Everic. "If a bit *cruel* of you, saer, playing a game you have no chance of losing."

"I'd only just learned the rules," Everic countered, taking the drink with a nod of thanks. And when Artris said nothing else, just watched him, Everic asked in his ever-blunt manner, "Do you need something?"

"Oh, many things," Artris agreed with a smile, though it didn't reach his eyes. "At the moment, just a small refresh of my memory—your eyes were *gold* when first we met, no? I swear we even spoke on the matter."

Everic stiffened. Before Reuben could open his mouth to intervene, however, he simply agreed, "They were."

Artris waited a long moment, as if Everic might say more—but eventually let out a small huff. "We simply *must* find a time in your busy schedule to speak further," he tutted, still smiling. "I'm sure not only *I* would be interested in your assets. My house's leader,

Magnatus Lenaphon, always likes to meet our potential partners in business."

Lenaphon. It wasn't a name Reuben recalled hearing yet, in all the conversations he took mental notes on over the last week and a half.

With Everic's short timeline in mind, the elvish man's offer was almost tempting. If not for what Reuben had sensed at the first parlor party, he would lean into Everic's space this very moment and softly cajole him to agree. But given Artris's intentions had felt like *suspicion*, not benign interest, it wasn't a risk worth taking.

So when he noticed Everic subtly glancing his way, Reuben didn't hesitate to purse his lips and, almost imperceptibly, move his head to the side.

Everic relaxed against Reuben, as if relieved. "I'm not looking for a partner," he answered Artris.

"Yes, from what I've seen, my good saer prefers to be the *sole* investor on any project he takes on," Reuben added with an appeasing smile.

Artris simply hummed. He was looking between the two of them now, regarding Reuben with a much sharper eye—his interest no longer simply carnal, it seemed.

It was strange, feeling at once flattered and wholly concerned by the fact someone had perceived Reuben as more than a pretty accessory on his client's arm. Reuben wasn't sure whether to act more flirtatious or more subdued to draw less attention to himself.

"I would say he's already found one," Artris chuckled at last, raising his glass to Everic. "Till next time, then, Saer Payne." He didn't wait for Everic, before taking a long drink of his wine and strolling off.

Once they returned to the carriage—Everic thoroughly searching it before helping Reuben in, even if his new guards had been ordered to stand on either side of the window and locked door—Reuben joked, "If all of High Ring society is like *that* one, I may just leave you to it once you get there."

"I may just give up on it myself," Everic said, throwing a twisted grimace at the small estate behind them.

"In that case, my other clients would be happy to have me back," Reuben teased, thinking of how he'd had to cancel his standing appointment with Caterina for the second time in a row.

Everic cocked a brow, then remarked, "Suddenly my desire for trite niceties and foppish company has returned."

He would have been the type of client with a possessive streak, Reuben realized. It wasn't exactly a surprise—many of Reuben's customers preferred never to be reminded of the rest—but the strange satisfaction he felt in return certainly was.

He liked this man *too* much, Reuben conceded to himself at last.

That didn't stop him from replying, "There are plenty of other reasons to keep them at bay—you could always send for me to play for you, saer."

Everic's lips twitched briefly into a smile. "We have another appointment with Delvanzus, the night after next," he reminded. "But I'll certainly keep that option in mind."

Despite Reuben's lack of time for his other clients, however, the nights he *did* work at the bordello were always booked. And with his body mostly recovered from the previous week's blood loss, and the chance to rest it almost every other night during Everic's appointments, Reuben knew better than to argue against more gold.

Nor had he endured another bad spasm yet, like he had after the carriage, that could justify a little voleris. So he put the bottles from his latest recurring order in the back of his vanity's largest drawer when they arrived, and resolved not to think about them. Even when he serviced seven clients in one night, his whole body left in a state of aching, Reuben could usually tell himself he had an evening off with Everic before he had to endure it again.

Following the parlor games, only three customers had booked with Reuben for the next night—but Zurnick, the last of them, had unusually paid for half of it.

Only a minute after Reuben saw the second customer out, sitting down to rub at his aching knees, he heard the next knock. And the orkish man grinned widely at Reuben as he was let in, looking rather pleased with himself.

Reuben *was* hard to book, these days. "It's been far too long, saer," he purred while shutting the door, turning back to stroke hands down the sides of Zurnick's large arms.

Zurnick put a firm hand on Reuben's waist, sighing out, "Been saving up quite a bit for you, Reubielocks," before ducking down to kiss him with a quick, wet enthusiasm. Meanwhile, his free hand moved to his trousers—not to unbutton them, but to pull something from his pocket.

Reuben stared down at the vial Zurnick presented, recognizing the shimmering, silvery liquid within, and swallowed hard.

"What have we here?" he murmured after a belated moment, forcing his eyes to rip away and look up at his client.

Zurnick's grin widened. "It was a costly canter, but I secured a deal with a Dijheri merchant last week. Figured it high time to treat myself," and he shook the vial between two fingers.

Reuben tried to smile. "Congratulations, saer," he said, stroking a hand along the man's flank. "And a wonderful way to reward yourself—I'm sure you'll enjoy it."

"Oh, but *you're* my reward, see," Zurnick chuckled, then squeezed Reuben's waist tighter.

Reuben's stomach flipped. "I'll take it with you, then?"

He couldn't count himself surprised, or even truly upset, when Zurnick shook his head. "I don't need help with virility, like you said," he replied, his smile growing playful as he led Reuben to the bed. "But I'll *definitely* enjoy watching its effects on you."

Reuben thought of Everic first, as he was guided to his knees. They had an appointment the following night, and he could imagine the disapproval, even *anger* that Everic would exude if he caught the scent of voleris. Given Reuben was about to drink a whole vial, there was little chance Everic wouldn't.

But it was Waron who intruded more viscerally into Reuben's mind, the moment Zurnick tried to feed Reuben the bottle. And even when he graciously allowed Reuben to do it himself—the earthy taste an immediate balm to Reuben's senses, as he drank down the concoction—Reuben's brief tranquility from its effects didn't last. Shattered into something confused, disoriented, and afraid, when the orkish man pulled Reuben's head back by the nape and Reuben blinked, realizing he must have lost time for however long he'd apparently spent servicing Zurnick on his knees.

Zurnick, on the other hand, was fascinated by Reuben's state. Quickly he pulled him up and onto the bed, grabbing Reuben's arm when he tried to twist onto his stomach. "Want to see what the locals mean about those 'starry eyes,'" Zurnick explained as he crowded over Reuben, his own gaze flickering eagerly across Reuben's face.

Given Reuben didn't remember many specifics after that—just Zurnick fucking him more than once, and with much more exuberance than usual—he could only assume the man had gotten what he paid for.

If that had been all it was, maybe Everic wouldn't have noticed. But when Reuben woke up just after dawn, his spine in a *fit* of pain from the long night and Zurnick's enthusiasm, all he could think about was escaping it. He had already failed to avoid the so-called poison—what was a bit more at this point? He already paid in precious cantergold for the supply—why let it waste away in his drawer?

Reuben staggered on shaky legs over to the vanity, fishing for the first vial he could reach within its depths, and gulped down the entirety of a second draught before he collapsed back into bed.

At last the pain faded, along with everything else around him. Then, like usual, Reuben drifted off to memories of Everic:

The sudden, foreign intrusion of two fangs in his skin; a strong arm pulling him in against a firm chest; Everic's lips during their last carriage ride, twitching toward a smile . . .

It was Isolde's voice that pulled Reuben from the murky, fevered version of sleep voleris afforded.

". . . mention it's Repose, and I don't see what *difference* it makes, if he's resting here or with your friend," she said, sounding not just cross, but suspicious. Reuben didn't make out any other voice, though Isolde replied after a few seconds in a disbelieving tone, "Will he? Then why does Reubie often look pale and *ill* after seeing him?"

Reuben cracked open an eye, taking in the dark window, the small light emanating from the candle in Isolde's hand, and Isolde herself, standing protectively in front of him. He couldn't quite see past her to who she was speaking with, though by the agitated, back-and-forth swish of a fuchsia tail coming in and out of view, he had a good guess.

And then Reuben sucked in a sharp breath, realizing it must be the night of Everic's next appointment.

Isolde turned back to him at the sound. "I'm sorry, Reubie—I didn't want to wake you, but Bev is *insisting*—"

"I'll go," Reuben interrupted as he sat up, ignoring the way his head spun until he could swing his legs over the bedside.

Isolde stared at him in disbelief. "You need *sleep*, not another appointment."

"I'll sleep there," Reuben promised, thinking of how short Delvanzus's last conversation with Everic was. On the other hand, imagining himself stuck here, trying to rest with a whole month's

240

worth of voleris still in his drawer . . . no matter how angry Everic was about to be, if Reuben was left alone he wasn't sure he could trust himself not to make the situation worse.

Isolde watched him hastily getting dressed for a few seconds, then threw a hand up in defeat. "It's clear I don't understand what's actually going on here," she said, glaring at both Bev and Reuben, "and apparently, *I'm* not supposed to," before storming out.

Bev took a few aborted steps after Isolde, her face twisted with regret.

"I can get there myself," Reuben offered.

Bev just gave him an incredulous look in response, watching him tie his shoes as if to find proof of the contrary. Reuben swallowed down the nausea in his gut and stood firmly on his feet afterward, giving her a reassuring nod.

"I'm feeling fine," he lied.

Bev considered him for a long moment. Then she shrugged out of her leather coat, moving around him to rest it on his shoulders. Signing what he was pretty sure meant, "It's a little cold, tonight."

Reuben softened, giving her a slow nod of thanks before they went their separate ways. And whoever Bev was—or why she was involved with Everic and his bloody plot—Reuben found no trace of worry left in him anymore, as he once again left his closest friend in her care.

# 16

# FAVORITE POSITION

Reuben regretted his decision the moment he walked out the bordello's front doors alone.

The air wasn't cold, really. Just carried the faint chill of nighttime in early autumn. But Reuben still shivered as he held Bev's coat tight around him and trekked down alone, his body out of equilibrium after two back-to-back doses of voleris. And besides the fluctuation in body temperature and the rolling of his stomach, his spine ached nearly as much as it had that morning. His evening out with Everic would be miserable—on top of pointless, given how little he could contribute to the vampire's schemes to seemingly upend the entire city.

Reuben should have just canceled and given his apologies later. He didn't have the fortitude to face Everic's anger right now. Even if Reuben's fear of the man had considerably lessened, the thought of so much as incurring Everic's disapproval still filled him with pressing anxiety.

Simply because he didn't want Everic to send for him less often, or not at all, Reuben tried to argue with himself. But it was more than that. He didn't want to lose Everic's gentle touches, or concerned frowns, or occasional smiles—ever.

Or, more realistically, for as long as Reuben could conceal the truth.

*No matter how many canters are in their purse, never let yourself need anyone more than they need you*, his mother had warned him just a year before her death. *Gold glitters the same—regardless of its source.*

Reuben had done his absolute best to ensure Everic was reliant on him like no other. But it wasn't enough. Reuben feared—no, he *knew*—somewhere in the almost-three months of appointments, he had come to rely on Everic in a way entirely unrelated to the man's piles of cantergold.

Ducking through the hollowed tunnels with a torch in hand, Reuben was too busy grappling with that truth to notice he wasn't alone.

"Reubie," spoke a voice from the shadowed storage room, nearly making Reuben jump out of his skin.

He whipped to face its direction with the torch held protectively out in front of him—though it was only Everic approaching out of the dark. The glow of his red eyes faded as he stepped into the torchlight, darkening further as they narrowed at Reuben.

"Why are you wearing Bev's . . . ?" Everic started asking, but paused, noting where Reuben was now staring: the other hidden door in this room, not only exposed this time, but with all its locks undone, the metal door open to reveal a black maw of an entrance that presumably led even deeper beneath the mountain.

Apparently there was *something* to the stereotype of vampires always dwelling in dark, dank places, Reuben thought before he pulled his eyes away.

He shivered at the drafty air in this room, and tried not to tense when Everic stepped closer and began scrutinizing him. "She stayed behind again, saer," Reuben explained, not acknowledging the door

243

behind Everic. Hoping, praying, Everic wouldn't deign to mention it either.

Everic seemed entirely focused on Reuben, luckily, lifting a cold hand up against Reuben's forehead. "Your eyes are dilated, and your body's feverish again," he observed, a frown beginning to line his face.

Reuben had already considered every kind of lie on his way here—but none would hold for long. So he braced himself and forced out the small, inevitable truth: "I've had voleris recently."

Everic's hand dropped. He took a wide step back, the shadows exacerbating his darkened expression as he responded sharply, "And Bev sent you here *on your own?*"

"The walk was fine, I'm just—"

"There is an entire criminal organization who wants me dead, who knows *you* are connected to me," Everic interrupted, his voice rising. "You've been put in enough danger without her getting *distracted* now."

At the rise in volume, Reuben shrunk in on himself. He almost considered admitting his sins—that the Allunata might want Everic dead, but only because of the intel they received from Reuben. And that, as little as he liked to think about it, someone out there was paying the Allunata to keep Reuben *watched*, not killed.

But even if he wanted to ruin any chance of seeing Everic again, Reuben didn't have the opportunity to speak. The vampire spun away and approached his usual door, not looking at Reuben until he'd unlocked and wrenched it open.

Reuben didn't wait for an order before hurrying past Everic inside. He only turned once he'd fit the torch in a sconce and placed his violin on the bed, ready with more apologies, and was surprised to see Everic watching from afar—standing just inside the doorway still and keeping the door open.

Reuben glanced over at the wardrobe. "I know you had that appointment with Delvanzus, saer—if you just give me a moment, I was going to change."

"Yes," Everic spoke in a short, stern tone, and Reuben blew out a breath before moving to where his new clothes were now kept, side by side with Everic's. But then the vampire ordered, "Change into a nightshirt, and lay down until I return," gesturing to the bed.

Reuben's hand paused in front of the wardrobe. "You—you sent for me to go *with* you, saer," he pointed out, a loud static of anxiety crowding his head at the obvious dismissal.

For all that he hadn't wanted to engage in Everic's heretic meetings with Delvanzus, letting Everic leave him behind felt like a much more egregious error—like a *failure.*

"I wouldn't have come if I didn't think myself capable," Reuben promised.

"And I sent for you at my discretion," Everic said, a dark current of anger, even bitterness, behind his words. "My whim, my *pleasure,* as you've said before. So—my whims have changed, and my pleasure is now for you to rest."

Reuben should have felt grateful. Instead his throat tightened, his chest constricting around a terrible, despairing emotion he didn't know how to name.

He couldn't look at Everic as he answered softly, "If that is your desire, saer," eyes lowered while he waited to hear the door shut.

It didn't. A few seconds later, Reuben's head snapped up, blinking at Everic suddenly in front of him—now with a much softer, sadder expression on his face.

"My desire, Reubie, is to see you *out* of these circumstances," he said, just as a hand slipped into Reuben's, squeezing gently. "Or at the least—to understand you better, and the reasons you find this life so difficult to let go of."

Reuben swallowed hard, though that didn't help the growing ache in his throat, the burning in his eyes. A weak, broken laugh escaped him before he replied, "I . . . I think I just keep finding more reasons, as you do, saer."

Everic's face twisted, then settled on something crossed between fondness and grief. When he lifted up their conjoined hands, Reuben watched in confusion—and then felt his entire body warm, as Everic leaned forward to press his lips against the back of Reuben's hand.

Nothing more was said before Everic left. But Reuben didn't need to be resting yet to know his mind would replay the moment many times in the future, like the melody of a new, favorite song.

The pleasant warmth faded in Everic's absence, of course. Reuben still felt a restless anxiety as he obeyed his client's simple request, stripping down to his undergarment before pulling one of Everic's large, loose shirts over his head. He set both Bev's coat and his violin on the bedside table before laying down, the feel of the firm mattress and linen sheets under him now familiar, comforting sensations.

Reuben couldn't seem to rest, however—and not only due to his aching spine.

He knew better than to trust, much less grow endeared to, the savior types. Even if Everic meant every word of his professed desire to see Reuben free, he was either dead by the end of his bloody business here, or would be forced to go on the run. Reuben simply couldn't grow attached to someone like this, much less their promises.

But that would grow harder and harder to avoid, if he let things like this happen—doing nothing at all for Everic save for taking up his bed and draining more of his coin. If Reuben kept allowing it, he would grow far too used to the indulgences.

When he inevitably cut off their arrangement . . . his heart would take far longer to recover than his finances.

So Reuben spent the next few hours thinking of ways to be useful. Some of them were viable options; should Everic have a single letter to write, for instance, Reuben could always help with the wording. Or if he didn't, Reuben could insist on playing a few songs for him instead—wearing just the man's shirt should only make the performance a more enjoyable show.

Reuben thought of offering his blood again, too, though he knew better than to actually bring it up without cause. And his later ideas were only imagined for personal entertainment: roleplaying as a snooty magnatus for Everic to practice interacting with; critiquing Everic's clothing now that Reuben had caught eye of all the latest fashion; helping Everic undress as he tried on different ensembles, then stopping at some point to stroke his bare chest, maybe even press him up against the wardrobe and kiss for an hour or two; pulling Everic into the bed and wrapping feverish limbs around him to finally warm the vampire up, hum song after song until Reuben could see what Everic looked like falling asleep . . .

The sound of the door jolted Reuben's eyes open, indicating he had managed to rest after all.

Everic entered the room smudged in dirt, but clearly in higher spirits by how lightly he stepped into the room and how mildly he regarded Reuben blinking awake. The vibrance of his now-green irises was also notable, indicating a recent meal.

"How are you feeling?" Everic asked as he crossed to the small table with a wash basin and began splashing his face.

"*Much* better," Reuben replied. He did a testing stretch to confirm, and felt a smaller, more manageable twinge in his spine. Then, noting Everic side-eyeing his movements as he washed, Reuben teased, "If it was your pleasure to see me in this *bed-rumpled* state again, saer, you need only have said."

Everic patted his face dry and ran a hand through his damp hair, his voice unbothered as he replied, "I will remember that for next time, then."

Reuben grinned widely in response, though he grew distracted whilst watching Everic shrug out of his coat—noticing not just dirt, but a fine, gray powder lining its edges. Quarry dust, perhaps.

The likelihood of Delvanzus wanting to meet in the Ravine was slim, but not impossible. All Reuben need do was ask—Everic would surely explain, considering he originally meant to bring Reuben along.

But that didn't mean Reuben *should* know, given what a liability Waron had made of him.

"I was thinking," he said, trying to distract himself instead, "I could weigh in if you had any correspondence to write?"

Everic shook his head whilst walking to the desk, draping the coat over his chair. "I don't have anything pressing."

"Perhaps a few songs, then? I don't think you've heard one of our crowd favorites," Reuben offered, reaching for his violin on the bedside table, "but it's perfect for travelers and newcomers to the city, Isolde and I have a small dance to—"

He paused, confused as Everic walked over and put a staying hand over his.

"I had something else in mind," Everic murmured, not quite meeting Reuben's eyes.

It wasn't an immediate dismissal, at least. So Reuben smiled and said, "Of course, saer." Waiting with equal parts intrigue and anticipation as Everic headed back over to the desk and opened a drawer, seemingly to retrieve something.

Everic stood upright after, his back facing Reuben for a drawn-out second. Then he let out a slow sigh and turned, holding a vial he was idly twisting between two fingers.

Briefly, Reuben's heart made an irrational leap at the sight—

perhaps Everic realized Reuben needed *some* comfort from his duties and pains, even if it was unhealthy—perhaps, he just wanted something else in return, for giving Reuben voleris—

But the clear bottle didn't contain any of the shimmering liquid famous for sending one's mind to the stars. Instead it looked to be a simple, clear-looking substance. Some kind of base oil, Reuben guessed.

Then, as the realization sunk in, Reuben felt a harsh, anticipatory flip within his gut.

In all his idle musings, he hadn't once considered the simplest, most rudimentary service he *could* offer. He hadn't used base oil to prepare himself before their appointment in weeks, either. Now Reuben felt rather silly for the oversight—even if he had no actual desire to laugh.

Instead, that strange *despairing* emotion returned, aching in his throat. Reuben could only hope he managed to swallow it down before the feeling showed on his face, as he spoke the teasing line he always did when a client presented a toy, or oil, or voleris to initiate sex: "What do you have for me there, saer?"

Then Reuben leaned to the side, slanting his body to let the shirt ride up and show off the curve of his backside.

Everic's eyes flitted to the part of Reuben's body on display, like always, though he replied with a question: "How is your spine feeling?"

"Perfectly at ease," Reuben assured—and, at the moment, spoke the truth. Even if the activity presumably ahead would retract that progress.

"So you won't plan to take voleris for it, upon your return?" Everic pressed further. And when Reuben briefly hesitated, he added, "You can stay as long as you need, until nothing is aching anymore."

Reuben let out a small huff. "If we're waiting *that* long, you'd have better hopes of haggling with the Priesthood vaults to make me your permanent concubine," he replied with a waggle of his brows. Half a tease; half a warning.

Everic, as he suspected, looked rather disgusted at the idea. Though his voice wasn't angry as he approached and asked, "You use it for pain the most, yes?"

Reuben nodded—inwardly correcting, when *he* chose to use it.

He kept himself loose, perfectly at ease like he'd claimed, when Everic sat on the bed and held out the vial as if in offering. Reuben just gave Everic a questioning smile, extending his bare leg to bump against the man's side.

In contrast, Everic looked nervous. For all his confidence in certain matters, perhaps intimacy fell more into the same category as social interactions for the vampire. And despite his long years of existence, there was still a chance Everic simply hadn't slept with anyone else since his long-lost husband.

"I can use my hands and this to help with the tension, if you're willing," Everic said in a very objective tone, nodding at the oil. "Not a perfect remedy—but massaging the pained area seemed to help before."

Reuben raised a brow. He had seen other stellas use base oil for such a practice before or as a part of the main service. But it was a pleasure Sidarchus hadn't bothered to teach and Reuben never learned otherwise. He'd long ago assessed it would be too physically rigorous for him to offer, on top of the already draining act of sex.

A *client* offering? Not impossible, even if it was certainly not something Reuben had experienced himself. But it could be a good excuse to receive permission, however unneeded in this case, to get intimate with another's body. And touching less intimate areas at the start might help Everic ease himself into the rest of it. Based on the short half-minute Everic had already massaged his leg once before,

Reuben was certain he'd be more relaxed as well.

So Reuben hid his surprise and just smiled wider. "How would you like me?"

Everic's eyes flickered up to meet his, still endearingly uncertain. "I'd like to focus on the areas that give you trouble," he said in a formal tone, "if you're alright with laying on your stomach for it."

"My *favorite* position." Reuben let out a soft, practiced giggle with the words—though when it came to penetrative sex, it wasn't even a lie.

He didn't wait for the go-ahead before pulling off the loose shirt and tossing a few pillows out of the way. Ignoring how his breath stuttered a little with more nerves, at the sound of one of Everic's boots being dropped to the ground behind him in the meantime.

They weren't the same kind of nerves Reuben felt around rougher clients or, *Zaldus guide*, Waron. It more reminded him of his first times with Sidarchus, so long ago now. Unsure of himself and worried about successfully pleasing the other person—though less in fear of retribution, than of simply not being enough.

Sidarchus had taught him quite enough in the first two years following his mother's death, of course. From taking Reuben's first innocent kiss, to gradually introducing intercourse, to eventually ridding Reuben of his remaining boundaries and shyness over the act of sex. And Sidarchus's mentorship still informed Reuben's actions to this day, down to the pose he laid himself out in now, arching his back to accentuate the curve of his arse. Which was covered only by a small strip of a lace-edged, linen undergarment, slitted open in the back for ease of access. Last, he laid on one side of his face, carefully splaying his hair to expose his neck and leaving his arms half-raised in a defenseless pose.

By that point, Everic's other boot was off—and as Everic's weight shifted toward him on the mattress, Reuben felt the vampire freeze, then heard the slightest intake of breath.

Presumably, taking in the sight of Reuben almost-naked and lying beneath him. And as Reuben waited for what Everic would do next, it was a struggle not to hold *his* breath, the worst case of nerves yet singeing through him.

Maybe they should have started out more personal than a massage, kissing and facing each other. If the silence went on too long, Reuben might just sit up and initiate it himself.

Then again, if Everic didn't want to be too personal, that could prove disastrous. Despite nerves and his strange despair, Reuben refused to ruin things now that they'd finally made it to this moment. Mostly, because he didn't want to have to anticipate it with Everic any longer.

Maybe, to a smaller degree, because he wanted to know what it was like.

What *Everic* was like.

It'd been the longest fifteen seconds Reuben ever endured, before he decided to prompt, "My lower back always gives me trouble," gesturing back towards his arse. Even if the truth was, *all* of it tended to hurt.

While Everic didn't reply, the words did seem to knock him out of his frozen state. Reuben heard the pop of a cork soon after, and felt the mattress shift before he saw Everic leaning closer in his peripheral—then, finally, the placement of oiled hands on his back.

Reuben jumped at the cold touch, though he quickly settled as Everic spread the oil out from his spine, along the contours of his back and the sloped area just before his buttocks. By the time the pressure of each touch increased, Everic's fingers had already warmed from Reuben's own body heat.

After that, Reuben found himself simply enjoying this part for however long it lasted. He didn't hold back the occasional groan of encouragement, when Everic's fingers found a place that was tight or tender. He kept his breathing deep and slow through the satisfying pain of each knot being kneaded away.

And as Everic added more oil, only to press more insistently up and down the muscle along Reuben's spine, he forgot to anticipate. He forgot to wait for what came next, right up until Everic's hands traveled lower and he heard the man ask, "Can I move this?" with a tug at his undergarment.

Reuben bit his lip, but lifted his hips in answer. His face warmed as Everic carefully pulled the lace down over the swell of his arse and Reuben felt his now-free cock hanging heavier between his legs.

If Everic noticed, he said nothing—only shifted himself once Reuben had settled to straddle Reuben's thighs, before his hands began spreading the oil onto either of Reuben's bare cheeks. Not between them yet, though Reuben couldn't help the way his breath was picking up at every touch, his cock stiffening further against the sheets.

Of course, Everic's next words put out the sparks of pleasure Reuben's body had been lighting up with. "Your spine feels strange," he said in that blunt, tactless way of his, trailing his fingers along the curve of it.

Reuben's mind struggled to process such an observation, much less answer. Not a single customer, in all his years regularly unclothed, had either noticed or deigned to mention such a thing to Reuben.

But then he forgot to respond, distracted when Everic's oiled thumbs pressed deep into the meat of his upper buttocks—making Reuben jolt from the pressure on his nerves, though he soon melted into the painfully good sensation. After a minute of that, Everic moved his thumbs to meet at the tailbone, ever-so-slowly traveling back up Reuben's spine.

Everic paused at the dimpled curve where Reuben's buttocks and back met, and said, "Especially . . . starting right about here."

"Oh?" Reuben said, half-muffled by the mattress, swallowing down a fizzy brew of embarrassment, arousal, and exasperation. "And . . . do you have much knowledge on bone structure?" he huffed whilst shifting uncomfortably, wondering what the man was getting at.

"I've seen my share of bodies," Everic answered in an offhanded tone, "and known a healer or two."

He said nothing more, his thumbs continuing their slow journey up Reuben's back, pausing every now and then as if noting another strange spot. And, with each deep press at those places, the pressure sent a dull, nerve-tingling pain up and down the whole of Reuben's spine. They were the areas along his spine always quick to ache and send sharp spasms, Reuben realized as Everic gave attention to them, the tensed muscle around each spot nearly as hard as stone before Everic's ministrations loosened them.

Reuben's erection didn't fade, but he grew less aware of it again the longer Everic continued, drifting in a pleasure-filled haze. Close to floating, it felt like, in the absence of aches and pains, which Reuben had grown so used to that the lack of them was nothing short of euphoric. And when Everic leaned to reach even higher and Reuben felt a brief, stiff pressure from Everic's trousers nudge the back of his arse, he had few nerves now about the vampire fucking him soon—in fact, his own cock twitched in response.

Everic never dribbled the oil between Reuben's cheeks, however, or unbuttoned his own trousers. His breathing sounded heavier, but he didn't so much as slide a slick finger inside Reuben, after what must have been nearly an hour of touching him, before pulling Reuben's undergarment back in place.

And Reuben truly wanted him to, he realized in despair. Not simply because it would even out tonight's *terribly* unbalanced exchange, either.

Reuben shivered in enjoyment as Everic's nails traced up and down his back before the touches ended—but end they did, leaving Reuben to swallow down his utter confusion before Everic saw it.

Everic already took his blood, his help with letters, his assistance in social settings. And nearly every time Reuben peered into the vampire's mind, attraction for Reuben was there near the forefront. Everic *had* to realize, the moment he asked for it, he could have Reuben's body as well—and tonight, thanks to his considerate efforts, without a worry for Reuben's discomfort.

What else had Everic done all this for?

Reuben carefully sat up as Everic left the bed, off to fetch a spare piece of linen to wipe off the excess oil. Reuben took the opportunity to adjust himself and situated a blanket over his lap.

Once Everic returned and knelt back on the bed, Reuben offered him a small smile, saying, "You've spoiled me terribly."

Everic grasped Reuben's shoulder, gently turning him away before focusing on rubbing the cloth down his spine. "Your back feels better?" he asked once Reuben wasn't facing him.

"Better than it has in a year, at the least." Reuben could only distantly recall the level of pain he'd lived with before Jophiel's experiment now, but he guessed, "Probably even longer than that. Truly, I can't thank you enough."

And that was the problem. That was why Reuben should have never come here tonight in the first place—*he* was supposed to be the one giving a service, not owing Everic for even more.

So when Everic lowered the cloth, Reuben turned back to grab his hand, begging, "Please, there must be *something* I can do for you tonight?"

Everic's hand was limp in Reuben's grasp, his eyes trained downward. "I'd rather see you return to me unpoisoned and in good health, than receive a thousand words of thanks."

Reuben's stomach sank as he let Everic's hand go. All this had been for his body, just not the way he'd thought—Everic simply must *hate* the taste of voleris, and went out of his way to prove Reuben had no excuse to taint his food in the future. It was far too kind a method, when he could just threaten to end their appointments instead . . . but for that, quite consistent with the gentle vampire's behavior thus far.

Reuben inwardly winced at the inevitable fight he'd need to have with Sidarchus, to get voleris off the list—and knew refusing customers' requests for it simply wouldn't be allowed—but still promised, "I swear, I'll refrain from ordering any more."

Only hoping, as he did, that it wasn't another promise he eventually broke.

"Good," Everic nodded. His hips shifted, as if uncomfortable—and upon glancing down, Reuben noticed the state the vampire was still in.

He didn't think twice before pressing, "That's not enough, though," daring to reach a hand towards Everic's lower thigh. Resting it a respectful, but not *too* far distance from the stiff strain in the man's trousers.

Everic's hand shot forward and covered Reuben's, as if to keep it at bay. "Reubie," he said in a low tone, glaring at Reuben now.

Reuben swallowed and decided to press his luck just a bit further—sliding his hand not lower, but around Everic's thigh to gently squeeze the inner, more sensitive part. "But I'd *like* to," Reuben argued meanwhile, biting his lip when he felt Everic's thigh twitch against his grip.

Everic's hand was tensed over Reuben's, though he had yet to pull it away. His glare had become more of a pleading stare, his lips parting around a few shaky intakes of breath. "Reubie, you don't . . ." he whispered, but then just frowned, not finishing the thought.

Reuben let his hand slide a little lower, closer to the stiff line of Everic's erection. His stomach grew jittery with nerves when Everic's hand merely slid down with it.

"I do," Reuben murmured back, despite not knowing exactly what he was arguing. "I want you *so* badly, Everic," was always a safe line to use, though never spoken so truthfully as it was now—and Everic's sharp hitch of breath in answer proved the vampire was discerning, but not *immune* to Reuben's practiced charms after all. "I've wished, imagined how you would touch me," he whispered, and reached for Everic's free hand with his own, guiding it around his hip.

Everic's arm was stiff, barely allowing the movement—but then he continued it of his own accord, grabbing Reuben with a wide, firm grip. Even abandoned Reuben's hand at his thigh in favor of wrapping an arm around Reuben's torso, his eyes flashing dark as he pulled Reuben up to straddle his thighs.

"Yes," Reuben hissed, grinning as he sat down against the erection beneath him and grasped Everic's wide shoulders for leverage.

Everic let out a soft, groaning exhale in response, eyes falling shut. And with the firm, steady pressure of his hand acting as a support against Reuben's lower back, Reuben only felt a small twinge as he made a grinding motion on the vampire's lap.

"I want you," gasped Reuben, warm and overwhelmed at feeling the hard line of Everic's cock rub between his cheeks. Though he came back to himself as Everic's grip tightened, and Reuben realized it was likely a matter of seconds before he lost all control of the situation. So he leaned in for a kiss before he didn't get the chance, murmuring, "I wanted this for *so* long, saer," just as he angled to press his mouth against Everic's parted lips—

Only to be wrenched off Everic's lap and onto the mattress, with such force and speed it was a wonder Reuben only bounced once.

Reuben winced at the jab of pain in his spine—then blinked in confusion when he didn't see Everic moving to hover over him. Nor did he feel Everic spreading his legs to kneel between them.

Reuben pushed himself up on an elbow and found Everic instead standing with a white-knuckled grip on the bed post, anger twisting his features.

Worse, with *disgust* in his eyes.

It was the same expression he'd worn after learning of Reuben's indentured status. No matter what he'd realized this time—it was clearly Reuben's fault once more.

"That was despicable of me," Everic said, low and shaky, his jaw clenched as he began stepping into his boots in quick, jerking movements.

Abruptly, Reuben wanted to laugh. "Just for touching me? I'm a *whore*, Everic," he said with a humorless scoff, not bothering to mind his tone. "This is what I do. This is what I'm *for*."

Never mind his wish for more.

"I know," Everic said, standing upright again with that same disgusted, heated expression. "I know. That is exactly the problem. *That* is what I can't forget."

"Oh, because it's so shameful a thing, to want someone like me?"

Everic's angry glare dissipated at the words—but his blank expression as he regarded Reuben might have been worse.

"How *could* I want you?" he replied in an abruptly neutral tone. Eyes narrowed, before he pointed out, "I don't even know your name."

Reuben stared at him, dumbfounded. A frigid cold began creeping up his spine.

"Saer, I . . ." he started, but found he'd already run out of words.

Everic gave a grim nod in return, as if that was all the answer he needed. "Goodnight, Reubielocks," he said shortly.

When he headed toward the door, Reuben didn't try to stop him. He didn't know if words would return to him at all, much less the right ones.

But the moment the door shut and he was alone, Reuben felt the despair encroach a third time and finally knew it for what it was: a hopeless, all-consuming sorrow he hadn't let himself feel in decades, that he wasn't anything more than the loveless, futureless, pointless *thing* that he was and always would be—until he was no more.

Reuben stared at the door and willed it to open back up again. For Everic to return, and unbreak every tremulous, fragile thing that had just shattered between them.

When it stayed closed, he shut his teary eyes and blew out a long, slow breath.

Neither of them should forget the nature of this business relation-ship, nor the *true* reason Reuben returned each night. Pretending otherwise was only a game that had hurt them both —and if he continued to let Everic blur the lines between hired whore and lover, it would only grow harder and harder to not believe the lie himself.

*Remember what you are, Reubielocks,* Sidarchus's warning came to mind.

Reuben had found the admonition terribly redundant, given the daily reminders of his profession, but he finally understood what his old mentor meant now.

He would *never* be a free man, or someone viable to love, or even a real friend.

In the end, he was Reubielocks—nothing more.

# 17

# GILDED FACADE

Probably, Reuben should have left early. If it was safer, he could have visited Daxus and Nahlia. Instead, he stayed the full night, then slowly got dressed, remade the bed, even sang softly to himself until another hour passed. By then it was clear even sunlight wouldn't force Everic's return. As Reuben exited the chamber, he decided he would just cover the 500 canters for Sidarchus.

He hadn't done a single thing worthy of gold anyways.

Whilst walking into the storage room, however, Reuben paused. The iron door on the adjacent wall was still exposed, left wide open.

He should have just ignored it and walked past. Overcome by morbid curiosity, however, Reuben hummed the incantation of *Light* on his mother's ring before cautiously stepping closer.

Perhaps because it was made of cantergold, the ring always shone far brighter than other items he imbued the spell with and hardly seemed to need a tune at all. But the warm light was not enough to fully pierce the darkness. Even once he reached the doorway, Reuben could only make out the beginnings of an arched tunnel carved out from the limestone, plunging deeper under the mountain as far as his light showed. The air smelled musty and old, an icy breeze tickling Reuben's neck as he stood at its doorway.

Reuben took a single step forward—and jolted at the faint but jarring sound of clanging metal on metal that echoed from its depths. Perhaps just someone smithing where the old dwarf-kind always used to; perhaps a clash of blades.

Either way, Reuben turned and hurried away as if a monster was at his heels.

Then startled all over again, finding Bev in the next room.

"Bev," Reuben sighed in relief, then rounded the table she was sitting at to face her, "I left your coat in Everic's room . . ."

His voice faded as she glanced up from her task, counting up cantergold into stacks with a small but empty, peculiar-shaped chest resting open nearby.

But it wasn't the items or task that surprised him—it was the dark, purplish bruise, swollen and shiny on her cheekbone and forcing her right eye shut.

"What . . . are you alright? What happened?" he asked, dropping his *Light* spell and taking a worried step closer. Then offered, "I know a quick healing tune that could help?"

Bev didn't respond as she shut the small chest. But when he reached out a hand, she stayed still, closing her eyes to allow it.

So Reuben improvised a few lyrics to the melody under his breath, *"If I was a lake / And my beau the sea / I'd carve us a river / For love to flow free."*

As he pulled back, her skin returned to its vibrant, violet-pink hue; Reuben felt a soft swell of pride when not even the slightest bit of discoloration or swelling remained.

Bev didn't look happy, however. Her head ducked down, shoulders hunched as she began sweeping her piles into a large linen bag. Then the infernal woman tied its drawstring shut, holding the sack out to

Reuben with downturned eyes.

"Some is for Isolde," she signed once he took it.

Reuben carefully tied it to his belt, still a bit worried as he nodded in thanks and began to leave.

Then, in his peripheral, Reuben saw Bev pull the small chest towards herself and reopen it—a wink of *gold* now glinting from its once-empty insides.

He stopped in his tracks, eyes widening. Hardly able to wrap his head around the implications of what he'd just seen.

Reuben hurried out before Bev could notice the reaction.

Of course, a chest that produced cantergold *did* explain Everic's bottomless funds. But Reuben had never heard of such a feat of magic. Crowdcraft could create the *illusion* of gold, maybe, and Zaldian godcraft could channel greater powers through the god-given material. Greencraft Reuben knew little of, save that it was grounded in matter the natural world had already provided. And devilcraft was simply the practice of evil, as far as the Gospel of Zald taught. Reuben had never experienced anything to counter those truths, unless he counted Everic's well-meant but still-terrifying charm.

Everic complained he didn't know Reuben, but *clearly* there was much more he hadn't told about himself, Reuben thought as he took his time heading back up to the main ring.

The vampire would likely explain now, if asked. But it was better for them both if Reuben stayed ignorant, blind, and focused on being helpful. Even more, on being "Reubielocks," and avoiding the curiosity and fondness that had corroded his perfect persona.

Reuben alone had never been enough—not in a very long time. He'd never made his mother happy, or successfully comforted her through her deteriorating illness. In fact, in the final days of her life, she regularly winced at the sight of him, and after a bout of spasming pain once said in a weary tone, *At least . . . I won't have to look upon that face again, soon.*

His only consolation was what he'd agreed to do in her last delirious hours. Humbly accepting the godcrafted Rite of Transference, cleansing her of her greatest sin before death: that of being a debtor. Which allowed Oriana the chance to enter the Embrace of Zald and His golden halls, the Zaldian priest at her bedside had explained, instead of eternal, icy darkness—for the small price of risking Reuben's own eternity.

The law assured he would be responsible for her debt in this life regardless. Why guarantee her eternal suffering, over the mere possibility of his own?

Of course, Reuben had more faith in his capabilities to pay off the amount at 14 years of age than he did now.

But *Reubielocks* didn't have a dead mother. He didn't have a mountain of debt, or pains in his back, or a fear of knives, or a problem with voleris. He wore beautiful clothing, danced and played his violin, and did everything in his power to please his customers each night. He was a gilded facade who laughed and teased and charmed, and in return was adored, admired, and lusted after.

There was little he wouldn't do, if it meant a cantergold.

When Reuben started showing through the cracks of the facade, *that* was when a high-paying customer discarded him. That was the moment he lost touch with his audience, forgot how to please, and made countless mistake after mistake. It was no wonder he'd made so many with Everic—for whatever reason, the vampire drew Reuben out of his persona far too often.

And he'd only suffered for it, Reuben thought as he neared the bordello. All Reubielocks needed was gold to be happy; if Reuben could remember that and even more, *embrace* such a mindset, he would be ecstatic right now about the savings he'd accumulated.

Everic's words about not wanting him wouldn't still be reverberating through his head, repeatedly stabbing him in the chest with each echo.

Reuben nodded at the bordello security guard he passed walking along the back alleyway of the Starlet Eye, trying to focus on the future. There was no surety as to when he'd get to leave the bordello again—Delvanzus's ball was about two weeks away, so Reuben hoped no longer than that—especially with how Everic left things. But Reuben should still make good on his promise to stop ordering voleris, the only pitiful favor Everic had requested in return for all his attentive care last night.

Reuben was just considering how well he could stomach a bit of uncomfortable intimacy with his manager to get the request approved, when he noticed a tall, hooded figure quickly approaching from a side alley in the corner of his eye.

His whole body moved on instinct—ducking and feinting backward, right before a long arm grasped the air where he'd just been.

Waron still caught his wrist a few seconds later, but that gave Reuben enough time to wordlessly hum the melody for *Soothe* in a hushing, pacifying murmur. Watching wide-eyed as the infernal man's other dark-veined, corrupted-looking hand reached to cover Reuben's mouth . . . and then faltered.

Waron's black, pupil-less eyes went half-lidded from under his hood, his body relaxing from its aggressive position.

"Guards! *Guards!*" Reuben yelled while he still could, trying to yank his wrist from Waron's grip.

But while *Soothe* briefly calmed harsher emotions like aggression and panic, it did nothing against complicated things like passion, lust, or obsession. Reuben wasn't surprised when Waron's grip grew less painful but held firm, even as his heart banged against his ribcage. He looked around desperately as Waron spoke in a slow voice, "I just want to talk, Reubielocks," and tried to crowd him up against the wall still.

Reuben didn't have time to wait and hope the security guard around the corner had heard him. So he let Waron pin him to the side of the building in order to focus, staring into Waron's eyes and singing as clear and melodious as he could, *"Mellifluous, diaphanous / Illustrious, euphonious,"* only praying to Zaldus that it would sound charming enough to work.

He felt tears of sheer relief spring to his eyes when Waron's grip loosened entirely.

"Such a pretty voice . . . from an even prettier mouth," the infernal man sighed with a small smile and glassy eyes. His hand released Reuben, reaching to touch his lips.

Reuben wrenched away. He'd bought himself an hour before Waron came back to his senses again—and Reuben should only need a few minutes.

He called again, louder and with more fervor, "Guards! *Help!*"

Since he perfected its melody at the age of 16, *Charming Words* was a much more powerful spell than any of his other tricks. If he got someone to fetch the piazza sentry guards, Reuben could force the damning truth to spill from Waron's lips about who he was and all he'd done. The Allunata's current leader would get arrested, undoubtedly executed—and, most importantly, Reuben would never have to see him or endure his touch again.

Waron frowned as Reuben moved away, following after him. "My client doesn't like how much you're sneaking off," he said, looking childishly upset that Reuben was out of reach. "You—I might just need to find you a new cage, little dove . . ."

Reuben reached the corner of the building and glanced down the long back wall—a bolt of panic running through him as he realized the guard must have rounded to the other side. "Who are they?" he decided to distract Waron with a question.

In any other circumstance, it would have been a satisfying thing to watch the spell do its work. Waron looked obstinate for a moment, but that quickly faded to reluctance, and just a second later relaxed into submission.

"Some higher up with deep pockets," he shrugged, getting close to Reuben again.

It was only then that Reuben noticed a strange mark burned into the pale skin centered just between Waron's collarbones: a narrow diamond with smaller, intricate shapes within, detailed in a way Reuben couldn't quite make out at this distance. He wondered if it was very new—or if, in his teary panic and then starry-eyed state during Waron's attack, he simply hadn't noticed the addition before.

As Waron took another step, it almost looked to Reuben like a piece of the twelve-pronged symbol embossed on cantergold pieces; that, or a geometric eye.

"They keep themselves anonymous," Waron kept talking, reaching up a hand again, "but—"

"Don't touch me," Reuben snapped. Once Waron's arm dropped, Reuben's eyes searched desperately for anyone else around. But the side alley Waron had come from looked just as empty.

"My turn: that leech you go to every other night—how *is* he keeping you alive?" Waron asked, his smile hazy but still edged in malice. "Or does he take turns on his servant girl as well? I've been meaning to track her down for some time . . . make her into a nice display, just like he did to one of ours . . ."

Reuben tried not to pay attention to the ugly words, unhappily reminded of the fact *Charming Words* couldn't make up for a charmless personality.

But it seemed Reuben would just have to bring Waron to a sentry official himself. "Come, this way," he said with a beckoning hand.

For the first time, Waron's inner will actually put up a fight. He took a step—then with great difficulty, paused and took a halting step backwards. "I—I've said what I needed to . . . even if I couldn't give you the—the *usual* attention you like, I shouldn't . . ." the imposing man muttered, and in shaky, hesitant movements, managed to start backing away. "Just know—if you keep up this habit of jumping into carriages, disappearing for days on end, I'll need to do something about it. I'll be *glad* to."

Reuben felt a conflicting flash of dread and relief, realizing Waron was likely about to run. "Wait, please," he tried to ploy, but couldn't even get himself to sound half-convincing. Not when all he wanted *was* for Waron to be gone.

"We're never far," Waron said, shaking his head as if to clear it. Then he smiled wider at Reuben, adding, "And if I know you at all, Reubielocks . . . you'll give me a reason to return for you soon."

Reuben could have kept trying to persuade him to wait—he very well could have succeeded, too—but the guard was still not showing up. Those usually stationed at the front of the bordello didn't seem to have heard his shouts either. And if Waron *was* apprehended . . . how likely was he to spill Everic's secret to authorities as well?

When Waron turned on his heel and strode back towards the alley, Reuben didn't call after him. He only watched Waron enter its shadows—and let out a small gasp of shock as, with a quick flash of the man's silver-handled blade, the shadows seemed to warp and swallow Waron whole.

For the second time in an hour, Reuben *ran*.

He kept a punishing pace even after dashed around to the front of the bordello and bursting through its doors, up the faded rug of the grand stairway—ignoring the security guards just emerging from the kitchens with what was likely their breaking-fast meal in their hands. And, once in his room, he slammed the door shut behind him, leaning against it while his chest bounced up and down around harsh, rapid breaths.

Reuben stared at every shadow in his bedchamber for a long, terrified minute, until his breathing finally steadied and *some* hope grew in him that Waron wouldn't reappear out of the dim.

But even once undressed and lying in his bed, he couldn't hope to sleep. His heart wouldn't calm, his spine ached once more, and three ghostly visages haunted his mind, howling over every other thought: Everic's look of disgust, Waron's anticipatory grin, and the vials of voleris that would take both of the painful images away, still waiting for Reuben in the vanity drawer.

He didn't end up sleeping a wink before the next night of work began.

Isolde acted distant over the next few days, but Reuben didn't know how to breach the distance. Especially considering the truth would only anger her and betray Everic further.

Still, he hoped good news would make up for that soon. Reuben hadn't carefully counted up his savings in more than a week, with how busy his current clientele kept him—but he knew the number was close to 10,000, nearing half of what Sidarchus said was Isolde's overall debt. If she put at least 10 cantergold of each working night's earnings towards her debt, like Reuben until recently, and dealt with a similar 10% interest rate, that meant the last three years of her labor had mostly paid for that steep accruing interest.

So if Reuben could turn 10,000 gold in to Sidarchus all at once, it should *more* than cut her years of indenturement in half.

He focused his imagination on the relief that would fill her eyes the moment he could tell her, whenever she gave him a look of discontent now. In the meantime, he kept performing well, taking on his usual amount of customers over the next few nights, and trying his absolute best to be nothing less, nothing more than *Reubielocks*.

More challenging, he tried to ignore the discomfort that rose up in him whenever any mention of the Hollows, or the Ravine, or the Zaldian Priesthood happened to enter conversation, quickly teasing or offering a compliment to change the subject.

Worst of all—he forced himself to at least get rid of his current stock of voleris, even if he couldn't face Sidarchus quite yet. It was easy enough to do in theory: dump the tiny vials into his chamber pot or throw them in the kitchen waste buckets downstairs. To avoid just putting it off, Reuben decided on the latter.

But in practice, he only made it halfway down the corridor before running into Gringoll, who stopped and exclaimed, *"Zald's balls,* Reubie—where are you going with all *that?"*

Reuben's hand clutched the six vials tighter. "Oh, I . . . I think they might have been mixed wrong," he lied. "Better not risk it, right?"

Gringoll took a step in front of Reuben. "Well, if they're just getting discarded, *I'd* be happy to take them off your hands."

Reuben hesitated. He discouraged Isolde from ever using the potion, if she could help it—but if Gringoll would be paying for his own supply anyway, was it wrong to refuse?

He didn't answer for long enough that the dwarvish man put a hand on his forearm, leaning in with wide eyes and a salacious smirk. "I could give you something in return?"

At that, Reuben recoiled, feeling a sick twist in his stomach. It was like being confronted with his own reflection after an overdose of voleris—except this image was even more visceral than the dark circles and reddened eyes a mirror exposed.

He pulled away from Gringoll's touch. "I . . . I wouldn't want anyone getting ill from a bad batch," he responded quietly.

Later, whilst emptying each vial into the waste bins, all Reuben had to do was think of the desperate, consuming hunger he could detect behind Gringoll's eyes to force his faltering hand to continue.

More days passed—long enough Reuben wondered if he indeed wouldn't hear from the vampire until closer to the guild ball itself. And when Everic finally *did* send for him, almost a week after Reuben's shameful mistake, it wasn't Bev who came. Reuben only belatedly recognized one of the new guards vetted by her as the tan-skinned, red-horned woman approached him in the bordello hall and casually stated, "The boss wants you this evening."

"Saer Payne?" Reuben checked, raising a brow at her bored nod. "Is Bev alright?"

"She's busy," the woman shrugged and, after Reuben hummed a quick tune under his breath, his crowdcraft discerned as truthful despite the vagueness.

So Reuben didn't question her further before grabbing his veil to go.

In the days he'd stayed indoors the mountain air had cooled considerably, chilling Reuben as it whipped through the alleyways of the city that night. Reuben thought of Bev offering her coat as he braced against it and, despite the little time they'd actually spent talking, found himself missing her quiet, stalwart presence. Even more so, when he realized the new woman was leading him to a certain small property in the main ring.

"Is there a reason we're going here?" he asked, clutching his veil against the blustering wind.

The infernal woman shot him a strange look. "Because he lives here?" she said, as if it was a stupid question. Reuben kept hesitantly following, reminding himself Bev had *approved* of this woman, before she stopped at the door and gestured at it. "The boss is already out with my brother Mezza, but he said they'd return shortly."

Reuben glanced at the darkened sky—it couldn't have been more than an hour since sunset, though the cloud cover made it difficult to tell—and did his best to believe her. His resolution to not let himself show through the cracks was already being tested, however, as he stepped inside the abode and heard the door shut behind him.

It was easier than last time to keep down his panic, at least. When Reuben found one of his new outfits waiting for him in the bedchamber, he imagined Everic selecting each piece from the wardrobe, transporting it here from the Hollows, and carefully draping the ensemble over the mattress all with Reuben in mind. The idea alone helped him to relax as he dressed in the ruffled blouse and buttoned a fitted green vest over it.

No Jophiel appeared, as usual. Reuben's fear seemed more like paranoia now, given just how many times he'd needlessly worried about her showing up in the past almost-three months without cause.

And despite how much Reuben hated what she had done to him . . . he would never have secured this job otherwise, he reminded himself.

When the guard led him out to the carriage that had just arrived and Reuben saw Everic speaking to the other infernal guard, a pit of nerves squirmed in his stomach. Crude memories intruded as well—*Reuben's hand inching down towards the vampire's clothed erection, climbing onto his lap to grind against it, Everic letting out a sharp gasp, grip tightening, eyes falling shut—*

Reuben ended up averting his gaze slightly, when Everic noted his approach and turned his way.

"Reubie," he said with a short, business-like nod. "Apologies for the wait."

Reuben wondered if he meant the last ten minutes or the past six days.

Regardless, he gave one of his perfect, demure smiles from under the veil and replied, "Oh never you mind, saer—as I've said, it's simply my pleasure to be here, so long as *you* have need of me."

Everic let out a slow sigh. "Needs can be nebulous things," he muttered, before holding out a hand to help Reuben up the carriage step.

This event was exclusive, invitations sent only to those already gifted a token from the silk merchant guild, and was held at the guild master's tall property just below the edge of High Ring. The main attraction was a three-roomed gallery featuring various Dijheri art pieces, including brightly-colored sculptures and a landscape painting that portrayed a blood-red desert with a stormy green sky billowing above.

As they toured the collection Reuben spotted the contrasting, monotone style used in Sazzera as well, of course, which focused more on portraying depth and religious iconography. One larger painting stood out in particular: a rare depiction of Zaldus, taller than any elf yet wider than any dwarf, covered in full, gold-plated armor as His hands cradled a burning phoenix in place of the sun, held over a jagged skyline.

Everic gave him a look when Reuben stood in front of it too long—and Reuben had to hold in a shiver as he tore his gaze away. "Impressively imposing," he recovered, managing a half-smile Everic didn't return before they moved on.

As the scattered attendants regrouped for a round of wine, Reuben made sure to tease and charm and impress without ever touching the vampire. And with Delvanzus missing, he enjoyed interacting with the infernal merchant, Saer Kapriyah, and the elvish mason, Saer Orlyn, the most. The two seemed to be close friends with each other and needed little prompting from Reuben to gossip about what prominent guests might be seen at the guild's grand ball.

By the end, Orlyn even offered, "I know a few of the gold keepers that will be present, if you'd like an introduction."

A successful outing, all told, though it didn't quite feel that way after when Everic said in the carriage, "I have further business—we can either drop you off at my main ring property or the bordello for the remainder of the night. Whichever you'd like."

In truth, Reuben wished to escape from the world a little longer, preferably in Everic's hideaway, and with Everic present.

But Reubielocks just smiled brightly and said, "I'd love a ride back to the bordello—thank you kindly for the offer, saer."

The next appointment was not a social event. Three nights later, with only three more to go before the ball itself, the other infernal guard—Mezza, if Reuben recalled correctly—showed up to take Reuben down to Everic's hideaway, all the while chatting away about the new things he'd seen in the piazza market that week, the fancy food "the boss" had his sister Zeya buy, and the multiple women he was trying to pursue at once now that he had the "pick of the city."

In Everic's slowly-expanding crew, Mezza was the first one who actually liked to chat a lot, Reuben observed. It should have been a breath of fresh air, even a chance to glean more information—but Reuben only found himself resenting having to play Reubielocks on the way there as well.

There was a purpose for him to focus on once he arrived, at least. When Reuben entered Everic's hidden bedchamber, he found the vampire scowling over a haphazard pile of at least a dozen missives on his desk.

Reuben relaxed, grateful to have clear parameters for the night. "That's quite an impressive queue you've buried yourself in," he observed whilst approaching. "Am I to dig you out tonight, saer?"

Everic's scowl faded into something closer to disgruntlement. He gestured at the nearby stool and sighed, "We may need to fetch a shovel."

With that, they spent more than half the night on correspondences—even despite setting aside three missives from Saer Artris to be ignored.

Both a headache and a sharp back ache had started to bother Reuben by the time Everic suggested a break. Reuben readily agreed when Everic offered to fetch refreshments, though nerves began to eat at him at the idea of unstructured time with the vampire again.

So he kept the conversation steered toward Everic's goals between bites, nodding at all the missives: "You have plenty of good connections with the upper working class, I'd say. But for the next step, our best chance is this ball. I'm afraid I only know a few of the dances, but I could try to show you . . ."

He trailed off when Everic started shaking his head. "Saer Delvanzus walked me through the easiest of them a few days ago."

Reuben blinked, and then swallowed down a small pit of jealousy before he smiled. "Wonderful. Otherwise, it looks like we have three potentials to focus on who should be present: two gold keepers that Saer Orlyn can introduce you to, and that estate manager of House Feluca who has investments in the quarry—am I missing anyone?"

Everic shrugged. "I heard there's a *chance* Magnatus Vyllorence shows, but it's not likely."

"The one with the highly sensitive arse?" Reuben remembered, smirking.

He quickly regretted it, however, at the fond amusement that flashed in Everic's eyes, and Reuben's heart panging with something suspiciously close to *longing* in return.

"The very same," the vampire replied, his lips edging toward a smile.

Reuben broke eye contact and focused on eating for a minute, though he hardly noticed what was on the platter whilst admonishing himself for already getting too familiar with the vampire again.

Everic filled the silence soon enough, speaking more seriously, "You haven't had any . . . safety concerns of late, have you? Any sign of the Allunata, at the bordello or around the area?"

Reuben nearly choked on a blackberry. "I—no, of course not," he replied in haste, ignoring the cold flashes of fear running down his spine in favor of searching Everic's face. And when he found little but the usual frown, pressed, "Why? Did you hear something? Did they come after you again? Is *Bev*—?"

"She's fine. We had a small run-in, since the last time you were here," Everic nodded at the room around them. "But the two fled soon after Bev caught them looking around the first few rooms— apparently searching for evidence of what devil I worship, from what she overheard," he said with a grim smile.

Reubielocks should have answered, *Oh, how frightful! I am utterly relieved you both survived such a dangerous encounter, saer.*

But when Reuben's mouth opened, he couldn't help but ask: ". . . Do you?"

Everic's smile faded. "I don't *worship* anything, or anyone."

After Reuben gave a hasty nod in answer, however, Everic's eyes softened—and Reuben's whole body stiffened as Everic rested a hand over his on the desk.

Everic said, "I do abide by what I personally believe to be right— just not out of any hope for eternal reward. Even the old gods would reject my soul now, I'm sure. But what is *good* . . . often eludes me." He sighed, squeezing Reuben's hand once before letting go.

Reuben bit his lip, unsure if he understood. He was far too frightened still at the idea of Allunata coming *here*, to this hideaway he'd considered a quiet oasis for some time, to focus much on Everic's vague words. And—more shameful—far too distracted by the simple sensation of Everic's touch, after almost two weeks deprived of it.

"You think more about it than many Zaldian acolytes, I'm sure,"

Reuben recovered with a small, tremulous smile.

Everic's expression darkened. "What is there to think about, when good and evil have already been strictly defined for you?" Then he turned back to regard the last few missives, declaring, "That's enough for tonight. We've made plenty of connections in the main ring's circle of influence. You're right—it's time to start setting our sights *higher.*"

# 18

# ACCEPTABLE TERMS

The grand ball at the Mason Guild Hall had been anticipated for weeks across the main ring. Besides taking place on the eve of the seventh trade council, it marked the first days of the new season, a celebration of summer toils giving way to an abundant autumn harvest. Even some of Reuben's clients like Caterina mentioned the event, though she lamented it being outside her own social circle.

On the night of its arrival, Reuben spent hours getting ready. For at least half of that time, he was applying rouge, kohl, and gold dust to his face, then weaving a few beaded strings and singular green glass beads into his hair—though he also switched out the piercings in his ears, buffed his nails, moisturized every inch of his body, and even spent a little time polishing his mother's ring before slipping it onto his pinky finger.

Given how important the night was, no time could be wasted on a walk through the city. Both Mezza and Zeya came to him just after sunset, together carrying in an absurd number of boxes that held the most expensive, elaborate ensemble he'd been fitted for yet: a green silk doublet and matching hose worn underneath a slitted, gold-embroidered pellanda in a deep, blushing rose color, its wide bombard sleeves reaching close to the floor. The tailor had even been so kind as to include a custom veil with it—a cluster of silk roses to pin in his hair from which a white netted material flared, dipping just low enough to shade Reuben's eyes.

When Reuben followed the two uniformly-dressed infernal guards down the staircase wearing the ensemble, he wasn't surprised when most of the bordello patrons in the hall turned his way, wide-eyed and openly staring.

"Yes, this is our most *sought-after* stella, the stunning Reubielocks, everyone!" Sidarchus announced to those nearby, meeting Reuben at the stairway's end. "You look stunning, my dear," he leaned in and said more quietly, eyeing Reuben with what surprisingly seemed like jealousy. "Be sure to tell me all the details when you return?"

Reuben nodded, though part of him strangely recoiled at the thought of confiding in Sidarchus further, especially with how stiffly Sidarchus smiled whilst waving Reuben off.

Finally they made it outside, Everic's carriage just a short distance away. And once Zeya helped Reuben into its cabin—Reuben taking extra care not to let the full-length piece snag on the step—he sat down only for his own breath to be taken away.

Everic always looked handsome in a weathered coat and his dark, shoulder-length hair mussed, of course. Just as he did wearing his more-tailored clothing to social events. But with his hair smoothed entirely back for the first time, the defined structure of his pale temples and cheekbones stood out on stark display. His eyes, a deep green tonight, widened at Reuben in return, playing off nicely with the dark, cobalt blue of his own pellanda, high-collared and patterned with silver coils.

"You look positively ravishing tonight, saer," Reubielocks said, whilst Reuben held in, *How I wish I could have stolen just one kiss*

278

*from you, that night.*

Everic blinked, regaining his composure as the carriage started moving. "Thank you—though I will look terribly underdressed with the likes of *you* at my arm," he said with an appreciative gesture towards Reuben.

"Hmm . . . perhaps a bit of kohl and rouge is missing," Reuben teased, nodding at Everic's face.

"I'll have to send for you a day prior to these affairs then, in future," Everic said, grinning wryly when Reuben gave him a look of confusion. "I wouldn't trust my own *blind* hand for such a task," the vampire pointed out.

Reuben flushed in embarrassment as he finally caught on. "It's not just a myth, then, about vampires and mirrors?"

Everic's smile faded. "No more than I am one," he muttered.

If Reuben had worried at all about how elaborate the tailor made his ball ensemble, he didn't once their carriage arrived. While the main ring boasted of far less wealth than High Ring, they certainly knew how to show off what they could—some wore large headdresses and plumed hats, while others had fur-lined capes trailing behind them, all with equally impressive doublets or gowns underneath their wide-sleeved pellanda.

The guild hall was decorated in the same extravagance, with gold-fringed curtains draped over the ballroom and curled around every pillar, hundreds of candles lit up in multiple crystal chandeliers. The huge room was still filling up with guests, but already the number intimidated Reuben—he didn't blame Everic for the tight grip the man kept around their looped arms.

By the time the hired musicians started up a lively dancing tune from a second floor balcony, it was a crowd someone could easily get lost in. Reuben was relieved when they finally found a few familiar faces, Saers Randal Kapriyah and Blanca Orlyn waving them over from the opposite side of the dance floor.

When they reached them, Orlyn shouted over the music, "What a fine turn out for the guild! Here—you *must* meet my friend, Saer Payne, this is Gold Keeper Antonia Dulfur . . ."

Antonia Dulfur was another rare human living in Sazzera, friendly and eager as they were introduced. She also seemed *extra* enthusiastic towards Everic despite his stiffness in return—and, just a few minutes into the conversation, batted her eyelashes as she asked, "Would you bless me with a dance, saer?"

Everic gave him a look of utter betrayal, when Reuben unlinked their arms to let the two go for the next set.

"I'm afraid Antonia might be interested in more *personal* connections than just business," Saer Kapriyah said around a wide, sharp-toothed grin as the three of them watched Everic and Saer Dulfur on the dance floor. The infernal man's adorned horns jangled as he swung his head to survey Reuben, waggling his brows while he asked, "Should we worry about her putting you out of a job, Reubielocks?"

Reuben observed the deep, lined grimace on Everic's face as he turned through the dance's next steps, and let out an indelicate snort. "I'd like to see her *try*," he huffed, thinking of his own failure to fully capture Everic's affections—despite getting all the way to half-naked and oiled on the vampire's lap.

Kapriyah and Orlyn both snickered in answer.

Afterward, Everic was quick to pull Reuben away and up onto a second floor balcony, already shaking his head before he said, "Not her."

Reuben hid a smile and placed a hand lightly on the man's forearm. "Did she not seem like a valuable contact? I don't think it would prove difficult, even for you, to charm her enough she introduces you to the magnatus of her house, and then you'd be one step closer to High Ring—"

"Not her," Everic repeated, his words clipped and short. "I'm here to do business, nothing more."

"Well, of course," Reuben agreed, trying not to sound impatient, "it's only that, when you're working with people, business can take many forms—"

"I am not so good an actor as *you*, Reubie, that I can easily pretend interest when I feel nothing," Everic cut in sharply.

Reuben opened his mouth, then shut it, swallowing hard. Wishing to deny it—but unable to, despite everything in him that wanted to scream, *I never have to pretend with you.*

It was a lie anyway. Reuben *did* have to pretend—he had to put on a smile, act as if Everic's words hadn't just cut him to the quick, and reply in a neutral tone, "That's no issue, saer. We still have two other candidates to consider for the night."

Saer Orlyn hadn't seen her other gold keeper friend yet, so in the meantime, Everic and Reuben looked around for Delvanzus, who had promised to introduce Everic to House Feluca's estate manager.

When the two finally found Saer Aldo Delvanzus, the guild master was not near the ballroom at all—instead, Delvanzus stood conversing with a small group in the same billiard room where Reuben had first met the dwarf.

At first, Reuben returned Delvanzus's bright, dimpled smile when they noticed Everic and Reuben approaching, relieved to see a familiar, trusted face. But Reuben quickly felt that smile fade as he noticed Saer Artris standing next to the guild master.

And then a strange *chill* ran over him, as his eyes moved to the individual standing on Artris's other side.

"Saer Payne, Reubielocks!" Delvanzus ushered them over, though if he hadn't been holding on to Everic's arm, Reuben wasn't sure if he could have kept his legs moving. It was hard enough not to stare as they approached Delvanzus, Artris, and the gold-and-white clad figure with them, who wore a sharp, tailored uniform far removed from the opulent designs of other guests, as well as a white headdress with an intricate gold mask hanging down to fit over their face.

*Five priests masked in gold*, Everic had said of those attending the trade council.

Reuben could only hope this wasn't someone so high-ranked—but he ducked his head and stared at the floor regardless, sweat prickling at his neck. In a panic, as he remembered he was wearing the least concealing veil he'd *ever* owned, and right in front of a high priest of the Zaldian Priesthood.

"I've been meaning to find you both," Delvanzus said once Everic stood beside them, a grin in their voice. "So many people to introduce you to!"

"Yes, and what are the chances?" Saer Artris agreed, sounding utterly pleased with himself. "This is my employer, the Magnatus Lenaphon, Head of House Luthur, High Priest and General of Security, who I was *just* telling all about you, Saer Payne—oh, and that whore always on your arm."

Reuben felt Everic stiffen, and quickly tightened his grip in answer, reaching up to lightly stroke the vampire's tensed arm.

"*Micah*," Delvanzus admonished in the meantime, and when Reuben snuck a glance up, saw how anger significantly hardened the guild master's usually round, jovial face.

"'Companion' is an acceptable enough term in polite company—so long as Saer Payne's status is unmarried, of course," came a smooth feminine voice from the masked figure, now certainly confirmed as one of the five high priests.

"Of course, Your Radiance," Saer Artris conceded with a smirk.

Everic blew out a sharp breath. With far too much heat to his tone, he said, "A *gilded* blessing, magnatus. You are far from the Aureate Cathedral tonight—especially on the eve of a council meeting. Are you here to seek perspective from the common man?"

There was a brief silence, made a bit unsettling by the expressionless mask staring at them all the while. Then Lenaphon Luthur cocked her head and replied, "Do you have perspective to give, child?"

When Everic didn't answer right away, Saer Artris jumped in, "Well, Your Radiance, *I* for one don't think we should just hand over cantergold plate armor to the Dijheri, if the matter comes up again."

Another guest in the circle agreed, "Even with the Ravine's expansion projects, it's a rare commodity, not to mention the craftsmanship required. There's little of equal worth Dijher could offer in return."

"But it is *far* superior to steel—stronger, lighter," Delvanzus argued. "And if they end up doing the fighting and we the supplying, is it not in our best interest?"

Artris chuckled, "Well, perhaps a few of their chattel would be worth the trade. Our indentured labor could learn a thing or two from their work ethic—"

"Slavery only ensures a forever-reluctant labor force," a dwarvish woman near Reuben countered. "Whereas indenturement encourages the sinner toward reform. Right, Your Radiance? When they are not beyond saving, of course."

"The Priesthood always leans towards mercy when we can," Lenaphon answered in a genial, diplomatic tone. "Though . . . there are more heretics and criminals than ever, I'm afraid, working in the dark and threatening our bright prosperity."

"Can't have that, not with a war incoming," Artris agreed around a pleased smile. "Especially considering how many in this city are—well, *predisposed* to devilcraft, if you understand," and his eyes flickered to the side—towards where the horned figure of Saer Kapriyah had just entered the room, Reuben realized with a small flash of indignation.

But he couldn't focus on his own anger. Everic's body had tensed so much Reuben worried a single word more would erupt him into a dark, devilcrafted mist. Reuben reached up and once again stroked the forearm still linked with his own, hoping the touch provided at least a small distraction, if not comfort.

Even as the group grew more passionate, talking over each other on the progressing topic, Lenaphon's masked face never moved. From here, Reuben couldn't see much of anything behind the small, diamond-shaped eye holes in the ornate mask . . . and yet somehow he suspected her gaze had not strayed from Everic since the conversation began.

Eventually Delvanzus spoke over everyone, "I'm sure we've given Magnatus Lenaphon much to think about before tomorrow! Now, I hear the minstrels are taking a needed break from their performing— shall we fetch a violin for you to play, Reubielocks?"

Reuben had no great desire to perform tonight, but he was enjoying the current social atmosphere even less. He was used to being the inferior person in any given group, of course, but trying to interact around a Zaldian priest was an altogether different feeling. Not just like he was lesser than the woman in front of him, as with everyone else—but like he shouldn't even *exist* in her presence.

He hadn't been useful to Everic yet, and many guild members in the room already were cheering at the chance to hear him again. So Reuben allowed Delvanzus to usher him over to the small performing area, a violin soon fetched for him from the various instruments available.

The violin didn't hold the same grooves and familiar weight as his mother's, but Reuben only needed a minute longer to tune and adjust the bow hair before he jumped into a set of upbeat numbers, taking the opportunity to read the crowd all the while.

It took a bit longer to channel through, but soon enough Reuben could *feel* through the violin like always: a merchant standing at the door, for instance, wondering where Reuben worked and how to book an appointment with him. One mason guild member near the back listening with a melancholic sort of longing, wishing to be standing closer to Saer Delvanzus in the crowd's center.

Artris's focus moved back and forth between Everic and Lenaphon with an anticipatory sort of excitement Reuben didn't like the feel of at all. And Everic—Reuben quickly skipped over a read of the vampire's emotions, telling himself to stop wasting time. He didn't want to know anyway, unsure if it would feel better or worse to sense no attraction from Everic anymore.

Then a thick, suffocating dread invaded his every sense.

Reuben abandoned his surveillance of the remaining crowd as his attention snagged on a familiar, *malicious* intent in its midst.

He strung out a note far longer than needed, eyes flickering desperately over the overcrowded room for a sign of Waron. Or even a *shadow*, given what he'd seen the infernal man do a week before—but the small room's abundance of candles, even at this late hour, left little refuge for darkness.

Reuben's fingers were beginning to shake at the overwhelming, unrelenting force of the feeling, too much to even play off as vibrato. More viscerally than he'd ever felt it—*angrier*, too. He finished his third song early with a distracting burst of illusory sparkles and abandoned the violin before the cheers had even finished. Then Reuben fled the room to avoid falling apart in front of the audience— or waiting around to get killed by one of them.

It was hard to find a single private space in the guild hall not already overrun by party guests. Reuben ended up between two pillars near the front entryway, shadowed enough that those heading up the stairs past him didn't notice Reuben leaned up against one with his head buried in his hands, forcing slow, shuddering breaths in and out through his lungs.

Or all but *one* of the passing guests didn't notice. Reuben jumped at the touch of a gloved hand on his own—glancing up to see Everic's shadowed face lined with concern.

"I'm sorry, saer," Reuben breathed out, glancing over Everic's shoulder fearfully, "just give me a minute, I'll return and we can ask Delvanzus about the estate manager—"

"You're shaking," Everic pointed out, taking a step closer and putting a barring hand against the other pillar—and perhaps Reuben would have felt trapped if it was anyone else boxing him in like this. Instead he relaxed at being further shielded from the masses, calm enough to even feel exasperated when Everic asked, "Was it what Saer Artris said?"

Reuben let out a sharp, disbelieving breath. "When he called me a whore? Everic, I call *myself* that."

Everic's eyes darkened. "No—about the indentured labor."

Reuben bit his lip, unsure of just how honest he *could* be. "Not that. No, someone in the crowd, they—I . . . I think they want me dead," his voice fell to a whisper at the admission.

Reuben thought of the three times he'd felt the sensation before: first, performing in the bordello hall, the very same night he'd met Everic. Second, during the private performance with Adina, if the hazy, drugged memory could be trusted. Third, just before Waron began cutting the truth out of him.

And now again—each time in an entirely new, unrelated context.

"Dead or worse, anyway, whatever that looks like," he finished with a shudder.

The lines on Everic's face deepened. "Who?"

"I don't—it's just a *feeling*, really. I don't know its source," Reuben admitted, biting his lip as he waited for a dismissal.

Instead, Everic took Reuben's hand and pulled him out from the alcove. "We're leaving," he declared.

Reuben stumbled to follow, eyes wide. Warmed by how quick Everic was to believe him—however undeserving—but worried now that he was making the vampire abandon all their hard work on a whim. "No, but—saer, wait—"

"Ah, there you are!" Saer Artris stood on the stairs just below them, wearing a bright grin. "Saer Payne: my house leader wishes to express great surprise and appreciation at the talent your *companion* exhibited tonight."

Everic glared and moved around Artris, replying, "She can send a letter."

Artris simply followed. "Oh, but she *insists* you both join us for an exclusive little party taking place next week. Your business interests have impressed me, and your whore's musical talents have impressed her—she will even deign to provide you a city pass, should you need it, so that you may enter High Ring and attend at her private estate."

Everic's eyes flashed; he turned back to face Artris with an expression Reuben could only describe as murderous.

"Thank you, Saer Artris," Reuben stepped in. "Please excuse my good saer—he finds the quieter, more refined parties far more enjoyable. We were just leaving, but please, send an invitation our way, no city pass needed."

Saer Artris's eyes narrowed at Everic before he slowly nodded. "Very well. Magnatus Lenaphon looks forward to making closer acquaintance with the both of you," he said, pulling a small token from his pocket and holding it out to Everic.

When the vampire didn't reach for it, eventually Artris sighed and held it out to Reuben instead.

The piece was embossed with cantergold and had been melded into the geometric, twelve-pronged shape of the Zaldian Priesthood, but otherwise seemed of similar size and weight to a guild token—and Reuben remembered then that the Priesthood had once been a guild as well, though he had no idea they employed the same methods for invitations and favors still. He curled his hand around the token and nodded at the gold keeper with a quick smile before turning away.

Now Reuben was the one pulling a reluctant *Everic* towards the exit, hopefully before the vampire did something unhelpful like rip out Micah Artris's throat in the midst of the guild hall.

When they reached their carriage, Everic ordered the infernal siblings in a sharp tone, "Take us to the main ring's edge," his expression stormy as Mezza unlocked the carriage door and Zeya went to ready the horses. Everic still did his usual search inside the carriage before nodding and helping Reuben up.

Once they were both inside, however, the vampire hunched over on the bench and put his head in his hands. "This was a mistake."

"It was a setback at most," Reuben assured, trying not to think about the familiar, malicious presence. "And if we risk going to Magnatus Lenaphon's estate, it's technically a *win*. However distasteful she and Artris are, there might be better connections to make at her party."

"Perhaps. But if anything close to *that* conversation is what awaits us in High Ring, I won't be able to swallow the filth they speak without losing my head, much less participate in it," Everic said gruffly, running a hand through his hair.

Reuben couldn't help but smile when, with a small jolt of the carriage, Everic's freed locks of hair immediately fell into his face.

"You said something similar about me, once," Reuben argued. "That you wouldn't—well, pay any of that mysterious gold you have, if it meant half went to the Priesthood vaults. Remember?"

Everic looked up, one corner of his mouth lifted. "If it meant some went *back* to the vaults," he corrected.

"Went back?" Reuben repeated in confusion, thinking of Bev's small chest—then blinked, staring at Everic in horror as he put the puzzle together. "You mean . . . ?"

"They have rooms and rooms of it locked away, just *sitting* there while they demand more from people like you," Everic said, sounding far too casual for what he was insinuating. "They aren't missing it. And with how many in this city they've ensured owe them, through taxes, tithes, and debt . . ." He paused, a sharp smile widening across his face before the vampire finished, "Well, it always returns to them eventually."

He wasn't outright saying it, but the truth was clear: somehow, the small chest was enchanted to take coins straight from the Priesthood vaults.

Devilcraft was enough to send someone to the pyre. But stealing cantergold, practically from Zaldus Himself?

Sidarchus was right, as always, that Reuben couldn't see Everic through to the end of his goal. And now Waron's threat added further to the risk, the longer Reuben stayed involved.

*I might just need to find you a new cage soon, little dove . . .*

But he could help just a little longer, until Everic gained a trusted connection in High Ring, Reuben bargained with himself. Just a few more appointments. Just another ball or two, before he gave the word to Sidarchus and bordello security began sending Everic's messengers away.

How Reuben would bring himself to go through with it, when the time came, he decided not to think about for now.

He swallowed down the last of his terror and pressed further, "But then—as you just said—you *did* reconcile with the idea of paying me. Surely there's a way to justify what you're doing in High Ring as well?"

Everic's eyes softened. "It was easy with you. You are only a victim in all of this corruption. More importantly, *a good person.*

An admirable one I'd say, whatever else I don't know about you. And I realized, wherever the gold ended up . . . it was the only power I could give, that you'd take for yourself."

Reuben barely avoided flinching at such words. He tried to tease, "My helpful blood, great beauty, and charming nature played no part, then?"

"You'd rather my motives were always so simple as that, I'm sure," said Everic.

And all at once, Reuben's memories of *that* night with Everic were painted over with a darker shade of guilt.

He already knew he was to blame for showing up in such a useless state, much less how the evening unfolded once he had. But now he understood a much larger portion of his mistake. Namely, that Reuben had seen Everic's physical reaction from touching him and made a simple, but tremendous assumption of the man's motives. And then he'd pushed, even *pressured* Everic despite clear indications of the man's hesitance.

And all of it motivated by his pointless fear of being just a little deeper in Everic's debt. Of forcibly trying to *simplify* what, if anything, Everic wanted from him, so Reuben could feel just a little better about himself.

*That was despicable of me,* Everic had said afterward—but Reuben knew who the despicable one truly was, now.

He stayed quiet through the rest of the carriage ride and the walk down to the Hollows, only murmuring a short, "Thank you, saer," when Everic unlocked the door to his hidden chamber and stepped back for Reuben to enter first.

They both took time undressing, given how many layers the ball ensembles had required—Reuben unthreading the beads from his hair as well. Everic unsurprisingly finished first and was sitting on the bed with a small frown when Reuben had changed into a nightshirt, washed his face, and turned to the other man.

"Everic?" he said softly as he neared, unsure how to broach the topic.

Everic had another subject to speak on, however. He stiffened and said, "I'll let you rest," nodding at the bed. "But first—tell me more about this person who wishes you dead."

"Oh—I told you, it was just a feeling," said Reuben, unwilling to consider if or how Waron had been in that room. Or worse, if he'd *still* been wrong somehow about the source of the dark presence.

Everic raised a brow. "Based on . . . ?"

Reuben hesitated. He had never told anyone about his music's insightful magic. It wasn't something Oriana taught him, or Reuben learned in any traditional sense. Even Isolde thought he just had a way with picking out intentions from their nightly crowd. Without the help of crowdcraft, however, Reuben couldn't boast of an innate intuition. He had believed the best in people for far too long before the hard whetstone of betrayal finally began sharpening his discernment. Besides his music, he held no great skill to perceive who in the crowd could mean an insignificant whore such ill will.

Everic didn't press, but neither did he excuse his question, seem-ingly content to give Reuben as much time as he needed to answer. He only watched with searching, curious eyes, until Reuben convinced himself he owed the man *some* small truth and stepped closer.

"When I perform . . . well, my crowdcraft doesn't always require a specific incantation for brief lights and illusions. Sometimes, it helps me read the feelings of those around me as well." When Everic raised a brow, Reuben flushed at the thought of all of Everic's feelings he'd intruded on, and hurriedly pressed on, "It was how I felt Artris had the wrong kind of interest in you despite his friendliness. Though that did us little good, I suppose. It's not *perfectly* reliable, but . . ."

"But it reinforces my trust in your opinion," Everic gravely nodded.

At the mention of *trust*, Reuben felt an even sharper pang of guilt and blurted out, "There's something else I wished to say."

Reuben bit his lip for a moment while trying to formulate the right words, ignoring Everic's inquisitive gaze.

Finally, he started in a formal tone, "First—I wanted to beg your forgiveness, saer, for my unprofessional behavior at the appointment before last."

Everic tensed. "No apology is needed," he said gruffly, eyes flickering away.

"But it *is*. I could tell you were uncertain. I should never have pressed—"

"I could have ended it with a mere word—"

"Just *listen*, please," Reuben interrupted in a sharper tone, waiting until Everic closed his mouth and lowered his shoulders in concession. "Thank you. I am terribly sorry for *my* conduct, regardless of what you did or didn't do," he continued, lacing his tone with as much sincerity as he dared. "And second: I swear, should you ever wish to touch me again, I would be happy to only follow your lead. Or—*or*, should you never, of course—just, in general," he stuttered, but plowed forward despite the deep grimace lining Everic's mouth, "I am here at your pleasure, Everic. I won't forget that again. Not ever."

In the silence that followed, Reuben watched Everic with bated breath, scrutinizing the unhappy twist to the man's otherwise stony expression.

At last, Everic sighed. "You've explained the problem much better than my pitiful attempt that night," he said, eyes averted downward. "And I am without Bev, for the moment, to help me articulate it any better." When he looked up and met Reuben's gaze, there was something both fond and sad to his smile, a quiet yearning in his dark eyes. "I forgive you, of course. And *I'm* sorry for my harsh reaction. I only wish . . ."

Reuben swallowed hard around the sudden hope threatening to surge up and take root in his chest. It was a pointless desire, he reprimanded himself, to hope Everic wished for the same exact, impossible thing Reuben did—that he *wasn't* Reubielocks, and could have a life, a future, or just a single thing for himself.

A heart to give, even.

But Everic only shook his head, not finishing the thought.

Reuben let out a soft, shaky laugh, twisting fingers through his loose hair. "I find I'm quite partial to your version of 'harshness,' saer," he said—then, remembering Everic's previous words, asked, "Though, where *is* Bev of late?"

Everic frowned and stood up from the bed. "Attending to her own business," he said whilst walking to the desk. Then added over his shoulder, "You remember Delvanzus's mention of disappearances in the Hollows, I'm sure. Tonight, what was said about the Ravine's expansion—it is no doubt related."

Reuben blinked, confused. "What do you mean?"

"The weak, sick, and elderly are disappearing first," Everic said, his face never more grim as he turned back to Reuben with a small parchment in his hand. Holding it out to Reuben, whilst continuing, "Those who are alone, with no connections to miss them. Those with any sort of criminal history, who aren't easy to defend. Though I've no doubt more will follow."

Reuben's hand trembled slightly as he took the bulletin. His eyes skimmed over the short declaration, THIS PROPERTY HAS BEEN ABDICATED TO THE HOLY SOVEREIGN STATE OF SAZZERA. GLORY BE TO ZALD.

He hardly heard Everic's voice continue over the roaring in his ears:

"You needn't be worried for now—those like you, already indentured and fulfilling a function in the city, aren't the target from what Bev has gathered. But there are plenty at risk, especially in the lowest rungs of the Hollows."

"Everic," Reuben tried to say, but his voice wouldn't work, his lips only shaping around the word. *The weak, sick, and elderly*, echoing over and over in his head.

"Bev has been working on an escape route for some time," Everic continued, oblivious, "but with the increased frequency, and now these bulletins, it's clear—"

"Everic, please," Reuben said, louder but still jagged and weak.

Everic stopped talking, though Reuben could hardly tear his eyes away from the parchment as it crinkled in his grip. He met Everic's concerned gaze briefly, and took a gamble.

*Your beauty is always improved when customers can look down upon it, Reubielocks.*

So Reuben dropped to his knees as he begged, *"Please—*Everic, I need your help."

# 19

# STRANGE CONVICTION

Reuben had thought he was *protecting* Daxus and Nahlia by not visiting them sooner. He'd seen the abandoned hollows, the extra sentry guards, even something getting nailed to a door—but only worried about the Allunata, not his own city targeting them. If he hadn't turned away weeks ago, *they* might have told him of the danger.

Now, as they hurried down the stairs and deeper into the Hollows, Reuben had only himself to blame if it was too late.

Since Everic pulled Reuben back up from his knees, heard his fears, then gave the short command, "Take me to them," the vampire hadn't spoken. Just waited, silent and wearing a stormcloud expression, as Reuben hastily dressed in some borrowed clothes and grabbed his few belongings.

Then Everic took Reuben's hand and nodded for him to lead the way.

Reuben always carried a pouch of late, containing his city pass, an extra key to Everic's chamber, some spare cantergold, and the guild token from Delvanzus. But the only thing he hadn't brought for the ball tonight was the one item he might truly *need* should his family be in immediate danger: his mother's old violin.

Returning to the bordello now wasn't worth the delay. Reuben consoled himself that he had a much more dangerous weapon in hand—and truly, the firm grip of Everic's hand in his was probably the only reason Reuben's panic hadn't shaken him apart from the inside out. He still bit his lip bloody by the time they reached the filth and squalor of the Hollows' lowest levels, never so dark and abandoned as it looked at this late hour under a waning crescent moon.

But not late enough yet for all to be asleep. Reuben's breath caught in his throat as he saw a warm light glowing from the little window of his family's hollowed abode.

Just then, the door opened. They were still a few paces away, but even in this dark Reuben recognized the ambling gait of Nahlia as she crossed the rim's narrow path, a bucket in hand. Humming to herself as she shook its contents over the rim and into the Ravine below.

Reuben stopped them, not wanting to startle her. "Nahlia?" he called instead.

The old elf jumped a little, her head swinging toward them as she held the bucket between her and the sound. But then her thin face wrinkled into a smile.

"*Zaldus guide,*" she admonished as Reuben walked closer with Everic still in tow, leaning the bucket on her hip. "What kept you, sunshine? Too late to help me with supper."

"Sorry, Nahlia," he breathed out around the beginnings of a smile, which spread across his face to match the large one already wrinkling hers.

Then she regarded Everic. "And brought us company to entertain, I see?"

Reuben let go of Everic as they reached her, too relieved to speak or explain quite yet. He simply slumped forward as she wrapped thin, wiry-strong arms around him.

"Good thing I always make a plate or two's worth to spare," she huffed, kissing his hair before smiling and beckoning towards the door.

Reuben followed without a further moment's thought. After he grabbed the door handle, however, he glanced to where Everic stood—and was surprised to see a raw, anguished grief on the vampire's face. Everic's head was bowed as if to hide it, but even through that straggly curtain of hair Reuben could see his eyes shut tightly, lips twisted.

"Everic?" Reuben asked softly, reaching a hand out.

Everic stepped backward. "I'll go get assistance, now that we know they're still here," he said, motioning towards the door. "Explain things to them."

"But what *is* going on?" Reuben asked, frustration leaking into his tone. He winced at hearing it, and tried to entreat like Reubielocks might instead, "I—I wished for *you* to assist, or else I wouldn't have cut our appointment so pitifully short, saer."

It was no surprise, however, when Reubielocks proved entirely ineffective in this unprofessional situation.

"This is the way I can," replied Everic with a short shake of his head, then added, "I'll return within the hour." Nothing else, before he turned and silently stalked back into the night.

Reuben's chest ached with both dejection and anger as he watched Everic go. He had to swallow down the urge to call after him, to bring up a dozen more questions, to demand Everic *stay*—to ask if he was alright.

But this was for the best. No one in his current life should join him *here* of all places, in the single refuge left for Reuben to be nothing but himself.

As Reuben entered, his nose was first greeted with musk from the chickens, followed by a leftover tinge of the sour Ravine smell, though both were muted by a lingering amalgamation of boiled eggs, shallots, and fresh bread. They'd managed to keep some of the tidiness Reuben left the place in, he surveyed whilst walking further into the candlelit room. Of course, it'd been just over two months since his last visit, instead of the usual three or four.

Nahlia's slow gait had just made it to the tiny kitchen alcove, plating what was left of the evening meal. Meanwhile, Daxus sat upright on their bed with a ripped pair of trousers in his lap, pausing his mending as he noticed Reuben's arrival.

"Our boy decides to visit when I'm *awake*, at last," Daxus said in a gruff tone, his bushy brows furrowed at Reuben.

Then his face gentled, a grin growing wide enough to see under his long white beard. Daxus put the trousers to the side, his short arms reaching out for Reuben.

Reuben was already hurrying toward him as the old dwarf said, "Come here, sunshine; let these old eyes take you in."

Reuben knelt on the bed and leaned down, ignoring his back's tired protest. It was worth the ache a thousand times over, to be pulled in and held so tightly, so lovingly, like he'd wanted for weeks—like he was an innocent, faultless child.

Especially after fearing he might never embrace either of these two again.

Daxus kissed his head and then regarded Reuben with dark, squinting eyes. His grin slowly faded into something more wistful, though the dwarf declared like he always did, "More handsome by the day."

Nahlia came back just then with two small plates. "Not unless he puts more food in his belly," she chided, setting them both down at the rickety little table. "They must be feeding you nothing but *mint water* up there, with how thin you've gotten." Then she frowned and glanced back at the door. "Your guest too shy for supper?"

Daxus's bushy brows rose. "Reuben brought a friend?"

*"Too shy"* was one way of putting it. Though Reuben wondered what Everic's reaction might have been, had he heard himself referred to not with the honorific of *"saer,"* or as Reuben's client, but as a friend. Someone like Bev, who he seemed to trust implicitly, to have an ease around, to even share dangerous knowledge with.

All things Reuben *couldn't* earn, even if he wanted to.

"He . . . he'll return shortly—there were a few things to attend to," he replied, moving to the table. When Nahlia still looked put out, he promised, "I'll introduce you all properly soon."

Reuben knew he should broach the topic of them packing and leaving soon. But he didn't know *where* they'd go, especially considering their frail age and Daxus's limp leg, and he didn't know exactly why.

And surely they had time now, Reuben thought as he took his first bite of bread. He didn't have to scare them with the unknown this very moment, if the two had stayed here peacefully up until now. Maybe they'd already heard the rumors or seen something, and it would come up naturally.

Or maybe Everic and Bev had been mistaken, and *only* criminals were being taken. Why would sentry guards care about a harmless old couple?

"I'm sorry my last visit was so short," he apologized, looking at the two for any signs of injury, illness, or further aging since he last saw them. "What all have I missed?"

Neither needed further prompting. While Reuben busied himself with easy eggs over Nahlia's thick homemade bread, they told him all about the last few months: every instance they'd managed to earn a half-piece mending clothes or selling eggs and bread loaves; the new errand girl they'd hired after the last stopped showing to bring them water from the main ring; and, of course, their eternal fight with rats stealing eggs from the coop.

"I could have hired a ratcatcher," Reuben chided himself out loud—even by his last visit, he'd earned plenty enough gold to do so. It was a pity *they* never did, considering the amount he left in the coin pot.

"Oh, don't waste your canters—we need something to complain about," Daxus brushed off. "Now, let's hear about *you*, Reuben."

Occasionally, he or Nahlia still asked. And yet, every time, Reuben saw how it pained them both to hear.

"Oh! Well—business has been very good. I've gotten paid at a much higher rate lately, and saved most of my earnings," he tried to assure in vague, digestible terms, though he felt the mood dampen before he even started. "I've been to some fancy social events that were enjoyable. And, um, I . . ."

"You made a friend?" Daxus prompted, smiling hopefully at him.

Reuben's mouth opened, though before he could think of a response, Nahlia said, "Hm, friend or *otherwise*," her long, drooping ears twitching like they often did when she was suspicious, "no one has been special enough to bring to us before. Who is this man?"

Daxus's eyes widened with delight. "Oh, a *special* friend—is that why the boy got cold feet?" he chortled, smiling knowingly towards the door. "Not that I blame him. I'm not in fighting shape myself, but Nahlia's stink-eye has cowed miners twice her size."

Reuben's face felt unbearably warm. "Not at all, he's just—I've helped him with a few things, and he's helped me," he said, purposefully vague to avoid ruining his family's opinion of Everic already. Nahlia's eyes still narrowed, so Reuben hurried on, "And now, he wants to help *us*."

Daxus looked even more hopeful. "Really? Is there some way that he can settle your . . . ?"

Reuben blew out a breath. "Few people in the entirety of Sazzera are *that* rich. No, but—" He hesitated, glancing between them before starting over with a question, "Have you two had any . . . problems? Any threats, any new reasons to worry at all in the last few months?"

The mood darkened this time. Nahlia frowned, her gaze flickering to the small niche above the washbasin where their coin pot was shelved. Meanwhile Daxus shifted uncomfortably, eyes fixed downward as if his beard was suddenly of interest to him.

Clearly *something* had happened since his last visit, Reuben could deduce from their reactions alone.

"What is it?" he asked, glancing between them.

"Oh, there's always something—but we've made it just fine," Nahlia sighed, patting Reuben's arm. Her drooped eyes looked weary in contrast to the small, warm smile she offered him. "And here's one less worry, seeing you again, Reuben."

Her smile faded at the sound of Daxus shifting loudly on the bed. Nahlia frowned in disapproval at her husband as Daxus slowly clambered to sit on its edge and swung out his short, stout legs.

"I think it best Reuben and I go walk the rim for a bit, my love," said Daxus.

"There's no need—"

"I'd know every inch of it blindfolded," Daxus reassured her, slipping his feet into sandals—nearby the crutch the dwarf then fit underneath his arm.

Nahlia glared. "You know what I mean, Dax."

"Whatever it is, you can just tell me now," Reuben argued as well.

"*Nothing's* happened," Daxus replied to them both, and though Nahlia's lips pressed together, she didn't argue. "Just . . . some things to discuss, son."

So Reuben sighed and got up to help the old man onto his feet.

Some things would never change—Daxus had taken Reuben out to walk the rim since he was old enough to stand on his own two legs. Often, to talk about things of only childish importance: why Reuben shouldn't have run off without informing someone, or why he needed to pay more attention to letters and maths, not just music, when Oriana came for lessons.

Just as often, however, the conversation was of lifelong importance: showing him why he should never lean too far over the rim; explaining the different parts and functions of the body; carefully describing Oriana's profession in more blunt terms, the older Reuben grew.

Of them all, the only walk he didn't remember with fondness occurred the morning Daxus gently explained that Reuben's mother wanted him to go live with her in the main ring.

Oriana had taken Reuben away the very next day.

In recent years, it was rare to see Daxus out of his bed, much less carefully limping out his door. Reuben wasn't surprised when they moved at a slow, inching pace for a few minutes, even as his heart ached with worry over how Daxus would manage to travel, if relocation *was* actually necessary.

"Always nice to greet the Ravine—I liked the achy shoulder-weight of a pick, you know, having a hard conversation with the stone," Daxus started with a wistful smile once they stopped, a statement he'd told Reuben multiple times over the decades. "I happily paid the sweat price, the neck cramps over the sluice box, when that shining reward waited to be shaken out from the cradle."

The way he talked about his old days as a miner often sounded like poetry, or even scripture to Reuben. Maybe, that was what the work used to be like.

But this wasn't the time to reminisce about the city's gilded history until Daxus finally arrived at his point. This time *Reuben* had something of great import to discuss.

"You and Nahlia are in danger," he stated plainly.

To his surprise, Daxus just nodded. "That last errand boy we had to replace?" He pointed a door further down the path, a smashed basket lying against the wall beside it. "I'm still worried about him. Nothing wrong with letting customers go, but he was a good kid, always on time; it wouldn't be like him not to tell us so."

Wary apprehension crawled up Reuben's spine as he surveyed the dwelling and the dark window above its door. "He lives there?"

Daxus sighed. "Doesn't seem to anymore. They always kept their door open at night to air out the animal smell, the Ravine stink."

Reuben took a few steps closer, a cold shiver running through him as he spotted a weather-stained, mostly-torn bulletin nailed into the shut door. The script was nearly illegible—but still recognizable.

"Sentry *swill* keep knocking late at night," Daxus continued, voice lowering as he glanced around. For now, the narrow path and branching stairways looked empty of any guards. "Saying there's no papers to prove we own our hollow. There rightly may not be. But Nahlia, she . . ." He shook his head, his wrinkled face cast down in sorrow. "She keeps paying them to look away."

Reuben's heart immediately tied itself in a dozen knots. "They already came for you," he whispered.

Daxus gave him a defeated look. "For the last six months," he admitted. "And they keep asking for more. Nothing will be enough soon, I think, but—but you *have* to know, we'd never wanted to use the gold in such a way. To *waste* it like that, especially with what—what you have to *do*—"

Reuben cut off Daxus's choked words as he ducked down, wrapping his arms fiercely around the man he would always consider his father. Tears sprang into his eyes, for now thanks to an overwhelm of *relief,* not the anticipation of saying goodbye.

Though only for a moment before he pulled back to meet Daxus's gaze and replied fiercely, "It was anything but a waste; I only wish I'd given you more. But my . . . my *friend* and I can get you two to safety soon. They're helping others as well—there's an escape route being made, apparently."

Daxus's brows pulled together. "Escape . . . escape where?"

Reuben bit his lip, standing and glancing at the path behind them. "I don't know much," he said, and silently cursed Everic for abandoning him without further explanation, "but I *do* know it's a better chance than staying here, relying on the mercy of sentry guards." He gave Daxus a pleading look, adding, "I just need you to help Nahlia understand."

"Oh, is that all?" Daxus huffed, leaning heavier on his crutch. "*I'd* like to understand. What is this route? How many have used it?" His dark eyes narrowed before he said in a lower tone, "How do you know this friend can be trusted?"

"He . . ." Reuben hesitated, having no idea how to explain, how to justify—

But then a familiar voice called behind him: "Most of your questions can be answered, but not here."

Daxus startled far worse than Reuben, his old eyes squinting frantically at the dark before Reuben turned to see Everic emerging from it. An infernal, horned individual was also coming down the stairway . . . though too short to be Bev, Reuben could already tell before belatedly recognizing Mezza.

Everic gave them both a short nod of acknowledgement, and without waiting for an introduction addressed Daxus: "Good evening. Mezza here can help your household pack the necessities, and explain what the journey entails." His eyes traveled further downward—noting Daxus's crutch—and with a slight frown, he added, "Also, discuss what route is safest for you."

"Mezza?" Daxus repeated. "And who are *you*?"

"Daxus, this is Saer Everic Payne, the man I've been talking about," Reuben hurried to say, stepping forward and swallowing down a sudden bout of nerves at these two meeting. He continued formally, "Saer Payne, this is Daxus, son of Calmus, former miner and refiner of the Ravine."

"And this one's papa," Daxus added, pointing a thumb at Reuben.

Reuben flushed, though Everic took the news in stride—he crossed over to the old dwarf and, without hesitation, held out his hand.

Daxus gave it a suspicious eye, but ultimately held out his own in return. Then both his bushy brows climbed up his forehead as Everic clasped their arms, placing his free hand over Daxus's wrist and pressing down on it twice in a gesture Reuben had only rarely seen people greet each other with when he was a child.

When they let go, Daxus was grinning. "You didn't say your friend was from the *Hollows*," the dwarf chuckled. "You trust him, then, sunshine?"

Reuben opened his mouth to refute Daxus's assumption, then thought twice. Especially when Everic made no move to correct him. It wasn't Reuben's place to say that the vampire *arrived quite recently in the city,* as Everic had first explained, much less give an opening for Daxus to inquire further.

And he had yet to answer the old dwarf's confronting question. But Reuben still didn't know where Everic actually came from. He still didn't understand what Everic truly wanted and *why* he was so intent on his goal to access and likely kill the Voice of Zald. He still found it disconcerting, Everic's abhorrence of Zald and everything Reuben had never once questioned his whole life.

He still felt it hard to bear, every time Everic's mood darkened and he stalked off, leaving Reuben fretful and alone.

In the end, he had no easy reason to trust the imposing, vampiric monster . . . only the evidence of a hundred simple, impossible kindnesses Reuben was still waiting to reach the limit of.

After a drawn-out second, he answered quietly, "He'll help us," and avoided looking Everic's way.

"Right, then," Daxus nodded, then took a few limping steps forward as he asked, "Mezza, yes? I don't suppose you grew up a hollow-dweller as well, son?"

"Did the horns give it away?" Mezza chuckled as the two started on the path back. "I know these parts better than my own nose; my family never stuck to one hollow for long, and there were a few with some back tunnels . . ."

Reuben intended to let them *all* walk ahead, then take a second and gather his thoughts. But Everic still stood there, watching him with an intense but unreadable expression.

When Reuben finally gave in and started walking, Everic fell into step beside him. "Could they be readied to leave tonight?" Everic asked.

It was a slow pace, given Daxus limping ahead of them, and the silence between them dragged on until Reuben sighed. "They don't have many things. It's just, *convincing* them to do it, and the journey itself . . ."

"You and Mezza will be able," Everic said firmly. "I'll stay back and keep watch, should any sentry patrol pass by until you leave."

Reuben stared at him, only half-aware that his feet had come to a stop. "Until *I* leave . . . ?"

Everic stopped as well, his voice quiet as he responded, "I told you, I understand how little blood has to do with love—with *family*." He took a fortifying breath, then continued, "Mezza can take you with them."

Reuben backed up a step. "I'm not going," he denied, and perhaps with too much volume.

"Something wrong?" Mezza called. He and Daxus were both a ways ahead now, looking over their shoulders curiously.

But after Daxus glanced between them, he waved a dismissive hand. "Eh, you two take your time. I'm a slow walker after all," he said with a short chuckle, raising his crutch pointedly. Then he turned back and continued his conversation with Mezza, "Now think on it, son, which of these women do you actually *like* . . ."

As Reuben watched them go, Daxus's voice fading out of earshot, he wondered if he could avoid this conversation by arguing that he and Everic *shouldn't* take their time, given the unknown urgency of the danger. But they were less than a minute away from Daxus and Nahlia's hollow; night had arrived with no sign of sentry guards banging down any doors.

And his reluctance faded into quiet, nervous anticipation, when one of Everic's hands slipped into his.

Everic took Reuben's other hand as well, making Reuben face him as he walked them off the center of the path. Closer to the rim and the blank pit of darkness beyond, the Ravine stink still present but fading now that its workers were finally at rest.

Everic paid the sharp drop no mind, leaning forward as he pressed, "These two are the loved ones you said the gold was helping, are they not? The reason you can't just leave the city. But if *they* are both escaping—"

"They have no city officials or bordello managers motivated to search for them, either," Reuben interrupted, hackles raised at Everic's insistence. "My presence would only add danger. And I have my friend Isolde to think of, too. I have . . ." He didn't finish the thought, much less the phrase before concluding, "I can't just leave this city, Everic."

A pained frustration glinted in Everic's eyes. "You *can.*"

Reuben's lips twitched into a bitter smile. His mother believed for most of his youth that they would be saved from their circumstances. If she could just get a city pass—if she could just send the right letter, to the right person—if she could just negotiate with Sidarchus's help to lower the interest—if they could just *run*, before her frail health failed her—

Her death was the will of Zald, Reuben remembered being told by the priest after she took her last breath. Whether doled out by the Priesthood, the city sentry, or nature itself, there was no escape from the dark consequences of sin.

"I owe the Priesthood vaults nearly 80,000 cantergold," Reuben told Everic finally in plain terms.

He felt some satisfaction at how wide Everic's eyes rounded in response.

But Everic was quick to recover with a sharp shake of his head. "That shouldn't stop you," he insisted, giving Reuben's hands a gentle squeeze.

Still unswayed. Still filled with that fiery, righteous indignation, despite his own murderous plans. Reuben couldn't believe it was an act after witnessing Everic's poor acting skills—but he couldn't imagine what fueled this continued insistence either.

He blamed it on his proximity to his family, his once-home, and the ugly reality of everything around them, for entirely discarding Reubielocks in that moment and stepping closer with the demand: "Do you *want* me to go?"

This close, Reuben saw the way Everic's face tightened, his whole body going still. His hesitation said enough—but after a long moment, Reuben felt cold thumbs gently stroke over his knuckles as Everic shook his head again.

"I would wish for nothing less," Everic whispered.

Reuben's breath hitched. If he hadn't already promised otherwise, he would have moved in and finally kissed the man, right there and then.

Instead he offered Everic a wavering smile. "The curse of Sazzera for us both, it seems."

Everic let out a shaky chuckle, and started to reply, "This city always was—"

But just then they both startled, Everic's words forgotten at the sound of a distant, alarmed shout from the path ahead—followed by a high-pitched scream.

# 20

# HEALING SONG

The scene in front of Reuben was streaked in blood.

Just within the dwelling's open doorway, an armored woman stood with her back to Reuben. A tear in her shoulder oozed blood, though the injury hadn't deterred her from holding Daxus by the arm, a sword pointed down at his neck. Even without seeing the front of her, Reuben recognized the gold breastplate likely embossed with a simplified crest of the city, worn over a black gambeson—typical attire of a Sazzeran sentry guard.

But the blood, pooled on the floor past their feet and streaked on the nearby furniture, clearly wasn't hers. Reuben stopped short at the sight briefly, then ran in around them, desperate to find its source.

Nahlia hadn't been injured, was his only thought for a moment as Reuben registered the sight of Mezza on the floor, blood rapidly escaping where the infernal man pressed a hand just below his collarbone. Another sentry guard stood over Mezza—the man's broadsword relaxed at his side, dripping red.

The guard had just turned and noted Reuben's hurried entry when a thick cloud of darkness billowed into the room.

In less than a second the candles snuffed out and the very air was choked of all light. Reuben heard others gasp and Nahlia cry out in fright—but he didn't freeze at the devilcraft this time. No more than a second later he lunged forward where Daxus and the first guard just stood, hoping to surprise her enough to get between them.

They hadn't moved far—a thick, familiar arm elbowed Reuben's hip, and the sentry guard started making harsh, frustrated sounds that indicated Daxus was in the midst of struggling already.

Reuben grabbed blindly for him. A sudden shout and then pained cries of the second sentry guard echoed in the darkness further back in the hollow, accompanied by the sound of more blood splattering on the floor. Reuben only used it to his advantage. When the sentry guard near him gasped at hearing the death throes of her comrade, Reuben chose right then to rip Daxus away from her.

Then cried out himself, staggering back after her blade sliced clean and wide across his thigh in retaliation—where Daxus's abdomen had likely been, just a moment before—and the scent of blood thickened in the air.

Just like that, the darkness folded in on itself and left the room visible again, the small candles relit. But what their dim light revealed was a snarling, red-eyed monster in the corner, blood dripping from its open, fanged mouth as it dropped its limp prey and locked focus on Reuben's attacker.

Nahlia screamed again as Everic pounced on the second guard. Daxus stood behind Reuben clutching onto his arm, while Reuben turned his head away and winced through the sounds of rending flesh and blood-choked screams.

But he could try to help another way. Mezza still lay on the ground, keeping pressure on his own wound. So Reuben pulled from Daxus's grasp and limped over to the infernal man. Without his violin once again, his magic wouldn't be nearly so powerful, but Reuben tried to focus just as hard without it, holding a hand over the wound. He sang the lyrics he'd made up for *Healing Song* when healing Bev—even added another verse for good measure: *"If I was a fish / And my beau a dove / I'd grow my own wings / To reach for her love . . ."*

By the second verse's end, the blood stopped dripping from between Mezza's fingertips. The pallor of his tanned skin improved, the tight, pained look in his eyes faded. Reuben sighed in relief, simply nodding when Mezza sat up and gusted out, *"Thank* you."

Silence fell; both guards laid in twisted, grotesque pieces on the floor, and the dark, hunched figure of Everic stood motionless over the nearest one. Reuben looked down at his leg, which was pulsing noticeably with pain now that the fear had faded, and wondered if he had any strength left to heal himself.

The peace didn't last more than a second, however, before Nahlia let out a gasp.

Reuben started to twist in her direction but froze at noticing Daxus, still standing right where Reuben left him. Both of his old, weathered hands were cupping his belly, however—holding together a wide, weeping wound now slashed across it. Daxus's face was ashen, nearly matching the color of his white beard as he stared down at himself and his innards peeking out.

The last slash of the guard's sword hadn't just found Reuben's leg.

"Daxus," Reuben breathed out in horror, right before his father dropped to his knees.

Reuben ignored the pain in his leg, his lack of instrument, and the sheer unlikelihood that crowdcraft could help such a terrible injury—everything but his need to reach Daxus right away.

He arrived in time to help the old dwarf gently land on his back, not face forward onto the blood-soaked floor. But even as he started to sing, Reuben knew that he couldn't repair such a wide, deep wound the way he had Bev's bruise, or Mezza's injury just now. Even if he could use his mother's violin and channeled every bit of his remaining energy and skill into the song, his music was never meant for more than parlor tricks.

*"If I was a lake / And my beau the sea . . ."* Reuben kept going anyway, hovering his hands over Daxus's gory middle as the pool of blood spread, as the dwarf's breaths grew scratchy and faint.

Over his singing, he heard Everic barking orders to Nahlia for a strong needle and flax string, to Mezza for the door to be shut. But Daxus was losing blood too fast. Reuben gave up on using his hands as a focus and instead put pressure on the old dwarf's wound, fat tear drops plopping straight from his eyes down onto Daxus's weathered shirt whilst he kept whispering the song over and over again—seeing no change, yet unwilling to admit defeat.

As he did, his eyes latched onto the sight of his mother's cantergold ring, bloodied a coppery orange on his pinky finger. Oriana discarded the token for Daxus and Nahlia to sell years before her death, but instead they'd held onto it, *just in case she ever asked for it again.* Or that was what Daxus claimed, anyway, when he gave the ring to a 14-year-old Reuben on the very same day he brought news to them of Oriana's death.

Her violin was an essential tool of the trade, but this bauble had no inherent use, or even significant value beyond its cantergold—just a small, discarded piece of his mother for Reuben to cling to. More importantly, a token and reminder during one of the worst times of his life, that Reuben still had a family to love and be loved by.

Was this another piece of himself he had to let go of, now?

Reuben narrowed his gaze and pushed his hands harder against the wound, latching onto something else entirely as he focused—and a tiny light flashed beneath his palms.

There was no time to be shocked. He felt Everic trying to pull his hands away, a threaded needle in hand, but Reuben stubbornly resisted. He kept whispering the song under his breath, putting every ounce of his heart into each word as the light glowed brighter—even seeming to illuminate the ring itself.

At that, Everic's hands dropped in surprise.

The blood was slowing and clotting, the wound closing. So Reuben continued for as long as he could—ignoring the pulsing, burning pain in his leg, the ache in his lower back, and the cold hand on his shoulder as Everic spoke roughly in his ear, "Reubie?"

Reuben kept his strangely-glowing hands pressed against the sealing skin as he saw Daxus's drooped eyelids flicker and the color of his skin return, as a flicker of warmth grew between Reuben's ribs—even as his body felt ready to drop to the bloody ground next to his father.

"Reuben," he finally registered Nahlia's creaky voice, chiding but gentle. "Reuben, that's enough."

At hearing his true name Reuben blinked and finally stopped his fast, breathy singing, his arms unlocking from the unrelenting position. His body slumped in exhausted relief as he broke out of the strange, frenzied trance, and fell back—only to be stopped by a firm arm and chest supporting him from behind.

His head slumped to rest against Everic's shoulder, his eyes slotting closed and his mind uncaring of the thick iron scent on Everic's collar.

Everic spoke into his ear again, his voice soft but urgent, "Are you alright? Can you—can you sing for yourself, now?"

Reuben meant to answer. But right now thoughts curled up and away from his exhausted mind, as shapeless and insubstantial as smoke. He was only vaguely aware of the ground meeting his back, something soft placed under his head before hands inspected his leg.

"Daxus?" said Nahlia, meanwhile.

"Not rid of me yet, love," croaked Daxus. "Though this time you've got our boy to blame for that."

Nahlia scoffed; the sound came out too choked to carry its usual bite. Reuben felt a weathered hand squeeze his, before the old elf demanded, "What did he *do*? Reuben, can you hear me?"

Reuben forced his eyes open, though Everic was the one who answered her. "He's exhausted from such a large amount of magic, clearly," Everic said in a business-like tone whilst ripping Reuben's trouser leg open, exposing the full extent of the wound. "Blood loss probably isn't helping either."

"At least you both got here in time—*fuck*, that went sideways quick," Mezza sighed.

Everic's voice answered sharp and short: "And it nearly cost you and Daxus your lives. We were *right* behind you—you should have kept calm, not escalated the situation and endangered the very people we came to help—"

"Enough," Daxus croaked gruffly from right next to Reuben. At that, Reuben dazedly turned his head to see the dwarf sitting up, giving Everic a dark, distrusting expression. "They'd cornered Nahlia. This one was a *bit* aggressive to move away their attention," he nodded at Mezza, "but not half so much as you, son, flooding the room with your *devilcraft*."

Reuben winced, but was unable to more than open his mouth before Everic grimly replied, "And I will do so again, should more guards have heard the screams. But for now, I'll stitch *this* wound, instead of yours, saer," he nodded at Reuben's leg. When his words were met with only silence and Daxus giving Reuben a concerned, wondering look, the vampire began doling out orders: "Now, you two grab only what you need and can carry for three full days of travel. Mezza, see how well you're able—"

But then Reuben arched his back with a gasp.

A burning pain split down his spine like he'd been sliced by a blade all over again. It centered on the middle of his back, though every muscle from his neck down to his lower legs seized with nerve-singeing pain, forcing a whimper from his lips.

"What's wrong?" he was half-aware of Everic asking in alarm, hands reaching around to touch his back hesitantly, and Reuben opened his mouth—only to cry out as another bout of pain split through him.

Everyone else began speaking at once.

"What have you *done* to him, devil—!"

"Hey, hey, saer, calm yourself, I'm sure there's an explanation—"

"I don't know what causes it, but I can get him to safety—"

"Put him on the bed, saer, I can heat up something—"

"Stop!" Reuben cried, then cringed again. He felt Nahlia squeezing his hand tighter as he hissed out between pained breaths, "Daxus, Nahlia—*ah*—there's no time, please, just—*listen* to him, hurry—" until his voice cut off, groaning as the waves of pain continued with relentless strength.

Whatever he'd done, it wasn't leaving Reuben tired like crowdcraft usually did—it felt like something was trying to *destroy* his body in response.

"Oh, my boy," Nahlia whispered, a hand stroking his cheek. Reuben cracked open his eyes just long enough to see the deep lines of concern on her face. But then she let go, firmly declaring, "He's right. I'll start packing, Dax; just what we can carry."

"If you harm him, then *Zald's light be quick to burn,*" Daxus threatened Everic in a growl, before Reuben heard him rising to his feet.

"Careful—"

"No, it's fine, love. I feel . . . better than I have in a *long* time."

Over the next minute, Reuben was distantly aware of the sounds of drawers opening, low murmurs and hasty feet moving across the stone floor, Nahlia checking on him once again. More vividly, he felt the painful, needling tug of Everic's stitches in his leg, though only amidst the ebb and flow of his spine's radiating pain, which always returned to distract him from the smaller discomfort.

After Everic finished with the needle he tore off one of his own sleeves and set about creating a bandage to tie around Reuben's leg—but there was little to be done about the entirety of his back.

When Everic spoke, a quiet anger in his voice, "What can I do? How can I stop this?" Reuben just shook his head hazily and bit his lip, trying to hide his pained sounds better. He thought of what Everic had resorted to last time, and found himself almost desperate enough to risk oblivion again.

The pain had died down somewhat, at least, by the time Mezza hurried over with a filled bag. "Daxus will be too slow for the main route," the infernal man muttered, glancing at both Everic and Reuben. "Even if we got them to the *Lantern*. Perhaps we could reach out to Saer Delvanzus—"

"Aldo is currently away, helping us elsewhere," Everic interrupted. "And I have no way of accessing the guild hall on my own, even if Blanca Orlyn is vetted now. You'll have to take them to the deeper refuge for the time being."

"I . . . I have a feeling at least one of them will put up a fight if I take them into the *catacombs* after seeing *you,* saer," Mezza said with a hesitant chuckle.

As Everic gusted out an audible sigh, Reuben blinked—winced at another spike of pain—but thought he realized the problem. "Everic, my pocket," he murmured.

"What?" Everic looked down at him, confused.

"I have a token from Delvanzus," Reuben made a weak tug at Everic's arm. "In my—*ah*—pocket—"

Apparently he'd assessed the issue correctly, as Everic didn't ask for further explanation. He searched both sides of Reuben's borrowed trousers, quickly making contact with the small bag Reuben kept his items in and spilling its contents out onto a clean corner of the blood-streaked floor. Then he plucked the octagon-shaped token from the pile and handed it to Mezza.

"Perfect," Mezza said to Reuben. "Thank you—*twice* over now."

"Just . . . get them safe," Reuben whispered, feeling lightheaded again.

"You and Zeya can take them by carriage to the guild hall," Everic ordered Mezza. "We will head to my hollow a minute after—a large group leaving at once would only attract more attention." And after Mezza nodded and returned to help Nahlia pack a second sack, he spoke quieter to Reuben, "I didn't know Aldo gave you extra tokens."

Reuben let out a pained chuckle. Carefully, he sat up on his own again and tried to tease, "They didn't give *you* any?"

Everic sighed again, turning to gather Reuben's items. When he handed the pouch back to Reuben, he admitted, "Aldo does . . . but I keep using them up."

Now was not the time to ask for clarity as to why, especially just to assuage a silly pang of jealousy that was distracting from his *actual* pain, Reuben told himself.

Then Everic's mouth thinned into a grim frown. "Can you manage the walk back now? We shouldn't linger any longer."

"Maybe—with assistance," Reuben admitted.

Then Nahlia approached again, and with Everic's help Reuben stood up on shaky legs to hug her. Her watery blue eyes were spilling with tears when the embrace ended and she took Reuben's face in both of her weathered hands, stroking his cheek. "We never meant to put you in danger," she said, mournfully regarding his bandaged wound.

Daxus looked even more upset, his eyes flickering in Everic's direction as he added, "But we shouldn't have to *leave* you in it either, son."

"It's alright," Reuben said, trying for a reassuring smile.

"You've certainly grown into quite the crowdcrafter," Daxus said, patting his belly and the puffy, pink line visible thanks to his ruined shirt. He gave Reuben a proud but sad smile as he added, "Thank you. We've missed your beautiful music, sunshine."

"I'll have to visit you both and play something proper again soon," Reuben said—though it was a promise he already knew he had little hopes of keeping.

Daxus grabbed him for one last, fierce hug—tight enough Reuben winced from another spike of pain in his back—and the dwarf whispered, "*Is* he hurting you?" before he leaned back with worry furrowing his white, bushy brows.

Technically, the answer was *on occasion,* even if Reuben consented to it. Psychologically, on the other hand, Everic was just as often soothing, assuaging, even healing Reuben's emotional pains as he was provoking, aggravating, and extending them. During this one singular night, he'd made Reuben feel both protected and abandoned, appreciated and criticized—wanted, and then entirely unwanted.

Just as much a contradiction as he'd been at the start. And yet, what did that matter when Everic was right here, not only cutting their important evening at the ball short on a whim of Reuben's *bad feeling,* but without delay trying to get Reuben's family to safety simply because he'd been asked to?

"I'm better off than I've ever been," Reuben spoke quietly, even if it was far more complicated than that. And, after glancing at Everic, decided to admit what he couldn't before: "I . . . I *do* trust him, Daxus."

Daxus slowly nodded—for better or worse, trusting Reuben in return.

Then, with a few more goodbyes to both Reuben and the four hens in their coop, Nahlia and Daxus were gone.

Reuben gratefully allowed Everic to sling his arm over the man's shoulders, after they'd waited for a minute to leave as well. But they only managed to get to the door before another jolt of pain made his knees buckle.

Everic caught him just under the arm before Reuben crumpled to the floor.

"*Zald's balls*," Reuben hissed, grabbing at Everic to try and regain his balance without aggravating the pain further. "I—I'm sorry, saer. I don't know *why* it's gotten so bad of late."

Everic's eyes narrowed, before he stated, "This may hurt for a moment."

Before Reuben could question him, one of Everic's arms shifted further behind Reuben's back, his other scooping under Reuben's legs. The quick force of it easily buckled his knees again, and for a split second Reuben was falling, only to be lifted into the air in Everic's arms.

Reuben cried out—in pain from both his leg wound and another sharp spasm from his back. Then he sagged against Everic, breathing out, "Good . . . idea."

"We'll see," Everic replied grimly.

He was right to be skeptical. The moment Everic took a step forward, Reuben felt yet another spike of pain light up his spine.

"Everic," he gasped, fisting a hand into the man's ripped shirt.

Everic immediately stopped again, regarding Reuben in his arms with a helpless look of concern. "We . . . I could try to carry you on my back instead?" he suggested, though he sounded as confident of the idea as Reuben felt.

"I trust you," Reuben replied, loud enough Everic would hear the words this time. He gave the vampire a pleading look, and when Everic seemed confused—though maybe hopeful at the words, too— Reuben added, "Everic . . . *I'm* asking, this time."

The line between Everic's brows deepened . . . and then smoothed out with understanding. Slowly, he nodded and leaned in.

The last thing Reuben saw was the man's eyes flashing a fiery, devilish red, before Everic rested his forehead against Reuben's and fulfilled his request with the gentle whisper: *"Sleep."*

# 21

# CLEANSING BURN

Reuben woke up in Everic's bed—alone, as usual.

Not for long before Everic came into the room looking muddy, tired, but assured with a platter of food for Reuben to eat. As he did, Everic washed up and explained that Nahlia and Daxus were hidden away in the guild hall for now, and Mezza would send word once they'd arrived somewhere safe outside the city. The Hollows were still abuzz with sentry guards, but based on their dead comrades' wounds they blamed it on a bestial monster that was apparently terrorizing the Hollows, not any mortal-kind.

The explanation and assurances brought Reuben some comfort after such a harrowing night, but not enough.

He'd nearly lost Daxus. Two sentry guards were dead. Out of nowhere, Reuben's back pain had flared almost as fiercely as it did during that fateful appointment with Jophiel. His family would never be able to return to their normal lives. And now all Reuben had left was Isolde in this city, and once he freed her . . . no one at all.

But Nahlia and Daxus would be taken somewhere safe, and only a dull ache lingered in Reuben's back now. So he stayed quiet and ate the platter of food as Everic talked, right up until Everic inspected his wound and remarked, "It's healed surprisingly quick over the past day or so; I'll need to take out the stitches. That song must have worked on you as well."

"A full day?" Reuben repeated, his heart skipping over a beat.

"Almost—you clearly needed the rest." Everic glanced at Reuben with fond, worried eyes that Reuben couldn't stomach meeting the gaze of for long.

*. . . if you keep disappearing for days on end, I'll need to do something about it . . . I'll be glad to . . .*

And now Reuben had disappeared from the Allunata's watch yet again.

He couldn't keep this up forever. Waron wouldn't *let* him, Reuben knew. And now that he couldn't deny Everic held some care for him—or at least a misguided desire to aid him—Reuben knew he wouldn't be able to forgive himself if his hesitancy put Everic in further danger as well.

"I probably benefited," he conceded as Everic began removing the stitches. Then, after a deliberate pause, added, "Especially if we *did* attend Lenaphon's private party this week."

The lines on Everic's face deepened. He stopped and stared at Reuben's mostly-healed wound, frowning—but Reuben had learned not to tense and assume he'd said something wrong, by this point. He simply waited for the vampire to think.

Once the task was complete, Everic slowly nodded. "I received the official invitation for her parlor party held in three days' time. It's a long affair, well into the evening. But with the war councils soon to start . . . you're right. I can hardly afford to be picking and choosing from so few chances at High Ring." His lips curled into a grim smile. "Besides—this way we can finally put to rest what Saer Micah Artris is *so* interested in about me."

Reuben was not as assured that interest could easily be *"put to rest,"* if Artris suspected Everic's vampirism—unless Everic meant *permanent* rest, which would hardly warm him to higher society.

Still, Reuben returned the smile. "In that case . . . there's much to prepare over the next three days."

By the time Everic removed the stitches and Reuben finished dressing into more borrowed clothes, pinning on his previous ensemble's flimsy excuse of a veil, they'd discussed everything from the time they should arrive, to the clothing they should purchase, to the names Everic should know, to the kinds of songs Reuben should play. Even what strategies to employ, to avoid Everic losing his temper when any conversation around them "turned despicable," as Everic termed it.

The last thing Reuben pointed out—that Everic would need to drink from him, given when the party started—was the only instance the vampire seemed to begrudge Reuben's advice, before he conceded and went abruptly quiet.

Reuben gave himself a quick *Healing Song* to finish off the wound— relieved, when no scar lingered—borrowed another plain pair of clothes from Everic, and took his payment without argument. Then there was nothing left but to brave the walk up to the main ring.

His fear had little to do with sentry guards patrolling about the Hollows, searching for some fanged monster. So Reuben kept to the widest, busiest streets until he arrived at the bordello, submitting to two different checks for his city pass before he was allowed on, in hopes of avoiding a darker threat. There was never any sign of him being watched or followed—still, Reuben eyed every shadow he passed.

He paused mid-step once inside the bordello, upon hearing an unusual amount of commotion above him.

It was the morning of Repose, Reuben belatedly remembered, with Sidarchus likely soon to start the queue for balancing their weekly finances. As he climbed up the stairs, however, he also heard raised voices, none of which sounded like Sidarchus.

Suddenly, Reuben's mind couldn't picture anything but sentry guards trying to take *Isolde* away next. The image spurred his tired legs quicker up the stairs.

Once he made it to the second floor and turned left, Reuben stopped short at the actual scene. The corridor was half-blocked by two men facing away from him; the hunched figure of Sidarchus, and a dwarvish man wearing bright gold-and-white attire, which stood in stark contrast to the dark wood, royal purple and blues decorating the stellas' corridor.

Clerics of the Zaldian faith were expected to wear some kind of gold over their plain white tunic, usually a tabard or a metal mantle, though sometimes just a gold-laced cord. This man wore all three, as well as a headdress—only missing the golden mask reserved for the highest of priests, Reuben noted as he took a few steps closer. Not a priest that had visited the bordello before, from what he could remember.

Thanks to their stance he couldn't see much further down the hall, but he could hear what sounded like Gringoll shouting hoarsely, "I don't accept! I don't accept it, Bittie! Stop—wait, no, she *can't*—"

Then Reuben hurriedly stepped aside as Bittie walked out of the corridor with two Zaldian clerics flanking her, her eyes teary but her chin held high. And, despite all the priests around them, with no veil shielding her gaze at all.

Briefly, she met Reuben's stunned face as they calmly moved past, Gringoll's sobs echoing after them—and Bittie gave Reuben a tiny nod before she took the first step down the stairwell and out of the bordello.

Another stella had joined the ranks of the Zaldian Priesthood, Reuben thought numbly, his mind flashing over the dozen other individuals he'd known in the last four decades who'd done the same. Sacrificing all their worldly goods, familial ties, and selfhood—even their very names—to enter the Embrace of Zald before death, and help others find His Golden Light.

Sidarchus turned to watch her go with a tight smile on his lips, though upon seeing Reuben it widened. "Oh, Reubielocks! What a relief you've made it in time," he said, louder to carry over Gringoll's sobbing as he gestured Reuben over. "You missed the sermon, but I know how important a quick health check-up is for each stella, *especially* our seasoned ones."

Reuben swallowed and went to stand near him, briefly nodding at the Zaldian cleric on Sidarchus's other side. "What happened?" he murmured, looking on at the pitiful sight of Gringoll being held back by Jemeye, though the dwarf stopped trying to pull free and fell to his knees, just then. A few more stellas were watching from further back in the corridor, various levels of pity and interest on their faces at the spectacle. Adina, near the back, looked strangely angry.

"You didn't see?" Sidarchus answered, his tone forcibly bright. "Our young Bittie has chosen a brighter, purer life for herself as a Zaldian acolyte. And *both* her and her brother's debts will be forgiven now, thanks to the great generosity of the Priesthood."

Reuben blinked to hide his surprise—it was a generous offer, especially depending on each debt's size. He couldn't blame Bittie for taking the only sure way out *and* managing to free her brother at once. Even if it meant she likely wouldn't ever see him again . . . or, if she did, would have to pretend not to recognize him.

"He will come to appreciate her choice in time," the cleric agreed sagely, and repeated an adage from the Gospel of Zald: *"The light may burn and blind, until at last we allow it to cleanse."* Then he regarded Reuben with a genial smile. "Are you ready for your visit, child?"

Reuben all at once felt self-conscious again of the veil pinned into his hair, the silk roses and netting a gaudy, irreverent display. Still, he nodded, beginning to follow—only for Sidarchus to grab his wrist, pressing a key into his palm as the house manager murmured, "Check on our Songbird, after? Her visit did not go so well."

Reuben looked back at Sidarchus in alarm, though the older man's eyes gave nothing away as he nodded at Reuben to move along.

After that, Reuben had never felt so impatient to get through his routine check-up in four decades. He stripped the moment he was allowed, spoke nearly over the cleric's questions, and answered as quickly as possible about the symptom list he'd memorized ten times over: each one indicating potential diseases and conditions prone to this line of work. Which was the same thing the cleric checked for as Reuben laid back and let the man examine his body, murmuring prayers all the while.

Like "*Grant this child eyes to see Thy Light, ears to hear Thy Glorious Song,*" as he examined Reuben's face and particularly the inner parts of his mouth.

Or "*Raise this creature out of sin and darkness, from the shadows that bind, O Brilliant One,*" when his hands moved lower, inspecting Reuben's genitals.

Finally, after declaring his body whole and healthy—*Glory Be to Zald*—the cleric washed his hands and stood at Reuben's bedside with a look of sad pity. "You've seen someone make a brave step today. What is it about the carnal pleasures of the flesh that hold *you* here still, child? Have you not seen how quickly such vices fall into void and darkness, even *devilry*, when not performed only in the virtue and glory of His Golden Light?"

Reuben, in the midst of sitting up, held in a wince. He'd been asked this question many times before and always gave a flippant reply or stayed silent, chanting his mother's warning in his mind and waiting out the cleric's patience until he was left alone. But it was harder this time—his mind flashed to both Jophiel and Waron at the thought of vices falling to devilry. Didn't his terrible experiences over the past year prove the Gospel of Zald correct? Did he only have himself to blame?

It didn't matter. His urgent desire to go check on Isolde overrode any of Reuben's shame and uncertainty—and forced him to rethink his tactics this time, to end this visit as soon as possible.

"I've seen what you describe," he replied, watching as the dwarvish man's eyes briefly lit with surprise. "And far too often. I . . . I *will* think on your words, saer, in the months between your next charitable visit. Just give me time."

It worked—the cleric gave his bare knee a proud pat and backed away. "*Pray* on them as well," he said with a kind, friendly look, waiting for Reuben's nod before turning to go.

Reuben threw on his dayrobe and grabbed his violin the moment the cleric left, counting out ten long, agonizing seconds until the man had hopefully left the corridor and Reuben could check on the last of his loved ones he had been so bad at protecting of late.

Upon unlocking and entering Isolde's room, Reuben only wished he'd somehow made the cleric leave sooner.

There were angry, bloody scores running up and down her arms, and noticeable strands of hair on the floor. Her eyes were wild as her head whipped toward the sound of the opening door, though they didn't focus on Reuben for more than a moment before Isolde curled in on herself, pulling harshly at her hair as she muttered something like, "I can't, they won't hear," and "the slayer still lies in wait . . . the woeteller always knows . . ."

Reuben let out a shaky breath and shut the door behind him. "Isolde," he tried first, and when she didn't respond he started humming his *Soothe* incantation whilst setting his case on her vanity and pulling his violin out, watching her shoulders slowly loosen by the time he picked up the melody with the bow.

Within a minute of his playing, Isolde stood listless but relaxed, her bloodied fingers no longer tearing at her hair and skin. She was swaying slightly on her feet with half-lidded eyes when he switched to his *Healing Song,* the wounds on her arms fading with it. Isolde didn't fight when he eventually stopped—just let out a soft, confused sound as he gently helped her into bed.

Reuben spent the rest of the day by her side. He stepped outside of her room only once when Sidarchus came for the bordello's due from the nights prior, but the house manager graciously allowed him to postpone their accounting meeting to the following day. Even with the bordello's usual cut, once Reuben added the rest of his recent earnings to his stash he could tell he was *past* the 10,000 mark, now.

He took an inkwell and parchment back with him, planning to spend the rest of Repose at Isolde's bedside. If needed, he could even tell Everic to visit the tailor without him the next evening, as much as Reuben wanted to go.

But only a few hours later, Isolde's soft brown eyes blinked a bit clearer. She said in a croaking, broken voice, "Virtues and vices, gods and devils."

Reuben sat up from where he'd been slumped in his chair and idly writing a few more lyrics: *Oh, have you seen the smile / They dress over their wounds? / Or heard their laughter sing / A melancholy tune?*

"Some water?" he said, offering the waiting goblet. Isolde did lift her head and try to drink, so Reuben kept a supporting hand over hers until she'd managed a few sips. Once she laid back on the pillow, letting out a small, exhausted sigh, he commented offhandedly, "You say that a lot."

Isolde blinked; her eyes grew even clearer, to his relief, before she frowned and asked, "Say what?"

"Gods and devils, virtues and vices," Reuben repeated.

Isolde pursed her lips. "Well, that's all they are, aren't they?" When Reuben just gave her a confused look, she sighed. "*Here*, they talk about all the gods as if they're like us. A family, with relationships and generations, life and death. Like the story that Sazzo and Klera birthed Zaldus on this mountain, that His coming was so great it created the Ravine—and that was why true gold started running through it."

Reuben nodded, having heard a similar tale many times before. The first scripture in the Gospel of Zald told of the old gods' union, a cataclysmic fusion of Sun and Earth that rent the earth in two a millennia before miners dared to delve within and the first of mortal-kind beheld His Golden Light. The first piece of true gold was found intact there hundreds of years later, larger than a mortal heart, shining so brightly it blinded, and *calling* to the miners until eventually they began to commune with it.

He knew he shouldn't encourage her to talk about Loethia in this state, yet Reuben couldn't help but prompt, "And . . . it's described differently, elsewhere?"

Isolde's eyes grew distant. "In the north, they simply teach that all other gods save the one true god-pair, Vash and Nereen, are false—or worse, devils. But . . . where I grew up, further south in the Empire, we didn't distinguish them that way." Her eyes slotted closed, then, as if picturing something peaceful in her head. "They were all bodiless eidolons floating undisturbed through the moors, until they'd been empowered by a vice or virtue of mankind. Usually, a facet of both." She looked at Reuben then, something terribly sad in her gaze as she murmured, "I still find it easier to see things that way."

"It certainly sounds . . . less intimidating, I think," Reuben agreed, thinking of the imposing image Zaldus made in that painting, a golden figure towering over the lands. "Just embodiments of us, only fed by the actions of mortal-kind? Not scary at all."

Isolde huffed. "If the old Loethian war stories hold any truth, it wouldn't make their followers any less capable of leveling a battlefield—or changing the entire trajectory of a civilization."

She glared at the closed door, then, hands fisting in the sheets. Reuben glanced that way as well, realizing that something specific about the clerical visit that morning must have set off her spiral.

Up until now, he never asked questions about her past—how she got involved in Loethian espionage, what her mission in Sazzera was for, or how her cyclical consignment into this peculiar, erratic state of mind began. Mostly because Reuben wanted to give her space, to never pry about personal matters. But as he took in the hunch of Isolde's shoulders, the angry, frustrated look in her eyes now, Reuben realized that desire had likely been more for his benefit than her own.

"Either way, we are still free to decide our own path," he pointed out gently. And, whilst watching the anger in her eyes fade into a sad melancholy, decided now was the time to offer his friend some hope as well: "I'm going to get you out of here, Isi."

Isolde's brow crumpled. "What?"

Reuben reached out and gently smoothed a stray strand of hair from her face. "With all the business we've been getting, and my new private client especially, I've saved up more than half of what you need."

She shook her head, frowning at him. "Reubie, you can't . . ."

"But I *want* you to have it. I'll go with you to give it to Sidarchus as well, to make sure there are no issues."

Reuben quietly worried about giving anything to the vaults that wasn't the full amount—even the larger payments he'd sent in the past didn't seem to have the same impact he thought they should. But *half* of what was owed, offered all at once? There was no way the vault's accounts shouldn't reflect the difference.

At his words, however, Isolde's whole body went stiff, her hands clawing into the sheets.

"Isi?"

"I've told you, Reubie," she said softly, staring ahead at nothing. "Gold can't solve all of our problems. *Certainly* not mine."

"No, I don't think you understand—"

"I'm an enemy to this place," she snapped, glaring at him. "No one, not even *you*, trusts me. Nor should you—too often my mind is not my own. I *hurt* people. I have, and I will again. And the Zaldians know it."

Reuben had been shaking his head halfway through her words, though all he could say was, "Everything will be easier, once you're free—"

"Free? What good is all your precious cantergold, if they never intend to let me go?" Isolde demanded, new tears welling in her wide, bloodshot eyes. "If they told me I was only kept alive to be the *bait* for my captain's return?"

Reuben stared at her in utter confusion. Isolde had received a merciful sentence despite being some kind of Loethian spy, Sidarchus told him three years ago. For reasons only known to themselves, the Priesthood decided that she was not worthy of death. Instead she'd pay a high penance serving the people of Sazzera.

But, criminal or not, every debtor was supposed to have the chance to pay their debt in cantergold instead of labor. It was why some crimes were considered only fees, and sins just minor faults—at least, to the blessed of Zald who could afford them.

If Isolde didn't even have the *option* to pay off her debt, instead of working here day in and day out for the next twenty years or more . . .

. . . then it wasn't indenturement at all, Reuben realized with a sick twist in his gut.

"That can't be right," he whispered. Then repeated louder, "That can't be true, Isolde. I'll—I'll talk with Sid—I'm sure there's been some confusion—"

"Talk with *Sid*," she agreed, eyes flashing with anger again. "Hear it in his smooth, palatable terms if you must. He's the one you seem to trust the most."

"That's not true," Reuben denied again, even whilst growing awfully nauseous at how little he could defend the claim.

"Just go." Isolde laid back against her pillow, eyes distant with that same tired sort of defeat she always had in this state.

Except Reuben understood at last *why* she felt so defeated.

"I'll check on you soon," he promised, like always. And while Isolde usually seemed comforted by the notion, this time she gazed up at the ceiling in silence.

It didn't feel like much consolation to him either, as Reuben entered his room and eventually opened up his drawer again—staring within it at the dozen precious, heavy sacks of *useless* gold.

# 22

# NECESSARY REMINDER

"Y ou'll only be asking me for an emergency supply halfway through the month," Sidarchus argued late the next afternoon at their accounting meeting.

Reuben had already dressed for his next appointment with Everic, expecting the carriage at sundown. But that wouldn't be long now. Along with the air cooling and autumn quickly settling in came the benefits of longer, swifter nights—for both stellas *and* vampires.

He stood just inside the door, hoping against hope to keep this conversation short, and firmly declared, "I won't." Even if they both knew he had begged Sidarchus for a late order of voleris before.

Sidarchus placed his quill down on the logbook and leaned back, watching Reuben with narrowed eyes. "What is this about, dear? It's been a year since you asked for a change to your usual monthly order, much less removed voleris entirely. If its effects are waning, why not simply order four vials instead of six? Or go back to just three?"

Reuben had mentally practiced this before entering: "My client . . . they say it affects my *taste*."

He tried to sell his nerves as bashfulness, looking down and biting his lip.

Sidarchus's mild chuckle indicated he'd bought the lie, though he still chided, "Need I remind you, they are not your *only* client, Reubielocks? Voleris is available to any customer who wishes to enhance their evening with you. If they wanted a normal prostitute they could visit a lowly brothel or go to the bathhouses—it is certainly no fault of ours, should someone book with the Starlet Eye and *not* expect a stella."

Clearly this wasn't going to be a quick talk. "When requested, I will of course keep taking it . . . but just for a month, I've promised to refrain of my *own* accord." Reuben forced himself to step closer, giving Sidarchus a plaintive, pleading look. Then shut off most of his mind as he put a hand over Sidarchus's weathered one, stroking the loose, veiny skin with his thumb. "I don't want to lose this customer quite yet, Sid. And if I come back later regretting it, you can charge me double—*triple* this time for the emergency."

Sidarchus let out a slow, belabored sigh. "I wouldn't do such a thing."

He rubbed his other hand over Reuben's with an indulgent smile, and for a moment Reuben thought it had worked—he made to pull away, ready to be out of this conversation.

But Sidarchus's grip tightened, keeping Reuben there. "*Quite* a particular client you have, though, on top of wealthy and dangerous," he continued. "How are things in that regard? As stunning as you were the other night, I'd avoid looking too posh here in the future— you might send the false impression to other potential clients that they can't afford you, dear."

Reuben tried not to show his annoyance at Sidarchus's sudden change of subject. "I usually change at my client's, so I'm sure it won't happen again, Sid," he assured. "And it is going well—but only so far as I've managed to appeal to their *tastes*."

Sidarchus didn't seem convinced. "Make sure it doesn't start going

335

too well. Gold is not worth being burned at the stake, dear. Need I say again, you *must* pull out before the situation grows dangerous—perhaps sooner than you think."

Reuben slid his hand up from under Sidarchus's, squeezing the older man's forearm as he walked around the desk. "I know," he murmured, heart sinking at the admission—because Reuben *did* realize, more with every passing day, that his time with Everic would need to end sooner rather than later.

And if Sidarchus knew the Allunata were threatening him for it, he'd make Reuben stop this very instant.

"You're right, Sid. I promise . . . I'll end it the moment there's a hint of danger," Reuben said, even as violent memories from his time with Everic flashed behind his eyes.

Sidarchus gave Reuben a long, considering look—then smiled, shaking his head. "You've always been quicker than most in this coop to molt your feathers. I suppose we can trust your instincts. But yes . . . very well. For the sake of your *particular* client." He dipped his quill and crossed out a very specific line from Reuben's next order, his other hand rubbing the back of Reuben's palm. "I'll simply keep some extra on hand, my dear, for when you've changed your mind."

Reuben bit down a grimace and allowed the touch just a little longer. "'Particular' is putting it lightly," he said with a conspiratorial wink in return. "And, speaking of making me taste sweeter . . ."

By the time their meeting concluded, the evening had already started—and passed just as quickly. With a rush order of clothing selected, fitted, and paid for to meet High Ring fashion standards, a formal reply written and sent to the General of Security, High Priest, and Magnatus of House Luthur, and another session practicing conversation tactics for the party itself, Reuben's appointment with Everic that night was packed with official matters right up until dawn's approach.

Reuben returned to the bordello feeling accomplished but unreasonably flustered, considering it'd been all business until right before he left, when Everic said, "Plan to spend the evening here, before Lenaphon's party," and stroked the back of one finger briefly down Reuben's cheek before turning away.

It reminded Reuben for some silly reason of the moment he'd wanted to kiss Everic at the Ravine's edge. Now it was all his mind could think about.

That, and the fact he'd told himself he would stop their appointments once Everic had a High Ring contact, anyway. What if they did find him one such person at this party, just two days away? How could Reuben justify continuing, when there already was *more* than a hint of danger thanks to Waron?

The fear ate at him—it was no wonder, when Reuben woke up in a cold sweat that evening after dreaming Waron had materialized from the shadows.

He had enough gold. More than he knew what to do with, given his failed goal to help Isolde, except just turn it all over to Sidarchus and hope there wasn't some unexpected fee to mitigate the ten or so years of labor the amount should remove.

But he still hadn't gotten enough of Everic, Reuben admitted to himself whilst inspecting the two small, covered baskets Sidarchus had left on his vanity desk. And perhaps, he hadn't gotten the chance to *give* anything of much importance to the man either.

Whether this was their last party together or not . . . Reuben would have a chance to change that at their next appointment, at least.

Two nights later, the baskets were empty and a pouch for the morning's party preparations was filled. Reuben wore his lavender shawl over a ruffled shirt and left the bordello with a small amount of melancholy—wondering all the while when he'd next get the chance to spend time outside its thick, isolating walls, should the party go too well on the following day.

Once he reached the vampire's hidden abode and entered, Reuben was surprised to find Everic in what could only be described as a *cheerful* mood. He smiled at Reuben's entrance, then spoke warmly, "Your family has made it out of the city," holding up a letter.

Reuben's heart leapt at the news. "Are they somewhere safe? Did anything go amiss?" he questioned in quick succession whilst hurriedly setting his violin and bag on the bed, crossing to Everic's desk. "Do they need money sent for food, or lodging, or medicine . . . ?"

"They're safe." Everic nodded at another letter open on his desk. "Mezza made sure of it. He said this one is for you," and he held the letter in his hand out to Reuben.

Reuben took it without question, carefully untying the twine that secured it before he drank in the unpracticed but recognizable scrawl of Nahlia's hand on the page.

*Reuben,*

*We hope your pains are gone, and you are healthy and safe. Aldo was a very kind host to us once they arrived, though only for a few short days. Then young Mezza led us through many dark, uneven tunnels, which Daxus kept tripping on, and I am not supposed to describe further. But we are outside again at last and today arrived in a quiet, spacious lodge with a few others. Mezza said we could stay and care for those who pass through here in the future. I hope we can—there are chickens here in need of tending.*

*We understand now that it's not safe to return. It might not be for a very long time. So we can only send in written word, how very much we love you. Always have, always will, since the day Zald finally blessed us and Oriana placed her little sunbeam of joy in our arms.*

*And we couldn't be prouder of you. No matter your mother's faults, the best decision she ever made was bringing you into this world. Do not forget that, and do not hide that beautiful light in you, sunshine. It is our prayer that Zald will unite us one day soon. Zaldus Guide Us till then.*

*All our love, Nahlia and Daxus*

Reuben wanted to ask about exactly where this lodge was. He wanted to know *why* Everic had agreed to do so much for him. He wanted to demand the vampire send all of Reuben's useless gold to *them* now, however little it would help Nahlia and Daxus in what sounded like a remote place.

But he put on a smile and merely said, "I can't thank you enough, saer. After this . . . please know that anything, *anything* within my power to give you, I would."

Everic gave a short nod, eyes shifting away—but not before Reuben saw a brief spark in them.

"There *is* something," Reuben guessed, trying not to grow excited. He wondered if Everic could already smell something different about him, despite being more than a hand's reach away—he hadn't applied his usual rose oil, in hopes of not drowning out a possible new scent.

Before he could decide whether to breach the remaining distance, however, Everic visibly swallowed and started carefully, "You don't owe me any information about yourself. I just . . . if you're willing, I *did* wonder if that was your given name," and then he glanced up, searching Reuben with pensive, dark green eyes, "what Nahlia called you that night."

Reuben's whole body went rigid.

In his panic to get to them, he hadn't spent even a moment to consider that Everic would be around the only two people who actually spoke Reuben's name aloud. And due to the awful pain that had lanced through him after healing Daxus, Reuben couldn't even remember *when* it had been said in Everic's presence.

"Reuben," Everic said slowly, as if seeing how the word tasted on his tongue.

Reuben shuddered. Right then, he felt caught between wanting to back away, and yearning to lean down and taste it from Everic's mouth himself.

He hid the small shudder behind a weak chuckle, shrugging and busying himself with folding the letter back up. "Barely different from what you call me already."

Everic nodded, and even looked somewhat relieved at the fact. But then he asked in a slow, curious tone, "Which do *you* prefer?"

Reuben stiffened again.

It was uncanny every time, how with such simple words Everic managed to find the cracks in his facade. Reuben had spent decades perfecting his words and intonation to squeeze every drop of gold and affection that he could from others, to deflect and dismiss his way through conversations, and in so doing had grown hardened to the same tactics being used on him.

But apparently that only left him vulnerable to this sort of tactic. No added charm or eloquence; in fact, it was Everic's *lack* of pretense that was to blame, for so often exposing that terrifyingly vulnerable place inside of Reuben he couldn't name.

Forcing him to confront another uncomfortable truth now: that he couldn't recall the last time a single person had explicitly asked for *Reuben's* preference.

He'd run out of humorous deflections. Reuben only felt a now-familiar despair tightening his throat while he struggled to reply. "I don't . . ."

And Everic simply *waited*, damn him.

Reuben should confirm he wished for Everic to use his stage name, or its shortened, more palatable equivalent. It *was* close to his true name. And if any other client was asking, he wouldn't hesitate; Reubielocks had always acted as a protective shield between Reuben and everything his work required him to do. Lately, it was his last safeguard to avoid making a dozen more mistakes.

But for whatever reason, *this* was the single lie Reuben couldn't stomach the thought of, much less speak out loud.

"I don't think I can answer that," he whispered. And his hands tensed hard enough to start crinkling the letter in his hand, as Reuben braced himself for Everic to press further.

Everic looked like he might. Discontent lined his mouth and between his brows, his eyes still searching. Silence stretched between them for a long, uncomfortable moment, and it took everything in Reuben not to fill it with empty excuses.

But to Reuben's surprise and utter relief, Everic gave a brief nod and turned his gaze.

"Zeya just dropped off the order from the tailor shop," he said in a blatant change of subject, nodding at a large clutter of finely-tied, paper-wrapped boxes Reuben hadn't noticed in the corner next to the wardrobe.

Reuben gratefully encouraged the distraction. With a forcibly-bright smile he stowed the letter away and walked over to inspect the order. "How exciting! I thought it would be impossible for her to outdo what she accomplished for us at the guild ball, but I'm happy to be proven wrong."

At best, he was hoping for a mild diversion from the tension of

Everic's confronting, unanswered question. But when he opened the first box, Reuben's breath caught in his throat—and he knew he *had* been proven wrong by her.

"Is it to your liking?" Everic asked.

Reuben stood back up, shaking out the carefully folded silk doublet. It was left unpadded to match the recent higher style, apparently, the fabric white but heavily embroidered in gold thread, with a large section of its back left bare save for a sheer, sparkling material and a few rows of dangling gold chains.

"It can't be a good idea for a whore to wear Zaldian colors," Reuben murmured as he fingered the delicate material—unwilling to admit he loved *everything* about the piece.

"You once said the same about going to a High Ring event," Everic countered, crossing over to join him. "And now you've been personally invited."

Reuben swallowed and set the doublet back in its box, standing and turning to face Everic without any real hope of arguing. But Everic had stopped behind him much closer than expected—and Reuben watched as the vampire stiffened, nostrils flared, eyes moving straight to Reuben's neck.

Everic was usually better at catching himself when he did it, quick to look away before it could count as staring. This time, his throat bobbed as his eyes stayed *locked* on their target. His voice came out sharp but slightly thick as he demanded, "Why do you smell like that?"

"Like what?" Reuben hid a smile and played dumb for now, shrugging. "I always add rose oil to my neck and wrists, I suppose—is it too strong this time?"

He pulled back his sleeve and held up his forearm expectantly for Everic to test.

The vampire's eyes flashed, staring at Reuben's bare wrist even as he flinched a step backward.

Given Everic *would* be drinking from him tonight regardless, Reuben felt only a small bit of guilt for the tease. "Alright, you've caught me—I replaced my voleris order with half a bushel of raspberries this month, since you're curious," he said with a small smile, lowering his arm. "And ate two baskets-worth in the last two days . . . though I didn't know how much of a difference it would make."

Everic ripped his eyes away and stood very still—not breathing anymore.

"I've told you," Reuben reassured, stepping closer, "I'm here at your pleasure, saer. And since you would finally be drinking from me again tonight, I thought . . ."

Reuben didn't want to cross any lines. But he did take one more step as his words trailed off, running a hand through his hair to make sure it was all cascading down one side and exposing the right side of his neck entirely.

Everic's eyes flickered up to watch the movement. After a moment his shoulders lowered and he hesitantly leaned forward, which Reuben encouraged with a blatant tilt of his neck.

A pleased stutter of breath escaped Reuben as the vampire finally ducked his head in and took a long, audible inhale through the nose, right where it hovered just above Reuben's skin.

Reuben brought a hand up, gently cupping the back of Everic's head to welcome him closer. Then, at last, he felt the vampire's lips brushing against his neck.

"Sweeter . . . but also bitter," Everic murmured, and Reuben shuddered at the cool wisps of breath on his neck. "A hint of something like rose, still."

Reuben swallowed hard, now the one worried about control—right then, he had to stop himself from reaching for the small of Everic's back and pulling him in closer.

He balled his free hand into a fist instead. "Sounds . . . nice."

With Everic's mouth poised there, it was both everything and nothing Reuben had expected to feel since the first time he agreed to give his blood to a vampire. The brief thrill of fear and anticipation, the primal understanding of danger, the vulnerable intimacy of a mouth brushing his neck—it was all there as expected, and would have been from the beginning should Everic have always used his fangs.

But thanks to everything that had grown between them in the months since, Reuben's fear was faint. Instead he felt abuzz with an anxious excitement, an eager impatience, and a twinge of arousal with Everic's lips there, still no more than a gossamer touch.

Then Everic leaned back, searching Reuben's face. "What did you do this for?"

Reuben's excitement faded. He couldn't keep that gaze for long—not without emotions he himself didn't understand growing too blatant on his face.

"Should I not have?" Reuben whispered, ready to take a step back.

Instead, he felt a finger carefully lift his chin, nudging his face up to meet Everic's eyes once more. "That's not what I asked," Everic pointed out, soft but firm.

Reuben bit his lip and tried to consider. The *why* behind whatever he did used to be so simple—always for gold and for his loved ones, which often was one and the same. What else would ever matter?

But Everic's gold was pointless to him now. Nahlia and Daxus were safe beyond his reach, and Isolde had turned out to be even more stuck in her circumstances than Reuben. Shaving off a decade or two of his debt would still count as worthwhile . . . but it had nothing to do with the burning desire to be with Everic every chance he got, to please him in ways he never asked for, and to touch and be touched by him at every given chance, Reuben admitted to himself.

Though he couldn't imagine saying all of that out loud. "I told you I wanted to thank you, and I do, but . . ."

"But I keep telling you there's no need," Everic finished when Reuben didn't, pulling back enough that Reuben had to drop the hand on his neck. "And you continue trying to give these—these *favors* in return anyway. Do you still think I will discard you? Are you so worried about whether I'll give you your pay?"

Reuben's first instinct was to apologize. Yet in meeting Everic's gaze, he could see there was not only confusion and frustration behind the man's question, but *grief* as well.

A grief akin to Reuben's own despair, he realized.

"Not at all. I—I just . . . I told you I'd been imagining it, how you might touch me," he stumbled through his words, ignoring the niggling shame worming through his gut at the tiny admission, the heat growing in his cheeks. "I liked the thought of us getting . . . close. That wasn't a lie."

Everic's face only darkened. "Unlike everything else you said that night?" he accused, frowning as he took a step back, likely about to make his usual move—walk off and abandon Reuben here alone for the rest of the night.

Reuben wouldn't allow it this time. He couldn't argue well without further dishonesty, but he refused to let Everic shut the door yet again, to leave even more questions and tension hanging between them—not when their time was so short.

So, without further thought for the consequences, he wound a hand around the back of Everic's neck and leaned in, his voice soft yet fervent as he said, "*This* isn't a lie."

Then Reuben brushed a kiss against Everic's lower lip.

He only pulled back a hair's breadth afterward; their lips hovered just short of touching again as Reuben waited.

Everic stayed still for a long, nerve-racking moment. And he would have every right to be angry. To push Reuben away, to never trust him again for what was yet *another* promise broken.

But then—to Reuben's surprise and utter relief—he tilted his head and returned the kiss.

Tentatively, gently, he kissed Reuben back, in a way that only made sense, given how the vampire had always touched him before. But after Reuben eagerly matched his movements, Everic deepened it— sighing out a gust of breath through his nose before strong hands were suddenly sliding up Reuben's back and threading into his hair.

Reuben's heart picked up in response. He quickly parted his lips for the next kiss, and a small groan escaped at feeling a cool swipe of tongue. Relaxing further, Reuben wrapped his other arm around the vampire's narrow hips, pressing their chests together as he kissed Everic Payne with more enthusiasm than he'd felt for the intimacy in a very, *very* long time.

Of course, Reuben had kissed too many people by now to call Everic the most technically skilled or practiced. Yet he also couldn't recall the last time his body had grown so warm and affected so quickly as the man held him tighter and, despite how careful Everic always was, started to kiss Reuben like he was aching for every taste— like he was *hungry*.

Reuben lost himself in the slow but building heat between them. He didn't want to just experience *this* with Everic, he realized in the midst of clinging desperately to the man, feeling a sharp curl of arousal as Everic sucked and gently bit at his lower lip. The reason behind his actions was actually quite simple. Reuben just wanted Everic, in every emotional, mental, and physical way he could have him.

He wasn't merely at risk of believing in the exceptional anymore, as Sidarchus warned—Reuben was *falling in love* with the dangerous exception.

When Everic's kisses slowed, his grip loosening, Reuben only felt a small twinge of disappointment in the face of this beautiful, terrible, distracting revelation. He let Everic rest their foreheads together, their elevated breaths mingling in the small space between them, and didn't allow himself to question everything it meant quite yet.

Instead, after he'd caught his breath Reuben angled his head to expose his neck again and whispered, "Please."

Everic's breathing all at once cut off. He leaned back and looked at Reuben's neck with what was clearly trepidation, despite the blown-out state of his pupils.

Then slowly, hesitantly—*hungrily*—he nodded.

He led Reuben by the hand to the bed, silent as they sat down. Reuben stopped to pull off his shirt, hoping to avoid any stains, but saw how quickly Everic's face was already clouding over with doubts, even anger, while he watched Reuben.

*Too careless*; *despicable*; those were the words he'd used to describe himself after their few intimate moments. And there was a high likelihood Everic was thinking something similar of himself now, even if Reuben could only guess as to why.

Taking a guess, he carefully leaned in with a hand on Everic's thigh and kissed him—just another soft press of lips—before murmuring, "Don't pay me for tonight."

To his relief, the anger and doubts fled Everic's expression as his eyes flashed with surprise.

Reuben continued, "Your generosity has always been so kind, but . . . this isn't for that."

Slowly, Everic took Reuben's hand in both of his, thumbs brushing up and down his knuckles. "What is it for?"

Reuben finally had the words now, even if he was terrified of them. Even if he questioned their validity, given he'd just now admitted them to himself, not to mention his very limited, deeply flawed experience with *love* up to this point.

He couldn't bring himself to say them out loud, however.

"For you," Reuben said, hoping these words would be enough instead. "For me. Only a moment, for . . . for *us*, and nothing else."

Everic considered Reuben's vague words for a moment. Then he sat under his knees and leaned over Reuben, pressing their lips together once more—his hand moving around to splay against Reuben's lower spine at the same time, gently helping him fall back. And once Reuben was lying on the mattress Everic stopped kissing him, letting go of Reuben's hand to brush a stray curl away from his bare neck.

"Stay *very* still," Everic warned, flashing Reuben one of his characteristic frowns.

Reuben answered with a smile as the bed shifted and the vampire crouched more intentionally over him. Letting his eyes flutter shut, as Everic leaned down and pressed a kiss against his neck.

Then he felt Everic's fangs sink in, and Reuben cried out.

Instinctively, he grabbed at Everic's shoulders. The pain came much sharper from this entry point, he was surprised to feel—though just as quick as it came, it left him. The initial animal fear still returned, intent on struggling against the predator at his neck. But this time he could anticipate and ignore it better, breathing out to ebb the panic. The soothing stroke of Everic's hand up and down his flank helped as well, even as the vampire kept a firm, restraining grip on the opposite side of Reuben's neck.

It switched to pleasurable at a swifter speed too, even before Everic's fangs pulled free. Something in the venom, Reuben guessed as his body went boneless, his thoughts growing hazy.

A far too genuine moan escaped him as Everic's bite ended and he felt the vampire begin to drink, the suction of his mouth at Reuben's sensitive neck a sharp yet pleasing contradiction of sensations. And Reuben felt a primal curl of satisfaction when Everic made a few low, needy sounds muffled against his neck in return.

On the other hand, Reuben's strength sapped away much quicker than usual. Or perhaps it was just easier to stay aware of what Everic was doing in such a vital place—Reuben never stopped feeling the tugging current against his lifeblood's usual flow in his neck. And with every suck of the vampire's mouth, he noted a headache forming as well, even though it'd been less than a minute since they laid down.

Reuben had to fight down the conflicting desire to keep Everic cradled here forever anyway.

"Everic," he whispered, then trailed a few fingers up and down Everic's back, enjoying how the man briefly shuddered against him. "Everic . . . I'm feeling . . . I think—"

Everic's spine went rigidly still before Reuben had managed to explain further. Then the vampire switched to laving a tongue against the sensitive bite wound instead, surging Reuben's senses back into a distracting, intensive pleasure. By the time he felt Everic's mouth pull away, Reuben was back to gasping and clinging to him, barely stopping himself from grinding up against the man.

Everic looked down at Reuben *terrified*, however, immediately dousing Reuben's arousal.

"Are you alright?" Everic demanded, a hand moving to finger Reuben's pulse and the other grabbing to feel his forehead and cheek. Everic's vivid, golden eyes were wide and fearfully flicking over Reuben's face. "Do you feel nauseous? How well can you breathe?"

Reuben swallowed—then winced, as that irritated the wound—before taking inventory of himself. But the only reaction he noted in his body, besides the flagging arousal, was a sudden desire to sleep.

"Just tired again." He tried to offer a reassuring smile, shaking his head—then blinked rapidly a few times as his head swam from the shaking motion, and corrected, "Maybe a bit dizzy. But . . . much better than last time."

His eyes widened, however, when Everic's face crumpled in response.

Without another word, the vampire dropped his forehead onto Reuben's clavicle. And when Reuben tentatively smoothed a hand down the back of Everic's head, Everic's next breath came with a loud hitch to it.

"Are *you* alright?" Reuben whispered.

There was a long beat of silence, before Everic admitted with a sudden frankness: "I killed him." His voice came out choked and angry, half-muffled against Reuben's chest. "Alphonz, my husband— the one time I drank from him, I didn't stop. I . . . I managed to get help and revive him. But even once I learned some control, I only ever drank from others after that, not him."

Reuben kept a hand in his hair, the other stroking up and down Everic's back in what he hoped was a soothing gesture. "You revived him," he tried to comfort, holding back a dozen new questions. "That's what matters."

"I'm still the reason he's dead," Everic whispered.

He lifted his head then, his golden eyes reddened and wet with tears. And Reuben didn't understand why he was saying any of this, what context if any it was supposed to provide—right up until Everic stroked a thumb along Reuben's healing neck and spoke softly, "I've grown weary of destroying the things that I love."

After months of seeing the man deny himself, Reuben had anticipated a confession or indulgence of physical desire at some point . . . but he'd never expected *this* from the ever-grim, ever-closed-off Everic Payne.

A hundred emotions bombarded Reuben in response. Fear, most prominently, and also joy, anxiety, even a touch of guilt, though he couldn't quite find that one's source. Hope as well, that *love* might be something reciprocal, if still budding, between them. Followed by deep incredulity, given how Everic's feelings were sure to change once he learned of Reuben's betrayal.

Quickly all of that faded into the background of his mind, however, considering Reuben still needed to respond and somehow assure the man. The quickest way would be to communicate his own nebulous feelings for Everic, even if he'd only accepted their reality tonight. Or much simpler, he could pull Everic in for another kiss, and hope that was enough to placate or distract the man until the morrow.

In the dizzy state of his mind and the panic of his indecision, Reuben did neither. Instead he fell back to instinct, sourcing an unserious, surface-level reply from his practiced persona: "Well, then it's a good thing I tend to heal so well, saer."

Everic's eyes shut, his jaw clenching. Almost like he was outwardly wincing at Reuben's words—and then Reuben realized Everic was, at a very *specific* one.

*It is a reminder to me of the imbalance between us,* Everic had told him months ago. Reuben hadn't thought much of using *"saer"* ever since, though, considering Everic had amended, *Keep using it. It is a necessary reminder, I think.*

"And—you are the most careful man I know, *Everic,*" Reuben continued, then stroked a hand along Everic's cheek, trying to ease the tension on his face. "There's no need for honorifics or 'reminders' now between us, is there?"

Everic reached up a hand to gently squeeze Reuben's wrist, stopping its movement. "So long as you are dependent, *enslaved . . .*" He shook his head, even as his voice betrayed cracks in that weathered wall of resolve.

Reuben only felt a deep, aching fondness—a growing *love*—in response.

But even if Everic knew for certain that power dynamics, obliga-tions, and cantergold had nothing to do with why Reuben wanted more with every passing day to hold and kiss him, make him happy far beyond the fleeting smiles Reuben managed to put on his face now . . . still, Reuben had little to offer anyone besides pretty lies.

Perhaps just one thing, he realized, swallowing hard.

It took him a moment to gather his courage, before he leaned up on an elbow and whispered, "Call me Reuben . . . just for tonight?"

He felt the tension in Everic's body, half-laid over him still, drain in response.

Then Everic let go of his wrist, smoothing it to cup the back of his hand and kiss the inside of his palm. "Reuben," he murmured against Reuben's skin—and sighed, sitting up. "You should eat something," he explained before Reuben's heart could sink, leaving him on the bed and heading towards the door.

By the time he returned with a platter, Reuben had changed into another borrowed nightshirt. He ate and drank dutifully what he was given, thinking hard all the while. But with the High Ring party looming over them, Reuben's mind scrambled to come up with ways to avoid losing Everic after all this: acting brash and rude around any of the prospective contacts they met tomorrow; continuing their appointments regardless of the party's outcome; somehow telling Everic of Waron's threat without incriminating himself.

None of his ideas would change the fact that he'd been blatantly lying to Everic, however. And nothing was sure to actually stop the Allunata, if he ignored the warning long enough and Waron decided to take him. Not when the man could break into the bordello, disappear into shadows, and watch Reuben whilst he was entirely unaware.

Reuben blinked back tears as he drained the last of his cup. That familiar despair had returned, ruining every good, hopeful feeling that the kissing and closeness and confession from Everic had just inspired. He tried to subtly wipe at his eye, but given how Everic was watching him eat like always, it wasn't a surprise when the vampire noticed.

"Reuben?" Everic spoke his true name again, this time in a worried tone—and it only made Reuben want to collapse into him and apologize for a dozen things he didn't have a hope of forgiveness for.

Instead Reuben pushed away the empty tray, then pulled back the bed covers and simply asked, "Stay for a while?"

Everic's eyes moved from Reuben to the bed with uncertainty. But whatever expression was on Reuben's face, it persuaded him—his eyes softened before he nodded, then moved to clear the tray and change out of his own daywear.

Once Everic had put on a pair of loose sleeping trousers and was laying just an arm's reach away, Reuben leaned in and pressed one last kiss against his lips—murmuring, "Sweet dreams, Everic."

Half-lidded and fanned under dark lashes, the vampire's golden gaze had never looked more beautiful to him as Everic answered, "Good night, Reuben."

Whatever else the new day would bring—intrigue and insult, truth and betrayal, blood and more blood—at least, for the first time since this business arrangement began between them, Reuben woke up in Everic's bed and didn't find himself alone come morning.

# 23

# HIGH RING

Likely thanks to the blood loss, he'd fallen asleep immediately and without a care—but part of Reuben's subconscious must have still braced for something to be initiated in the middle of the night.

"Reuben?"

His mind felt hazy, his body overheated and restless from some fragmented memory-turned-dream as his eyes blinked open to the pitch dark. Most of the dream was lost now, though Reuben remembered the end too well: Sidarchus sneaking in to visit him, just as he had after the first time Reuben tried voleris. Except this time Reuben wasn't 14, and Everic was still sleeping there next to him, adding to his dizzy distress as he heard a voice in his ear telling him to *be good, relax, you'll like this . . .*

Everic's low voice next to him asking, "Reuben?" a second time was what finally snapped him out of it.

Reuben realized he was fisting the blanket in both hands, his breathing heavy, his body abuzz with both anxiety and a discomfiting sort of arousal over something he hadn't thought about in years—no, *decades.*

He wasn't alone in his dead mother's bed this time, though. Reuben shifted and reached out blindly into the darkness, stuttering out a sigh when he found the sturdy, comforting shape of Everic not far on the other side of the mattress. He thought no further before scooting forward and wrapping his feverish limbs around the vampire's still form, hiding half his face away into the cool, soothing slope of Everic's bare chest until the tension drained from his body.

Everic, on the other hand, didn't breathe. But after a moment of perfect stillness, he shifted his limbs until he was carefully holding Reuben, and a minute later whispered, "The candle went out . . . should I go light another?"

Reuben swallowed down the pit of shame forming in his throat, and only clung tighter to the man in answer.

At what felt like a much more natural hour to his body, Reuben woke for a second time to find Everic still there in his arms—though clearly not the *whole* time, given the three new candles lit on the bedside table. Reuben was only thankful, however, as the light helped him see Everic's hand resting nearby, which he interlaced with his own.

Everic allowed Reuben to maneuver their joined hands over the vampire's pale chest in silence. And in the first sleepy minutes of waking, Reuben didn't mind the quiet between them either. He was busy remembering all that had happened the night before—even more, what *didn't* happen—and found himself filled with both relief and regret as late morning brought with it a cold light of awareness onto his situation.

Relief, that Everic hadn't stormed off again and Reuben didn't ruin possibly their final night together by kissing him.

But even more, *regret*, that such a pointless, distracting revelation had intruded during the otherwise lovely last night he'd planned for them.

Perhaps he could just ignore it. After all, what did Reuben even know about that kind of emotion? His only experience with something close to romantic love thus far was early and immature, in the midst of his youth. Even then, whenever Reuben looked back on his younger self's needy desire for Sidarchus's attention and affection, his willingness to please the older man without even gold as an excuse, he only felt a sharp uneasiness.

Sidarchus had said he loved Reuben too, on occasion, only to treat him the same way he did to this day—like little more than a naive, stupid child.

And this situation was arguably worse. If it was the right word to use, *loving* someone who was a client, not to mention a vampire, not to mention planning to assassinate the country's leader . . . surely Reuben would only regret it more, this time.

Trying to distract himself from such thoughts, he decided to break the silence. "I was out too quickly to see how a vampire falls asleep."

A tiny scoff pushed out from the chest beneath him. "It's a rather boring, efficient affair," Everic said, his voice quiet but content in a way Reuben wasn't sure he'd heard before. "I close my eyes, go very still in both body and mind. Then . . . simply decide to open them."

"No nightmares?"

Everic's arms tightened around him for a moment. His head angled, cheek resting against Reuben's head. "No nightmares. Though . . . no dreams either."

"Hmm." Reuben began examining the various scars along Everic's knuckles and palm, tracing a finger over each tendon and line shaping the pale hand—and found new lyrics quickly form in his mind as he hummed to himself: *Oh, have you traced the scars / That prove their battles won / Yet make the mind forget / The war is truly done?*

As he ran a finger over a thicker, bumpy line curving down from the outer edge of Everic's thumb, Reuben mused: "I just realized, all these scars . . . but I haven't noticed anything like a bite."

He kept his eyes down, prepared to move on to a new subject if this one was pushing things too far.

But it seemed, for all there was left to know, Everic's misplaced trust in him hadn't faltered yet. "Not all of us have bite scars," he answered. Then ran nails up and down Reuben's back, drawing out a heavy, relaxed sigh from him as Everic continued, "Particularly the older vampires."

Reuben considered this with a contemplative frown. Of course, vampires *were* a far newer and therefore less known phenomenon than the old monsters and shapeshifters of legend. With how rare it was for any devilish creature to survive long in the holy, protected city of Sazzera, all the legends he knew were gleaned from the recountings of the destroyed coven and its vampiric leader as told in the Gospel of Zald.

Perhaps Everic never had a vampiric master who bit him—perhaps he simply died, and happened to be chosen by whichever devil was responsible for creating this new, hauntingly beautiful type of monster.

Reuben brushed his thumb over the nearest scar again. "And all of these?"

Everic did stiffen, then.

"You don't have to tell me—"

"War," Everic answered lowly, however, at last confirming Reuben's suspicions. When Reuben lifted his head, he took in the grim expression on the vampire's face, and opened his mouth to apologize. But not before Everic continued, "The first one, anyway . . . back when I had the ability to scar. But that's—"

Reuben hastily cut in, "I didn't mean to pry—"

"I'm sure it's little surprise." Everic met his eyes, then. The gold in them was less stark this morning, though still vivid enough to distract Reuben until the vampire spoke again. "I . . . I know you said you were happy to remain in the dark about these things. And there is danger in knowing them—but I am not sure it would mean any *more* danger than what I have already put you in. Only things I would not hide from you, should we . . . well, should we continue any notion of *this*." He nodded at Reuben laying half-over him with an uncertain frown.

Reuben swallowed, an anxious fluttering in his chest at the mere idea of continuing this "*notion*." He loved the thought of being able to kiss and hold each other if he did return for another appointment; he also feared it, for the inevitable failed expectations and countless mistakes he would have to fret over, and worse—the terrible sense of loss, once it was over.

But having all his suspicions about Everic confirmed, the moment he asked for it . . . did any of that matter to him now?

More than likely, Everic was a Loethian soldier sent here to kill Sazzera's leader and weaken it for invasion. Should he succeed, many more than the Voice of Zald would die, and certainly the whole city would suffer.

But did the city not already suffer? And was it not *Sazzera* that had threatened Reuben's loved ones or was still holding them captive, not the devilcrafted monster currently in his arms?

On the other hand, vilifying any one side of an argument had never served him—he didn't need to have *any* opinion, Reuben comforted himself for now. Everic would execute his plan regardless. And no matter how Reuben felt about it, they *couldn't* continue this notion, this intimacy. Not for very long.

In the meantime, however, he couldn't bear seeing any measure of grief return to Everic's eyes. So after a beat of silence while he considered, Reuben smiled and reached up with his free hand to cup Everic's sharp jaw, leaning in to brush a kiss against his mouth.

His stomach sank when Everic put a staying hand on his shoulder before he could—then fell even lower as Everic reminded, "I'm paying you for today, remember?"

Reuben opened his mouth to argue, but found himself unable. Even if he had some savings to be irresponsible and frivolous with now, he shouldn't keep offering what he did last night. In the end, gold was still his only excuse for being here.

The truth was, even when he *didn't* embrace Reubielocks—Reuben couldn't escape him, either.

After that, Everic kept quiet and reserved throughout their morning preparations. Perhaps Reuben had gone too far, asking about the scars—or Everic was regretting every line they'd crossed the night before.

And maybe Reuben *would* have been better off not knowing what his true name sounded like in Everic's voice, or what it felt like to be held by him. Maybe then it would have been easier to focus as he helped with smoothing and tying back Everic's hair, and put some of his own gold powder on Everic's eyelids and cheekbones —instead of getting lost in memories of kissing the man's lips.

Or at least, less painful when Everic moved over to the wardrobe and said, "I have cloaks we can walk through the Hollows with, Reu— *Reubielocks*," frowning as he corrected himself.

Reuben fell quiet as well, avoiding eye contact as they both dressed and put on the unassuming cloaks. Last, he grabbed his violin and took one more second to memorize the candlelit room, just in case, before nodding his head at Everic to go.

The cloaks helped both with concealment, given how conspicuous their outfits would make them in the Hollows, as well as combating the mild chill of the early autumn day. Of course, by the time they reached the top of the main stair where Mezza and Zeya would bring the carriage, Reuben was glad for the cool breeze, out of breath and overheated from the cheery midday sun as they approached.

The two infernal siblings stood at attention, acknowledging Everic with low nods. Once Everic nodded back, however, Zeya hurried forward to Reuben and wrapped him in a tight hug.

"Thanks for saving my idiot brother," she whispered. "Bev *said* you were a good one." And as she pulled back, Mezza shot Reuben a wink from behind her.

Everic was giving them both a stiff, disapproving look, though it faded at seeing Reuben's surprised but smiling face while Zeya turned back to the horses.

While Mezza opened the door and they both entered the carriage, however, Reuben's smile quickly fell as he thought of the few allies they'd have at the event today. Everic himself sat and stared out the small window with a shuttered expression, content to maintain the silence between them rather than review strategy, it seemed.

But given Everic was paying for him today, as he'd so *helpfully* reminded, Reuben still had a job to do. And Reubielocks would never let such a harmless thing as physical rejection stop him from earning his pay.

"Such an exciting day!" he started. "I didn't ask last night—did you ever hear word of whether Saers Blanca Orlyn and Randal Kapriyah would be attending today?"

Everic blinked hard, as if pulling himself out of a spiral of thoughts, before he met Reuben's gaze. "I . . . Blanca Orlyn will be accompanying Aldo, yes. Kapriyah didn't manage an invite, unfortunately, but Aldo says there is a good handful of magnatus and high society members that the guild has some acquaintance with."

That was a good start—but not enough with how little time they had. So Reuben pressed further, "Any that are close with the Priesthood, with the Voice?"

Everic frowned. "Lenaphon has been the city's head over Sazzeran security, including all sentry units and military troops, for more than a century now."

Reuben blinked, surprised—though now he did vaguely recall Saer Artris mentioning "Head of Security" as one of her titles upon their introduction. Still, she hadn't seemed very old, from what little her masked figure gave away, and such a high position wouldn't have been handed to someone without plenty of experience.

"Also, Delvanzus confirmed with me yesterday—she is one of the five officially on the council," Everic added.

Reuben's eyes widened. "Then . . . if you gained her favor quickly, *she* could invite you to observe a council meeting?"

Everic gave a stiff, unhappy nod. "It sounds like it. Though, as confident as I am in *your* talents, that is still a very large 'if' given my one interaction with her so far."

Reuben shrugged, offering him an encouraging smile. "You weren't friendly, but you stood out and questioned her in a sea of bootlickers," he pointed out. "She didn't give us an invitation for nothing, and with the reasoning we've practiced, I'd say you have a good chance of persuading her. Sometimes it's smart to play by the rules—but, like I've told you, some unconventionality, a bit of *interest*, can take you far."

"If I have your melodic tongue nearby, anyway, to bend the rules in my favor," Everic stipulated, his eyes crinkling around a small smile.

It quickly faded once Reuben returned it, however, morphing back into a worried frown as Everic's eyes strayed back to the window.

They ended up riding together in silence for the next twenty minutes, stopped or slowed at times as the carriage moved through the busy streets of the main ring up to the highest sector of the city.

There was an issue at the High Ring gates further halting their progress—sentry guards arguing with Zeya about something, by what muffled words Reuben could hear from within the carriage.

361

After a minute Everic let out a sharp, annoyed breath and pulled out the Zaldian token from Artris as he wrenched open the door, jumping out to intervene.

The argument ended soon after, all but Everic's voice dying down. Reuben heard apologetic murmurs and then Everic's curt reply, "I'll make sure House Luthur hears how you've treated their guests," as he moved back to the open carriage door, fuming as he ducked and climbed back inside.

Everic's expression was stormy as he sat back down. "Our first taste of *High Ring hospitality*, I think."

Once the carriage started moving again, Reuben fiddled with the more-complicated veil the tailor had fashioned for the occasion, guessing that the likelihood of coming across a Zaldian priest just tripled. He had already fastened the curtain of crystal and gold beads to the cuffed jewelry capping the points of his ears, but now slipped the band down from his hair to rest dangling from his brow, more fully obscuring his eyes.

He was distracted trying to tighten the ear caps when Everic suddenly said, "I should never have involved you in any of this."

Reuben froze for a second. Then he slowly lowered his hands, swallowing hard as a dozen worries and inadequacies crashed down from just those few words.

"What do you mean?" he asked, trying not to panic. Remembering how often Everic's anger turned out to be self-directed, he tentatively encouraged, "We're *so* close to getting you an invite to view the next council, I can feel it."

"And then?" Everic countered. "I knew this mission could cost me my life—what's left of it, anyway. But you . . ." He paused, looking pained now. "I cannot see a future, whether I fail or succeed, where the eye of suspicion *doesn't* turn your way."

Considering Reuben was already being watched by some anonymous higher up, he wondered if it would make any difference. "You've said it yourself, saer," he said around a wavering smile, "I'm a talented actor. I'm sure I can talk my way out of it, should I be accused."

Everic regarded Reuben with those ever-searching eyes. Then he said, blunt and to the point, "If today goes well, and I do somehow secure an invite to the last trade council—you *must* run. You must be long gone, for your own sake, by the time I enter the Cantara Circle and complete my business with the Voice. Do you understand?"

Reuben did, even if he wished not to. But hearing the danger laid out so plainly now, Everic himself admitting the likely fallout of his goals, all while now knowing Reuben had come to *love* the man . . .

He couldn't help but argue, "There has to be a safer way; you still have countless war councils your target may show up at once the matters of trade are over. Or, if there is no safe method, surely we can find an alternative . . ." He trailed off as Everic began shaking his head.

"There is no alternative to her death," Everic said through gritted teeth. "Only once the Voice is gone from this city, will its tyranny no longer be eternal, and regular mortal-kind can decide whether to continue what she's done or start anew."

"Then at least with more discretion," Reuben conceded. After considering Everic's words further, however, he had to question, "If she's immortal, like you—what makes you think you *can* kill her?"

Everic's eyes shifted away from Reuben again. "Sometimes . . . a thing's strength is also its weakness," he muttered. "I can explain more, but not here. Just—trust me, something like *her* shouldn't exist. The amount of suffering she's caused . . ." He trailed off, looking all at once old and weary.

Reuben bit his lip, glancing out the window, and felt a jolt of surprise to see they were now passing *trees*. What seemed like a forest, almost, except the branches were neatly trimmed and the trunks grew in uniform rows.

"It seems *some* are living quite well for themselves under her rule," he said, catching glimpses of a grand white mansion through a red and gold canopy of autumn leaves, just before the road began curving in that very direction.

"And any who are not prospering can easily be labeled as sinners," Everic replied lowly, both of them watching as the mansion of House Luthur grew closer in their window's view. Once it curved out of sight as the carriage reached it, he glanced back at Reuben, eyes narrowed. "Will you truly consider it this time? *Please?*"

Reuben couldn't pretend to misunderstand. "Running?"

At Everic's nod, Reuben looked away, hoping to think of some further excuse, some reason to explain the stubborn, gnawing desire to *stay,* beyond wanting to just be there for Isolde, or avoid bringing danger to Nahlia and Daxus, or even his blossoming love for Everic.

*Freedom is the only song a person must fight to sing . . .*

But Reuben had never been much of a fighter. And with a real foe that couldn't be flattered away or paid with gold, what more could he actually offer to save those he loved? So long as Reuben remained so powerless, wasn't fleeing the only option besides surrender?

Before he could think on it further, the carriage came to a stop— and their first party in High Ring commenced.

When Mezza opened the carriage door, Reuben took in a perfectly manicured lawn sculpted around the tall, columned mansion, with people spilling from both sets of open double doors.

Everic had already unfastened his cloak and left it on the carriage bench. Reuben followed suit while Everic climbed out, then adjusted his beaded veil one last time before taking Everic's hand to step down—and felt a smile curling at the corner of his lips when Everic took in his ensemble with an expression akin to the one he usually wore whilst staring at Reuben's neck.

The tailor had done an excellent job with Everic as well, of course: his angular features had been perfectly accentuated by a suit coat with a sharp fit at the shoulder, lapels with the left side flared out in an asymmetric style, all of it in differing shades of black and slate gray with violet accents. Even more, his collar had been left bare, the ruffled black shirt beneath the coat plunging down in a deep, v-shaped neckline.

Despite the misstep of this morning, Reuben didn't care to be subtle as he eyed Everic's form—and silently promised himself he would try to offer physical affection at least *once* more this evening, especially if it was to be their last. For now, he very properly grasped Everic's arm just below the elbow.

Reuben couldn't deny the property was magnificent. Especially once they passed the guests out on the manicured lawn, entered, and found themselves in a grand chamber of such impressive size, it made the bordello hall and even the masonry guild's ballroom feel like tiny shacks in comparison.

There was obvious iconography marking the high house's religiosity as well: most stunning, a huge mural painted on the ceiling of the sun and clouds over a dusky blue sky, currently aglow thanks to actual sunlight coming in through second story windows. And all throughout, the moulding and ornamentation of the architecture was themed to depict the sun and an array of fiery birds and winged celestials with smooth, empty faces, who carried baskets bursting with riches—all of it sculpted from stone and gilded with gold.

Thanks to the size, the crowd wasn't as packed as the guild ball, though while Reuben navigated them through the clusters of guests he felt far more intimidated by these people: gold rings on every finger, precious stones pierced all across their ears and face and draped in chains from their neck, jewelry sewed into most of their gold-spun pellanda and headdresses. One woman let out an open laugh, showing off two golden front teeth fitted to the rest with a thick, gold band, which Reuben guessed was a status statement after he saw others with the cosmetic replacement as well.

He wondered what a *ball* would be like, if this was how the High Ring elite presented themselves at a mere parlor party.

The only ones who were more simplistic in their garb either wore the white and gold uniform and headdress indicative of the Priesthood, or a black uniform with gold badges pinned to their chest. Knowing her status as Head of Security, Reuben could assume he was surrounded by the highest-ranking sentry officers in the city.

But no matter if the party guest was dripping in finery or wearing prim, decorated uniforms, the looks sent their way—particularly, *Reuben's* way—confirmed all of his worst fears. He'd grown far too comfortable amidst the relaxed, liberal circles of Saer Delvanzus's acquaintances in the heart of the city.

Now, they stood on one of its highest peaks, and Reuben had never felt so small.

On either side of the huge, two-story room, grand winding stairs led up to the second floor and its balconies, hugged by archways on either side that led into further corridors that guests were walking in and out of. Etiquette stated they should find the hosts before being introduced to anyone else—but Reuben wasn't upset when they ran into Aldo Delvanzus long before ever catching sight of Micah Artris or Lenaphon Luthur.

"My good friends! What a gilded blessing to see you here," the guild master said, standing up from their seat with a flute of mulled wine as Everic and Reuben entered an expansive, multi-sectioned billiard room.

Reuben felt Everic's arm relax just as relief coursed through him as well. "Aldo," Everic said with a small but genuine smile. "And

Blanca—?"

"You just missed Saer Orlyn," Delvanzus smiled, waving towards the door. "She was quickly swept up in one house member's offer to tour this impressive construction—a mason's delight, to be sure." They leaned closer, adding in a softer voice, "You missed Saer Artris as well, who wished to be informed of your arrival."

"How flattering," Reuben smiled, then glanced pointedly at Everic.

"We have no wish to avoid him tonight," Everic said around a grimace.

"Yes, by all means," Reuben added, "tell the gold keeper we are happily partaking in the festivities and grateful to be here, should you see him before we do."

In the meantime, the first step of the plan *was* to enjoy the party. Which meant, with Delvanzus's assistance, getting Everic acquainted enough with the guests whom the guild master knew in order to get invited into a few party games.

Despite Delvanzus's amiable nature and seeming friendliness with many in this room, however, very few showed interest.

"Saer Payne has already invested in a few of our guild members' more exciting projects," Delvanzus said while introducing them both to a dark-skinned dwarvish woman—less fancily dressed than most, though still with multiple gold rings hooped through each of her chin-length locks. "I was not surprised when Magnatus Lenaphon invited him and his lovely companion to expand interests with the houses of High Ring."

The woman's eyes flickered to Reuben for just a moment before she replied in a careful, polite tone, "Cantergold speaks for itself—though I didn't realize House Luthur made such . . . *unconventional* friends."

Only a minute later, she made an excuse to go converse elsewhere. As more reacted the same, Reuben found his optimism about this event wilting. Everything he'd worried about at the beginning, when Everic asked him to expose himself to society, was at last coming to pass. He should stop their appointments even if Everic *didn't* get an invite tonight—which was growing more and more likely, the longer he stayed on Everic's arm.

When Saer Artris entered the room and noticed them an hour later, Reuben braced himself for things to grow worse.

"Ah, two of our most special guests," Artris greeted as he approached, dressed much more decoratively than Reuben had seen him before with emerald paint on his lips and his blond hair braided in a long tail behind him. "I admit it—after weeks, I was beginning to think I'd *never* receive a response from the mysterious Saer Payne, much less ever see him walk these halls." He smirked, gesturing at Everic. "And yet here you are."

"Magnatus Lenaphon received a response from me," Everic corrected, then pointedly looked past Artris to the door he'd come from. "Where is she?"

"Yes, I'm afraid we've yet to see our distinguished host *once* since our arrival," added Reuben.

"Oh, she comes out to mingle at some point during these events," Artris waved a relaxed hand. "Usually for the music. You'll just have to keep an *eye* out." He pointedly glanced back and forth at Everic's golden eyes before continuing, "As I'm sure many today will be watching you. Come—*I* can help you meet some of High Ring's most notorious 'ne'er do wells,' saer."

Saer Artris remained mostly insufferable—but there was no denying the gold keeper could wield an impressive level of charm when he chose to. At his introduction, the group of High Ring elite and military officials he brought Delvanzus, Everic, and Reuben over to seemed either neutral or pleased at their introduction, regarding Everic with mild curiosity and entirely ignoring Reuben.

Which was fine with him. Reuben only felt grateful to no longer be hindering Everic's success. And thus far, the topics were mild in comparison to the guild ball's discussion on slavery, not requiring him to smooth over any bad reactions from Everic as the conversation and mulled wine flowed. At least, not until it had moved from the price of imports to the best cobblers and cordwainers, then finally to the impact of yet another difficult harvest from the Steppes.

"We might have to start sending enforcement, just to make sure the workers aren't skimping," a gold keeper said with a shake of her head.

"It's a wonder the Loethians ever wished to conquer such an unfruitful wasteland," one uniformed sentry huffed.

"It was *made* a wasteland," Everic countered, to which several members of the group gave him disapproving looks.

Reuben straightened and thought quickly on his feet. "Oh, I don't know if even these esteemed guests are *quite* so traveled, saer," he said quietly to Everic, though still audible to the group—trying to sound both chiding and amused as he reached with his other hand to rub the stiff tension from Everic's arm.

But Reuben had miscalculated, thinking he could so easily put people like this on the defense.

"Travel cannot make up for *history*," the dwarvish woman from earlier contradicted in a patronizing tone, looking at Everic despite answering Reuben. "Our houses have been caretakers of these lands for centuries, human."

A sentry officer, his black uniform decorated with a litany of golden badges, did address Reuben directly with a sneer: "Indeed. Best keep such vapid flattery in your master's *bed*, not polite society, harlot."

They'd practiced what Everic would do, should any one person or discussion grow loathsome enough to threaten his composure. But when Reuben didn't feel a quick, double squeeze to his arm, indicating he should interrupt and start asking people flattering questions about themselves to divert the conversation, he wasn't surprised—as foolproof as he'd thought the tactic before, right now it would only prove the sentry officer right.

"Or better yet, why not *play* for us, Reubielocks?" Artris interceded, giving Reuben a nod towards the nearest corner of the room. Then he smiled at the group, suggesting, "It might not be quite the time or the place for musical performance, but it wouldn't hurt to have some background ambience for a few games at the billiard table, no?"

Reuben deflated in relief as everyone agreed, the brief tension dispersed. Except for in Everic, of course—who seemed even *less* willing to let Reuben's arm go now than when he'd been asked to dance the week before.

Reuben nearly had to pry his arm free until Everic released him with great reluctance, his golden eyes almost entirely shadowed by his furrowed brow. "Are you sure?" he muttered—and didn't look appeased when Reuben nodded.

Then Artris, not yet moving over with the group, took a step forward. "His music will be better suited for this atmosphere, saer. Performances in High Ring require a bit more . . . refinement, let's say, than a party tune and a pretty face—as pretty as that face may be," he explained, eyes wandering over Reuben before reaching a hand towards the hair curling down his chest.

Reuben had felt nothing the last time Artris touched him. But this time, perhaps because he'd gotten used to Saer Delvanzus's friends— even more, the recent memory of Everic's hands to compare with less welcome touch—Reuben briefly felt the urge to cringe backward.

Before Artris could more than stroke Reuben's hair for a moment, however, he gasped—Everic's hand suddenly grasping his wrist in a tight, gloved grip.

"Mind your hands, or I will," the vampire growled, his expression all at once murderous as he stepped closer. Then gave the appendage a small but pointed shake, before letting go.

Artris winced, as if Everic had just pressed on a bruise. "Such *sentiment* over a low-born whore," he murmured, lightly rubbing at his wrist. "One might begin to think there are other reasons you bring him, Payne."

"Oh, my good saer simply prefers my interest to stay *exclusive* during our outings, saer," Reuben quickly tried to smooth things over. "My sincerest apologies for the misunderstanding—I would be deeply honored to play for you all."

Of course, he still worried Everic would attack Artris without him staying between them. But as Reuben retreated to the corner and began preparing his instrument, he was relieved to see Everic stand on the opposite end of the billiard table from Artris.

And within minutes the phenomenon of Everic's excellent accuracy and hand-eye coordination took center stage, only a few guests bothering to glance up when Reuben's first song started. While these people were clearly more experienced, that didn't stop Everic from beating them 3 for 5 rounds the first game. Reuben was starting to wonder if vampirism had even more perks he wasn't aware of—or else Everic's precision could be blamed on the training he'd mentioned before, now used for party games instead of war.

Quickly, Reuben and his music melted into the background. In the meantime, he tried to play soft, soothing melodies at slow tempos, with small five-minute breaks in between segments so his fingers didn't tire too quickly. He was further glad Everic bit his neck, not his wrist, so the only aches to expect by the night's end would come from too much standing.

But as soon as Reuben concentrated harder through his music, using crowdcraft to tap into the intents and emotions of those in the billiard room, he had to stop for a break much sooner—an icy dread of recognition needling down his spine as he felt a very *specific* presence once more.

When he felt it at the ball, Reuben had been too overcome by sheer shock and terror to try identifying its source in the crowd. Here, at midday, with only a couple dozen people in the room, there was no conceivable shadow for Waron to hide within. The dark presence *couldn't* simply be him, even if Reuben felt it during the man's first attack.

He forced down the dread when nothing else happened, and started playing again a few minutes later. Steeling himself, Reuben decided to spend the next hour and a half going through the aura of every single person in the room, including those who entered and left it, with meticulous scrutiny. Starting with the obvious suspects like Artris, who emanated both anger at Everic and a smug satisfaction within himself, for whatever reason—but no particular intentions of harm towards anyone, much less Reuben.

The others held even less intentions of note. The dwarvish woman was truly worried about the fields she owned in the Steppes, while the sentry officer was embarrassed at losing to Everic so many times. When Saer Orlyn returned with a small group still gushing over the architecture of the second floor's terrace, and people divided into smaller groups to play cards, Reuben even tried those he had no suspicion of. He was glad when Blanca Orlyn only emanated a relatable anxiety about attending the elite event and missing Randal Kapriyah's companionship—and felt utterly relieved when Aldo Delvanzus emanated the usual amiability and sharp assessment of the guests around them.

Everic . . . Reuben tapped into his feelings, and wished they were alone again so he could soothe the anger, worry, and discomfort bleeding from the vampire's presence. Reuben looked over at their table as he continued to play, and was glad to see the vampire's face betrayed little of such feelings at least, his golden eyes studiously focused on the cards in front of him instead of the conversation at the table about avoiding something called a stripling tithe.

But then Saer Artris reached forward to gather the cards from the table center, his sleeve riding back on his wrist to expose a very unique mark burned into his flesh.

In the split moment Reuben saw it, the mark looked red and angry at the edges, as if recently added. But still clear enough for him to recognize the eye-like, geometric symbol with small etchings within it—just like the symbol on Waron's chest.

Reuben's knees felt weak. There was a roaring in his ears. Still, he forced himself to play on and focus his mind even harder, this time on that specific point in the room.

His music echoed back awareness of something powerful. Something angry. And something *familiar,* yes . . . but not in the way he'd first assumed.

The presence had never belonged to an old, angry client he already knew, Reuben understood now. The familiarity ran older and deeper. Like an awakening instinct, or an inherent pain passed from mother to child.

Maybe it didn't simply want him *dead*, like he'd assumed.

But it certainly hated that he was alive.

Reuben ended his current set one song early, feeling a bit faint. He needed to find somewhere to sit down, to gather his suspicions, to *think*. After he set his mother's old violin on a display case nearby, he met Everic's gaze across the room—who always looked his way when the music stopped—and managed a hasty smile to assure the man before he looked for a place to rest his feet.

The room had filled further, however, despite the amount of people still conversing in the great hall. Any empty seat Reuben spotted was surrounded by other people he would have to introduce himself to and converse with. Blowing out a breath, Reuben decided to try the music room for some privacy, exiting the closest doorway.

Instead, he came face to masked-face with Magnatus Lenaphon of House Luthur, just about to walk in.

"Sae—Your Radiance," Reuben stumbled over the right honorific, ducking into a low bow as the expressionless golden mask stared back at him.

"Reubielocks, companion of Saer Payne," Lenaphon replied in a neutral, smooth tone. She wore a slightly more decorative ensemble today—long gold bands on her forearms, delicate chains draped and braided over her chest from one side of the mantle on her shoulders to the other. Her gloved hands clasped in front of her as she added, "I see you are not at his side, presently."

"Oh, just needed a quick minute in the powder room," Reuben lied. Then, remembering their goal, offered, "Though I know my good saer would love to speak with you, Your Radiance. If you'd give me a moment I can go fetch him—"

"That can wait," Lenaphon said, as if simply stating fact. "I wish to speak with *you*, child." She nodded over her shoulder towards the unlit corridor she'd emerged from, and said, "Come. Let us pray together."

# 24

# RADIANT GAZE

Without another word, the high priest walked away, simply expecting him to follow. And even a month ago, Reuben very likely would have done it without question.

Now, he found himself hesitating for just a single, dangerous moment—glancing back through the open doorway.

Though Everic had sat purposefully to see the corner where Reuben stood performing, that position put his back to the doorway where Reuben stood now. And no matter how Reuben willed the man's head to turn, Everic stayed stiff and motionless in his seat.

"Is something the matter?" Lenaphon asked. She stood further down the hall, her voice's usual smooth, genial inflection now carrying a testing edge to it.

Reuben bit his lip. "I—I just know Saer Payne *deeply* wished to have an audience with you, Your Radiance," he tried again. "He has great interest in what the council is accomplishing, and how his business might facilitate the new proposals that are laid forth."

Lenaphon held out a gloved hand. "Then come, and I will hear you advocate for him as well."

Reuben glanced again through the doorway . . . but perhaps this was their best option. With his smooth flattery and pretty lies, he could secure Everic's attendance without the vampire needing to so much as grit his teeth through a prayer.

Everic would soon be thanking him for it, Reuben reasoned with himself as he turned and followed.

The high priest led them down the corridor at an unhurried pace, then turned left into another even further shrouded in shadow. Then she whispered, *"Father, guide our way,"* and a single ring on her finger brightly shone.

They passed many doors along the hallway, not stopping until the large double doors at its end. "I assume it has been a long time since you properly knelt in supplication under the Golden Light of His Eye," she said, nodding at the doors. "Or perhaps you *never* have entered a prayer chapel."

Reuben had never even heard of the term. Given that harlots and adulterers weren't allowed in usual chapels or the Aureate Cathedral, however, he murmured, "No, Your Radiance–and I wouldn't wish to sully it with my impure presence."

"This one is for my private use," Lenaphon said, pulling out a key to unlock it. "I have brought far more sinful things inside than you, child."

The assurance brought more foreboding than comfort. Reuben swallowed and didn't respond as the doors opened, following her in—though he had to squint as sudden bright light flooded into the shadowed corridor, burning into his eyes.

Once he finally adjusted, Reuben took in a room around the size of his own bedchamber, with the same sun symbols and golden moulding along the windows, ceiling, and flooring as grand hall. But the little chapel's uncanny radiance was accomplished thanks to the sheer amount of square mirrors patterned on the walls and sloped ceiling, reflecting and enhancing every mote of light coming from the tall windows, the skylights—and now Lenaphon's ring, as she stepped up to a small altar centered in the room with a wide, shallow bowl carved into it.

"Did you know the Gospel of Zald never states why *'all the harlots and adulterers and impure shall veil their eyes before the priest and the saint, the innocent and the child?'*" she asked in a mild tone, standing over the bowl.

Given the two places he grew up, Reuben had only heard the Gospel of Zald paraphrased or quoted. Certainly, he never held a rare written copy of it in his own two hands. He'd never entered a place of worship either; his only interactions with the Zaldian Priesthood were their regular charity visits to the bordello.

Of all the rules sourced from it, Reuben knew this one better than any other—and yet had to shake his head at Lenaphon's query, confused to hear the reasons he was taught might *not* have been from the text itself.

"It is not a mark of shame as some like to treat it," Lenaphon said, gesturing for him to stand across from her. "It is a protection, you may have heard. Eyes indeed expose the soul; they are first to shrink under Zald's pure light. A veil symbolically protects the innocent from being corrupted by the sinful . . . but much more literally, protects the sinner from the *saint*—from the pure celestial power of a blessed one's gaze, which might smite and wither unworthy souls at a mere look." Once Reuben hesitantly stepped closer, she said in a flatter, harder tone, "Though few are pure enough to earn such a title as saint, in recent times."

Reuben didn't know why he was here, or what this morbid explanation was for. Even so, a terrible, cold dread began pooling in his gut, adding to the fear and confusion already there as she spoke.

"A merciful practice, then, Your Radiance," he tried to agree in a pleasant tone, though it came out faint and weak to his own ears. So Reuben switched to an upfront, emotionless tone instead: "As are the proposals of the council. Merciful and wise—from what *Saer Payne* has told me, anyway. He's had growing interest in them and the value of friendly trade agreements with Dijher, these last few months."

The ornate golden mask gave absolutely nothing away as Lenaphon stood there, presumably scrutinizing him after he answered. Then her head turned downward and she muttered quietly at her wrists, *"Grant your body bend at my will,"* a flash of light emanating from the diamond-shaped eye holes of the mask before the wide gold bands around her wrists glowed as well. Reuben blinked in disbelief as the glow faded and the bands became unnaturally malleable whilst she pulled them off.

"The council may be merciful, yes—but Zaldus is not a god of mercy," Lenaphon countered. "Just as light seeks to fill every corner of darkness, just as *gold begets gold begets gold*, He is a god of expansion, of abundance. And so it is by nature, not compassion, He seeks to flood even the darkest of souls in light."

After Reuben gave a hurried nod of understanding, she continued, "Good. Now, before you prattle further about matters that do not concern you, we must offer a prayer and assess the light within *your* soul. Hold out your wrists, child."

There was no point in questioning why. There was no hope of defying a Zaldian priest, much less one of the exalted leaders with power over the whole city. This woman was one of only five priests who had been appointed to such a station. She was one of the few individuals in existence who might even have seen the *Brilliance of Zald, God of Gold and Light* with her own eyes.

And yet, he found himself hesitating again.

"Do you understand, or shall I repeat myself?" Lenaphon said, voice edged with impatience.

"No, of course, Your Radiance, I'm sorry." Reuben reminded himself of the goal behind this meeting as he held out both of his arms wrist-up.

Briefly, he was distracted wondering how many times he'd offered up his blood to Everic in such a similar, vulnerable position—and then Lenaphon pushed his hands through the metal rings and he felt them all at once meld tightly to his skin.

But Everic had always checked for Reuben's willingness, and always stopped when Reuben made the smallest protest. Reuben was just terrible at speaking up.

Here, Reuben stared at his wrists in horror and only started to ask, "Your Radiance, please, what is—" before he was cut off.

"Kneel and place your hands in the bowl," she ordered, and nodded at the altar.

Reuben glanced down, noting the bundle of tinder currently in the offerings bowl, and realized he was already shaking his head. "I—I hold nothing but reverence and awe, for Zald and His blessed ones," he tried again, "but I am not prepared for such a test. Given what I am, surely it can be *assumed* my soul is filled with shadow and darkness—"

"'What you are' has yet to be decided," she said in a hard tone, betraying anger and derision behind it. "And I grow tired of making guesses and watching for signs. Place them in the bowl."

Reuben's hands were shaking as he knelt. He had just rested his forearms along the edge of the carved-out bowl when Lenaphon waved a hand over his wrists and muttered, "*Grant your body unite once more.*"

The cuffs glowed again, though they didn't loosen on Reuben's arms. Instead, the moment he tried to shift he realized that they'd been *melded* with the gold surface of the altar. Entirely locking

Reuben's hands in place where they hovered anxiously over the tinder.

Then Lenaphon pulled out ceremonial pieces of flint and steel from a lower cavity in the altar, her intent clear.

Reuben's fear took hold of his mouth. "My hands are of no use to *anyone* burnt, Your Radiance," he protested, voice rising as sparks caught from her first few strikes and the tinder beneath his hands began to smoke. "You are wasting precious time, and once Saer Payne notices my absence—"

But Lenaphon spoke over him, "*Grant your spirit purify,*" this time with a hand hovered over the small wisps of orange fire licking the tinder.

With another flash of light, the flames flared up into something much faster, brighter, and paler.

Reuben had only seen it in action once—but once was still enough to recognize forged fire.

He wrenched backward uselessly, his supplicating tone forgotten. "Stop—*NO*—"

"*Calm* yourself," Lenaphon spoke sharply over him, putting away the fire-starting items and rounding to his side as the forged fire flared hotter and brighter. And quickly it rose higher, encroaching towards his flesh despite how Reuben tried to curl his fingers back or flinch his bound hands away from it. "It will take but a moment," she said as she leaned in to watch.

Reuben didn't see how that was any comfort, remembering how quickly Everic's face melted off.

He desperately wished for strength to break free. He was sorely tempted to sing *Charming Words*, even if that utterly ruined Everic's chances the moment the charm ended. Instead, Reuben just tried to calm himself, starting in a whisper, "*An autumn crow knows, always where to go,*" even as his voice broke when he reached the last line of the verse: *"The phoenix can feel, when only fire will heal . . ."*

A fearful cry escaped him again as Reuben felt the first feather-light touch of flames brush over his fingers, and he yanked his body against the golden bindings hard enough to hurt his shoulders.

And yet, though he felt its heat when the small pyre rose higher . . . Reuben's hands never burned.

He went still with disbelief as the white-gold flame flickered up and curled around his hands, no more than tickling his skin even as it consumed every bit of the tinder offered. A harmless caress.

Was this a trick? Some test of faith? Reuben glanced at Lenaphon for an explanation, but as always, her masked face revealed nothing.

In the quick half-minute it took for the unnatural fire to consume everything possible, the tinder nothing more than a fine pile of ash, he hadn't felt even a tiny singe. Despite that, his breathing came out fast and ragged, the only sound in the quiet room until Lenaphon straightened and brought her hands up to her face.

Then Reuben's breath cut off for a stunned moment as the high priest removed her mask—and Lenaphon Luthur looked down at him with the bright, golden gaze of *three* eyes.

Otherwise, the face behind the Zaldian mask was an unassuming one. Her skin held a pale pinkish tone, her nose was small and upturned, her lips pursed above a strong, round chin. She didn't look any older than Reuben despite her age, though as her headdress came off with the mask he saw her ears weren't so long as Nahlia's, the one pure-blooded elf Reuben knew. A shock of pale, golden hair was carefully plaited in multiple sections along her temples, connecting at her neck into a tight bun.

But the extra eye, narrower than the normal two and sitting centered above her brow on its side in an irregular, vertical fashion, naturally took up most of the attention. No iris, just a golden pupil shining a bright light that was *searing* with intensity—and yet didn't feel foreign at all to Reuben.

It was the same light that Reuben conjured in the dark. The same color as the flash before his tiny, necrotic cut had disappeared in the carriage. The same glow from his hands, when he miraculously healed Daxus.

There was a bone-deep familiarity to it, as well. A recognition that Reuben didn't quite understand—and certainly didn't put him at ease. Not when the gaze *also* held the exact same malicious, sourceless intensity he'd felt so many times in the past three months—except now, it finally came from a very obvious, clear direction.

Belatedly remembering her earlier warning, Reuben blinked out of his shock and forced his gaze downward. Even with the beaded veil obscuring his vision and presumably protecting his soul from a gaze of *"pure celestial power,"* it was hard to look at for long without wanting to shrink.

But Lenaphon grasped his face firmly by the jaw, forcing it up towards her. Her two lower eyes narrowed to match the third, before she tugged harshly at one of the little connecting chains to his veil.

With a small clink, the material fell from his face and onto the stone floor.

"Look at me," Lenaphon ordered just as Reuben was about to squeeze his eyes shut. He still kept his gaze down, terrified, until the elvish woman said in a softer tone, "My gaze alone won't be the thing that hurts you, child."

Perhaps he shouldn't have believed her. At the implication something else *would* hurt him, however, Reuben didn't see why she would lie. So he very slowly, very incrementally moved his eyes to meet her gaze—and still, felt nothing.

Lenaphon looked down at him with distaste, but also a strange satisfaction. "I was right," she murmured, her two normal eyes flickering over his face. Then her hand on his jaw tightened. "Where did Father's blood manifest? What aspect were you marked with?"

Reuben didn't understand either question, but tried to say, "My father—I don't, I don't know who he—"

Suddenly Lenaphon's hand was around his neck, squeezing tight as anger, disgust, and *malice* burned in her eyes. "Then tell me this: which one of my wretched sisters hid you from my sight for so long?"

Reuben tried to speak around the constriction: "I—I don't understand, please Your Radiance—your sisters, who . . . ?"

"Your *mother*, boy," Lenaphon corrected sharply, and the third eye's light glowed brighter. "Who is she? Gabrelus? Eriel? Surely not *Azrael*?"

She thought they were related somehow, it seemed, though Reuben had to shake his head at each of the names offered. "She was Oriana," he rasped.

Finally, Lenaphon released his neck.

Then, despite how foolish it was to let fear shorten his temper *now* of all times, Reuben glared as he cleared his throat and added, "I don't know *what* house in High Ring she came from, just—just that she became indentured, and then gave birth to a bastard—me—and remained in the bordello until her death, 48 years ago."

Lenaphon didn't react to the name itself. She only stared at him, a sharp line forming between her faint, blond brows after his explanation. "An offering born outside the Cathedral . . . that isn't possible," she murmured.

For the first time in the course of this conversation, Reuben's curiosity overrode his fear. "Did . . . did you know her?"

But then Lenaphon reached down, and suddenly her hands were everywhere. Prodding, pinching at his face and neck, digging at his scalp, squeezing hard at his arms and shoulders as her extra eye flashed with light, over and over again while the harsh, uncomfortable search continued.

Reuben only recoiled at first, confusion overtaking any other emotion, right up until she reached his spine. Then he gasped and cringed forward towards the ashes as her thin, bony fingers dug into his back. Pressing and jabbing at the very points along his spine that Everic touched weeks ago, though certainly not to soothe them—Reuben let out a whimper as her fingers prodded sharply and at a strange, painful angle, isolating one of Reuben's most tensed spots. Then she let out a gust of breath, as if surprised, before roughly pinching the area, isolating a hardened section branching from either side of his spine between her thumbs and forefingers.

"*No*—what—*stop*," he gasped. But managed to keep in any cries of pain before her torturing touches ceased and Lenaphon rounded to face him again.

She no longer looked angry, but *disturbed*, as if he appeared as strange to her as she did to him. "You should have been offered back to Zaldus on the day of your birth, child."

Though he still understood little, Reuben flinched at these words.

From a very young age, he knew that his existence had ruined his mother's life. His conception, at best, was an awful accident that played a large role in separating Oriana from her family, ruining her already fragile health, and sentencing her to die in a whore house. And at worst . . .

"A diluted, deformed male kindred," Lenaphon continued sharply, "and put away in a brothel, no less, where you've likely created even more broken things for me to track down and dispose of."

Overwhelmed with both fear and lingering pain, Reuben no longer felt in control of his tongue. "You're mistaken—I am *not* my mother," he replied in a bitter tone. "Any good prostitute knows how to avoid offspring, Your Radiance."

Lenaphon's lips pressed together. "We'd best hope," she replied, before her two normal eyes narrowed again. Rounding to face him from the opposite side of the altar, the high priest removed her glove and reached a hand towards his face, murmuring, "But as far as disposing of *you* . . ."

She only pressed a thumb lightly between his brows—but Reuben flinched as a sudden, searing light shone from her third eye, burning into his own eyes and blinding them entirely.

In the eternity that followed, Reuben felt as though he'd been struck by lightning, then thrown on a pyre. A sharp, nerve-searing sensation burned into his mind and across every inch of his body— like a thousand stinging ants crawling up his skin, or a downpour of red-hot coals blistering his soul. Perhaps all of it at once.

Somehow, no smoke billowed from his skin, even as his whole body shook and his mouth fell open around a silent, empty scream.

For the second time in a short span of months, Reuben expected to die.

Then the light faded. Her extra eye returned to its usual glow, and Lenaphon's thumb shook slightly against his brow before her hand dropped.

The high priest backed up a few steps, her normal eyes wide. *"Grant your body bend at my will,"* she whispered.

Reuben felt the metal around him finally loosen.

He didn't waste a second to wrench his wrists free, staggering back onto his feet despite the black spots still swimming in his vision, the weak state of both his back and his knees. His breaths came out ragged, though the searing sensations had disappeared, and as Reuben examined himself he saw no physical indication the pain he'd just suffered had been real.

Lenaphon watched him with incredulous wonder, all the while. "Your blood is not diluted at all," she said, though it sounded more like an accusation.

Reuben blinked hard, keeping a hand on the altar until his legs felt strong enough for him to walk, then hopefully to *run*.

In the meantime, he heard himself weakly agree, "I . . . I *have* been complimented on the strength of it before."

Lenaphon's face hardened. "Very well. If you will not *die*, for now you will at least cease conniving and disappearing into the night—especially with that *shapeshifter* always impersonating our kindred."

So she still didn't know what Everic was; Reuben wanted to sag with relief.

Instead, he straightened. Despite her anger, Reuben could feel the dynamic in the room had shifted. Lenaphon—one of the most powerful individuals in the whole city—had just tried to divinely dispose of him, and somehow failed. A high priest of Zald had used an impressive display of godcraft, but for all the momentary torture of it, seemed to have done less permanent damage to Reuben than some of his past clients.

"You will no longer require careful watching, because you will not leave the Starlet Eye Bordello for anything but public events or by my invitation," she continued in a testing, threatening tone, "or I will apply my *own* mark on you to watch from."

If the presence of her eye hadn't already been so familiar, these words alone told Reuben that he'd found the anonymous *higher up with deep pockets* Waron described, who discreetly hired the Allunata to watch Reuben. This mark she spoke of must have been the brand on Waron and Artris's flesh. All of which meant every time Reuben felt a malicious, disembodied presence, it had been *her* watching him through someone else.

Reuben put away that realization for now. With her here and watching his every move with malice, but behind that, *terror*, he knew her threats were small. If she wanted to kill him the normal, less moral way, she already would have. And who knew if such a mark would even last on Reuben's skin—never so miraculous as

Everic's undead regeneration, or else Reuben would have noticed long ago, but still quick to heal and never scar?

He might even be able to bargain with her. Agree to her terms, and in exchange, get Everic his way in to access the Voice of Zald.

Or, if Reuben wished to be uselessly sentimental . . . even demand to know about his mother. His *father*, if blood was what tied Reuben to all of this.

But Reubielocks had been paid for one thing, tonight.

Reuben swallowed hard, mentally said goodbye to Everic's peaceful hideaway in the Hollows, then forced his voice to steady. "I would do all that you ask willingly, Your Radiance . . . if you extended an invitation to my good saer, Everic Payne, to witness the last trade council."

Lenaphon stared for a long moment—made twice as long, for the extra eye gazing at him.

Then she cocked her head, eyes narrowing. "I cannot tell if you are ignorant or simple, trying to bargain with a high priest of Zald."

Reuben shrugged and pretended nonchalance. "Or you could *attempt* to put your mark on me," he said with more confidence than he felt. "But I don't scar easily."

Lenaphon glared. Despite that, she didn't call his bluff—just took her mask and headdress from the altar, carefully putting them back in place on her head.

Once her strange face was hidden once more, Lenaphon let out a slow, steadying breath. "Let us return you to the festivities, then," she said. "And . . . should you obey me, your devilish shapeshifter shall receive his invitation shortly."

Then the high priest reached down and picked up his discarded veil from the stone floor, holding it out to him.

# 25

# MOTHER'S WISDOM

Without another word exchanged, Reuben followed the high priest on weak, shaky legs out of the private chapel. He struggled with the beaded veil's clasps as they walked, his fingers numb and fumbling. When it was finally back in place over his eyes, however, Reuben's hands still felt restless. He barely resisted the urge to rub at his bruised wrists, or the pounding ache between his brows, or the lingering sensations of a hand on his neck as they moved down the corridor.

Lenaphon didn't bother to godcraft any light this time; the illuminated end of the dark corridor acted as a guiding beacon for their return. With his vision impeded again, Reuben squinted to watch his footing in the dark.

Still, he invited the obstruction of the veil for once. It provided distance from Lenaphon, the crowds ahead, and all he had just endured and witnessed with his naked eye—and with that distance, *perspective*.

Thanks to his strange blood and a lineage even Lenaphon didn't seem certain of, he'd survived a gaze he clearly should have perished under. Just as important, he succeeded in completing a nearly impossible objective: with lies, pretense, and charm, Reuben just secured the final key to Everic's goal—or, more accurately, Reubielocks had.

*And* with the small price of his few current freedoms. But Reuben was quick to swallow down that sorrow for now. Even beyond Waron's threats or Sidarchus's admonishments, he had always anticipated the loss to come. He never truly entertained Everic's kind but pointless pleas for him to flee; from the start, he'd saved up for *Isolde's* freedom, not his own.

Perhaps he always understood that if his own mother—born into an abundance of wealth and family and connections—still wasn't able to run, then a bastard born in a brothel stood no chance.

As for the loss of *Everic* . . . whatever fondness or budding love Reuben might feel, it didn't matter. From the start, Everic's singular goal was to kill the Voice of Zald—even if he managed to survive the task, he'd surely have to flee.

None of this was about Reuben. It never had been.

Reuben walked with steadier feet after that, numb determination settling his nerves as they reached the end of the corridor and turned right, walking back to the candlelit area behind the northern stairs.

Lenaphon stopped short for a moment in front of him, a stiffness to her spine indicating her surprise at the small group that already noticed their arrival. She nodded briefly at her staring guests and walked past at a quick pace with a gesture for him to follow. Reuben still felt lingering, critical eyes on his back as they turned away from the billiard room's doorway, instead heading toward the great hall and the sound of familiar, elevated voices.

"—*don't* tell me, then I will break down every door until I find them *myself*," said a low, thunderous voice Reuben would know anywhere.

He hurried around the corner after the priest to find Everic standing a few steps up the stairway, his forearm rigid under the staying grip of Delvanzus's hand as the guild master looked up at

Everic with concern.

Everic's face betrayed no concern. His eyes were dark and murderous under a shadowed brow as he stared down at Saer Artris—who stood at the base of the stairs and answered, "I swear I don't know where they've gone, but I'm sure—"

Then the shadows fell from Everic's face as his eyes alighted on Reuben.

Everic hurried down the stairs before Artris could continue, hitting the gold keeper's shoulder none-too-gently with his own and entirely disregarding Lenaphon as he passed them to reach Reuben.

All eyes in the nearby vicinity moved from the spectacle Everic had made, now to both Magnatus Lenaphon and Reuben's appearance. Once Everic stopped in front of him, gripping his upper arm tightly as if worried Reuben would disappear again, Reuben offered a quick smile—though he couldn't block out the growing background mutters of the crowd musing things like, "Perhaps she rebuked his *incongruous* color scheme," and, "Even priests need to relax once in a while . . ."

Lenaphon might have heard them as well, for the high priest waited no further before half-raising her arms and addressing the crowd. "Good evening, children!" she said, genial but loud enough to be heard by all in the hall's near vicinity. The buzzing crowd quieted in seconds. "I have just returned from a rather *illuminating* private communion, and feel impressed to remind you all: none, not even those of us righteous enough to prosper and shine under the discerning eye of Zald, are wholly pure."

While she spoke, Lenaphon's head moved as if slowly surveying the crowd. Reuben shivered when her mask faced his direction—and briefly he could *feel* her hidden eye piercing into his once more.

"As every light touching this imperfect world must cast a shadow," she continued, her gaze thankfully moving on, "so the sins of darkness ever encroach upon mortal-kind, creeping at our backs until they are absolved and burned away from our hearts." The high priest's mask was unreadable as ever, but Reuben thought he heard a trace of reluctance to her tone as she continued, "Nevertheless, they *can* be burned and cleansed under the Golden Light of His Eye—as I have now from this man. A harlot and a debtor, yes . . . but a child of High Ring as well."

Reuben felt more eyes turn his way as Lenaphon gestured in his direction. And even without the help of music, he could feel *curiosity* begin to replace the crowd's judgment and derision as they regarded him now.

Only for a second, at least, before the high priest ended the impromptu sermon. "Now—let us banish the darkness in our hearts through the uplifting arts as well!"

A few more looks moved in Reuben's direction—some unabashedly interested, like Artris, others simply confused—before the group followed Lenaphon under the opposite stairwell's arches, presumably to the music room.

Clearly, Lenaphon had said what she did to save her own reputation. But it was strange for Reuben, still considering how to charm and flatter and use this situation to further Everic's standing . . . even whilst knowing the *true* destination of Everic's climb up the social ladder had already been reached.

Despite a few lingering gazes, it seemed no one was quite willing to approach them anyway. Reuben couldn't find it in himself to be disappointed; all he wanted right then was to drop his head into the crook of Everic's neck and be *done* with these people.

Everic waited no further to lean in. "What happened? What did she do?" he said, quiet but urgent in Reuben's ear. "Are you hurt? Should we leave now?"

Reuben opened his mouth, then quickly shut it.

Lenaphon hadn't hurt him in any lasting way. Or, more accurately, both she and her test *couldn't* by some stroke of luck or fate—or blood.

*It's waiting there in your heart, in your blood . . .*

He shivered, no longer able to doubt Isolde's words had been inspired by *something*, even if she always dismissed them.

"Nothing happened," Reuben said, though internally he added, *nothing permanent.* "I'm gilded as gold, saer—and actually, I have some *very* good news to share."

Everic's golden eyes flickered over his face, tight with worry on top of suspicion.

"With any luck, you should receive a rather significant invitation within the next few days," Reuben promised and, hoping to distract from further questions, stroked a few fingers lightly down the long, bared neckline exposing Everic's sternum.

His smile twisted ruefully when, as always, Everic's motionless chest jumped around a sudden breath in response.

Everic slowly exhaled and caught Reuben's hand, briefly holding it captive there against him. "Tell me everything once we leave, then," he said quietly whilst interlacing their fingers.

Reuben hesitated—and that on its own was telling. How many times had he made up stories out of thin air in the last four decades, and not lost a wink of sleep over the deception? As if there weren't enough signs he'd let his unprofessional feelings go much, much too far, this growing discomfort, this *guilt*, whenever he had to directly lie to Everic should have warned him weeks ago.

Reuben only managed to give one nod, far from convincing before he hastily changed the topic instead: "I believe I left my violin behind, if we could go fetch it?" Then he nodded at their friends lingering a few paces away. "And after, we could go and listen to the music with Saers Delvanzus and Orlyn, who look to be waiting on us."

Everic didn't spare the two a glance. "Are you sure you're alright to stay?"

Given how little Reuben wanted to end the night and commence the conditions of his new deal with Lenaphon, he at least could put genuine feeling into the words, "I would hate to end our evening so soon, saer. Besides—I'd *love* to know what Saer Artris could mean by performances being more 'refined' here."

The music, to Reuben's surprise, was neither dreary nor boring despite being far different from Reuben's usual performative party tunes or folksy ballads. In fact, all of the High Ring guests who stood up to play over the next hour displayed just as much if not more talent and technical skill than Reuben, and tackled far more complicated, intricate numbers than most he had ever heard or bothered to compose himself.

Well, perhaps not *ever* heard, Reuben silently corrected himself after the next number. It was a young violinist with a harpist's accompaniment, performing a slow, emotional number Reuben distantly recognized. And as he listened further—noting things like the perfect, lilting movement between notes, the equal clarity and strength to each double or triple stop—and realized who he'd once heard play the same piece, tears burned in his eyes.

While the violinist played on, Reuben's heart swelled around an old ache; all he could think about was his mother.

He thought he already knew how much she'd lost. But somehow it cut even deeper after speaking with Lenaphon—who now further confirmed Oriana's suffering was all thanks to a *"diluted, deformed, male"* child who apparently *"should have been offered back to Zaldus"* the very day he was born.

But for all that Oriana never could love Reuben the same way Nahlia and Daxus did, she was the one to send him to their loving home. She was the parent who taught him music, who shared all her hard-earned wisdom, who never lost hope of a better future—and, even on her deathbed, reminded him to always keep fighting.

Reuben did his best to remember her lessons, as harsh as they were, all throughout his life. He'd even done well, up until the last few weeks. And that was when everything had gone so wrong.

Maybe the reason he started taking these risks, made mistake after mistake, and ended up in this dangerous situation was because he had the hubris to discard her simplest admonition: *Never let yourself need someone more than they need you.*

Everic squeezed his hand, glancing at Reuben when he tried to subtly wipe at an eye. But Reuben kept his gaze downward, only hoping that he was finally making a decision Oriana would approve of, whatever came next.

Few guests, if any, ever clapped at the end of each number; Delvanzus's enthusiastic applause sitting on the other side of Everic continuously set them apart in that regard. But at the end of this one, Reuben made sure to join them.

"Between you and me, Reubielocks," the guild master said in a conspiratorial tone, once performances concluded, "I still much prefer the bright, *invigorating* style of your music." Then they held out a hand, cupping it when Reuben followed suit to press a familiar-shaped token into his palm. Delvanzus's cheeks dimpled as they explained in a much softer tone, "If you or any more delightful members of your family need passage in the days ahead," nodding at Reuben's hand before letting go.

"Thank you," Reuben said, gripping the guild token tightly, though he only managed a weak smile as he realized he'd likely never see Aldo Delvanzus again either.

Everic's voice next to him interrupted the miserable thought. "Thank you, Aldo. Keep an ear to the ground once we depart?"

"Of course! I'm sure there will be plenty of interest expressed now that Magnatus Lenaphon has spoken in your favor," Saer Delvanzus agreed, winking at Reuben.

Reuben's gut sank at talk of departure, and he opened his mouth to argue—but what more *could* be accomplished tonight, now that he had the council invitation secured?

He knew the true reason for his reluctance to end the evening, and there was no place in Reubielocks for such sentiment.

So Reuben nodded and kept smiling. He clung to Everic's arm tighter than needed as they made their way out of the music room, subtly glancing for Lenaphon's position in the room.

She didn't notice their exit—her masked face was inclined away, leaning back from Artris's pointed ear as if she'd just whispered into it. Artris nodded at her, his face unusually serious as she turned back to a group of guests. Meanwhile, her gold keeper hurried out of the room ahead of Everic and Reuben. He had rounded the southern stairway and was halfway up the steps, by the time they also reached the vaulted grand hall of House Luthur.

Reuben didn't have it in him to worry or wonder long about what timely errand she'd sent Artris on, however. Not when, as they stepped out of the mansion, he remembered the carriage ahead of them only had one more stop.

It was barely past sunset. Sidarchus expected Reuben back late tonight, but now he would easily get there in time to perform with Isolde. After that, Reuben wouldn't leave the bordello ever again, save for public events and by *her* invitation—whatever that meant. And as soon as Everic concluded his bloody business at the last trade council, and was killed or forced to flee, what desire would Reuben have to disobey her anyway?

With shaky hands, Reuben unclasped the little chains to his beaded veil the moment he sat down in the carriage. Everic sat across from him, a frown sharpening the vampire's face again as he waited. Likely, for Reuben's explanation to begin.

The words stuck halfway up his throat. He'd been so desperate to make himself useful, to leave Everic with everything he wanted. But should Reuben have worked harder to persuade Everic against such a rash, dangerous assassination attempt instead?

Had his bargain with Lenaphon just sealed Everic's death?

The moment the carriage was in motion, it seemed Reuben had run out of time to speak first. "What did she say?" Everic waited no further to prompt. "Where did she take you? Why did she want a private audience in the first place?"

"She . . ." Reuben paused, reminding himself it was too late for lies on that front—her council invitation would get delivered to Everic's official main ring residence regardless of what Reuben claimed now. "Magnatus Lenaphon said she will send you an invitation to sit in and witness the last trade council meeting," he admitted slowly, ignoring the other questions for now.

Everic's eyes widened—but then he leaned back, wearing an incredulous frown. "To the *council*? Already?"

Despite the thrill of terror the thought inspired, Reuben probably *could* explain—all of it, from Lenaphon's demands down to Reuben's first weak-minded betrayal. He'd almost managed to redeem himself from exposing Everic's vampirism, after all; Lenaphon already implied during their conversation that she would have no reason to continue hiring the Allunata, once Reuben agreed to her terms. By some stroke of luck, Waron had never reported Everic's nature to his anonymous employer either, and likely never would get the chance now thanks to Reuben's actions tonight.

But as distrust persisted on the vampire's face, Reuben knew the nebulous truth behind *why* Lenaphon wanted so much surveillance on him was far more damning to reveal than if Reuben crafted a thousand more pretty lies.

So he kept his body relaxed, his tone light as he started with an almost-truth, "I told you, your unconventional interest carries weight." Then, rolling the guild token around in his fingers, Reuben laced in the first bit of blatant fabrication: "She took me aside hoping to learn more about you. Luckily, I managed to quickly distract her with other information," and back to a half-truth, he finished, "then I used the tactics we'd discussed to start proposing your attendance."

*A lie is best served between two easy, digestible truths.*

Everic's eyes narrowed. "She knows your mother was of High Ring now—did she not interrogate about *you?*"

"She didn't—well, she asked a *few* questions, but that was the most of the information I gave up about either of us, I swear," Reuben appeased. He twisted his lips into a soft, reassuring smile as more lies and half-truths spilled out of them, as quickly he might play an improvised riff to a familiar chord pattern: "She found both of our bloodlines of interest after that; perhaps it matters more than I realized, in High Ring. I think the intrigue of your quick rise in social circles and extreme wealth was enough for her to grant your request . . . though it may be safer to simply go to the council meeting, scope it out, and seek a second invitation before putting yourself in such danger, saer."

*In conflict, conceding a smaller, less-important thing often distracts the other party away from the original issue at hand.*

As ever, his mother's wisdom proved true, even if the lines on Everic's face deepened into a grimace at the alternative Reuben offered. "I will . . . consider it," the vampire replied stiffly. "If you think a second invitation could be secured, anyway. I trust *you,* even if I don't trust her."

Guilt ate at Reuben's heart like acid, corroding his resolve.

But if he ignored Lenaphon's bargain and continued helping Everic, she would simply find him a more secure prison. Or if he tried to run, even with the aid of a powerful vampire, he wouldn't just be hunted for trying to escape debt anymore.

And if everything Lenaphon insinuated about Reuben was true, who knew if Everic would *want* to aid him still.

No, tonight had to be his last with Everic. And without a chance to advise him in future, Reuben found himself desperate to curtail Everic's reckless plan while he still could. "If you don't think it's best to trust her . . . might the danger be *too* great to attend?"

Everic's gaze returned to him, his expression flat. "Not at all. I always knew what this mission might cost, what meager chance I'd have of survival afterward, should I actually get access to the Voice of Zald and *could* exploit her weakness."

The soul-scalding force of Lenaphon's strange eye came to mind, and Reuben held in a shudder. "Then I hope you are just as informed of her strengths," he murmured. And considered, just for a brief moment, if he *should* find a way to warn Everic about the high priest's abilities, even if it meant wrapping up the information in even more lies.

But Everic's eyes darkened with a knowing gleam. "Far too informed of them—I told you this morning, I've seen war," he replied slowly. When Reuben gave him a questioning look, Everic explained, "The first was a very large, infamous one in this city . . . over 200 years ago."

It took Reuben a few moments to understand—to realize it wasn't Everic's previous hints about himself, but *history*, that Reuben's mind should be using to fill in the gaps.

Yet what other notable war could he be referencing, than the Loethian invasion more than two centuries prior? The war which culminated in one final, devastating attack of Loethia upon the Sazzeran Steppes, when all hope was lost until the moment that the Voice That Spoke From the Golden Mount turned the tide of the *Battle of the Steppes*, sent the empire's armies fleeing north, and stepped into the light of history?

"You were there?" Reuben whispered.

Just then, the carriage slowed to a halt, voices starting up outside. Both Reuben and Everic tensed, waiting in silence for another disturbance—Reuben white-knuckling his violin case as he remembered the exchange he saw between Artris and Lenaphon, and suddenly feared another of her hired Allunata would burst in through the door, their bargain no more than a trick to make him let down his guard.

After a few muffled back-and-forths, however, the carriage jolted back into movement without issue; it seemed the sentry guard were more inclined to allow the carriage out of High Ring than within.

And if anything, Reuben reminded himself, Artris was more likely to be sending word to call *off* the Allunata now that Lenaphon had no use for them.

Everic's expression remained dark after Reuben's question, especially now that twilight had deepened closer to night. But it also looked weary, slack with grief as the carriage rolled on.

Now Reuben was the one with questions. "Everic . . . are you saying you *saw* the Voice of Zald stop Loethia?"

The vampire had never looked more his age as he answered in a soft tone, "I saw . . . *blood.*" His hands balled into fists in his lap, Everic recounted, "The battle had gone on gory and grim all morning; neither side was giving ground. But then, right at midday, we heard screams growing louder from the south. I turned to look, was nearly blinded, but I . . . I witnessed a winged being of light, flying up in the midst of the battlefield and crying out in a beautiful, terrible voice. Then everyone—*everyone*, no matter which banner they fought under—started crumbling, bleeding from every orifice. Arrows flew at her, spells were flung, it didn't matter. The blood . . ."

Everic visibly swallowed before he continued in a lower, aggrieved tone, "Where it wasn't boiled into fumes by the blaze of white fire ringed around the *creature*, it became a sea. So, so many bodies . . ." He shook his head. "And any who were unlucky enough to not immediately die or drown in their own blood laid there senseless and rotting for days, until their wounds or a simple lack of water did them in instead," he finished in a whisper, a far-off horror shining in his eyes.

Reuben had no words, at first.

There was little surprise that Everic's perspective painted the Voice of Zald in a less-than-holy light. But somehow, Reuben hadn't expected such a *grisly* contradiction to the noble story of the Voice of Zald's first and greatest triumph.

"No wonder you want her dead," he answered in a soft voice.

Everic blinked, his gaze seeming to return to the present. "This isn't simple vengeance," he countered sharply. "A being of such power— never aging, ever healing, leveling armies, seemingly immune to any magical craft . . ." He paused, then let out a short, angry breath. "Her tyranny is reason enough for what I must do. But should she be involved in a *greater* war, like what will soon be proposed? I fear this land would take a millennia to recover from the blinding scourge."

Hearing the words *"blinding scourge,"* it was hard not to think of Lenaphon. And at Everic's brief list of the Voice's powers, Reuben was reminded of how extraordinarily young the high priest looked for being Head of Security longer than a century . . . likely never aging as well.

Reuben could guess she'd be immune to forged fire. Perhaps her special eye was not powerful enough to raze down armies—but it was clear she had great abilities surrounding surveillance, and was likely to thank for how tight a grip the Zaldian Priesthood and sentry guard kept around the city.

But if *Lenaphon* was the same kind of being as the Voice of Zald . . . A *"broken thing,"* she'd called Reuben—yet also her *"kindred."*

And for all his weaknesses, forged fire had failed to burn him on two separate occasions. He'd healed from the tiny cut of the Allunata's cursed blade; Everic himself had questioned Reuben's origins before, considering just his blood was enough to protect an unholy vampire from both necrosis and the sun.

Reuben swallowed hard, then spoke in barely more than a whisper, "Everic . . . that was more than two centuries ago. There—there may be more than *just* the Voice of Zald, by now."

"With such capabilities?" Everic countered. "There could be descendants, some mixing of bloodlines since then, but *nothing* akin to the likes of her. Sazzera would have conquered all of Monmark by now."

*That vivid gold in your eyes is a feature I've only seen in the most blessed of Zald,* Artris had told Everic at their first parlor party. Now, Reuben couldn't help but think of the other high priests on the council as well, and what *their* headdresses and masks might be hiding.

He desperately wanted Everic to be right.

Still, Reuben had to question: "But . . . if there were more?"

Everic's eyes narrowed. "Do you suspect Lenaphon?"

"I can't be *sure,*" Reuben denied quickly, even as his stomach flipped at the murderous glint in Everic's gaze. "It's just suspicious, her time in such a position with how young she seems, and her questioning the gold in your eyes. She mentioned that she shared a notable bloodline with a few sisters, too," he added just a small piece of truth at the end, watching closely for Everic's reaction.

The vampire blew out a sharp breath, his dark brows furrowed. "I would hope she is just a descendant, then. If not . . ." There was naught but a glint of gold left in Everic's darkened eyes now, his voice low and biting as he stated, "If there *are* any others out there, lying in wait for their god's command, ready to massacre thousands—far too powerful to be allowed among the common mortal . . . then, one way or another, they *all* must die."

It wasn't till he heard the answer that Reuben could admit to himself why he'd asked—foolishly hoping to be proven wrong.

*Trust me, something like* her *shouldn't exist,* Everic's words from just a few hours now reverberated in his skull.

And when Reuben still tried to argue with himself, to list in his head all the ways he was weak where the Voice of Zald was nightmarishly strong, Lenaphon's words echoed back, accusing, *Your blood is not diluted at all . . .*

Dread pooled in Reuben's gut as Everic's murderous gaze turned from his, softening as he grew deep in thought.

Reuben found it hard to breathe as he waited. Perhaps Everic was just considering the fact he might face more than the Voice of Zald at the council, and would heed Reuben's advice to take a slower, more practical approach. Or much better, he was deciding to give up the venture altogether and run while he still could—go back to wherever he came from in Loethia and build a quiet, content life in the shadows, maybe even find a real partner for himself who actually had a life and a heart to offer him in return.

Worst and most likely, however, Everic was considering how *"one way or another"* he could personally ensure the death of any and all persons akin to the Voice of Zald.

Unknowingly, the death of *Reuben,* if Lenaphon's test could be trusted as truth.

Everic had not realized Reuben was on that list yet. But once he did, Reuben could only hope Everic surmised the same pitiful truth Lenaphon had hours before: whatever blood ran in Reuben's veins, he was little more than a liability, not a threat.

He didn't suddenly lunge at Reuben at any point during the carriage ride, at least. Everic just sat there stiffly, frowning out the window as the road grew bumpier and the last remnants of twilight cast a deep gray shadow over the louder streets of the main ring's middle tiers.

Regardless, Reuben sat there in silent, anxious fear, flipping the guild token over and over in his hands, entirely oblivious to the time slipping away until the carriage lurched to a stop—the window framing a small piece of the piazza square still magically lit and abuzz with commerce at this time of evening.

Just like that, their last appointment was over.

Reuben realized he was ending their agreement almost the same way he'd started it: terrified, on edge, uncertain if this Everic Payne might soon be the death of him.

*Almost* the same, because this time the fear was only one string in a conflicting knot lodged heavy in his chest, tangled now with both a fragile love and a faulty but lingering *trust* in the vampire.

A trust that left Reuben hoping, if or when Everic learned all of the truth, he wouldn't come for Reuben—for the sake of their once-mutual fondness, if nothing else.

When Everic continued staring out the window, his eyes in some aggrieved, far-off place, Reuben cleared his throat. His voice still felt thick around the words, "I—I suppose this is goodnight, saer."

Everic startled a bit. His mouth was a sharp, thin line as he glanced at the door, which he then reached for and opened instead of answering Reuben—but only to lean his head out.

"On to the main stair!" he called to the infernal siblings at the driver's seat over the busy street noise, before ducking back in and shutting it.

Reuben stared at him. "Saer? I told my manager I'd return—"

"I'll send word and compensation to him," Everic interrupted, not quite looking Reuben's direction. Despite that, Reuben spotted worry, even a hint of *guilt* on Everic's face as he vaguely added, "I need you to stay one more night."

Reuben was terrified of what the guilt could be for. "He—he'll be expecting the amount from last night as well," he hastily tried reasoning. "I should at least go explain, get money to pay for it, and check if my schedule can be rearranged."

"Your slaver is always more than permissible," Everic dismissed. Then his jaw clenched, his gaze shifting away. "And *I'll* cover last night's payment."

Reuben's heart cracked, as if someone had just plunged it into a bucket of ice.

"Everic," was all he could whisper—the warm, rose-tinted memory of every kiss they'd shared the night before now stained with confusion and pain.

When Everic finally returned his gaze, it was with a stiff mouth and a hard expression, identical to the face he'd worn the first night they met. "I have been careless for far too long," the vampire stated grimly. "But I fear it is time to use *all* the tools at my disposal—and hope, however damning the means . . . perhaps this nightmare I created will finally end."

With that, the carriage wheels began moving again, rolling Reuben away from the bordello and down towards the Hollows below.

# 26

# WORSE MEASURES

Reuben hadn't kissed him for the cantergold.

And he made sure Everic *knew* as much by declining the usual payment last night. Reuben assured in every way he could that—unlike the other times he tried initiating intimacy between them—each touch and kiss was motivated by nothing but true desire.

Now, Reuben could only assume Everic was rejecting that truth. He wanted a strictly professional relationship. No notions of anything else, however unlikely they would have been to entertain.

On the other hand, he just said he *needed* Reuben—for the first time, insisting on one more night for his own sake, not Reuben's well-being. In any other circumstance, that should be something to celebrate. A sign that, despite his faulty heart's best efforts to put him at a disadvantage, Reuben had managed Oriana's simplest advice after all.

*Never let yourself need someone more than they need you.*

Then why did he feel so heartbroken?

At the least, there was no reason for Everic to suddenly insist on paying for last night if he already planned to kill Reuben. Reuben should just relax and be glad their last night had extended into two. He should feel secure in the knowledge nothing had changed between them despite the piling dangers, deceptions, and complications.

But as they rode back to the main stair, Reuben had to keep blinking back tears as he realized he'd *wanted* things to change.

He managed a smile once the carriage stopped and they both put on their plain cloaks, though Everic's downcast gaze didn't see the effort. Instead, the vampire's expression remained steely, hardened—as if he was about to do something regrettable.

Reuben couldn't blame it on the chilled mountain air when a shiver ran down his spine.

Everic still grasped Reuben's hand as they walked—down the main stair briefly before he angled left into an alley, away from the sentry guards stationed ahead. Then Everic led them through winding paths and stairs, down into the sulfuric stink of the Hollows by the same route Bev used to take Reuben.

Despite his fluctuating waves of fear, Reuben wasn't even marginally tempted to try and run. Not at the thought of challenging the grim resolution on Everic's face. A charm would soften it—but the mere idea of using a spell in defense against *Everic*, this man he'd begun to favor over any other, even considered trusting with his useless heart . . . Reuben swallowed the lump building in his throat and just gripped Everic's gloved hand a little tighter.

Everic didn't have to find out the truth. He hadn't learned about any of Reuben's other deceptions yet. Reuben just needed to make sure, whatever the vampire was bringing him back for, he didn't give Everic any sign of his fear—even if he was meant to sit there and offer advice as Everic started plotting the death of *anyone* akin to Lenaphon or the Voice.

If Reuben focused on deflecting his own emotions, diverting any attention turned his way, Everic should remain none the wiser.

"Did you want to talk strategy for attending the council?" he asked somberly, trying to match Everic's tone and behavior as they reached the last stairway.

*If ever you cannot present a work of art, show them a mirror instead.*

Everic's mouth twisted into a deeper grimace. "Among other things," he agreed, though that told Reuben less than nothing. As they approached the open entrance of his hollowed abode, Everic added, "I never wished to damn you with knowledge—but I fear we will *both* be just as damned without it."

Despite the continued vagueness, Reuben thought he understood Everic's worry now. He *did* feel damned by knowledge: condemned by a single piece of truth about himself he never asked for or sought out, but that Everic's dangerous life and Lenaphon's sadistic test had forcibly uncovered.

Information about *Everic* was a good distraction, however. And no amount of ignorance about the vampire's past would save Reuben from High Ring's scrutiny now. So, as they ducked inside the first stables room, he took a fortifying breath and asked, "Is there more to tell of, then, after the battle?"

Everic's hand clenched in his. "*Much* more," he muttered, before tugging Reuben further into the pitch dark. "My death, to start."

Reuben could barely see once Everic opened the first door and led them through, his eyes straining as the hollow reached complete darkness in Bev's small living area.

He clung to Everic's hand. "And . . . a devil chose to bring you back?" he whispered, remembering Everic's claim of having no bite scars.

Then Reuben realized he'd have no way of even seeing if Everic nodded or shook his head—so he whispered the quick lyrics, *"Silently she guides / Beacon in the night,"* until his mother's ring brightly glowed and chased away the shadows.

Everic flinched ever-so-slightly away from him, squinting at the light—though with far less wonder than the first time he saw the spell, and much more scrutiny.

Reuben's stomach dropped—he'd unintentionally drawn attention to himself already. Crowdcraft could create illusory, weak bursts of light, of course . . . but the light he could craft, especially on Oriana's cantergold ring, more resembled the steady warm glow of Lenaphon's spell than his other flashy tricks.

Everic couldn't know that, Reuben tried to reassure himself as Everic's gaze swung back to the illuminated storage room ahead. But Reuben still felt weak at the knees as Everic led them further in, almost not hearing Everic when he answered belatedly, "I didn't want to die. I wanted to warn the city, find that being, and drown her *light* in darkness." His lips curled into a snarl around each word. Though it faded some as he explained, "In my half-mad, half-dying state, after days laying there, I . . . I manifested something that attempted to save me."

He kept the last part vague, not directly answering the question, but Reuben was no fool. If another vampire hadn't turned Everic, there was only one other suspect.

Everic was one of the very first vampires, then. Whichever devil had originally crafted the monster—likely Everic *knew* them.

"And after?" Reuben prompted as Everic revealed the door to his hidden abode.

Everic's lips twisted into a dark, humorless smile. "After, I gorged on any of my fallen enemies or comrades that still drew breath," he said sharply. Then dropped Reuben's hand to reach for his pocket, pulling out the key and unlocking the door. "It took me six years wandering the wilderness before I was more than a mindless wraith, attacking anything with an ounce of blood." Everic paused as he gripped the handle, his shoulders lowering. "When I finally managed that . . . I had enough presence of mind to remember my home, and slowly found my way back."

With that, he opened the door and strode within. Everic had already thrown off his cloak and was shrugging out of his suit coat, by the time Reuben hesitantly entered and let his presence illuminate the darkness.

There were the extra candles, half-burnt on the bedside table. There was Reuben's clothing neatly folded on the bed. He'd even left his lavender shawl, still draped over one of the seats. Everything exactly where he left it that morning—mere hours ago, when Reuben's fears were indefinite and his blood was just a strange, useful anomaly. Reuben stared at it all, and felt a smaller sting of guilt that Everic would have returned to this sight alone, oblivious that Reuben never intended to return for any of it.

Though Reuben's throat tightened around a dull ache as he realized he'd now have to take it all back, erasing any evidence of his short existence in Everic's life.

Everic, meanwhile, had moved over to his desk. When he grabbed his weapon belt slung over one arm of the chair, buckling it around his waist, Reuben forgot his melancholy and felt the next rising wave of fear.

"Saer . . . I still don't know why you need me here tonight," he reminded.

Everic shrugged on his usual old weathered coat with haste. "If I cannot trust the Voice of Zald's death to be enough, these plans—your dangerous involvement in them—will all have been for nothing. My death will be for nothing." He reached back and tugged at the leather cord holding his hair back, running a hand through the freed strands and sighing. "And *if* it is not enough, as I fear, I need that truth confirmed before I rely on worse measures than myself. Your perspective and observations will greatly help—though I don't expect you to approve of what I do next."

Everic glanced at him, softening as he finished, "Nor will I fault you for it . . . should you wish to end your involvement, after this."

Reuben relaxed. He thought he understood at last what Everic was so hesitant to share—for all that Reuben wasn't loyal to the Priesthood, how would any good Sazzeran citizen react to the knowledge someone was working for their enemy nation?

If that was the damning truth, it was nothing unexpected.

"Loethia is providing you aid, then?"

Everic paused in the midst of pocketing his ring of keys. "Loethia?" he repeated, raising a brow at Reuben. Who felt confusion contort his expression in return as Everic answered, "None of this has to do with Loethia."

All at once Reuben's confidence fled, the fear returning with a vengeance.

Though he should have hid his reaction better—another flash of guilt twisted Everic's features as he watched Reuben's face.

"But . . . what other 'measures' could you use?" Reuben whispered.

Everic's dark gaze moved to the door behind Reuben, his face grim. "First, we should determine if they're necessary."

He moved past Reuben through the still-open door without further explanation, apparently expecting Reuben to follow.

Reuben already had a sinking feeling about where they were headed, even before he grabbed his shawl—intentionally leaving his violin, just in case he needed an excuse to run back. Then he followed Everic back out, nervously twisting his mother's shining ring as they returned to the storage room.

Despite his correct assumption, a cold dread still trickled into Reuben's veins when Everic approached the back wall, crossing to one end of the storage shelf in front of it. With a single push, the wood slid smoothly out of the way.

They both stood there for a long moment, regarding the heavily-locked iron door it revealed.

"By the time I died on that battlefield," Everic softly broke the silence, an old grief in his eyes, "I was first commander of the 3rd Sazzeran legion. Fighting for the blessed city of Sazzera and the freedom of my loved ones—my parents in the Hollows, my brother at his forge, my husband operating in a medical tent behind the front lines."

Reuben's head whipped to the side, staring at him in shock as Everic continued, "If the Voice had controlled her power enough to just kill Loethians that day, not her own people . . . or if I had *stayed* dead on the battlefield . . . perhaps this city would look entirely different now."

He said nothing else, pulling out his ring of keys to undo each lock by the light of Reuben's ring—and Reuben just stood there, dumbstruck, trying and failing to wrap his head around this single piece of information.

All along, Everic had been *Sazzeran*. Wherever he'd lived over the last couple hundred years since, he was born and raised in this city when it had only recently expanded from an important mining town into a city-state of growing influence. Its initial government of landowners and merchants was established just a century prior to the Loethian invasion, and the Zaldians . . . they had only *just* grown popular during Everic's lifetime, right before the Voice won the battle.

Or, if Everic was to be believed, before she obliterated the battle-field entirely.

But before he could ask where Everic had been since then, if not Loethia, a terrible realization dawned on Reuben right as the vampire turned a key into the last lock.

Everic forced open the heavy door, which groaned and squealed from the strain as it slowly revealed the same arched tunnel and fathomless darkness that Reuben had hurried away from once before.

This time, however, he could fathom it. Or at least, Reuben thought even more on Sazzeran history, and all that once transpired in the deepest depths of the Hollows according to the Gospel of Zald—only a decade or so after the beginning of Everic's undeath.

Reuben should have suspected from the beginning, or put it together after noting Everic's ire for the Priesthood. At the least, he could have guessed once he'd seen the vampire's powers. He was sure, if he told his manager of Everic's nature, Sidarchus would have made the connection right away.

But Reuben had been blinded by Everic's favor, his kindness, and his good, if not harmless, intentions. He couldn't see the pattern of what was right in front of him: an ancient, vengeful vampire, hiding away and plotting in the Hollows, all with the goal to take down the Priesthood of Zald.

There was a chance Everic had only been a member of the coven that once terrorized the lower half of the city . . . but remembering his powers, his lack of bite marks, and even more, his commanding nature in times of danger, Reuben would be fooling himself to ignore an even greater likelihood.

And yet he still found it hard to swallow the idea that the quiet, careful man before him—a person who hated social events, had to be reminded to breathe, and got flustered just at seeing Reuben's outfit tonight—was the same vampiric master who had created and controlled a legion of bloodthirsty vampires two hundred years ago.

When Everic finished pulling the heavy, creaking iron door open and then turned, holding a hand out to Reuben, his limbs felt frozen.

Everic didn't know he should want to kill Reuben yet, he reminded himself. The vampire just asked for Reuben to share his perspective and observations with whatever lay beyond this tunnel—the remnants of his coven? Or something *worse?*—and had promised Reuben could then end his involvement without issue.

Surely Reuben could trust him still, if only at being a bad liar?

Just one more job; just a few more pretty lies. Then Reuben would return to the bordello before Lenaphon was the wiser, avoid ever seeing Waron again, and leave behind forever the dangerous, damning knowledge of Everic Payne.

Resolved, Reuben met his eyes—not a mote of gold in them, after just a day without his blood—and forced himself to grasp Everic's frigid hand with a nod.

"The first masons who built the Hollows carved these tunnels nearly a millennia ago," Everic said as he led them deeper under the city. "Then, when it became tradition to bury, not burn the dead under the old god Sazzo, dwarves began carrying them down here, expanding tunnels and carving out new wings to accommodate the influx. Returning to hold feasts with their dead loved ones, wandering deeper to connect with their greencraft or commune with the earth god."

Whilst he spoke, the limestone walls began to change—decorated in skulls and femur bones and carved into shelves on either side of them, each containing piles of dusty, ancient remains. They passed more and more as they walked, until the walls were filled with endless stacks of niches from the ground all the way up to the ceiling.

Reuben shivered, and not just because the musty air was growing colder with every step. "Those weren't its only uses," he murmured.

Everic gave a short nod. "In the winter and foul weather, beggars would find alcoves to sleep in," he continued. "They were used for secret meetings too, by guilds and criminals and devilcrafters alike. Some still are. Though certain sections are too small for anyone to traverse but children—or shapeshifters. And many others are too dangerous for anything but monsters."

They were coming up on a section of the tunnel that briefly widened, opening up into an alcove that looked far more used by the living: a furnace carved into one corner and an empty trough next to it; a work bench littered with bits of metal, wood pieces, and half-used candles; tools engraved with strange markings hanging from wall hooks; more storage in one corner, including boxes and a sheet-covered mirror. Most strange to Reuben: a large anvil with both a dark blade and a shattered hammer abandoned on it.

That was, until he caught sight of a pair of large, reflective eyes watching them from the shadowed tunnel that continued ahead.

Suddenly every one of Reuben's fears from his first night visiting Everic came flooding back—shapeshifters, devilcrafters, vampires, and all the cave-dwelling monsters of legend that were fabled to infest the deepest parts of the Hollows.

But before Reuben could so much as open his mouth to warn Everic, the reflective eyes blinked and disappeared back into the darkness. Reuben wondered if it'd been just a trick of the light, or a manifestation of his growing panic turned to paranoia.

He didn't have time to consider further before Everic led him past the benches and anvil, ignoring the strange little workshop in front of them in favor of moving to the corner filled with storage. There, Everic approached the standing mirror and, with one sharp tug of the wrist, pulled off the old fabric to reveal a tall, single sheet of mirrored glass.

The mirror was arched and finely made, reflecting Reuben in perfect detail with his too-wide, frightened eyes, his curls windswept from the walk—and his hand, glowing with his mother's ring and clutching at nothing.

Everic paused and stared at the empty lack of himself, not even his clothes showing up in the mirror. "The Zaldians collapsed or blocked off every entrance they knew of. But some, like Bev's ancestors, had built personal tunnels that still connected with the main network. So they hid them, used them sparingly, and avoided where the priests had buried the monstrous coven."

Most of the catacombs were inaccessible, Reuben had learned from a young age, ever since the Priesthood destroyed the old coven. But if the immortal creatures had merely been *buried,* not destroyed . . . left to rot, for 200 years . . .

When Everic glanced over, his searching eyes flickering over Reuben's face, Reuben didn't bother to mask his horror. "Where they buried . . . you?"

Everic's eyes flashed with a murderous glint. "Not well enough, it seems," he said before pulling a knife from his belt.

Reuben staggered back from the brandished weapon with a gasp. Only for confusion to diffuse his terror as Everic pierced the dagger's tip deep into his own forefinger until it welled with blood. Then, with a grim set to his mouth, the vampire reached out his wounded hand and smeared the blood in a strange pattern onto the mirror's surface.

Geometric, like the symbol of the Zaldian Priesthood, though more reminiscent of a teardrop than a sun before Everic's bleeding hand dropped. Then Everic muttered in a soft, rolling tongue, his eyes lighting up like coals. The symbol exuded a fiery glow in response, blood hissing against the glass and somehow sinking into it.

Reuben took a slow step back. "Everic, what is this?"

But even before the mirror began to magically warp, Reuben knew devilcraft when he saw it. This time disturbingly similar to when Jophiel once smeared her blood into glyphs on his body—except then, the searing magic had sunk inside of *him*.

Everic stared at the mirror, his jaw set. "I need to be sure, before I consider waking up the rest—and out of anyone, *she* will know if the Voice of Zald is my only threat, and how best to fight any others." His gaze softened but remained resolute as he entreated Reuben, "Just help me explain what has happened. Tell her about the things we've accomplished and learned . . . and whatever you saw this evening that has you so scared, now."

But Reuben had already frozen after the first sentence, his heart in his throat.

He might have become a master at his mother's wisdom, but he still found himself slow to catch onto his old mentor's advice: *Don't expect an exception to turn out exceptional.*

Everic stood apart from every other client Reuben had known, yes. But that was never a reason to trust him. In actuality, it was a sign Reuben shouldn't have agreed to this at all—not since the moment he heard that name on the man's tongue.

Everic had *sworn* she'd have nothing to do with this. *She's nowhere near the Red Road anyway,* he had reassured.

But Jophiel didn't *need* to be nearby, apparently.

And if she was an expert in matters of blood, as Everic claimed in the past—if she herself had been the one to detect Reuben's hidden nature, enough to recommend him to Everic in the first place—he was a dead man the moment she opened her mouth.

Reuben retreated two more steps, quelling the urge to just flee as a form began taking shape in the mirror. "Saer, I—I left my violin in your chambers," he said, using his planted excuse as he began turning away. "Just give me a moment, I'd feel much better about this if I could fetch it—"

And then Everic was right in front of him, hands gripping his upper arms. His eyes still so *kind* somehow as he said, "However she scared you before, she has no power here, I swear—"

"*Please,* Everic—"

"I won't involve her at all, I just need information—"

"Run away with me," Reuben blurted out, not realizing till it was out of his mouth that he didn't just mean from this chamber, but out of the city itself, away from this terrible place that had wrapped binding chain after chain around the both of them.

And once he had, all his hopes latched onto this new, even more dangerous bargain, cupping Everic's face with both hands and pleading further, "Don't do this—*don't* ask her, and we can run and forget all of this together—give up our reasons and find a quiet place to live far, far away, just—just, *please*, Everic, don't . . ."

But Reuben was already out of time.

"Everic," a familiar voice spoke from the mirror, soft as silk.

Jophiel had been summoned.

# 27

# UGLY TRUTH

E veric stood in front of Reuben, obscuring his view of the mirror and its occupant. But just her voice seemed to pierce the air like a knife, cutting Reuben off.

Everic didn't turn yet to address her. His eyebrows had drawn together as he stared at Reuben, looking pained and upset by his sudden, desperate pleas . . . even a touch *uncertain*.

Reuben kept cupping his cheeks, and felt the tiniest flicker of hope.

But then an old familiar grief lined the vampire's face. "It's my fault the Zaldians became so powerful," Everic said, placing a hand over Reuben's and gently pulling back from his touch. "I can't run from that, not when I alone have the means to end this nightmare. Not when I can save everyone—save you—from *them*."

Reuben's eyes filled with tears. "So determined to be the savior," he whispered, the words bitter on his tongue.

Everic shook his head, that fierce conviction returned to his eyes. "I was always meant to be buried. This time, I just have to make sure the right people go down with me."

Then Jophiel's voice rang out in the chamber again, though in a light, friendly tone: "Everic? You brought someone else with you, I see. It's been months—do you have news, maker?"

Everic's shoulders stiffened. Slowly, the vampire pulled back from Reuben so he could turn and acknowledge the woman in the mirror.

Reuben didn't allow it.

Something irreparably broke in him as he tightened his grip on Everic—the damning words already waiting on his tongue.

"*Mellifluous, diaphanous,*" he sang, slow but clear. Everic froze after just the first few notes and moved no farther. "*Illustrious, euphonious . . .*"

Everic's eyelids had drooped to half-mast by the time Reuben finished the first line, his head leaning into the hand cupping his face. And if that was not evidence enough of the charm's hold, the vampire now regarded him hazily with an expression that revealed what Reuben had only caught guarded glimpses of before: fatal attraction, open admiration, and unabashed adoration, all of it centered on the sight before him.

Maybe even *love.*

Reuben felt a tear drip down his cheek as he continued needlessly, reaching to brush a strand of hair out of the vampire's adoring, hazy eyes while he sang in a softer voice, "*Oraculous, symphonious / Aliferous or luminous / It matters not, the words I smith / All beautiful, all sure to miss / The wonderous, miraculous / Joy of knowing you exist.*"

"Everic?" Jophiel's echoing voice repeated.

Everic blinked, though his gaze was still glassy, his voice unnaturally at ease as he responded, "Jophiel, thank you for answering—"

"Don't speak to her," Reuben quickly ordered, and watched with both guilty relief and despair as Everic opened his mouth to argue, his brow crumpling in confusion—and then all at once it relaxed again, the vampire nodding with an easy sort of complacence.

"Oh *dear,*" Jophiel said, sounding amused. "It seems Everic Payne has at last turned into a puppet himself. Is that you I hear,

Reubielocks, hiding in his shadow? I'm glad to see he took my recommendation—though I wouldn't be *shocked* if he'd accidentally drunk you dry by now. Come, let me see how you both fare."

Reuben still couldn't see past Everic's wide shoulders, but that changed too quickly for him to have any say in it. Before he could order Everic to stop, the vampire stepped aside, allowing Jophiel to see them—and for Reuben to see her.

For a moment, he thought he'd misremembered everything about the woman. Or was so terrified his eyes had started playing tricks on him, morphing the traits of his two least favorite clients into one. For Jophiel had been short of stature, not looming taller than both Everic and Reuben where she stood in front of a dark, shadowed backdrop Reuben couldn't make out further. And she had been elvish, not maroon-skinned with large, bat-like wings furled behind her. Certainly, he would have remembered the multiple horns sprouting from different places on her head, curving and interweaving together like a pointed wreath.

But Reuben still recognized the features of her face: the arched curve of her brows, the wide shape of her red mouth. He *vividly* recalled that smile—last directed his way at the very end of their appointment, in a moment his pain-addled mind had entirely blocked off until the memory forcefully resurfaced now:

*Warm lips pressed to his forehead. A smile down at him, the teeth too sharp this time, before Jophiel leaned forward and whispered into his ear, "You did very well. I do so hope you survive this, Reubielocks of the Starlet Eye—it seems you have many more talents yet to prove . . ."*

"Everic, make her leave," Reuben begged, ripping his gaze away from that face before a worse memory intruded.

"I . . . I can't . . ." Everic took a step forward, then seemed to struggle with himself, shaking his head.

"The blood-rune should keep for a few more minutes," Jophiel explained, a smile still in her voice. "The only way you could end it early is by shattering the old family heirloom—and I doubt your little melody is *quite* persuasive enough for him to allow that."

Never had Reuben been more tempted to just run. But *Charming Words* wouldn't erase Everic's memory of this next hour. If Reuben simply fled without an explanation, he'd only leave the ugly truth to be spoken from *her* poisonous lips, instead of his own. What hope did he have of Everic not hunting him down, then?

At the realization of what he had to do, Reuben faced Everic—whose sole focus already was Reuben, his half-lidded eyes seeming to use every ounce of concentration the charm still allowed to search Reuben's face, to read his expression.

"You're so frightened," Everic said, frowning deeply. And when tears quickly obstructed Reuben's vision again, running down his cheeks, Everic very carefully reached out and brushed them away. "So filled with fear, it's making you sick."

"I'm sorry," Reuben whispered back. "I'm so sorry, Everic." His hands clutched at the vampire's chest and arm, as if that could save him from drowning in the sinking pit he'd dug for himself. "I—I lied, in the carriage. Lenaphon took me—she *tested* me—and I . . . I'm like them. Like her, and the Voice."

Everic blinked hard, shaking his head as if to clear it. "You . . . ?"

"I am," Reuben whispered. "And not just—just a *descendant* of someone like the Voice. Lenaphon had terrible abilities, and she couldn't kill me. Please, I swear, I'm *not* a threat, but . . . I can't come here anymore. I have to do what she says, now."

Everic started shaking his head again before Reuben even finished. "No," he denied, anger briefly tensing his expression before it faded back into hazy submission—and then flared up, only to be doused again, and *again*.

Reuben's fractured heart sank at the sight of *Charming Words* doing its work so well. Saving him from the one person he might have allowed to be his savior.

After enough times Everic wrenched out of Reuben's grip, resisting the charm enough to glare at Reuben before once again it dulled on his face. "No," Everic repeated himself hollowly, his shoulders hunched as he stared at the ground. His hands clenched, reached for his weapon belt, relaxed—and clenched again. "How . . . I need to kill . . . ?" he whispered to himself, hair half-obscuring his face.

Jophiel's laughter interrupted, then. Objectively, it was a soft, innocent sound—but all it reminded Reuben of was the quick rending of flesh, the hot splatter of blood.

Reuben met her bright red, pupil-less gaze with a bitter resignation. "Did you know?"

"You'll have to be more specific, I'm afraid—"

"Did you already know what I was, and just *chose* to keep him in the dark?"

"I knew you were special the moment I heard your voice," Jophiel answered the first part, her smile flashing a set of red-tinged, sharpened teeth. "But when the ritual you helped with worked *so* well . . . I made further assumptions, I suppose."

"Ritual?" Everic repeated, directing his confusion at Reuben. "What did you—you *helped*—but . . . *ugh*, my head . . ." He shook it as if trying to dislodge the charm by force. Then regarded Reuben with an expression far worse than anger.

"I didn't know," Reuben denied, and reached out a hand only for Everic to step back. "Please, I didn't know about any of this—"

"You've *charmed* me," Everic accused, right before his eyes dimmed again, the devastated betrayal in them flattening into something more numb.

Reuben knew then that he'd lost him. It shouldn't have hurt so terribly, when Reuben never intended to keep him—but even the good memories he'd wished to hold onto were now painted over in ruin, as Everic spoke through gritted teeth, "I shouldn't have believed . . . I should have done this on my own."

"Hah! He never could have handled this task alone. *You've* witnessed that, I'm sure," Jophiel countered, smiling at Reuben. "But if I'd told him specifics at the start, well—I'm afraid he wouldn't have let you survive past your first meeting." She made an amused nod toward Everic, who had begun pacing in an erratic, jilted manner, as if every few steps he needed to remind himself what he was pacing about.

And Reuben knew she was right—though in his fear he lost control of his tongue, snapping at her, "*You* didn't manage to kill me."

Jophiel's pupil-less eyes flashed. "Oh, I wasn't trying to then. But powerful as a celestial-blooded godling may be, Reubielocks—you are nothing *without* that blood," she said, pressing clawed hands right up against the mirror as if no more than a flimsy sheet of glass separated them.

And at the final word *"blood,"* her smile widened much farther than it naturally should, nearly splitting her face. Lips parted around a long, wet, ruby-red tongue that flickered out, and Reuben watched in dumbfounded horror as it licked along *multiple* rows of grinning, pointed teeth in her horrifyingly large mouth, further coating them in a red, viscous substance that began dripping over her lower lip.

"What *are* you?" he whispered.

Jophiel's mouth closed, though she didn't bother wiping at the blood-like liquid still running down her chin. "Was I less alien than expected, till now?" she said, watching him hungrily. "I take after my maker, I think. Creations like Zald may grow in power thanks to mortal-kind's silly, corruptible ideals—but we so-called devils are born of the pure essence of your *truths*." She regarded Everic, her gaze growing fond as she added, "And I am his truth."

Reuben glanced at Everic as he backed away, but Everic's face betrayed no horror at her words or appearance. He only looked dazed still, and behind that, angry. His hand was resting on the pommel of his sword, his eyes no longer hazy with love, but a dark desire for blood.

And despite how badly Reuben wanted to beg, to plead, to craft *more* pretty lies until Everic's gaze grew soft with adoration for him again—he was wasting precious time. He had to flee while he still had the chance.

"Yes, run little godling! Run while the charm still holds," Jophiel laughed, her voice echoing after him as he took flight out of the alcove and back the way they'd come.

But then louder footsteps joined his in the tunnel. "Reuben—?"

"*Stop*," Reuben yelled behind him, and it was only in hearing his voice so hoarse and broken that he realized he'd started sobbing.

"*Reuben—!*"

"*Don't* follow," he shouted with more force.

At that, the footsteps slowed and came to a stop.

And Everic wouldn't follow again until the charm's end, Reuben tried to comfort himself. But there was no comfort to be found with each gasping breath that dragged in and out of his lungs like knives as he ran, the tears stinging hot and blinding his vision, the light from his mother's ring flashing and warping the shadows into disturbing shapes as it moved with his swinging arms.

Reuben was numbly grateful for the thick, well-made boots this ensemble came with as his feet pounded hard into the limestone floor, mitigating the immediate ache in his spine. He still had to slow by the time he made it out of the catacombs and through the storage room, trying to catch his breath—but that only allowed the overwhelming despair to take over until he dropped his *Light* spell on the ring and forced himself to keep moving.

His eyes were too teary and swollen to catch it, when a shadow snuck in past him at the hollowed dwelling's entrance.

Reuben had to slow again after just a few stairways. This time he focused solely on breathing in the cold fresh air for a minute and tried to not think at all. Until he looked behind him, of course, and remembered he was about to be hunted by an angry, ancient vampire—a man he realized he'd fallen in *love* with, just this time last night—and was headed exactly where Everic would expect to find him.

But if he didn't return to the bordello, he risked not only Sidarchus sending sentry guards to search for him, but much worse, *Lenaphon* tracking him down.

Reuben pulled out the guild token, wondering if he would be a fool to try trusting Delvanzus. He imagined himself running on foot all the way to the guild hall, begging to be whisked away somewhere and for Everic to never be informed—then laughed brokenly at himself when he *still* felt a pointless resistance to leaving the city.

He was just like his mother in that way. Forever waiting for someone else to come save her, forever following arbitrary, isolating rules just to survive each moment. Reuben thought he'd been smarter to never truly hope for his *own* freedom, like she had—but ended up twice as foolish, wishing for something even more impossible.

And now here was the truth of him laid out, an uglier reality than his constant betrayals, failing body, or inherent bloodline all put together: Reuben could make himself indispensably useful to those around him for a time, craft a whole persona to attract fleeting adoration . . . but how could something *born* unwanted ever be worth holding onto?

What was he worth, besides cantergold?

Time and time again, life only gave him one answer.

With that, Reuben's feet slowed to a heavy walk. He paused and took extra time fashioning his shawl to drape over his eyes, then made his usual route back to the Starlet Eye—wondering if Everic would catch up to him before he even arrived. By the time he entered the bordello's open double doors, he almost wished Everic had.

Performances had just finished. Bordello patrons were all about, eating or waiting their turn for an appointment, some flirting with the stellas who were between customers, everything business as usual. Sidarchus unsurprisingly sat hunched at the main desk, examining a very large bag of canters when he glanced up and noticed Reuben headed towards the stairway.

"Reubie!" He waved him over, grinning as Reuben reluctantly obeyed. "You've arrived just in time, I—"

Sidarchus paused then, taking in Reuben's face from under the shawl's shadow. His graying brows crumpled together with concern before he hurried around the desk.

"Come, dear," he murmured, putting a gentle arm around Reuben and ushering him toward the back rooms.

Reuben didn't resist as he was led into the house manager's office and directed to a chair before the older man set the heavy coin bag on his desk. Sidarchuse returned to dab a moistened handkerchief at Reuben's cheeks and lower lids, until the gold powder that had likely streaked and smeared from his tears was gone.

Then Sidarchus pet a gentle hand through his hair, fixing its flyaways and regarding Reuben with open pity. "You ended the arrangement tonight?"

Reuben numbly nodded—though when Sidarchus tucked him into a hug, his eyes burned painfully with tears once more. He twisted away, ending the embrace early, and whispered hoarsely, "I . . . I think I need the night off."

Sidarchus's eyes widened, then narrowed. "Are you sure that's wise? I know it sounds hard to work right now . . . but often the *only*

cure to sorrow is distraction. I think especially in your case, Reubie—
tonight is a chance to prove to yourself you can earn a lucrative sum,
regardless of with whom. I already have your schedule booked for
you."

"Sid," Reuben pleaded, his voice choked, "please, I can't—I *can't*—"

Sidarchus clicked his tongue, then cupped Reuben's head again,
pressing him into another tight embrace. "I understand," he said
softly into Reuben's hair before he pulled back. And then returned
to his desk, taking something out from a lower drawer.

Upon recognizing the slim bottle in his hand, Reuben felt a sinking,
resigned, but also *relieved* sensation in his gut.

"I told you I'd keep extra on hand, just for you," Sidarchus said,
holding it out.

Reuben's back was aching. His mind was on fire. His future . . .
one way or another, it was about to come to a swift end.

What was one more promise broken?

He accepted the bottle from Sidarchus, uncorked it, and swallowed
the sour, earthy mixture without a second's pause.

Sidarchus smiled, a brief look of relief slackening his weathered
face. "Good boy. Now, up you go," he nodded towards the door.
"You'll feel better soon with a draught for starry dreaming and some
gold weighing your pockets after. I promise."

Reuben said nothing in response. He left the office, trudged up
the stairs, and went to his door with no intentions of doing more
than undressing and passively opening his mouth for any customers
tonight. Perhaps he would go back down and ask Sidarchus for
a second bottle too, if this one didn't block out faces and recent
memory well enough through the entirety of the miserable work
night ahead—supposing Everic didn't barge in and cut it permanently
short.

He already felt his body loosening, at least, his thoughts dissipating faster than usual by the time he reached his room. Reuben entered the dark chamber with slow, unsteady steps, eyes drifting toward the bed—and then stumbled to a stop.

He stared, dumbfounded at the sight before him: Isolde, gagged and bleeding on the opposite side of the room, her hands held in place above her head only by a knife, which had been pierced through both palms and embedded into the wall.

The light from the hall shrunk into nothing before the door clicked shut behind Reuben.

Then a wide, constricting hand gripped his shoulder as Waron chided from the shadows, "You've kept us waiting, little dove."

# 28

# PIERCING NOTE

He never retrieved his mother's violin, was all Reuben's slowed mind had time to think before he felt steel pressed against his neck.

"Fight me or scream, and the next knife goes in her middle," Waron continued in a pleasant voice.

Reuben gave a short, tiny nod. Otherwise he remained frozen, still staring at Isolde across the shadowed room where she was pinned to the wooden inner wall, blood dripping from her pierced hands. More of it darkened her hair and ran down her face, from which she looked back at Reuben with wide, pain-filled eyes.

Reuben couldn't let himself be gagged as well. Lacking a strong conduit without the violin, he would once again have to rely on just his voice—but before risking a charm, he needed to comply, appease, and play this new game until he learned the rules well enough to bend them and get Isolde away from Waron.

Even if that meant going with Waron himself.

Most importantly, he needed to stay *focused*, Reuben chided himself when he heard a click from the door's lock, and realized he'd been standing there with his heart racing and his mind doing frenzied laps, not even noticing Waron had retracted the knife or moved away.

Where Waron had gotten a key, Reuben didn't know—and his foggy mind didn't have time to consider before an imposing figure rounded in front of him.

Waron peered down at Reuben's face greedily, using the blunt edge of the blade to stroke Reuben's cheek. "Already pliant and eager for me," he observed with a smile. "I didn't expect your friend here to intrude on the moment, but this does rather simplify things, doesn't it?"

Only a minute after drinking the vial, Reuben already felt strangely unfocused. But he played it up further, letting his eyes go half-lidded as he repeated in a soft, confused tone, "S-simplify, saer?"

Waron chuckled. "You come with me, I leave her alive," he said very slowly. Then, just as the knife tip reached the edge of Reuben's jaw, he twisted the blade—smiling wider when Reuben flinched from the quick sting. Reuben heard Isolde let out a desperate noise of protest, though Waron spoke over the sound, "Though I'm afraid it's too late for your leech or his servant. My people had already made plans to cleanse the Hollows of him, and now that our services are no longer required to keep watch on *you* . . . who was I to stop them?"

Everic and Bev were also in active danger then, Reuben understood with a nauseous flip of guilt in his stomach. Still, he kept his expression loose and unreactive, hoping to behave drugged enough Waron would let his guard down.

Waron stepped in closer, smearing a thumb along the new bloody cut on Reuben's jaw, and smirked when Reuben sucked in a pained breath. "I didn't inform the High Ring client of his *exact* nature, of course—didn't want my sweet Reubielocks burned with him," he sighed before his hand dropped. "I've never wanted to see you hurt, you know."

Reuben ducked his chin and looked up at Waron through his

eyelashes, letting the voleris smooth out his emotions and maintain his complacent exterior even after hearing such a *ludicrous* claim.

"Thank you, saer," he whispered.

Waron's grin grew smug. "But I *do* enjoy seeing you open and honest about what you truly want." He pointed the bloodied knife to Reuben's vanity, ordering, "You have a minute to grab your things."

Reuben was eager for the chance. Maybe now he wouldn't have to leave—if his act was convincing, he could delay enough to put Waron at ease and allow distance between them. Just a few steps away and then, if he sang clear and confident enough, he could get out a few notes and charm Waron like last time before his mouth could be clamped shut—or worse, Isolde got stabbed.

Waron likely remembered last time as well, however, and still held him at knifepoint. So Reuben kept his movements slow as he took off his shawl, folding it into a makeshift holder for the items on his vanity. And while grabbing things at random, he tried to consider his options should he get the chance to sing.

He could use *Charming Words* for a second time tonight, though it wasn't guaranteed to stop Waron from hurting Isolde, so another *Soothe* to pacify the man first would be important. Perhaps after that, Reuben could go a step further and sing *Lullaby,* just to give him a minute to free Isolde, grab the key, and run—or try to, anyway, given how exhausted Reuben would be by then. And then they could alert bordello security in time for him to get disarmed, and then inform the sentry guards the Allunata's leader was tied up in his bedchamber, and then Waron would be taken away, and imprisoned and likely burned at the stake, and then—and then—

"Yes, that too," Waron prompted, sounding amused.

Reuben blinked hard, trying to force his mind out of its anxious circles.

His body was leaned forward, his hand hovering over the larger base oil bottle on the vanity's surface. The rose and salve oils were already stashed in his shawl, alongside a decorative hair comb and a random handkerchief from the drawer. Reuben didn't recall grabbing any of them. Meanwhile, a knife tip was idly tracing up and down his spine, playing with the tiny chains artfully looped there.

With a hard swallow, Reuben finally connected his mind with his shaky, hovering hand and added the base oil to his pile, nauseous at the thought of its use.

"All ready?" Waron said when Reuben reached for nothing else. The infernal man didn't wait for an answer before grabbing Reuben's upper arm to tow him away.

But Reuben still felt a stubborn, unjustified desire to delay things further.

"Wait!" He dared to pull against Waron's grip and, before he was punished, opened the vanity dresser's deepest drawer more fully—revealing a dozen gold sacks lined up in two neat rows at the very back. "I . . . I've wanted to leave, saer . . . been saving up to . . ."

His power of speech was *actually* failing him now, no acting required. Reuben could feel his body swaying too, only the harsh, painful grip on his arm keeping him upright. But he'd guessed correctly—Waron released him, his pupil-less eyes widening with a bright interest down at the gold.

"*Zald's balls,*" Waron swore with a disbelieving chuckle, "it seems you won't cost me anything after all. Hurry—add it to the pile."

Reuben clumsily obeyed, not fighting his disoriented, unbalanced state to slow things down as he reopened the makeshift sack on the vanity dresser's surface.

And yet, what was the point in stalling? Shouldn't he get Waron away from Isolde first, before he risked a fight?

He was holding on to useless hope, to traitorous *trust,* Reuben silently reprimanded himself as he pulled out each heavy bag and tucked them into his shawl. After everything that just happened—after Everic proving he *was* in cohorts with Jophiel, and watching him struggle against Reuben's charm with murderous intent—part of Reuben still foolishly believed if Everic turned up and saw Reuben in danger, he would forget his anger and intervene.

But the hour for *Charming Words* to fade was already over, with no vampire in sight.

Reuben forced himself to move at a quicker pace. He managed to gather up the corners and tie them together, but when he tried to pick up the makeshift sack Reuben immediately lost his balance pulling against its new weight—nearly hitting his head on the dresser again before he slammed a hand on its surface to catch himself.

Waron stepped in and picked up the heavy sack instead with a short chuckle. Then he said, "This will certainly soothe my people's sensibilities about our new caged little bird," as he tied it to his cross-body belt. Without further ado, Waron put a hand on the hilt of his silver-handled sword, the other grabbing for Reuben's waist. "Just a short step into the shadows now—"

And Reuben panicked. In lieu of fighting, he simply dropped, his entire body becoming dead weight and falling to the floor before Waron could get a good grip on him again.

Everic hadn't come. Everic *wouldn't* come in time—he called himself things like harsh, rash, and too quick to action, but Reuben had seen the hurt on his face. He was probably still talking with Jophiel and coming to terms with Reuben's betrayal, making new plans before taking action. Or worse, thanks to Reuben he was already in danger and getting attacked by the Allunata.

There were only two options: Reuben could either comply with any and all of Waron's sick whims through the next few hours or days, and hope he somehow found a way to claw out from the dark pit he was dragged into . . . or he could try to fight now.

Reuben started humming the wordless melody of *Soothe* just as Waron huffed, reaching down for him.

But Reuben's slowed mind had weighed his options a moment too long. He saw the infernal man's pale face flicker just for a moment at the melody—and then his boot delivered a sharp kick to Reuben's back in retaliation.

Anywhere else, and Reuben might have just let out a short moan. But as searing pain lit up and down his spine, the cry that escaped his lungs was far too loud. He wasn't surprised in the slightest when Waron slammed a hand over his mouth before Reuben could choke it down into whimpers, pressing the knife against his neck again. He was only grateful the man hadn't thrown it at Isolde instead.

Reuben looked up at Waron with teary, apologetic eyes, and tried to say, "I'm sorry," against the hand.

Waron sighed down at him. He replied, "I know you are," with a shake of his head. "But now you've proven there's still one last, unfortunate measure to take before we can go," and he took Reuben by the arm—

—and then Reuben blinked and found himself sitting on the edge of the bed, lightheaded and dizzy, Waron leaned over him with fingers brushing his lower lip as Waron finished saying, ". . . a pity, as I do enjoy that pretty whore-mouth."

Reuben was losing time at longer lapses now, and his heart pounded against his ribcage at the realization, his breaths ragged as he saw Waron's hand go to his belt, where Reuben's sack of belongings had been tied alongside the silver-handled sword and a half-dozen knives. Then Waron sheathed the current knife in his hand and replaced it with a tiny, wide, much-too-familiar one—the same blade that had been tied inside of Reuben's mouth weeks ago.

Isolde was screaming, Reuben distantly heard, though her gag muffled the sound too much to hope anyone else would hear. Her body twisted and bloodied further against her awful constraint in Reuben's hazy peripheral, until the sight was eclipsed by Waron leaning closer.

A wide hand gripped Reuben's jaw, forcing his head up and his mouth open.

Reuben blinked slowly, and found himself in a very familiar position—his mind foggy, someone touching him, his gaze fixed up at the wooden top of his dead mother's four-poster bed.

"Sometimes it's best just to take the temptation away," he heard Waron sigh.

He'd never gotten the chance to sing Everic his song, Reuben thought in a haze before he distantly registered cold steel pierce into his tongue. His mouth filled with a salty, iron taste.

And then the harsh grip disappeared.

Waron quickly twisted away, and just in time—or else the blade in Isolde's blood-soaked hands would have sunk straight into the middle of his back.

Reuben straightened his aching head just in time to see the blade rip into the heavy sack at Waron's hip instead. Reuben's belongings tumbled out, bottles shattering and cantergold scattering as Waron whirled around and the contents spilled in an arc across the floor.

Waron jumped back and away from her, a snarling scowl on his face. Isolde's eyes were dark and wild in answer as she righted herself from pulling the knife free, barely managing to keep a grip on its slippery handle. Her gag now lay like a necklace against her throat.

She wasted no time to lunge forward, attempting to stab him again. Waron blocked her with his forearm. But Isolde redirected the force of it into her own momentum, ducking and stabbing into his thigh. He roared, swiping at her with the tiny blade in his hand—and by now Reuben had only just registered the pounding pain in his tongue, it was all happening so fast—before Isolde ducked, though this time the knife *did* slip from her bloody, terribly-wounded hand as she wrenched it free, clattering to the floor.

Waron stared down at Isolde with a cold malice as he sheathed his tiny blade.

Perhaps thanks to his terror, or else his unlucky familiarity with Waron, even in this drug-addled state Reuben could anticipate what would happen next.

Right when Waron's hand went to unsheathe the silver-handled sword, Reuben thrust himself forward, putting his body between his attacker and his friend—and felt a morbid kind of satisfaction as the blade slashed the upper half of his chest.

Then Reuben gasped, pain searing across his skin.

Waron sucked in a breath as well. "You stupid, *stupid* thing," he breathed out, looking even a bit remorseful as he stared at the long cut already bleeding red into Reuben's thin white doublet.

It *was* a stupid, irresponsible gamble to make, based entirely off of conjecture and a much less dire injury. If Reuben died of a necrotic wound, he would only have himself to blame. But he could only hope Isolde was using this distraction to *run*, out the window if she had to, as he intentionally staggered forward to lean on Waron.

Waron caught him by the shoulder, frowning at the wound still. "I *did* wonder, what with all the interest about you," he murmured, then glanced down at his sword, "but even *Soul Bleeder* wasn't sure . . ."

Reuben should have known better than to think Isolde would leave him, however. It seemed she'd used the distraction to reach for the knife, as out of nowhere she lunged upward with it in her hand once more—which Waron barely managed to parry with his larger weapon.

He pushed Reuben to the ground before attacking her; Isolde impressively twisted just in time to avoid the blade, and a small back-

and-forth began near the window. The two seemed well-matched despite the greater reach of Waron's sword, and Reuben belatedly realized that if Isolde was sent to Sazzera as a *spy*, she likely had been trained in many ways before ending up in her current circumstances. It was a wonder how Waron had managed to subdue and pin her to the wall before.

To assist, Reuben tried to hum *Soothe* again—but just the vibrations sent a shooting pain through his badly-wounded tongue. He winced, sucking in a breath at the pain, then choked on the blood ever-running down his throat. Ultimately, managing nothing but a few wet coughs.

Without the ability to sing or speak, what other use did he have? Just his body now, Reuben thought, readying himself to stand up and intervene once again.

But he'd barely made it up off one knee when Waron feinted to the left, making Isolde think she had an opening, only for her to perfectly expose herself to the force of his true attack: slamming the hilt of his sword on her outstretched, wounded hand.

The tiny moment of exquisite pain distracting her was all Waron needed before his dark blade stabbed forward an instant later.

As Reuben watched the devilcrafted blade sink into Isolde's abdomen, time seemed to stop.

The sharp, pulsing pain across his chest and in his tongue was forgotten.

The hazy edges to his vision cleared.

He opened his mouth as if to channel through his voice—but even if Reuben could sing, he had never once crafted words or composed a melody that would order *death*. So, in his half-delirious state, Reuben channeled through something else entirely.

He'd used his mother's ring like a focus when he somehow succeeded in saving Daxus. Even now, Reuben *could* sense a connection, a new door to beckon magic through . . . but it wasn't enough. Not *nearly* enough. Reuben's senses instinctively reached out even further, and latched onto more and more of the same material: the thousands of cantergold pieces spilled across the floor.

Right as Waron pulled his blade free from Isolde's abdomen, the room lit up with all the brightness of a noon-day's sun as Reuben opened his mouth and *screamed.*

The scattered cantergold trembled, emanating the light—and so was *he*, Reuben realized as he let out the single wailing, piercing note.

An instant later, the glass in the window burst. Both Isolde and Waron doubled-over, dropping their weapons and covering their ears.

But Reuben didn't want Isolde hurt. So he stood and strode towards Waron, trying to push the growing, burning sensation in his chest specifically out at Waron's hunched form—*directly* into his blackened soul, if Reuben could somehow manage that.

And then, after three eternal seconds, Reuben closed his mouth.

The light faded, both from him and the thousands of gold pieces littered amidst the blood and shattered glass. A warmth lingered in Reuben's chest, and he noticed a tingling sensation at each location of his injuries. His mind felt clear again; his eyes finally took in the chaos of the room for the first time.

Most vividly, Reuben beheld Waron and cringed back in disgust.

Blood ran from Waron's nose, trickled out of his mouth and ears, dripping in red tears down his cheeks from eyes clouded by burst blood vessels. Waron stumbled to stay on his feet as he groaned and held his head. He looked so terrible that Reuben didn't think much of turning his back on the man to check on Isolde—only to feel a harsh, clinging grip on the decorative chains draped along the back of his doublet.

"R-Reubielock-s-s . . ." Waron gasped, his voice thick and rattling.

Reuben gasped—then gave a cry of *anger* before he ripped away from Waron's grip. And when the delicate chains broke, his old client just crumbled to the ground.

Reuben didn't spare him another glance before hurrying to Isolde's side.

# 29

# SOUL BLEEDER

I solde had fallen to one knee, cradling her middle when Reuben reached her. "Slayer in the dark," she whispered to herself, her lank, bloodied hair hiding her face.

More blood dripped from between her fingers. "Isi, let me see," Reuben ordered, his tongue still throbbing but miraculously usable again.

He nudged her hands away at the site of the stab wound—such a small entry point, that were it a normal wound Reuben would feel confident in his abilities. But then Isolde began to sway as more blood trickled out.

Reuben helped her lie back on the floor. Then he reached for his half-ripped shawl lying nearby and folded it into something he could press on the wound. And despite the grisly miracle he'd just performed, all he really knew to do now was sing the same words for *Healing Song* he'd first improvised for Bev: *"If I was a lake / And my beau the sea / I'd carve us a river / For love to flow free . . ."*

His voice sounded terrible, his consonants warbled—but Reuben sagged in relief when the bloody holes in her hands closed up, the glassy look in her eyes clearing.

He stopped after a minute to lift the makeshift bandage, and found the bleeding injury from Waron's *Soul Bleeder* was the only wound that showed no improvement.

"*If I was a fish / And my beau a dove,*" Reuben kept going, pushing every bit of feeling he could into each word. He even tried to use his mother's ring again as a focus through the next stanza, "*I'd grow my own wings / To reach for her love.*"

The smallest of bruises on Isolde's neck faded by the last word . . . and yet the stab wound looked unchanged the next time he checked.

No, that wasn't true—as Reuben paused to more fully inspect the area, he saw a blackish coloration had started to rim the edges of the injury, even a small amount of dark ichor leaking out with the blood.

"*No,*" he denied, and sang the song all over again, this time ignoring her gasp of pain to press his hands right up against her abdomen as he had with Daxus's gut wound.

But Daxus had been cut by a sentry guard's broadsword, not an Allunata's devilcrafted blade.

Only more black ichor leaked out by the song's conclusion. Reuben's breath hitched; a tide of hopeless dread washed over him as he realized the small wound had *widened.*

The first time he watched someone die from this ugly injury, it had taken the assassin far too long to gasp out her last breath after Waron abandoned Reuben on the bed. The corrosive black ichor continued to pour out of the wound for even longer after, burning into the floorboards right up until Isolde found Reuben tied up and bordello security hauled the body out. The first time, Reuben had simply been horrified, cringing away from the sight.

This time, it was *Isolde* . . . and it took everything in Reuben right then not to break down and sob.

"Reubie, it's alright," he heard Isolde whisper. As Reuben glanced at her through his tears, her face was ashen. "The woeteller warned

441

me. I knew."

Reuben stubbornly shook his head, clinging to one last hope. "You saved me—now it's my turn to save you."

He grabbed the bloody knife she'd dropped on the floor and—unlike the first time he held a blade to his skin—felt no hesitation before he cut deep into his palm. But it was the same drive then that propelled him now, perfectly clear to himself at last: there was little Reubielocks wouldn't do for a cantergold . . . but Reuben would do *anything* to keep those he loved safe.

So he grit his teeth through the burning pain. Then he prodded Isolde's slack mouth open, squeezing his newly-wounded hand just above it.

A few trickles of blood dropped into the back of her mouth before Isolde grimaced, shutting it and weakly trying to twist away from his grip. Which Reuben didn't stop, watching with bated breath now for his blood to do something his songs couldn't.

A flash of light briefly lit the room again . . . but it was only from the slash in Reuben's chest, not Isolde's wound.

His blood would exert its power to save *him* from necrosis, while at the same time abandoned his dearest friend to a slow, agonizing death.

Reuben tried to push out a sound again around his hitching breaths, unwilling to admit defeat. He only got out, *"If I was—"* before his spine twisted in sudden agony.

Just like the first time he'd healed from a necrotic wound, the miracle came with a terrible aftershock: mind-rending, nerve-singeing pain. Reuben crumpled and fell to the floor between a deathly-still Isolde and a pitifully-groaning Waron, gasping and then crying out as the torturous sensation shot down his entire spine and jolted through his legs.

The cost of this magic wasn't simply exhaustion or pain. But it wasn't trying to destroy him either, like he'd thought while suffering in his family's old hollow. It was working itself through him, *into* him, sourced and centered on his mid-back—and Reuben's cries crossed over into screams when he felt a sickening *shift* within his bones around the spot.

His vision whited out.

After that, reality faded in and out. Cold air was blowing in from the broken window, the smallest balm as it brushed over Reuben's sweat-sheened skin. There was urgent knocking, then banging and shouting . . . all of it coming from the locked door, before a muffled voice interrupted and the banging stopped. Meanwhile, Waron was making small retching sounds; more blood had pooled around him the next time Reuben's eyes could focus and glance the man's way.

Finally, the pain receded enough for Reuben's awareness to return—and with it the sick realization that Isolde hadn't made a sound.

With aches shooting through him at every motion, Reuben dragged a hand under himself to sit up and check on his friend . . . and despite seeing her shallow breaths, felt the last of his hope fade.

A dozen black veins now spidered from the widened wound in her middle, oozing almost entirely ichor now. The inky liquid dripped down her abdomen, eating away at her dress and onto the wooden flooring, where small drops had already begun to sputter and hiss.

He'd failed her. Just like his mother—Reuben had promised himself to help them both, and yet while his broken body stubbornly persisted on, his very existence was what had weakened and slowly killed Oriana over time. In his mother's final moments, all he could do was hold her small, cold hand as she moaned nonsensical things, delirious with pain, "*I didn't have time . . . please, I only ever wanted her . . .*"

Tears streamed down his cheeks as he took Isolde's hand the same way now, cradling it in both of his.

Freedom, especially for Isolde's sake, had been well-worth fighting for. But Reuben had done all the fighting he could, and only ended up exposing her to danger, driving a wedge in their friendship, and saving gold she couldn't even use.

Now, all that was left . . . was to lose.

That was, until the small crunch of glass alerted him to a new presence.

Reuben sat up, too tired to feel more than a tiny stab of fear at the thought Waron was somehow healed and ready to finish them both off. But Waron still lay on the floor, twitching and writhing.

Instead, Reuben met the large, reflective eyes of a shadowed beast. Feline, sleek and black-furred, the color barely standing out from the clear night sky behind it. The huge creature sat perched on the windowsill, its size at odds with the tiny noise the impact of landing there had made. Reuben stared, uncomprehending for a brief second, save to wonder if these were the same watching eyes that he spied in the catacombs.

Then its form was obscured by a thick cloud of darkness.

The black cloud billowed through the window, spilling past the beast into the room. So dark and complete as it filled the space that, for a moment, Reuben saw nothing at all. Then the rolling mist gathered and swirled back in on itself—reforming into the imposing figure of a red-eyed, blood-splattered Everic Payne.

Those red eyes immediately swept across the room, and Reuben cringed in on himself in anticipation. But Everic's scrutinizing gaze paused at Waron's bloodied, crumpled form before ever reaching Reuben. The vampire's nostrils flared, eyes widening as he took a single step backward at the gruesome sight.

Before Reuben could react, the feline beast behind Everic gracefully leapt from the windowsill. The shape of the dark, four-legged creature twisted and unnaturally warped, mid-air.

It landed next to Everic entirely changed, wearing the usual dark leathers, small gray horns, and warm, fuchsia-toned skin of a very familiar, quiet infernal woman.

In any other circumstance, Reuben might have laughed. Surely nothing should surprise him ever again after tonight: Everic was the vampiric master of a legendary coven; Jophiel was a devil he somehow manifested; it only stood to reason that Everic's other closest ally would turn out to be something like a *shapeshifter*.

"Isolde," Bev breathed out, rushing over on two feet.

Glancing down at Isolde's limp form, Reuben pushed down his lingering shock for now. "Please," he appealed to her first. "Please, I'll do whatever you want, Bev, just—she's *dying*."

Reuben's words seemed to knock Everic out of his frozen state. "Move out of the way," the vampire ordered, striding over as well.

Reuben hurriedly obeyed, shifting to kneel at Isolde's head and wincing—both at the lingering protests of his back, and the way Everic avoided looking at him as he took Reuben's place. Bev was already at Isolde's other side and lifting the makeshift bandage, her tail swishing in agitation behind her as both she and Everic inspected the wound.

Bev sucked in a breath at the sight.

Everic just leaned back, his face grim. "It's too late. If it was her arm, perhaps . . . but this has pierced things that can't be removed."

Reuben felt a new wave of tears burn painfully at his eyes, and was surprised he still had any left tonight. "It's my fault," he replied numbly around hitched breaths. "If I had just gone with him . . ."

Bev stood up and let out a wordless shout before pacing away. Everic gently placed the bloodied, ichor-stained shawl back over the wound. Reuben just took Isolde's cold hand again, wishing to hold her through these last few moments.

Then Bev noticed Waron still moaning, twitching on the ground, and all at once her face twisted from grief into rage. Without warning, she reached down to scoop up his silver-handled blade from the ground, then thrust her arm forward—stabbing him straight into the heart with *Soul Bleeder*.

Waron let out the weakest, most pathetic little gasp, before finally going still.

Reuben shuddered and looked away—and accidentally met Everic's gaze, who was frowning deeply at him before his red eyes shifted back to Isolde. Probably remembering he was supposed to kill him, Reuben reckoned, feeling a tired little jolt of fear at the reminder himself.

Then they were both distracted as Isolde coughed weakly, and dragged in her next breath after a belated wait. Each shallow inhale sounded like it took more effort than the last.

Reuben pressed his face against the back of Isolde's hand, trying to comfort himself that he'd join her soon.

But when Bev rounded back to them, her face was stormy and determined as she said, *"Blood."*

She must have remembered what Reuben's blood did for Everic, months ago. Reuben opened his mouth to explain that he'd already tried, that his blood was likely useless to help anyone but a vampire . . . and then he realized Bev was staring at *Everic*.

Who glared at her in return—though when that didn't seem to intimidate her, his face crumpled into something pained and guarded instead.

*"Your* blood?" Reuben realized.

Everic shook his head, though his eyes avoided directly meeting either of their gazes. "It won't save her, Bev. It will damn her."

"You know that's not true," Bev denied with a few simple hand signs, repeating it till Everic noticed while she gave him a flat, unimpressed look.

Everic's gaze narrowed, his voice sharp as he accused, "Are you so desperate for answers from the woman, you'd risk *this*? A fledgeling vampire is a dangerous, volatile thing at best—even if we kept her under my authority."

Bev's face softened. "It's not that," she whispered, tucking Waron's devilcrafted blade into her own belt—and though Reuben didn't know much of the context around their words, he could see in her dark eyes, turning on Reuben now, that her motivation came not from a need for *"answers,"* but a simple, heartfelt desire to not let Isolde die.

A desire he shared. And if there was no other answer to healing such a fatal wound, besides *this* . . .

Reuben squeezed Isolde's cold hand tighter. "Will it work?"

Everic grimaced. "Her body may reject it. And *if* I drank her blood—which I'd need to, first—there's a good chance the necrosis would infect me as well."

"Then . . . you would need *my* blood afterwards." Reuben's stomach flipped at the thought of Everic's fangs near his neck right now.

Finally, for the first time since he flew in through the window, the vampire intentionally met Reuben's gaze. "Likely, yes. So I'll leave the decision up to you."

A thousand questions flew through Reuben's mind—where she would go, what she would eat, how she would be kept safe—but every second he wasted to ask them was one less before Isolde was gone from him forever.

Isolde's next breath hitched, catching on itself. Bev and Reuben both looked down at the dying woman with desperate terror.

"Do it," Reuben heard himself agreeing.

*"Now,"* Bev said, louder than he'd ever heard her speak as she knelt down at Isolde's other side.

Without another word, Everic took one of Isolde's limp hands and lifted it to his mouth.

Reuben watched in silent awe and horror as the vampire bit into her wrist—Everic briefly grimacing as he did—and drank Isolde's corrupted blood.

It only took about fifteen seconds before she let out a final gust of air.

And in the single moment that followed, Reuben started to panic, opening his mouth to protest that Everic had just *killed* her . . . but was distracted by the sight of Everic biting his own wrist. No, *tearing* it open, reminding Reuben of his own instinctive fears when Everic first used his fangs on him.

Then Everic held open Isolde's mouth as Reuben had done minutes earlier, his pale face stony and his shoulders rigid with tension while he pressed his torn, bloody wrist against Isolde's slack lips.

Bev let out a gusted sigh when Isolde suddenly stirred to life, and Reuben watched in frozen shock as his friend began actively swallowing the blood offered, and eventually started *sucking* at Everic's jagged wound. Isolde even let out a weak whimper a minute later as he pulled it away, before she went still—cold as death in Reuben's grip now.

"It's finished," Everic said into the quiet after. For a single moment, his still-red eyes softened as he regarded the pale, deathly visage of the woman he'd possibly just turned. And then he started, "We need to get her out of here, somewhere underground—"

"I can," Bev signed. Her face darkened, her hand briefly clenching around the pommel of Waron's blade before she scooped Isolde up into her strong arms.

Reuben swallowed down the request to see her again, just one last time. Instead he simply pressed a kiss to the back of Isolde's hand, whispered, "I love you," to his first and only true friend, and let go.

Bev and Everic said nothing else—just gave each other firm nods before she stood up and, still holding a limp Isolde, backed into the darkest corner of the room.

Then, with a small flash from Waron's blade, the shadows twisted around Bev and Isolde . . . and left nothing behind.

Except for Reuben and Everic, of course.

Reuben made himself turn to face the vampire. As silly as it was, given he was likely about to be drained dry, he whispered, "Thank you," whilst pulling his tangled hair over to expose one side of his neck.

Because Everic *had* still come. And Isolde was hopefully saved, even *free* of this place—if not quite alive.

"Don't thank me yet," Everic answered darkly.

Reuben steeled himself. He didn't try to scream or run again, but his fear had found its strength once more, coiling harsh and tight in his gut at the prospect of death—as it had ever since the moment he bowed his head at 14 years old and submitted to the rite that would save his mother's soul.

Still, of all the ways in which he could die before he met the fate that debtors were promised, his soul lost in a frozen, endless darkness forevermore . . . what more could he ask for, then to have it begin as a short, relatively painless pull into sleep, facilitated by someone he might even love?

Especially if he could feel Everic close to him, one last time.

So Reuben didn't offer out his wrist. He just requested, "Please . . . here?" and with a tilt of his head, more fully bared his neck.

Everic was still as stone for a long moment, his expression unreadable.

Then, slowly, the vampire nodded. He twisted to more fully kneel in front of Reuben; his hands reached out to grip Reuben's nape and shoulder.

But after he'd moved closer, Everic paused, his gaze briefly flitting over Reuben's face.

Here at the end, Reubielocks completely abandoned him—Reuben couldn't force even a tiny smile. He only managed to return Everic's nod, waiting silently until the vampire leaned in with parted lips.

Then Reuben shut his eyes tight as he felt Everic's fangs pierce his neck, not expecting to ever open them again.

# 30

# CHOOSING TRUST

E veric kept a firm grip like always, keeping Reuben perfectly
still as he bit down, then began to drink.

Not that Reuben had any intention of fighting him. He
only fought his own instincts, trying not to tense, trying not to think.
Just sink into the inevitable, however little he felt ready to face it.

But Reuben couldn't quell that same aching despair that Everic
specifically seemed to unearth from growing like a thicket within
his chest. Choking and piercing his heart, denying Reuben even the
peaceful death he'd hoped for.

If only he'd been strong enough to actually save Isolde, before the
only option left condemned her to darkness. If only Lenaphon's
malicious eye never spied him out in the crowd, recognized what he
was, and hired the Allunata after him, so Waron might have forgotten
about him—or at least, Reuben might have considered fleeing with
Daxus and Nahlia when he had the chance.

If only he could have just enjoyed a few more weeks with Everic—a
few more days, even—before the ugly truth so rudely intruded on
them.

*Loveless. Futureless. Pointless.* No matter how well Reubielocks let him pretend otherwise, that was all Reuben had been and could be, since the moment Oriana mistakenly brought him into the world until now, his very last.

His eyes remained shut when the sharp, pulling pressure of Everic's mouth slowed barely ten seconds after it started. Reuben just sniffed and blinked back tears, assuming this was a mere pause before the vampire continued.

But then Everic's tongue swept across the bite marks—unless Reuben was entirely mistaken, now sealing the wound shut, like always.

When Everic's lips pulled away, Reuben remained wary with anticipation. He stayed stiff where he sat, his breath quick and uneven when a cold forehead rested against his skin.

Everic kept his face tucked there in Reuben's neck for a few seconds longer. "You taste like voleris," he finally spoke in a quiet, subdued tone.

Reuben winced, realizing the problem. "I'm sorry, saer, I—"

And then further words died on his tongue, his thoughts going entirely blank as he felt Everic's arms wrap around him.

The vampire breathed in deep—his first noticeable inhale since arriving in Reuben's bedchamber—and then his body drained of tension as he gusted out, "I feared I might never see you again."

At that, a dangerous, hopeful relief threatened to overtake Reuben's fear.

He couldn't make his arms move to embrace Everic in return, however. Neither could his mind simply accept Everic's words for what they implied. Reuben wasn't sure he was *capable* of assumptions right now, too many shocks leaving him numb and wary in the face of more.

"*What?*" was all he whispered against Everic's shoulder.

The arms around him briefly tightened, before Everic pulled back and met Reuben's gaze with golden irises once more. "Bev still hasn't figured out where the Allunata's headquarters are."

Reuben relaxed just an increment. While every color looked beautiful on the vampire, he found he associated this particular hue with memories of safety, affection, and warmth.

"It might have taken days, *weeks* to find where he took you, if you weren't dead by then," Everic continued. "Though . . . I suppose you are harder to kill than you look."

His face darkened as he glanced over at Waron's body.

Reuben recalled Everic's description of the dying soldiers after the *Battle of the Steppes*, and his stomach turned with a whole new kind of guilt.

"Not by you," Reuben argued in a weak, rasping voice. He couldn't simply trust in Everic's current behavior—not after witnessing the man's barely-restrained anger in the catacombs. "My body healed in ways I don't rightly understand tonight, but if *blood* is what gives this kind of power, you were right. Jophiel is right. You are the perfect person to kill the Voice, to end anyone like her, and . . . and clearly I'm just like her," he said around a constricted throat, nodding towards Waron's body. "Waron's blade did nothing—but *you* can drain and finish me off easily, Everic."

Everic glanced at Reuben's neck—and Reuben felt another flip of fearful anticipation as he waited for the vampire to lean back in and do just that.

"Yes . . . and if *you* wished, you could have ended me quite quickly yourself tonight," said Everic. "But you didn't. You charmed me, admitted you'd lied to me, told me you have the same nature as the very thing I woke up to destroy—and then simply left me back there, unharmed. Not even ensuring I wouldn't come after you."

Reuben didn't respond, confused for a moment.

Then, slowly, he recognized Everic was right. To ensure his own survival, he could have at least attempted to kill Everic while he was vulnerable in that charmed state. Objectively, Reuben probably *should* have.

It simply never crossed his mind to hurt Everic—or anyone, really. And he'd never once attempted to, right up until Waron hurt Isolde in front of him tonight.

A tiny half-smile raised the corner of Everic's stern mouth as he watched whatever was happening on Reuben's face. "I'm only sorry we couldn't get here sooner. How are your injuries? This wound is shallow but needs to be cleaned, at the least," he nodded at Reuben's chest, "your hand is cut, is there anything more pressing—?"

Reuben quickly shook his head. "I'm fine for now," he assured, in awe at the fact Everic was *still* worrying over him like always. Meaning he hadn't entirely lost favor somehow, even after charming the vampire and revealing he was kindred to the very thing Everic hated. And if that was true—if all Everic wanted was something like more control over Reuben, not his death—now was Reuben's chance to play along and use his mother's rules to make sure Everic needed him more than ever.

The recent memory of Everic fighting against *Charming Words* intruded then, however, making Reuben wince. He was so convinced before, that forgetting Oriana's wisdom had caused his worst mistakes with Everic—and yet, treating Everic like just another untrustworthy client tonight had ensured disaster.

Perhaps Sidarchus's advice could be leaned on instead? After all, Reuben was already on his knees . . . then again, so was Everic.

Reuben felt the beginnings of a smile on his lips as Everic kept looking him over for injury—though it died as he took note of Everic's bloodied coat in return.

"Are *you* alright?" he asked in belated alarm. "Waron, their leader, he said the Allunata were on their way to attack you—have they already, or did something else go wrong—?"

"Nearly two dozen ambushed us, yes," Everic confirmed grimly, "only minutes after you left. Bev and I killed enough to send the rest fleeing back into the tunnels. I wanted to make sure you weren't attacked on your way back—but then we *did* learn from a dying one that their leader was after you, so we traveled straight here." The vampire sighed, mournfully shaking his head. "Though not in time for your friend. I'm sorry for dragging you into this—"

"No—Everic, it's *my* fault they attacked," Reuben interrupted.

His heart pounded against his ribcage when Everic gave a confused look in return. But even as everything inside him forged by his mother's wisdom—everything that made up *Reubielocks*—inwardly screamed at Reuben to never put himself at someone else's mercy . . . Reuben had no desire to use his facade a second longer.

If Everic was going to kill him, or punish him, or at the very least abandon him because of the truth, let it be now or never.

Either way, Reuben couldn't stomach even one more pretty lie.

"I . . . I *swear* I didn't know anything about my blood when you first hired me," he whispered, looking down. "But Lenaphon somehow could tell. She hired the Allunata to keep track of me. And after I started leaving to meet with you, Waron, he—I didn't *want* to tell him, but . . . the night before the assassin attacked you in the carriage, he was waiting for me here, just like tonight, and he—he *interrogated* me . . ."

Everic said nothing after Reuben's shaky voice trailed off. But when Reuben dared to glance up, the vampire's eyes were glowing with a murderous light.

Reuben flinched hard as Everic's arms moved—but only to wrap around him again. And this time they pulled Reuben forward, tucking his head under Everic's chin. Distantly, Reuben noted that Everic smelled like blood, earth, and leather . . . and behind that, maybe just a hint of cinnamon.

"It is some small comfort, I suppose," Everic replied, "that you didn't deliver him any *less* of a slow, painful, excruciating death than I would have."

A hitched breath escaped Reuben's chest in answer—and he couldn't say if it was closer to a laugh or a sob.

But as badly as he wanted to collapse into Everic at last, he tensed further with a shudder. "Everic, I *lied*," he protested in a choked voice. "I promised you at the very start, but I couldn't keep my word—I told him exactly what you are. That's how they found out, why they've been tracking you, trying to attack you. And I should have told you, I was just so afraid, I—"

"You *should* have told me," Everic agreed very sternly, though quite mitigated by how gently his cheek rested against Reuben's hair, his hand stroking Reuben's arm. "Then . . . that means Lenaphon knows after all?"

"Waron didn't tell her," Reuben answered, pulling back to reassure him. "She guessed you were a *shapeshifter*, and that only based on your changing eyes, I swear."

Everic raised a brow. "Then she knows nothing about shapeshifters," he huffed, before his expression sobered. "Though the information is still out there now, for her and others to find."

"Yes," Reuben whispered. "I'm *so* sorry."

He should have been relieved that Everic wasn't reacting with anger or violence. But when the vampire didn't reply, Reuben's fragile hope began to fade again.

"And I . . . I understand, if you never trusted me again," he finished, pulling from Everic's embrace and staring at the ground.

Everic replied in that simple, blunt way of his: "I never trusted you to be truthful. You didn't even wish for *me* to speak the whole truth, when I offered to tell you everything after the carriage attack."

At that, Reuben's heart sank. *I trust you,* Everic had assured him more than once—and it was admittedly strange, that Reuben felt far more betrayed upon hearing this than at seeing Jophiel's form appear in the mirror.

"I—I suppose I shouldn't mourn the loss of something I never had to begin with, then," he replied with a small, humorless smile.

There was a loaded beat of silence. Then Everic requested, "Look at me?"

Reluctantly, Reuben obeyed.

And found the vampire regarding him with nothing but an open fondness softening the edges of his eyes and the lines of his face. Even *more* genuine than the besotted way Everic had looked at Reuben while charmed—if only because his mouth was still curved in that characteristic, endearing frown of his.

"No, I didn't trust your word. But I trusted your heart," Everic declared, gently reaching to take both of Reuben's hands. "I trusted your good intentions, your desire to help your loved ones, to put others before yourself—even if to an *unhelpful* degree, I would argue in some cases." His thumbs brushed back and forth over Reuben's knuckles, a line forming between his brows. "Should we continue any semblance of our former agreement, I would need more transparency . . . but I never stopped trusting in *you.*"

The tension in Reuben's body finally dissolved away. He slumped forward as wave after wave of relief, affection, and joy swept over him, breathing shakily through the onslaught as he took in Everic's words and found he *couldn't* reason them away.

Thinking no further, Reuben closed the remaining distance and kissed Everic's frowning mouth.

After only a few soft presses of their lips, however, Everic pulled back and murmured, "You don't *need* to kiss me," interlacing their fingers as he assured, "my trust in you came regardless, perhaps in *spite* of any physical intimacy—"

"Needs can be nebulous things," Reuben whispered. He gave both of Everic's hands a small squeeze and smiled, admitting, "I don't think I truly stopped either. I've been far more distrusting than you, but . . . even once you brought me to Jophiel, I wanted to believe you'd spare me—and after I ran, and Waron was about to take me . . . I still hoped you'd come."

The line between Everic's brows deepened, his mouth opening—but a light, tentative knock at the door intruded before the vampire could reply.

"Reubielocks? Saer?" Reuben heard the muffled sound of Sidarchus calling in his bright, friendly customer voice. "There were complaints of a large disturbance earlier, I had to calm everyone down . . . does all bode well?"

Everic's eyes narrowed at the door as they both rose to their feet.

Quickly, before Everic could say a word, Reuben took a few steps forward and called back, "Thank you, Sid! All is well—just a small incident."

"Oh! Truly? Nothing we can't clean up, I'm sure," Sidarchus said, sounding surprised. "Very well! Apologies, saer, I won't further interrupt your last few minutes with our most *exclusive* stella."

Waron's appointment was almost over, it seemed.

Reuben wondered how much Sidarchus knew. If he'd just been paid off to ignore the fact Reuben had blacklisted Waron, and was ignorant to Waron's full intentions . . . or had *some* idea, Reuben thought as he remembered Waron having a key to his door somehow.

At that reminder, Reuben turned and tried not to breathe or look closely at Waron's body as he crouched down, ignoring the strange, painful *shift* that happened again in his spine as he searched the dead man's pockets.

Meanwhile, Everic repeated, "'A small incident?'" with an incredulous look at the body and mess around them.

Without trouble Reuben found the key, quickly pocketing it as he shrugged, "I improvised." Then he turned back to Everic with the warning: "And I'll have to be *quite* untruthful in a few minutes once the sentry guards show up—about the window, the body, *Isolde* . . ."

Reuben swallowed down the grief still lodged in his chest for his dear friend, forcing his mind to not dwell on her uncertain fate for now.

Instead he searched Everic's face and said, "The question is—should the story include you?"

Everic hesitated. "That *is* the question. I can go now, and never return," he motioned at the open window. "Or I can help you run, and try to ensure *anyone* who searches after you, high priest or otherwise, meets a swift death. Or . . ." He took a step closer, his gaze scrutinizing in return. "We could decide together, what happens next."

Reuben bit his lip. Just an hour ago, with his life seemingly hanging in the balance, he would have quickly agreed to the first offer without argument—or maybe even risked the second. But now . . .

"How exactly would we do that?" he asked softly.

Everic gave him a small, sad smile. "For starters . . . what do *you* want?"

At this very moment? Reuben wanted to kiss him again, he didn't say.

Generally, he liked the idea of running and never looking back . . . but not at the cost of leaving Isolde *or* Everic behind, Reuben could admit to himself now. Or Bev either, by this point, and soon enough that list might grow to include Delvanzus and more of Everic's allies as well. And that was the true conundrum of this city—ever a miserable place Reuben should want to leave, yet inexplicably tied to everyone he loved.

But before he could consider further, there was one more matter to resolve.

"What does *Jophiel* want you to do?" Reuben countered.

Everic's eyes narrowed. "I didn't ask. Her machinations do not concern me. We are tied to one another, as she alluded to—but I *swear* to you, I am not beholden to her, nor she to me. She is not involved in my goals, either; I only wished to use her expertise tonight on the matter of blood."

Then Everic's frown grew troubled as he continued, "Though I realize now, your concern over her at the start wasn't simply to do with her otherworldly appearance. I should have asked more questions about your first meeting with her—you may have charmed me, but I still heard that she involved you in some *ritual . . . ?* Was it to test your blood—?"

"It doesn't matter," Reuben quickly interrupted, moving back to the floor to start gathering the coins and half-empty gold sacks. Internally, he had to slam the door on a dozen memories of that night that wished to creep from the dark corners of his mind.

Everic just let Reuben's short, defensive answer hang in the air and silently knelt down to help.

Truly, Reuben had *no* desire to detail every moment of that horrible day right now—or ever. And he didn't see how recounting it would do anything but justify why he was afraid, why he'd been worried about her involvement in the first place. If Everic was to trust him, he shouldn't *need* to further explain.

But Reuben also didn't want to slip back into dishonesty and avoidance all over again. So as they swept the coins and bags into one great pile, he forced out in a voice barely above a whisper, "I can . . . *try* to explain more, at some point . . . in time. But for now, if you say she won't be involved, then . . ." He forcefully shook his head, holding in a shudder. "I just wish to *never* see or speak with her again, Everic."

Everic didn't look satisfied when Reuben glanced his way. But neither did he press Reuben for answers; a flash of guilt twisted his pale face before he nodded lowly and said, "I'll never put you in that position again. I swear it. I . . . I deeply regret that I didn't ask you first, tonight."

A hesitant smile curled Reuben's lips in answer. They were quite the pair—neither managing to keep their initial promises at the start, neither giving the other enough reason to continue trusting . . . and yet both still stubbornly choosing trust anyway.

The vampire's tone grew even more regretful as he continued, "And I wouldn't blame you if that's not enough. You know who I am now. You have some notion of the terrible things I've done, and what I am *still* capable of, should the need arise. If you wish for more information about the war, the coven, Jophiel, before you decide what you want . . ."

Reuben dropped the last few pieces in the pile, pausing and glancing towards the door. "I doubt we have much longer before I'm checked on. And I have plenty of things to share with *you*," he pointed out, thinking of Lenaphon's eye, the sisters she'd mentioned, the bargain they'd struck. "There's simply not enough time, but I—depending on what *you* want—I think—of course, to be safe—"

He cut himself off, realizing he was still avoiding the question. And after a lifetime of defaulting to the safest, easiest option for either his loved ones or himself, it was hard to even consider something else.

But as the question hung in the air between them, Reuben understood his discomfort: it wasn't just other people, who never asked for his preference. He hadn't allowed *himself* to consider what he truly wanted in a very, very long time.

For nearly fifty years, his only focus was the game of survival, clinging to the rules his mother left him as tightly as precious cantergold. He used them to play and keep himself in the game, to outsmart other players, and especially to put up safe walls, protecting his own mind from the hopeless state of his circumstances. How else would he have made it through the last nearly five decades?

But somewhere along the way, the rules had also become their own kind of cage, Reuben could see now. Barricading him from real connection, self-respect, his own simple wants—locking away his true self entirely behind *Reubielocks.*

*You keep playing, when you should be singing,* Isolde's cryptic warning came to mind again.

Taken literally, the power Reuben had recently discovered through his voice far outweighed what he could do with his mother's old violin. But now he was reminded of the *"singing"* Oriana told him about on her deathbed, words that stood in stark contrast to most, if not all, of her previous advice:

*Freedom is the only song a person must fight to sing . . . and that is why we must. You must keep singing, Reuben, so long as your voice is still yours to lose.*

Reuben had entirely misinterpreted his mother's last, most important guidance, he realized. They were never meant to encourage him to keep his head down, work hard and unceasingly, and never protest until finally, one day, he endured long enough to earn the needed cantergold to pay his debt.

After all, ending his indentured servitude wouldn't free Reuben from a city that preyed on all its people—from Nahlia and Daxus, who toiled for decades in the darkest reaches of the Ravine, to his indentured mother, once born into the gilded privilege of its highest tiers.

Freedom was worth *far* more than gold.

When he met Everic's eyes again it was with fear—but also determination.

"I want to fight," Reuben declared.

Everic regarded Reuben solemnly. Then he nodded, a rueful smile curving at one side of his mouth. "The curse of Sazzera for us both, then," he quoted Reuben.

Reuben smiled back. "Besides, I couldn't *never* see you again anyway," he said, putting on a lighthearted tone and poking a finger into Everic's chest. "I need my violin fetched from your bedchamber—*and* you just turned my friend into a vampire."

Everic only looked more rueful. "There is much to resolve between us still," he agreed.

"And we will—but while we're discussing things I'd like," Reuben continued, and was pleased when the encroaching grief on Everic's face retreated, a faint curiosity overtaking it as Reuben spoke. "In public spaces, my stage name works well enough. I don't have any surname or the standing for an honorific. But in private, I . . ." Reuben paused, feeling inexplicably nervous before he offered, "I *would* rather you used my true name, from here on out . . . *if* you'd like."

Everic went very still. Then he slowly reached out a hand, brushing the back of his scarred knuckles down Reuben's temple, then his cheekbone, then carefully down to his jaw, lingering just above the recent cut Waron left there.

"Reuben," Everic murmured at last, his fingers unfurling to rest at the side of Reuben's neck—right where he'd bitten down, two nights in a row. Brushing the tiny, already-healing pinpricks there as his golden gaze flickered over Reuben's face, then lingered on his mouth.

"One last thing," Reuben whispered. "I know I don't need to, but . . . I *want* to kiss you right now."

It was no wonder Everic's body so often felt stiff, Reuben thought once the vampire leaned over all the cantergold he'd paid Reuben for the last three months and did just that. There was a reason Everic always tried to be so careful. His lips moved with immediate passion, his hand at Reuben's neck shifting to pull him in by the nape, and Reuben finally understood what his music was always trying to tell him—that, behind that hard but thin barrier of control, Everic Payne was simply an ever-storming tempest of passion: rage, obsession, hunger, hatred. *Love.*

And by some miracle Reuben no longer felt fear, but a small thrill in his heart at capturing a small piece of that volatile passion for himself—only kissing Everic more enthusiastically in response.

Until he had to pause for breath, of course, and giggled when Everic shoved half the gold pile aside to lean in closer, repeating, *"Reuben,"* in a breathless voice as he pressed kisses against Reuben's neck.

Reuben wrapped arms around Everic's shoulders and felt his body shiver in response, both with arousal and a strange, burgeoning emotion he didn't know how to place at first. Like mourning something he never had, combined with the joy of it finally gained— like grief mingled with relief, or the taste of bittersweet.

He had been kissed a thousand times over . . . but *only* as Reubielocks, until now.

When Everic's lips trailed up towards his ear, whispering the name yet again as he did, the feeling overflowed in a physical way; Reuben dropped his head to rest on Everic's shoulder as tears painfully burned and leaked from his eyes.

Everic stopped. "Reuben?" he repeated. His hand rubbed Reuben's lower back, the vampire's voice hesitant as he asked, "Does something hurt? Or did I . . . ?"

Reuben let out a teary laugh, pulling back to smile at Everic's worried face. "No, no, I'm *happy,* it's just—I've just realized . . . I *hate* 'Reubielocks.'"

A tiny smile formed on Everic's face, though only for a moment before Reuben kissed the quirk of his lips and eagerly fit their mouths together once more.

And as they held each other tighter, lips sliding and hands stroking the lines and curves of the other's body, Reuben mused at how different Everic was in this state, instinctively starting to gasp and sigh, to breathe heavily under Reuben's touch—as if, with every kiss and caress, Reuben was putting the life back into him—

But then knocking came from the door again, this time more forceful and quick. A sound Reuben knew well: imposed on the rare occasions he couldn't get a customer out the door in a timely manner himself.

"Time's up!" came the muffled warning of a bordello security guard.

Sidarchus's softer voice said something as well, though Reuben didn't quite hear as he hurriedly jumped up from where he'd half-climbed into Everic's lap—wincing as he felt his spine shift yet again, though it felt strange, almost like a *release* of tension now, if still a painful one.

Everic noticed, giving Reuben a concerned frown as he rose to his feet as well. But there would have to be time for questions and hypotheses and explanations about this *and* a whole host of other subjects—later.

Reuben nodded at the open window and urgently reminded, "You *can* still leave and avoid any trouble. I swear I'll be fine." When Everic looked incredulous, he added with a wink: "You should know by now—just a few charming words, and my 'melodic tongue' will have shaped this all in my favor."

The worry on Everic's face softened into fond exasperation. He glanced at the door, then back at Reuben. "Perhaps so . . . but what do you want?"

Reuben felt another small thrill—not just at being asked, but at the realization that what he wanted right now was dangerously simple.

He let out a shaky laugh when Everic kept standing there, patiently waiting for an answer like always, as if bordello staff weren't about to burst in and decide for them.

Reuben shook his head at the gentle man, the imposing monster . . . and then hesitantly offered Everic his hand. "Stay for a while?" he requested, just as the click of a turning key sounded from the door.

Everic took his hand and carefully kissed the back of it—and Reuben didn't need a single note of music to hear the truth in the vampire's low, soft voice as he said, "From now on, Reuben of the Starlet Eye, I'm here at *your* pleasure."

# A Killer's Heart

*Oh, have you met the souls*
  *Whose eyes live far away*
  *Deep in the bloodstained*
  *Of darker yesterdays?*

*Oh, have you felt the calm*
  *They cling to, lest they storm*
  *Or climbed the icy walls*
  *They build to guard their warmth?*

*The soldiers and fighters*
  *They always touch lighter*
  *For once in a battle*
  *That grip squeezed much tighter*
  *A fight it must be*
  *a war set apart*
  *But lucky are those*
  *to win a killer's heart*

*Oh, have you traced the scars*
  *That prove their battles won*
  *Yet make the mind forget*
  *The war is truly done?*

*Oh, have you traced the scars*
  *They dress over their wounds?*
  *Or heard their laughter sing*
  *A melancholy tune?*

*The warriors of bygone*
  *Forgotten, but live on*
  *In darkness you'll find them*
  *far from their land's new dawn*
  *A fight it must be*
  *a war set apart*
  *But lucky are those*
  *to win a killer's heart*

*A fight it must be*
  *a war set apart*
  *But lucky are those*
  *to win a killer's heart*

The story continues in Part II of *Circle of Sixths* . . .

# EUPHONIOUS

(Free chapters posted weekly on Patreon!)

**Loved the story?**
Write a review on Goodreads or other platforms, and help spread
the word to the reading community. It would mean the world!

Enjoy a <u>free</u> bonus short story available for download at
imogenpyre.com:

*Wretched Desire: A short story*
"It was hard to know exactly who he'd been, before he died and
woke up a blood-crazed monster. But one thing he knew for certain:
Everic Payne had always been a selfish man."

# ACKNOWLEDGMENTS

First and foremost, to the online readers who followed the unpolished serial chapters of *Mellifluous* as I posted them week after week, cheering me on and believing in this obscure little story: You are better than gold.

Next, to Tinuviel: you can't read, but I have to acknowledge how much of my writing happened with you asleep in my lap, refusing to let me leave my desk for hours. I'm not a fast writer, but you're not a fast napper—so, as always, we two are in perfect symbiosis. You're curled up in my lap as I'm typing now, and I think it's safe to say only time could deepen my love for you.

There are so many other people that have helped along the way: Emma and Ashley, for always believing in my dreams even when I've questioned them; my fandom community for encouraging me to go for it; Linnea, who I hope never reads this, but has helped me stabilize my work-life balance tremendously so I had enough spoons to write; the two agents who gave me personalized feedback, which showed me how to polish the story into something I'm proud of; and of course, all the people who've been awful or broken my heart—thanks for fueling my angsty, grimdark fiction!

An extra big thank you to each of my beta readers who read the roughest version of this story, and who were kind enough to poke holes into flimsy parts of the narrative and still gush about its redeeming qualities. And most of all, my deepest gratitude to Amanda for acting as an alpha reader, beta reader, editor, proofreader, sounding board, and supportive friend, especially as I reached the home stretch of editing this behemoth. You kept me sane enough to get *Mellifluous* publish-ready, rather than throw it out the proverbial window. All remaining issues, anachronisms, errors, and grammar mistakes are most *certainly* my own.

One last, selfish little acknowledgment: to me at the very emotional age of 13, raging to my diary that I'd never write a book again after the family computer died and took my draft with it. I proved you so, so wrong, and aren't you glad for it?

# ABOUT THE AUTHOR

By day, Imogen Pyre works as a writer and editor for a professional association. By evening, night, and weekend, they are writing transformative and original fiction, developing lore and worlds for TTRPG roleplay, and running a Patreon and Discord server for their readers.

Pyre is part of the LGBTQ+ community, an ex-member of a high-demand religion, and an avid fan of all things queer fantasy since the very formative age of 7, when their dad yelled at the TV screen that Frodo and Sam should stop acting gay for each other.

MELLIFLUOUS is their debut novel.